Length of Days

Louise Lenahan Wallace

ALL THINGS
THAT MATTER
PRESS

Quote from Charles Dickens' *A Tale of Two Cities*, copyright 1999, Dover Publications, Inc.

Quote from Robert Browning's "Song" from *Pippa Passes*, contained in *My Last Duchess and Other Poems* by Robert Browning, copyright 1993, Dover Publications, Inc.

Verses from Stephen Foster's "Jeanie with the Light Brown Hair" contained in *Popular Songs and Folk Songs* by Stephen Foster, Dover Publications, Inc.

ISBN: 978-9966634-8-9

Library of Congress Control Number: 2016946255

Cover image adapted from Civil War Christmas by Thomas Nast
Cover design by All Things That Matter Press

Previously published as Days of Eternity, Treble Heart Books, 2007.

Thank you to the Union County Historical Society in Marysville, Ohio, for your generosity in providing me with information about Civil War era Marysville. Especially to Charlie Thompson and Viola Hill, my deep appreciation for helping me bring that long-gone time to life.

Love,

Louise

Length of days, and long life, and peace,
Shall they add to thee.
Let not mercy and truth forsake thee …
Write them upon the table of thine heart.

~Proverbs 3: 2-3

PROLOGUE

1857

The two men, black frock coattails snapping in the breeze that pushed their beards up over their eyes, finished smoothing the dirt over the grave. Hoisting their shovels, they discreetly backed away, leaving the tall, mustached young man and the fair-haired child alone to mourn their dead.

Beneath her bonnet brim, four-year-old Charity Michaels' gaze slid from the mounded earth up to her father's eyes. Normally as blue as her own, they were now so grief stricken they appeared black. Ethan Michaels, sun-browned fists crushing his Sunday hat, stared at the grave. The late October wind gusted past, setting still bright oak and maple leaves into skittering flight. Beneath the dark blue coat Mama had finished making for her only last week, fingers of cold pushed around Charity's knees.

She shivered. She wanted to touch Papa's hand, to feel his warmth, but was afraid to distract him from his attention fixed so fiercely on the raw, glaring earth.

She knew those two men with shovels had buried Mama under the mound of dirt. After supper last night, Papa had perched her on his knee and explained that Mama was in heaven with Charity's baby brother. Confused, she had searched his grief-ravaged face, so frighteningly different from his usual contented expression. She had thought about Mama, how she never sang or laughed any more after baby Andrew died. Faced with pain far beyond her years, she had tried so hard to understand. "But if Mama's with Andrew, she isn't sad now, is she?" When she said that, Papa looked like he was about to cry or something. But Papa never cried, not even the time he hit his thumb with the hammer. That time he had just said a lot of funny words. But last night, right away, he had gently touched the silky wisps that framed her face. With her curly blond hair and big blue eyes, everyone was always telling her she looked just like Mama.

"No, Charity, Mama isn't sad now. She's happy again."

Before she could question further, he had set her on her feet. "It's your bedtime. Go find Mrs. Abrams to help you. I'll be along soon to hear your prayers."

Standing beside Papa now, the toes of her kidskin boots smudged with dirt from the grave, Charity remembered the question she had wanted to ask last night. She shivered again in the chill air, and Papa suddenly scooped her up in his arms, his short brown mustache tickling as he pressed his cold cheek to hers.

Lifting her into the buggy, he wrapped the lap robe around her. Snuggling into the welcome warmth, she caught a last glimpse of the grave as the horses thrust forward. A single maple leaf, scarlet burnished in the afternoon sun, fluttered onto the mounded earth. Gazing at it, the question she could not put into spoken words came to her again. *If Mama's happy, why is Papa so sad?*

CHAPTER ONE

1859

Zane Edwards stooped for another chunk of firewood from the split pile. As he straightened, he saw his wife step onto the back porch from the kitchen of the white painted farmhouse. Unaware of his presence, Larissa Edwards paused on the top step as he had done minutes earlier and looked to the breath-taking sunrise filling the farm world.

South of the barn, Mill Creek's rippling surface reflected crimson streaks splashing the skyline beyond the sugar maple grove. All around, farm animals stirred to the beginning of the day. A mother duck led her fuzzy, new hatched brood among the rushes at the water's edge. In the pasture, the oxen grazed stolidly, seemingly indifferent to the fact they would soon be trudging in front of Zane's plow. Clover, the Guernsey milk cow, chewed her cud placidly, flicking her tail at the first early flies.

Larissa drew in deep breaths of the dew pearled morning. Zane started to call to her, but changed his mind, allowing her the freedom of private moments of communing with nature. Still unaware of his presence, she descended the steps. Wandering along the flowerbed bordering the porch, she bent, intently studying the bright patches of blooms.

Zane knew a carefully selected bouquet of daffodils and bluebells would grace the breakfast table when they sat down. He smiled. No matter how rushed or hectic her schedule, she always managed to add a bit of brightness, if no more than the russet of shingle oak or the butter yellow of sugar maple leaves at year's end, to their living. Swelling contentment of the just born day, of the budding springtime farm world around him, of everyday existence shared with Larissa and thus lived to the fullest, welled within him. "'God's in His Heaven,'" he murmured, once more bending over the pile of firewood. *Mr. Robert Browning sure hammered the nail straight on that one.* All was right with the world.

A little later, brown hair still combing damp, face and hands scrubbed after the early morning chores, Zane pulled out his chair at the breakfast table. He saw then Larissa had arranged the flowers in the dark green bowl her parents had given them as a wedding gift. The vivid blue and sunny gold of the blooms lifted from the deep green as from a bed of ferns.

His lips quirked at such a whimsical notion. His Pa had cussed him out good for such fancifying when he wasn't much higher than the table, here. Had told him the day's work wouldn't wait for such nonsense as sketching the barn cats or Jumper the ox at the plowing. He hadn't tried his hand at it since that long ago tongue lashing, but sometimes, as now, wistfulness came over him at the loss of the dream.

He pulled himself up sharply. Larissa, deep blue eyes puzzled, watched him, and he realized ten-year-old MacCord and five-year-old Rose waited for him to take his chair so they could also be seated. "The flowers are real pretty, Rissa." The glow that lit her face was worth a hundredfold of any picture he could have produced on paper.

He took Mac's hand on one side, and Rose's on the other as Larissa did the same at the far end of the table. Head bowed, he said the words of his own Pa before him, "Almighty Father, we thank You for this day, for this food we are about to eat, and for all the blessings You have bestowed upon us. Help us be worthy of Your goodness. Amen."

"Amen," Mac and Rose echoed as their fingers squeezed his, then released.

Zane reached for the platter of fried eggs and glanced at Mac. "So today's the big test day, is it, son?"

Dark blue eyes apprehensive, Mac took the basket of biscuits from Larissa. "Yes, sir. Miss Sullivan said she'd grade my test before school's out, so I'll know for sure this afternoon. If I pass, may I go tell Doc Rawley before I come home?"

Still brushed by his father's long-ago disdain and the death of his own dream, Zane spoke with quiet assurance. "Of course you can. After all, he'll be waiting to hear whether he has a new helper or not. Just remember, Ma and I know however you do, it'll be your best. We can't ask more of you than that."

Mac continued to look troubled. "It's just that I want this so much," he blurted, turning red at revealing his heart.

Larissa patted his hand. "We know. We want it for you, too. But we're proud of you, no matter what. Don't forget that," she said sternly, so that he finally smiled.

***

"Come on, Mac. Hurry up!"

Mac tugged at his cap brim and tried unsuccessfully, for the third time, to ignore his younger sister. Darting in front of him, she skipped away on the path that skirted the edge of Cowbell Swamp and led through damp, ferny places. Without raising his head from the book he was reading as he walked, he mumbled, "We have plenty of time before the bell."

"But I want to get there so I can jump rope." Framed by green calico bonnet strings, her lower lip protruded dangerously. "You don't have to read that book again. You read it last night."

"Do so have to read it again. You heard Pa and Ma. I have to get a hundred percent on my test."

She was not to be put off by such a trifle or by his inattentiveness. With five-year-old persistence, she bobbed in front of him again so that he stepped on her. That worked. He gave her his full attention as he told her through gritted teeth, "Rose Edwards, cut it out!"

"But Mac," feminine ingenuity switched to flattery. "You'll do good. You always do, and I want to jump."

Masculine pride refused to be cajoled. "You know Ma and Pa said I have to get a perfect score on this test or else I can't work in Doc Rawley's office after school. That was our agreement."

"Don't know why you want to work there." She made a sour face. "All that blood."

"If I'm going to be a doctor, I got to start practicing now. There's an awful lot to learn," he explained with older brother superiority.

"Will you know it all if you read that book?" She eyed the one in his hand with new found respect.

He started to explain this was a history book, but thought better of it. "If you don't quit flapping your jaws, and get going, you won't have time to jump," he warned.

She squealed and took off as fast as her sturdy little legs would carry her. "I'll race you," she flung back over her shoulder. "And I'll beat you, too."

Mac rolled his eyes in disgust at the ridiculousness of the challenge, but increased his pace to keep her in sight as she skipped ahead, following the path beside the flower sprinkled meadow.

He trudged along through the springtime morning budding around him in this year of 1859. The sun brushed warmly against his shoulders after the snow and ice filled winter just past. Vaguely, he noticed red-spotted white buckeye blooms and the new leafed green of towering walnut and hickory. He smelled the elusive fragrance of violets, but paid no attention to the sky as deep a blue as his eyes or the frisking squirrels as flame bright as the unruly mop of hair curling from beneath his cap brim. He was aware only that this was Friday, and his parents, after weeks of pleading on his part, had finally agreed to his helping Doc, if he kept up his school grades. His elation flattened. If he couldn't remember the names of the thirteen colonies, the date and order they were admitted as states, and their capitals, all his beseeching and studying would be for nothing. Sighing, he opened the book again.

Ahead of him, Rose flew into the yard edging the brick schoolhouse and dashed away to join the rope jumpers. Two boys about his own age promptly waylaid him. "Hey, Mac, look what I found." Ian Hollister, big for his eleven years, thrust a garter snake at Mac.

"He's a beaut, Ian." Mac set his history book on the bottom step beside the dinner pail Rose had abandoned. "Can I hold him?"

"Not yet. Bruiser and me been waitin' for you. We're gonna have some fun."

"We sure are," Theodore Damon chimed in gleefully. Only his mother and Miss Sullivan, the teacher, dared call him by his birth name. Others who tried learned swiftly how he had come by his nickname.

"See that new kid?" Ian jerked his head toward a little girl who, hands clasped behind her back, wistfully watched the rope jumping. "Says her name's Charity. Well, we're going to show her some real charity." Mac registered a swift impression of big blue eyes and blond hair braided and tied with pink bows that matched her dress and bonnet. She looked about the same age as Rose.

Even as Mac glanced her way, Ian and Bruiser swaggered toward her. Realization flashed and he yelled, "Don't do it!"

Bruiser sliced off Mac's protest by planting himself in front of the child and demanding, "We got a test for all the new kids who come to this school. You know what it is?"

Bashful Five blinked mutely up at Towering Twelve.

"Well, this is it." As he blurted the words, Ian whipped the snake from behind his back and thrust it at her. "Here, hold it."

Her reaction, in the boys' opinion, was downright disappointing. She merely stared at the snake. The snake stared back.

"You gotta hold it. You want to come to this school, you got to pass the test. What's the matter, you a scaredy cat?" Ian again thrust the snake toward her, this time so close its tongue flicked her cheek.

Up to now she hadn't made a sound, and neither Ian nor Bruiser possessed enough sensitivity to realize that her eyes were dilated with horror. When the snake's questing tongue brushed her face, she opened her mouth to scream but nothing came out. She stumbled backward, frantically dodging, but her feet twisted from under her. She landed, with a loud, messy splash, face down in a mud puddle the size of a young pond.

Ian and Bruiser got their wish, then.

Scrambling onto her hands and knees, she shrieked. And shrieked again. They were such thorough screams that, the students found out later, even Mr. Obadiah Beldane at his blacksmith shop down the far side of the road heard her.

Mac stood as paralyzed as the other children by that tormented wailing. Indignation finally jolting him, he yelled, "What're you guys doing?" and thrust the shocked boys aside. Bending, he stretched his hands to the bitterly sobbing little girl. "Come on. I'll help you."

Through her tears, however, she saw only another boy, bigger by far than herself. "No snake," she pleaded.

He held up his palms. "Look, no snake," he promised.

Warily she eyed Bruiser and Ian, who started snickering.

Mac rounded on them. "You guys better shut up."

Still snickering, the boys elbowed each other. "Mac's got a sweetheart," they chanted promptly, loudly, and in unison.

Face burning, Mac again reached to Charity. She took hold and he pulled her up with a loud squishing. Ian thrust the snake at her again. Mac let go of her and gave him a hard shove. "Get that thing out of here."

Ian stumbled but promptly shoved back. This time Mac, with a loud, messy splash, fell flat on his back in the muck. He landed right beside Charity. She had still been off balance when he released her hands and she had, unfortunately, again splatted into the puddle. With a bellow of rage he started to rise, but a sharp command halted him.

Authority, in the form of Miss Sullivan the teacher, had finally arrived. At forty-three, Charlotte Sullivan had taught long enough that she had instructed the parents of some of her present pupils. Firmly entrenched in spinsterhood and a whalebone corset, gray-streaked black hair twisted into a no nonsense knot at the back of her head, she had lost the soft roundness of youth, both in body and in temperament.

Upon entering her school world domain, a pupil's first lesson consisted of reading the gleam in her black eyes and melting into the woodwork accordingly. Even the boys taller than her five-foot, eight-inch frame respected her rule. The second lesson a student absorbed was that, having cut to the heart of a problem among her pupils, she passed judgment with unyielding fairness. She pushed her way through the group of awe struck youngsters. "What is going on?" She caught sight of Mac ensconced in the mud hole beside her newest student, both children dripping pathetically. "Oh, my," she added faintly.

Silence stretched, a silence so total and ominous, the plup of mud as it slid from Mac's hair into the puddle vibrated the springtime air. Rose's piping voice finally shattered that awful quiet. "Ian and Bruiser's got a snake. Ian shoved it at that new girl and made her fall in the mud. Then he shoved Mac in."

The two boys began to edge away. "Ian, Theodore, come back here. Your parents will certainly hear about this," Miss Sullivan added tartly as Mac took Charity's hand and hauled her to dry land.

Escape obviously hopeless, the boys abandoned their effort. "We was just funnin'," Bruiser said sullenly. "She fell in the mud all by herself. Mac shoved Ian before Ian shoved him." He broke off at Ian's glare. "Well, he did," he finished defiantly in the face of Ian's total lack of appreciation for this defense.

7

Ignoring the boys for the moment, Miss Sullivan surveyed her two muddy, dripping students. They were so thoroughly covered with muck that, had she not already known, she would have had a hard time naming either one. Only Charity's big eyes, peeping through the mud mask like a bewildered raccoon's, and the bright mop of hair even Mac's head to toe dousing couldn't dull, gave a clue. The expressions on their faces—Miss Sullivan didn't know whether to laugh or cry. Wisely doing neither, she merely said briskly, "You two need to go home and clean up. Charity, can you walk to the hotel by yourself?"

Mac retrieved his cap from the ooze. "I'll take her, ma'am."

Sticky wet though he was, Miss Sullivan patted his shoulder. Turning to her other students, who were beginning to murmur among themselves, she announced sternly, "Everyone else inside. Time for class to begin. And get rid of that snake!"

***

Mac set off, slowing his stride so Charity could keep pace. "Why're we going to the hotel instead of your house?"

"Pa and me live there."

"You live at the hotel?" Mac was suitably impressed. "I ate supper there once. It was for sure grand. You just moved here to Fairvale, didn't you?"

She ducked her mud smeared chin. "Ma died and Pa was real sad and we moved here."

Mac didn't know what to say about her Ma dying, so he told her he lived on a farm three miles east of town.

She fingered the wreck of her dress, and her lower lip trembled. "I especk Pa'll be real mad. He told me not to get my new dress dirty."

"It wasn't your fault. Bruiser and Ian can be awful mean sometimes. You didn't have to be scared, honest. It was just a garter snake. It wouldn't hurt you."

At memory of the snake's tongue flicking her cheek, her eyes dilated again. "But a snake bit my Ma, and she died. I don't want to die!"

Mac stared, speechless, as her full meaning sank in. "This snake wouldn't hurt you," he repeated, dazed. "Ian and Bruiser won't tease you again, either," he vowed.

Approaching the corner leading to the hotel, she scrubbed her wet cheeks with her fists, smearing the mud more thoroughly than before. "I'm scared."

Mac, taken aback by the quaver in her voice, stared at her. "Scared of your Pa? We'll tell him it wasn't your fault. He won't be mad."

"Yes, he will. He's mad all the time now." Then, more strongly, "I'm not going home."

Mac hadn't a clue why her Pa should be angry, but who could figure out grownups? Of two things he was certain. She had made up her mind, and she wasn't going home. She had her small feet planted firmly, now, and she obviously had no intention of budging. As a matter of fact, she looked remarkably like Brindle, their old cow at home, who sometimes set her feet and refused to let him drive her to the pasture. The glare of challenge in Charity's eyes, now, looked distressingly familiar. Dismay swamped him.

What am I going to do with her?

CHAPTER TWO

Mac knew one thing for sure as they stood in front of Morey's Cabinets and Furniture, with Charity's determined little knees stubbornly locked against his urgent, and hopeless, tugging. *We can't stay rooted to the boardwalk forever. Maybe the mud hole wasn't such a bad place for her, after all.*

His exasperation and embarrassment were increasing by the moment. Their progress through town had not gone unnoticed. Smiles, stares, and outright chuckles greeted them at almost every step. Besides, the mud was drying, causing intense itching in some very inconvenient spots. Mac scratched the back of his neck, pondering Charity doubtfully.

There was really only one choice. "Come on." He grabbed her hand, almost pulling her off balance as he dragged her down the steps off the sidewalk. His initial tactic succeeded. She had no choice but to follow him. As soon as they reached the brick paved street, however, she dug her heels in again, nearly jerking his arm out of the socket.

"I'm not going home." The gleam of challenge abruptly became sparks of fire.

Girls. And he'd figured his sister Rose was a pain in the—He dug at the base of his neck again and tried to scratch the back of his left calf with the toe of his right boot. He didn't know which was worse, the itching or the sputtered amusement continuing to trail them.

"Charity, you got to come with me," he hissed. "You keep standing here, your Pa will see you, sure."

She glanced furtively toward the hotel and back to him. "Nope."

Surprise had worked before. Grabbing her hand, he yanked her along with him. This time he got as far as the mouth of the alley between the hardware store and the saddle shop before she dug in again. But at least they were shielded from all those grinning grownups.

"Look," he panted, "if you won't go to your home, we can go to mine. I got to get cleaned up, too. I don't guess my Ma would mind if you come along. She'll know what to do."

The fire sparks in Charity's eyes changed swiftly to a glow of hope. This time when he tugged at her hand, her total lack of resistance almost knocked both of them off their feet. Still clutching her grimy little fist in his, he led her carefully along the alley, threading their way among stacked up crates, barrels, and mounds of garbage.

Twice Mac halted, pulling Charity against the wall when doors ahead of them opened. The first time, Mrs. Phineas put her cat out. She never even glanced their direction. The second time, Mr. Jake Barton, who did odd jobs around town, and Miss Ella Willis, who did laundry for people, stood framed in the doorway. Mr. Barton tried to kiss her. She giggled and attempted to shove him away, although Mac didn't figure she attempted very hard. She finally succeeded in shutting the door on Jake, who glanced up the alley, but didn't see the children crouched behind a stack of barrels. Setting his hat more firmly down on his forehead, he sauntered toward the street, whistling jauntily and definitely off-tune.

Only after Jake Barton's whistling had faded in the distance, Mac rose to his feet. Motioning Charity to follow, keeping close to the wall, he sidled to the end of the alley. Peering out cautiously, he saw no one. Grabbing Charity's hand, he zigzagged north to Centre Street and another block east to the edge of town. Giggling, they made one last dash, crossed the wooden bridge over Mill Creek, and gained the shelter of the trees bordering the village.

On the road home at last, safe from curious eyes, the two made no pretense of hurry. After all, what was waiting for them except a history test and a spanking? They had Miss Sullivan's permission, too, although Mac declined to examine that one too closely. He pointed out the cottontail burrow he'd discovered three days before. They lingered at the edge of Mill Creek and he showed her how to skip stones, shaking his head woefully as hers repeatedly plopped on the first jump. They stood stock still in wonder as a doe and two fawns emerged from the trees and crossed the grassy meadow not a rod in front of them before melting into the foliage on the other side.

Passing Cowbell Swamp, he told her how it came to be so called. Long ago an untended cow wandered past and, tempted by the lush foliage, ventured too far out and mired in the middle of the swamp, sinking before she could be rescued. "Now," Mac said solemnly, "sometimes on summer evenings, you hear her bell clinking as she grazes. But no matter how much you look, she's never there. Just her bell clanking. Over and over and over," he finished mournfully.

Charity shivered and gazed wide eyed at the shimmering water. "Poor cow," she said softly, obviously missing the entire ghostly point.

Mac didn't know whether to laugh or be disgusted at such a tenderhearted response to his haunting tale of woe. Before he could decide, she darted off, chasing a dragonfly that flitted past. He heaved a disappointed sigh and followed. *How could my storytelling go so wrong?* He always shuddered, no matter how many times Pa told it. Would he ever figure out how girls thought? He was beginning to doubt it.

His dormant conscience finally stirred. "Guess we better get going. Come on, I'll race you to that maple tree." She accepted the challenge so promptly, she literally left him in the dust. He beat her, but he was frankly panting when she caught up to him. She was scarcely even out of breath.

"You run fast. For a girl," he gulped.

"I like to run," she said innocently—and unnecessarily.

Back planted against the maple, he tried to look as if he didn't really need to breathe that hard.

As they neared the farm, he caught sight of his father, plowing. Hope of edging past him unnoticed proved futile, for Zane saw them at the same time and waved them over. "Come on." Mac took Charity's hand again and helped her over the furrows and humps. She apparently had supreme trust in his assertion his parents wouldn't be mad. She hopped along, perky as a chipmunk. He, on the other hand, was beginning to feel a shade doubtful. *What if*—There was no time, however, for further speculation. Arms crossed, scowling ferociously, Pa eyed their approach.

They stood silently in front of him. He regarded them just as silently. Finally, Mac ventured a weak, "Hi, Pa." And, seizing opportunity, "This is Charity. She's new at school."

"Hello, Charity," Zane said solemnly.

She bobbed a curtsy as nonchalantly as though she were entertaining in the parlor, not standing mud bedraggled in his cornfield-to-be.

"We fell in the mud." Mac ventured his carefully reasoned explanation, but the sternness in his father's eyes halted his attempt.

"You'd better get on to the house. I expect Ma will want to see you." Zane watched them retrace their path across the bumpy ground. Only when he was certain they wouldn't hear, he allowed his sternness to melt into a choked chuckle. He didn't know exactly what had happened, but they both looked like they'd been held up by their heels and submerged. Achilles had fared better, since his dipping took place in plain water, and his heel, at least, had escaped the dunking. *I doubt there's an inch so fortunate on either of these youngsters.*

Mac halted at the back steps. "Maybe we better call out, first," he suggested from past experience. He hallooed to his mother, and again, before she appeared in the doorway.

"Mac? What's wrong?" Her panicked questioning died. She stood speechless, her face a peculiar pink shade, for a full five seconds before slowly descending the steps. She reached out to shake him but speedily changed her mind. "MacCord Edwards, what have you and Rose been doing?" She found her voice but stopped in confusion as she realized the second small mud pile wasn't her daughter.

"This is Charity. We fell in the mud," he explained again, and also quite unnecessarily. "This is my Ma," he added helpfully to Charity, who bobbed another curtsy as casually as though Mrs. Edwards were used to greeting pathetic little heaps of mud who showed up on her clean doorstep.

Larissa smiled a weak acknowledgment. "Where's Rose?" she

demanded anxiously of her son.

"At school. Miss Sullivan sent us home to get cleaned up. Charity said her Pa'd be real mad, so I told her she could come home with me, that you'd understand," he offered hopefully. "She doesn't have a Ma."

Larissa started to protest his open handedness, but broke off as his last words sank in. After all, they were here, now. She could scarcely send the child home, wherever that was, with a "No, thank you." She swung into action. "I'll start heating water for baths. Mac, go to the barn and get out of those filthy clothes. Charity, are you wearing shoes and stockings? Take them off. You'll have to come into the house for a bath, but we can try to keep some of this dirt outside." Even as she scolded, she sat the little girl on the step and helped her tug off her wet shoes.

Mac, shoulders drooping, started for the barn, but his father waylaid him. "Hold on, son. I'll get a quilt to take with you." He edged past his wife, who was working on the second shoe, her face screwed into a combination of disgust and determination. He dropped his hand to her shoulder as he passed, and she glanced up. Mac saw his lips twitch, her jaw stiffen in an unreadable between-parents look.

He turned away dispiritedly. He was itching furiously now from the dried mud. His parents were angry with him after all. *But what else could I do?*

The barn, with its good odors of hay, animals, and leather, enveloped him comfortingly. He started shucking his stiffened clothing, but paused as a shadow filled the doorway, became his father silently extending a quilt. Mac wrapped it around his suddenly shivering body and sank into the fragrant bed of a stall. Pa hunkered beside him and reached for a handful of straw. Selecting one, he began breaking it into pieces. He glanced sideways. "Want to tell me about it?"

When Mac eyed him doubtfully, he reached to tousle the boy's hair, releasing a flurry of mud flakes. "Come on, now. It can't be that bad."

Yes, it can. Nevertheless, Mac plunged in. About Ian and Bruiser and their snake, the mud puddle, and Charity's not having a Ma, and being afraid to face her Pa. It tumbled out rather jumbled. When he finished he kept his eyes on a patch of blue quilt that was just like the stuffed pony Ma had made for him years ago when he was little. He had lugged that fool horse everywhere he went.

"Sounds like you've had quite a morning." Pa's voice erased the past, bringing Mac back to his present woes.

"I'm sorry, Pa. But I just couldn't let 'em pick on her like that." His voice trailed off at the strange look in Pa's eyes. He hung his head again.

Zane, quilt, mud, and all, enfolded his son in a swift, hearty hug, and ruffled his hair again, loosing another storm of mud flakes. "You did good, son." His voice seemed to stick and he cleared his throat, repeating gruffly, "By jingo, you did real good."

Relief flooded Mac, but honesty and worry forced him to add, "I guess Ma's pretty upset."

"Probably. I think she just finished scrubbing the kitchen floor. But I reckon when it gets explained to her, she'll see the way of it."

Sitting in a shaft of sunlight, wrapped in the quilt and in the comfort of Pa's words, Mac drowsed. He drifted back to awareness of Ma's voice, talking to Pa, and rubbed his eyes with his fists, not remembering for that first moment how he came to be huddled in the straw.

"I've never seen so much mud in my life." Was Ma scolding? Uncertainty held him rooted to the spot. If he hadn't known better, he would have sworn she was laughing.

Pa's deep chuckle answered her, and the knot in Mac's stomach smoothed. "We still have one to go." Pa motioned with his thumb toward the stall as Mac, trying to get to his feet, tripped on a fold of the quilt and flopped back down onto the hay.

Ma knelt beside him and removed a wisp of straw from his hair. "Pa told me what happened."

"Are you mad with me?"

She smoothed a mud-stiff lock back from his forehead. "Of course not. But Charity still has to face her Pa and explain it all to him."

Mac's eyes clouded. "She said he'll whip her if he finds out. That's not fair."

"Lots of things in life aren't fair, son. But it doesn't mean we can avoid the truth." Pa spoke with quiet assurance.

"May I go with her when she tells him?"

Mac waited while his parents exchanged a glance that was, again, to him unreadable, before Ma smiled. "If you're going calling, I suggest you leave a few pounds of mud here at home. Then her Pa might be just a little more inclined to listen."

He jumped up, stumbled over the quilt again, and nearly lost the whole covering. He made a grab for it as Pa reached out and swung him up into his arms. Safely ensconced in the blanket, the weight of responsibility off his shoulders, he became once more a ten-year-old boy deeply loved by his parents. He let Pa carry him to the house, and while Charity sat outside on the porch step, he bathed and put on clothes that were wonderfully mud free.

***

Clean and itchless once more, Mac and Charity started back to town to face her father. "Your Ma's nice," she remarked as they trotted along. "She said I could borrow Rose's dress and hair ribbons and everything.

She said Rose wouldn't mind." Smoothing the red checked skirt, she asked anxiously, "Do you especk she will?"

"I don't guess so. If she does, you can always shove her in a mud puddle."

Giggling, racing, they scampered into Fairvale. Again crossing the little wooden bridge over Mill Creek, they skirted the public square, a grassy expanse from which the town radiated. As they neared the hotel a second time, Charity began to lag once more.

Mac, determined to forestall another heel setting session, urged her to get it over with. "He can't be mad, now. You're all cleaned up. Ma said she'll wash your dress and stuff, so you don't have to worry about that." She didn't look noticeably convinced, so he added, "You can't avoid the truth, you know. You have to face it, even if it doesn't always seem fair."

Abandoning the last shred of hope, clutching his hand in her cold little fist, she slowly followed him into the hotel. "That's my Pa, over there," she whispered, pointing.

Mac had to blink first, to adjust his eyes from the bright sunlight of outdoors to the darker interior of the hotel lobby. Keen disappointment stabbed him. He had halfway expected, from Charity's attitude, a fierce old man stomping his feet and breathing fire, with maybe a tail and horns thrown in for good measure. *No tail or horns.* He was old, to be sure. *He's every bit as old as Pa.* The only smoke in evidence curled from the pipe resting in the holder on the desk. His brown hair, mustache and short beard were no different from those of the other men in town or on the surrounding farms.

When he glanced up and saw them framed in the doorway, Mac noticed his eyes were as deep blue as Charity's, and just as filled with sudden anxiety. "Charity, what are you doing here?" He handed a key to the young couple standing by the desk. "Room Four. Up the stairs, turn right." As they moved away, he hurried to his daughter.

In spite of himself, Mac panicked. *What if Charity was right all along?* He realized abruptly he didn't even know what to call her Pa because he didn't know her last name. Her father solved that problem as he descended upon them.

"Charity Michaels, what have you been doing? Why aren't you in school? And where is your new dress?"

Voice quivering, gripping Mac's hand so tightly he was sure she was going to break the bones, Charity blurted, "The snake licked me, Pa. I fell in the mud. And Ian pushed Mac in and we went to his house—Mac's—and his Ma gave me a bath and washed my hair and braided it and here's my shoes." She thrust them at her father. Caught unaware, he grabbed them by reflex and speedily discovered they were still damp with mud.

He looked from the shoes in his hands to the mud on the front of his black dress coat, to his young daughter who, having "faced the truth," waited mute and wide eyed for punishment to swoop.

He regarded her in total silence while he digested her rush of words. Still in total silence he turned away. The children exchanged a glance, Mac's bewildered, hers a frightened I told you so. They watched in petrified fascination as Mr. Michaels bent down behind the front desk. He straightened, a copy of the Fairvale *Tribune* in his hands. He placed the paper on the carpet and gingerly set the shoes on the paper. Dusting off his hands, he took a step toward the children, but halted as an elderly, bearded and mustached gentleman entered.

"You will remain here until I've assisted this guest." His face set in unmistakably stern lines, his voice came with ominous quiet. Behind the desk, he pulled aside a green velvet curtain on golden rings that rattled loudly against the rod, and motioned Charity to obey. "You, too, young man. I'll want the complete story." They edged past him and, with a final rattle-knell, he dropped the curtain, slicing them off from view of the lobby.

The windowless little room, evidently the hotel office, contained a desk and chairs. A book with ruled lines, writing, and numbers covering its visible pages lay on the desk. Mac's flustered glance confirmed they'd come in through the only door. Charity shivered wordlessly as they sat down. An awful feeling of doom swooped over him.

Before he could think of anything to say, the curtain swished back and Mr. Michaels, seeming ten feet tall to the fearful youngsters, stood framed in the doorway. He glanced at each of them. He let the curtain fall. "I want the entire story, from the beginning." His voice, still frighteningly quiet, held the same no tolerating of nonsense tone. "You, young man." His blue eyes and chilled voice pinned Mac like a butterfly on a board. "You, I presume, are Mac." At the boy's single nod, he continued, "Since you seem to have figured to a large extent in this escapade, I suggest you tell me precisely what transpired."

Mac wasn't entirely certain about the first part of the sentence, but he harbored no doubt about the command expressed in the second half. Sliding to his feet, gulping, he plunged into his explanation. Mr. Michaels said nothing the whole time. His eyes, however, flashed a fire similar to Charity's when he heard the part about the boys shoving the snake in his daughter's face. At Mac's explanation why they went to the farm instead of coming here to the hotel, incredulity replaced his scowl. Mac stumbled through to the end, feeling he had told it very badly. "Just please don't be mad with Charity," he finished miserably.

Silence stretched while, with that still baffled expression, Ethan Michaels regarded his unhappy daughter. "Charity," he said roughly, "come here." She eyed him apprehensively, but obediently scooted down off the chair. She stood before him, her gaze fastened on her bare toes. He knelt to her level, reached to tilt her chin up, and saw the misery in her blue eyes. "Oh, Charity," he murmured, more to himself than to her, and held out his arms. Stunned, she threw herself against him in a choking hug.

Mac balanced on one bare foot, then the other. *The history test, even the mud puddle, would be better than this.*

After an eternity or so, Mr. Michaels stood, holding a beaming Charity, her arm clasped tightly around his neck. He reached to put his free hand on Mac's shoulder. "There's been an abundance of misunderstanding here. It's long past time Charity and I had a heart-to-heart talk. For now, thank you for assisting her when she required it."

A huge balloon of relief swelled inside Mac. He didn't understand Mr. Michaels' abrupt change of attitude, but he realized that, furious as Charity's Pa had been earlier, he wasn't mad at either one of them, now. Obviously, it just indicated one more way of a grownup that he couldn't hope to figure out.

***

At supper that evening, Mac related the climax of his adventure.

"So Charity didn't get into trouble after all?" Pa passed the plate of roast. "She was certainly one mud caked little girl when she was here."

Mac swallowed a bite of cornbread. "Mr. Michaels said he'd like to come by tomorrow to get Charity's clothes and meet you. He wasn't mad with us at all after we explained."

Rose giggled. "You're lucky. Miss Sullivan got madder than a wet hen at Ian and Bruiser. She yelled and said if they ever did anything like that again, they couldn't come back to school." Her voice suddenly sobered. "She told us Charity's Ma got bit by a snake and died, and that's why Charity's so scared of snakes. I don't blame her." She shuddered. "I hope you don't get bit by a snake, Ma. You won't, will you?"

Larissa touched her daughter's soft hair reassuringly. "I have no intention of it. I don't like snakes, either."

Pa's eyes twinkled. "If a snake ever bit your Ma, she'd just bite it back." He cleared his throat. "And now one more matter. The history test. Did you take it, son?"

Mac looked rueful. "I sure did."

Rose bounced in her chair. "He got one hundred percent. May he be a doctor now?"

Pa and Ma exchanged glances. Grinning, Pa put a big hand on Mac's shoulder. "Yes, Rose, he can be a doctor. It'll probably take a little more studying, but it appears you're on your way. We're proud of you. For more reasons than one."

Mac basked in the glow of praise, but slumped his shoulders in sheer relief that this day was almost over. He couldn't remember ever being so tired.

CHAPTER THREE

Upon their move to the farm just after he and Larissa married, Zane realized the place needed more than simple "dirt farming" in order to succeed financially. Grown to manhood hesitant to speak his innermost thoughts and feelings — that long-ago tongue lashing about wasting good work time mooning over picture drawing had left its mark upon him — he had faltered in voicing his fancy notions to Larissa. Those early days, he hadn't yet learned that confiding in her completed an essential part of his deepest self and did not, as he'd feared, shout of weakness. He'd told her, haltingly, his thoughts of raising blooded horses for sale.

Her enthusiastic response amazed and amused him. She admitted that, growing up around her father's livery stable, she rode horses of every description from the time she could walk. Because she became a "proper young lady" before meeting him, he hadn't known of her expertise. Contemplating the possibility, however, he allowed how it suited her personality. Still, several years passed before the full truth struck, causing him to chuckle wryly. *No wonder she canters ever a furlong or two ahead of me in our daily living. She's had a lot of practice.* They had started small, carefully establishing the bloodline. Over the years, their combined knowledge brought a stable of Morgan horses now attracting attention in far flung counties of the state.

Thus, the morning after Mac's mud puddle adventure, the family rose early to take advantage of the bright spring day. Farm work was a never-ending session. Zane and Larissa required both children to help with the chores. Rose cleaned tack and fed and watered the chickens without prompting. She helped with housework and, at five-going-on-six, would soon become the family's chief producer of knitted stockings.

Regardless of Mac's embryonic medical career, Zane and Larissa expected him to continue his full share of home chores, including riding the horses out for their daily exercise. More than once within the children's hearing, Zane told Larissa, "While they're young, teach 'em to work hard and finish what they start. When they're grown, they won't shy away from sweat and calluses."

One day, Mac asked Zane if his Pa used to say that to him a lot, too. Startled, Zane realized how he was echoing his own father's words. It seemed like he'd heard them at least once every day during his growing up years. Echoing the words was one thing. Echoing the harsh tone in which they'd been spoken was quite another. After that, he kept a watch on what he said, and how he said it. Not for the finest wheat harvest this side of heaven would he imitate his father's disciplinary methods.

For sure, he wasn't afraid of sweat and calluses, and he was gratified to know that his children weren't, either. On this blue and green April morning, plowing the cornfield, father and son had full opportunity to display both.

This year Mac could reach the handles of the new John Deere plow, so he was learning how to lay out a straight furrow—and also discovering the skill required for something so simple looking. Zane shook out the lines set around his waist and clucked to Buck and Bob and off they'd go, a furrow cut behind them clean and straight as if he'd laid a plumb line. When Mac tried it, the oxen started reluctantly and kept going only if he prodded them and yelled, the furrow behind wavering like Zeke Pritchard had stepped it off after one of his "medicinal purposes" drinking sprees.

By mid morning, it seemed to Zane that they'd been plowing all day and half the night. Having had to sternly quell his sympathy as he watched Mac struggle, he felt as tired as he knew the boy must be. Even so, deep pride filled him at his son's determination to get it right. As he assured Mac that his furrows were, indeed, getting straighter, a voice hailed them. They turned and Mac recognized Charity and her father in a livery stable rig stopped on the road fronting the cornfield.

"Appears we can call a halt, son." Zane sleeved sweat from his eyes. "Don't know about you, but I'm more'n ready."

Mac shucked the lines from where they rested on his shoulders because he wasn't tall enough to set them about his waist like his father. Zane, with compassion born of having been there himself, watched as the boy tried, unsuccessfully, to hide his relief. Under the straw hat, Mac's mop of red hair was sweat pasted to his forehead. His blue shirt and dark pants stuck to him as firmly as if he'd been dunked into Mill Creek.

Charity, in a green dress and bonnet, looking like a part of the springtime morning, hopped from the buggy and waved a greeting across the furrows.

"Good morning, Miss Charity." Zane removed his battered work hat and saluted her with a friendly grin.

She bobbed her little curtsey to him and, hands clasped behind her back, added shyly, "Hello, Mac."

Realizing that his son's tongue had suddenly acquired a dozen knots, Zane strode forward, drawing their other visitor's attention from Mac. The man had stepped from the buggy and spoke apologetically. "Perhaps we've arrived at an inconvenient time."

"Not at all. We're just getting ready to take a break. You must be Charity's father. I'm Zane Edwards." He stuck out his grimy, sweaty hand and pulled it back ruefully.

With no hesitation, Ethan Michaels grasped it firmly. "I farmed back in Sanilac County, Michigan, before we moved here. Never met a hard working man yet harmed by a little dirt." He winked at Mac. "Now mind, I said a little dirt. I gather you and Charity between you had enough mud to grow the finest stand of corn in Michigan or Ohio." Mac grinned at the friendly teasing.

Over his visitor's shoulder, Zane glimpsed Larissa and Rose picking their way across the bumpy field. Larissa's soft chestnut hair was tucked tidily into the thick bun at the back of her head, and the tendrils usually framing Rose's face showed the dampness of their recent combing back into her braids. As though they hadn't been toiling over a hot washtub only minutes before, clean aprons covered their Saturday work dresses. Just as Zane was teaching his son the finer points of plowing a straight furrow, Larissa was teaching her daughter the reality of hard work and the sometimes grim necessity for seeing a task through. Rose was also learning that moments came when only a fresh approach—a crisp apron, flowers so new picked they still held morning dew on their petals as they graced the breakfast table—would do. "Hyacinths to feed the soul," Larissa called them.

After giggled greetings, Rose and Charity scampered away. Zane circled his arm about Larissa's waist. "My wife, Larissa. Rissa, Mr. Michaels."

As Larissa tilted her face to their guest, who was considerably taller than her own five-foot, one-inch frame, Zane saw something spark, deep within their visitor's shadowed blue eyes. Remembering Rose's story of his wife's death, Zane sensed the awkwardness of the situation. Even so, he couldn't banish the swelling of his heart. It occurred each time he observed the glow lighting Larissa's face as he introduced her. Even after all the years, while his words stated the commonplace, his tone unashamedly acknowledged the complete joy he found in their marriage. Smiling, she reached out her hand. "Mr. Michaels."

He removed his hat, shook with her and dropped his hand back to his side. "A pleasure to meet both of you. And please, call me Ethan. I just dropped by to return Rose's dress and to thank you again, all of you, for assisting my daughter yesterday. You have a fine son." Mac reddened and scuffed a dirt clod with his bare toe.

"We appreciate hearing that. We've worked hard to bring them up responsible. It's good to know we're getting results. Mac," Zane added, "why don't you take the horse and buggy into the shade and water the mare? And take a breather yourself. I'll call you when it's time to start again."

Released and relieved, Mac trotted toward the buggy and the patiently standing gray mare.

Ethan's eyes followed him. "You can indeed be very proud. I

21

understand he's the only one yesterday who even attempted to help Charity." His voice held deep appreciation and undisguised bitterness.

Zane, knowing the rage he would feel were Rose thrust into that situation, forgot the earlier awkwardness and put his hand on Larissa's arm. Which one of them he was reassuring by this touch, he wasn't certain. He turned to her and she raised her head. The love and trust in her eyes distracted him. Not noticing Ethan's sharp intake of breath at her response, he spoke with his usual courteous warmth. "Thank you. Now, why don't we go to the house where it's cooler?"

Larissa promptly reinforced the invitation. "I have fresh doughnuts and buttermilk."

Zane, watching Larissa, didn't see Ethan's sudden bleakness as he tipped his head in grave courtesy. "I accept with pleasure. I've always had a special fondness for doughnuts."

Later, the men tramped the fields, talking of stock and horses, crops and soil, of differences in farming methods between Michigan and Ohio. Ethan paused by the corral gate, stooped and picked up a twig. "You have it all," he said quietly, head bent, carefully examining the bit of wood in his fingers. "A good family and a good farm." He hesitated as if searching for words. "I have no right to initiate such a topic, so I'll mention this once and never again. What you have here—it's what Nettie and I had. A man who's been there can tell." His grief filled eyes suddenly met Zane's squarely. "Thank God every day of your life for what you have. Don't ever take it for granted just because it's here." His voice trailed off and he gazed a long way out across the grass-lush pasture and the grazing horses.

Zane had no words that could even begin to comfort him. Silently, he placed his hand on Ethan's shoulder.

That night, Zane and Larissa in bed, her head nestled under his chin, his arm warm and strong around her, Ethan's words returned and an icy fist punched his belly. *How does he stand it?*

***

That late spring and summer, life was full to the brim on the Edwards farm. Besides the never-ceasing work cycle, they saw a great deal of Charity Michaels and, when he was not busy at the hotel, a lesser amount of her father, Ethan. Charity and Rose, so close in age, had become fast friends. Larissa, without stepping over the bounds of friendship or demeaning Ethan's relationship with his daughter, quietly began to supply some of the mothering the little girl so desperately needed, and the child took on a new bloom of joyful living.

Ethan, for his part, never intruded on the family's privacy, but he showed up at odd hours, invariably about chore time, to pick up Charity. He always pitched in to help with whatever work was in progress, doing it with the ease of long practice, skillful as Zane himself.

Zane became concerned about Ethan's doing so much. As the summer wore on, he became very nearly a hired hand. "Except without pay," Zane lamented to Larissa, now so much his source of counsel he could only wonder at those early tongue-tied days and his young foolishness. "He's doing the work of a hand, but he's not getting anything in return. Except sweat and calluses. Do we offer him a wage? I wish we could hire him on permanent, but our own pockets aren't that full."

Larissa sewed steadily on a new dress for Rose while he fretted and paced. When he had run down a little, she rested the material on her lap. "I don't think he's doing it for pay in the money sense. You said he had a farm before Nettie died. You also said he's—" she ducked her head over her sewing to hide her smile and made her voice male gruff "'—good as me at the work. He doesn't question, just does.'"

Her eyes, all laughter gone, met her husband's. "Perhaps you should put yourself in his place for just a minute. How would you feel if you lost this farm? It's your right arm. Take you off the land, you'd wither like a tree pulled up by its roots. I suspect it's the same with Ethan. He'd literally lost the ground his roots were in and he was drying up. Then he came here, began doing odd chores for you. He's living again. He's nourished. Not the same, of course, as farming his own place, but he has a start, now, toward life.

"As for payment, he's no fool. He sees how good it's been for Charity, being around Rose. She's blossoming, and happy, like a child should be. He can't repay you for that, in money, any more than he can pay you for his own new interest in life. So he's giving back the only way he can. Zane," she rested her hand on his, and her eyes were misty, "let him."

He regarded her a long moment. "What would I ever do without you?"

She laughed and picked up her sewing. "Just don't ever expect to find out."

***

After his discussion with Larissa, Zane stopped fretting and accepted Ethan's welcome assistance with the farm and horse work. His presence freed Mac, now past his eleventh birthday, to give more time to school while it was still in session. Later, he spent increased time helping Doc Rawley in his office and accompanying him on his innumerable visits about the countryside.

Doc, in his early fifties, had a bushy head of black-graying hair, an equally bushy, graying beard hiding his mouth, deep frown lines between his eyes, and a strong tendency toward grumpiness. He could be, and was, stern to the point of harshness when Mac blundered a task he figured the boy should have mastered. "In this business, sometimes your first go-round is your last. You don't do it right that first chance, they're going to be dead a mighty long time." But he was infinite patience itself as he detailed a new technique to his deeply absorbed student. Sometimes he even waited on the edge of the schoolyard for class to be dismissed so he and Mac could discuss a finding in the newest medical journal.

Mac learned early on that not only was he allowed to voice his opinion, Doc Rawley expected him to, whether it tallied with Doc's view or not. "You got to use common sense, too," Doc insisted. "Don't fry the boot for supper just because it's what came up on your line. But don't reject, either, without careful thought. It just might be a new kind of fish."

He waved a medical paper at Mac. "Take this article about this fella named Lister, talking about infection, saying it's what causes so many people to die after surgery. Is he a quack? Lot of high thought of doctors insist he is. But why do we lose so many patients after operating successfully? We'll have to chew this one a little finer. I'm betting we haven't heard the last of him or his new fangled ideas."

Initially, Mac's duties had consisted mainly of sweeping the office and dusting the few medical volumes on the shelf above the desk. A stickler for cleanliness, Doc even out rivaled Ma. He'd laid it on the line, the first day. "Some doctors say clean or dirty don't matter. That the patient'll get well or die on our skills and according as God wishes. Maybe so. But I can't see it does any harm to give Him a hand now and then. I've noticed He seems to appreciate it more if the hand is clean."

True or not, Mac couldn't decide. He knew only that for all his hard bitten grouchiness, Doc saved more patients than he lost, and his community trusted him implicitly.

Most doctors learned medicine as Mac was learning it now, by apprenticeship. Doc, however, had been to medical school, all the way to the University in Pennsylvania. After a long, three-year course, he had even worked for a time in the Pennsylvania Hospital. The medical books came from there. Doc expected Mac to read the books, not just for information, but to make him realize medical knowledge was on going. Practices accepted as ironclad fact only twenty years ago were now outdated and must be avoided at all costs. He encouraged Mac to ask questions. "You got to learn by doing," he insisted. "All the fancy books in the world aren't going to teach your fingers how much fever is too much for Retta Hill's baby, or your ears that the wheeze in Old Man

Tucker's chest is lung fever, not consumption."

Mac scrubbed bottles for Doc to fill with medical concoctions from his pharmaceutical stores, kept eyes and ears open when patients came to the office, and eagerly awaited his first call to tend someone in the country. Only then, he felt, would he be fully initiated into real doctoring. The first several weeks, however, his deepest wish went unfulfilled. All the farm calls came when he was not in the office. Doc told him to keep his britches on, the time would come soon enough and probably be highly inconvenient at that.

Sure enough, on a gloomy Saturday morning, the skies a curtain of gray and thunder growlings vibrating in the distance, Ham Tolliver burst into the office. "Close the door," Doc growled in greeting as he continued to bandage his patient's arm. "You want us all to come down with sneezing fits?"

"You gotta come quick, Doc," Ham gasped. "One of the Packer girls has stomach cramps and is painin' somethin' awful. I was coming to town and when I passed their place, Cleet hailed me. I told him I'd come straight for you."

Doc grunted.

"Don't know which gal," Ham admitted. "I just tore for town when Cleet said she was bad off."

Doc grunted again and told Mac, "You might as well try your hand at this. I don't guess Hank, here, will mind being practiced on."

Hank Carter, on the receiving end of a broken arm, courtesy of his horse, Hazel, who'd thrown him against the corral gate earlier that morning, managed a weak grin. "Go ahead. I don't see as you can make it hurt much worse. Ain't my first broken bone. Don't reckon it'll be my last."

"Told you last year when she busted your leg to get rid of that fool—"

"Doc!" Ham Tolliver protested.

Doc, his eyes on Mac's hands, didn't turn, but he snarled, "I heard you, Ham. But I got to finish with Hank, here, first. Even if he probably knows as much by this time about bone setting as me." He added bitterly, "Leave it to a Packer to have a bellyache—tighter, Mac, that's better—on a rotten day like this. Probably too many green apples. Packers don't die. They just reproduce."

The Packers, a hard scrabble family living on a hill farm four miles outside town, were not noted for either their prosperity or their efforts toward that goal. Their skills, rather, leaned toward promoting arguments that usually ended up in fistfights, and producing with monotonous regularity a new offspring each year. Thus, while Doc's attitude did not exactly ooze Hippocratic idealism, it was understandable.

Mac finished splinting Hank's arm and waited for Doc to check his work. Doc inspected it carefully. "You know," he told Hank casually, "this boy'll put me out of business one of these days. You're fixed up good as if I'd done it. Lucky for you he's learned right off, since you refuse to get rid of that fool mare," he added sourly.

Hank grinned. "She's not bad, Doc. Just feisty."

Doc snorted.

After releasing Hank with instructions to go home, rest, and "stay off that danged beast," Doc gathered his equipment, preparatory to aiding the Packer girl's bellyache. "Calomel and ipecac. We'll probably have to flush her out," he said bluntly.

Mac ducked his head to hide his grin. Not only Packer males possessed a fighting bent. The females undisputedly held their own against any comers, usually with rocks. If Doc was pondering ipecac, he'd have his hands full. Doc sensed rather than saw his amusement. "Go ahead. Snicker. We'll see how full of chuckles you are after we finish. Well, come on, Boy. No doctoring education is complete until you've passed the Packer test." He opened the door to a curtain of rain and a growl of thunder. Pulling his hat lower, he addressed the sky. "This is Your doing, not mine, so don't tell me. You're the one invented Packers in the first place." Doc's acquaintance with the Almighty might not include many sessions inside a church, but he was always bluntly honest in his opinions.

The ride to the Packer farm was miserable.

Huddled in his corner of the buggy, Mac tried to avoid the worst of the rain, a hopeless attempt because the wind gusted it in sheets right at them. Bella, Doc's piebald mare who could out-ornery him any day of the week, was reluctant to forge ahead in the face of so much water, and Doc had to keep clucking to her. Their mackintosh overcoats weren't much help keeping them dry. The wind kept snatching the corners, lifting them gleefully for easy insertion of the rain fingers. The thunder growls were closer now. Lightning zigzags surrounded them. Doc glanced sideways at his pupil. "I'll drop you off home when we go by. No sense both of us getting soaked." He had to raise his voice over a fresh gust of wind.

Mac shook his head violently. "No, please. I ain't that wet. I want to go with you."

"Your Ma'll have a fit, she finds I had you out like this."

"She don't have to know. I won't tell her. Unless she asks," he compromised. "Besides, I'm with you. She already knows that."

Doc studied Bella's dripping rump. "I've done fool things in my time. Thought I'd filled my grain bin, but I guess not. All right, but if you catch your death of cold, do me a favor. Come back and tell your Ma I tried to talk you out of it. Or else she'll be the death of me."

In spite of the discomfort he had just denied, Mac managed a watery grin.

The Packer farm, unsightly enough in the cheerfulness of sunshine, was positively dreary when squatting in the rain. The yard, for once bare of Packers, was a sea of mud. Cast off litter made little islands in the muck. A few chickens, scrawny, bedraggled, and thoroughly soaked, pecked optimistically at the scattered garbage. Doc pulled in close to the hipshot porch, upon which Packer pocketknives had inflicted an array of designs, and hallooed.

No answer.

Doc glanced at Mac, who shrugged in equal puzzlement. He hallooed again at the top of his lungs, so that Bella twitched her ears irritably. The sagging front door suddenly jerked open to reveal Ma Packer. She weighed at least two hundred pounds and graying hair straggled from the careless bun on top of her head. Her wrinkled, stained dress looked as if she had attempted to clean up the front yard with it, and failed. Her hard brown eyes held no friendliness as she snapped, "What d' you mean, screechin' like that? I just got these young'ins settled down and now you come along hollerin' fit to wake the dead. I declare I don't know what's—Get back inside!" she interjected, using an ample leg to bar the doorway from a horde of young Packers attempting escape. The muted rumbling behind her swelled.

Doc did his best to keep control of the situation. "Miz Packer, I'll put my horse in the barn and come back to the house. Mac, why don't you hop out here—"

"Yes, yes, in the barn. Pa's waitin' f'r you." Ma Packer gestured impatiently, flung out her leg again, and roared, "I told you to stay inside, you little—" The door slammed.

"On the other hand, Mac, why not come with me? A few more gallons of water won't make you any wetter." Doggedly finishing the instructions Ma had interrupted, Doc turned Bella toward the barn that, if ramshackle, showed better care than the house. Pa Packer gestured vigorously from the doorway, but the gush of wind and rain drowned him out.

"Been waitin' f'r ya. Thought ya'd get here a smart time ago," Pa greeted them graciously once they drove close enough to make out his words. Doc flicked a glance at Mac's dazed expression. The boy was, undeniably, getting a full taste of Packer hospitality.

"Well, git down, git down. Cain't do no doctorin' from there." Pa Packer, dingily gray of hair, bushy of beard, and a skinny shadow alongside his hefty wife, motioned impatiently. Expertly aiming an amber stream of tobacco juice, he hit a foraging rooster's comb. Ignoring the ensuing squawking and flapping, Pa eyed Doc critically as if waiting for his excuse justifying such tardiness.

"If you'll give my horse a rubdown, we'll get on to the house," Doc suggested optimistically as he stepped from the buggy. "Which girl is sick?" His attempt at enlightenment totally failed, for Pa, ignoring his question, was literally dragging him farther back into the barn.

"This way, Doc, and shake a leg. She's right bad off." Mac, frankly owl-eyed by this time, carrying the medical bag, followed in their wake. "Here she be. Now do somethin', quick!" Pa gestured toward a dim-lit stall, from which sounds of labored breathing emerged.

Doc glanced in and confirmed his darkening suspicions. On a meager bed of straw, stretched out on her side, ribs heaving with effort, lay a mule. Face purpling with indignation, he stared from the mule to her master. "You mean to tell me you dragged me out here in the middle of a storm that would have floated Noah's ark, for a mule? One of your girls was supposed to be sick."

"Glory be, no." Pa was genuinely shocked. "One of the young'ins comes ailin', Ma c'n always fix 'em up. But this is my Angel girl. She needs to be took good care of."

Doc glared from the mule to Pa, but the man obviously wasn't joking. He glanced at Mac beside him, whose eyes were all but popping out at this turn of events. Doc sighed. "Told you this would be an education. I just didn't figure on how much of one. Well, we better get to it." He began rolling up his sleeves. "Pa, I want warm water, lots of it. It's up to you to see I get it. Not hot, just warm. Boy, she's going to kick like a mule. See if you can find some rope to tie her legs together."

Mac, with a strong premonition of Doc's choice of treatment, leaped to obey and came back with some frayed pieces, undoubtedly the finest the barn had to offer. Doc eyed them dubiously. "Guess they'll have to do. Let's hope her kicking mood's been doused by all this rain. If not, we're in for a high time." He helped Mac secure the mule's legs. "This fine specimen of muledom has a dandy case of bloat. Probably been eating sweet clover. Know what we're going to do?" He cocked an eyebrow at his pupil.

Mac nodded solemnly. "You're gonna flush her out. But you aren't gonna use ipecac."

"You catch on quick. Let's just hope this mule isn't as smart."

Pa brought two buckets of warm water. "This good, Doc?" In his deep anxiety the temperature be exactly right, his hands shook, sloshing water onto his feet.

Doc tested it with an elbow. "Feels fine. Now you get over here and hold her legs down. I'm not aiming to be kicked into eternity by any outraged Packer, even if it is a mule." Mac choked and buried his crimson face to hide his laughter.

The barb flew right over Pa's head. "She wouldn't kick you purposeful," he said earnestly. "My Angel wouldn't." Mac's face turned redder still as he made a peculiar coughing sound.

"That boy ailin', too? We should tell Ma. She'll fix him right up, she will."

"He's probably taken cold, coming out in all this wind and rain. His Ma'll have my hide for sure." Doc's gallant rescue of Mac didn't impress Pa.

"Young'ins now days ain't got no starch. Take my Zeeb. He's about of an age with this'n. Had 'im plowin' t'other day. He griped the whole time about how much work it was."

Doc's eyes met Mac's in a flash of mutual realization. Undoubtedly, Zeeb had been doing all the plowing while Pa was sitting in the shade with his jug. Doc wondered, in unholy wickedness, if Angel, too, had been lounging while the boy pulled the plow for her. He could just picture her stretched out on her back, tipped against a shady tree, front legs crossed behind her neck, Pa's smirking grin on her face. All this time his hands were as busy as his thoughts. Now, "Stand back!" Mac dove to the side as Angel gave a tremendous lurch.

Pa was grinning from ear to ear. "You do have a way with animals, Doc." It was his highest praise.

On the way back to town, Doc studied Mac huddled silently in the corner of the buggy. "Quite a morning, wasn't it?"

No answer.

Doc peered from under the buggy top at the sky. "Looks like she might be clearing up." He paused and flicked the reins. "What's your opinion of doctoring, now?" He might as well get it said. "It was rough, no doubt about it. But that's what practicing medicine is, and no getting away from it. It's not glamorous. Most times it's not even pretty." A long-drawn moan from the corner of the buggy interrupted him. *Hell's fire. Is the boy going to cry? I gave him credit for more sand than that.*

The low groan came again and Mac doubled over, his whole body shaking. After a shocked moment, Doc realized Mac was laughing so hard tears were streaming down his cheeks. "We thought—it was—one of the—girls—and it was—his precious mule!"

Doc slapped his knee and his own mirth rolled out, peal after peal. Bella finally turned her head and gave them a disgusted glare. He eventually managed to catch his breath. "You'll do to ride the trail with, Boy. You surely will."

CHAPTER FOUR

Summer became fall. Mac's education continued. Bumps, sprains, fevers—he came to know them all on a first name basis. He learned, too, what it was to watch long hours beside a patient's bed, to wish fiercely for ability to stay the cold hands of death, and, in the end, to know that wish futile.

"It's something you'll never become hardened to. Leastways you better hope you don't," Doc said to the youngster huddled miserably in the corner of the buggy.

Mac's response was a thready whisper. "Mrs. Theron said the baby was a year old last week. She took her first steps on her birthday and then giggled so hard about doing it she fell smack on her bottom." His breath snagged in his throat. "How can the Therons go on? Memories should be happy. How can remembering things like that make them anything but sad?"

"They'll deal with it," Doc said harshly. "And so will you. You have to, or you won't be any good to anybody when they need you most." The harshness softened. "Put it in a corner of your heart and mind—not buried, you've got to acknowledge it—but don't dwell on it. Life has to, and will, go on. Just make damned sure what you gave was your best."

Mac sat a bit straighter and grubbed at his tear stained cheeks. His eyes lost a little of their glazed expression.

"You're learning an awful lot, awful fast," Doc said quietly, "but let me tell you something. Once you've faced death, fought him hand to hand and won, you can't ever be afraid of him in the same way. Losing just makes you that much more determined to win next time. And most times, you do. We're healers, Boy. We have the gift of life in our hands. No matter what happens, don't you ever forget that."

But events that fall of 1859 and spring of 1860 were whirlpooling into a cataclysm over which life and death were to seem merely pawns for the giving or taking.

Mac and Rose knew by heart Zane's favorite story of the Presidential contest of 1840. How Martin Van Buren's Democratic party accused Ohio's Whig candidate, William Henry Harrison, of wanting only a log cabin and lots of hard cider. Ohio voters promptly responded with torchlight parades in which cheering citizens drove wagons hauling log cabins, while other townsfolk rolled cider barrels through the streets.

Now even that drama paled into insignificance beside this modern day calamity of state snarling and tearing against state. Throughout that summer, tempers soared, the political climate among Fairvale's eight hundred sixty-seven citizens every bit as volatile as that of cities boasting much larger populations, every bit as warm and humid as the corn growing weather hovering over the countryside.

Men gathered in front of stores, at road crossings, at corners of maturing wheatfields to discuss the pros and cons of Northern abolitionist and Southern sympathizer. Cincinnati and other southern Ohio towns enjoyed strong cultural and economic ties with Kentucky and the slave South. Some Fairvale citizens had relatives "down there," so earliest sentiments were divided. John Brown's capture of the arsenal at Harper's Ferry, Virginia, on October 16, 1859, and his subsequent conviction and hanging for treason, heightened the quarreling.

Occasionally, older boys actually exchanged blows. A surreptitious time or two men, who in years did not have the excuse of being called boys, did so too. Miniature battles were won and lost in Fairvale even before President Lincoln declared war. Those disputes, however, were settled with fists and feet, weapons much more ancient than the guns later used to settle the national argument. No lasting physical damage was done except for Skinny Hawkins' chipped front tooth, and Obadiah Beldane's black eye that swelled shut. The puffiness made it hazardous for a week or so for the horses Obadiah shoed for a living, because it affected his depth perception. But the many-hued bruise healed, and the hooves that he pared a little crookedly grew out without harm to the equine owners. Only Skinny Hawkins' front tooth remained chipped. The country, unfortunately, would not emerge so unscathed from its dispute.

Mac, shuttling from home to doctor's office to the farms of patients, heard so many rumors mixed with a few facts, he didn't know what to believe. Pa, usually so calm, made no bones about his feelings. Was a declaration of war necessary to bring the dissenters into line? Then so be it. If it came to such an assertion, would anyone really be so eager to fight? This feuding had been going on for decades … Here something Mac did not identify for many years crept into Pa's voice. If it came to war, all those arguments about slave or free, in the Union or out of it, boiled down to the one certain fact of a man doing his God-given duty. At which talk Ma turned pale and very quiet.

Doc, on the other hand, violently opposed the whole notion of war. Not for political reasons, but because, as he put it, "I've spent thirty-five years patching up the human body, and now these fools want to shoot little bits of metal at each other and undo in a split second what I've spent most of my life trying to preserve. The lop-headed idiots!"

Mac, helping Doc cleanse and patch, also heard the views of those townspeople sympathizing with the Southern states. Through all the talk of state's rights and dissatisfaction of the increasing dependence of Southern economy upon Northern shipping and manufacturing, Mac caught a thread that puzzled him as much as that catch in Pa's voice when Pa talked of a man doing his duty. The men discussing the Southern viewpoint did not stress duty as a major issue. Rather, they seemed much more concerned with honor and the disgrace and dishonor of failure to support the Southern part of the country.

Mac, floundering in depths far beyond his experience, wished he could ask Pa and Ma about the difference, but, for the first time in his life, was afraid to approach them. Talk about the war now brought a look to Pa's eyes as if he were far away from them. When he returned to the present, his eyes held unbearable sadness. Ma got so quiet at those times it was almost as if she, too, had gone far away. Frightened, unable to fully comprehend their adult grief, Mac concluded that only by keeping silent could he keep them close.

One evening while Mac and Ethan curried the horses, unable to contain his bewilderment, he asked Charity's father. Ethan, suddenly intensely concerned with working a burr out of Pegasus' mane, did not answer for a long time.

"That question holds no easy response, Mac. I would to God there were. Maybe, then, we wouldn't be caught in all this turmoil." He studied the tines of the currycomb. "One could say that honor and duty are the same ideal—two parts that make up the way men think—just as the husk and the silk both make up an ear of corn. But it's not that easy. They aren't the same, any more than the husk and silk are when you peel them off the ear." As his thoughts shaped, his hands stilled on Pegasus' mane. "It has, I think, to do with the way a man looks at life and his place in it. Your Ma and Pa taught you when you do something wrong, admit it and take the consequences." Mac nodded. "They've taught you to feel a personal responsibility for what you do. You performed the action. It's your duty to accept the outcome. Now, as I understand it, Southerners look at it as a measure of disgrace, rather than as an individual consequence. The action is weighed in the eyes of other people. To dishonor is to shame, not just the immediate circle of folks, but also the ones perching on the branches of the family tree for quite a distance back."

Mac, struggling to comprehend, felt Ethan's hand on his shoulder. "If you can't grasp it, you're not alone. Men much older than you are wrestling, too."

Mac hesitated, but puzzlement won over politeness. "How come you understand so much about it?" He ducked his head in swift embarrassment at his rudeness. Ethan didn't answer for a long moment. Feeling the hand on his shoulder tighten, he looked up. Ethan was staring at something far behind Mac.

"My wife and I moved to Virginia, to a little town called

Fredericksburg. I was a tutor there before we went on to Michigan, where Charity was born." Ethan tugged at his beard and smiled. "Ancient history, I know. But I had time to observe the Southern viewpoint. Now we better get this currying done or Pegasus and Andromeda will grow new coats before we finish tending the old ones."

***

It was a confusing, frightening time, even to those well past their eleventh summer.

Larissa listened to her husband's vehement outbursts, to his explanations and vows of loyalty to his country, and went about her work, and prayed.

Charity listened as her father and Mr. Edwards, over the milk buckets and hay forks, engaged in long discussions. Too young to grasp what they were pondering, she understood only too plainly that if "It" happened, Pa would go away and leave her. "I'm awful scared, Mac," she confided one evening as he filled a water bucket at the well.

Balancing the bucket on the curb, he saw, in spite of near darkness, her worry-pinched expression, and all his own insecurities rippled to the surface. How could he possibly reassure her when he was scared spitless himself? Grasping the bucket bail, he lugged the water toward the house. "Come on, Speck," he threw over his shoulder, using the nickname he had bestowed on her when she was too young to pronounce "expect" but seemed to use it in every other sentence. "I have to finish my chores." She trotted confidently beside him, unaware of his inner turmoil. *Why does she think I always have all the answers? Doesn't she know I'm just as scared as she is?* Shame zipped through him. If Pa went away, Ma would still be here. If Charity's Pa left, who would she have?

Ma stepped onto the porch, sparing him the necessity of answering. "I'll take the water in, Mac. Pa wants to start evening prayers, so he and Charity's Pa can go to a meeting in town." She spoke calmly but her hands, taking the bucket, trembled. He knew, then, it was a soldiers' meeting. Mr. James Hawkins had organized a local troop company, and Fairvale citizens were planning, even before a declaration of war, how the town would be taken care of with its men gone.

Pa, Mr. Michaels, and Rose were in the sitting room when Mac followed Ma in, he in turn trailed by a subdued Charity. Pa, in his leather armchair beside the fireplace, held the Bible open to *Micah*. Ma sank into her oak rocking chair on the other side of the hearth and drew Rose onto her lap. Mac sidled over to the high-backed walnut bench facing the fireplace and scrunched into the corner Ethan wasn't already occupying. Charity leaned against her father's knee. Pa slanted toward the candle on the square walnut table beside him, adjusted the book to catch the flickering light, and began reading in the resonant voice that had stitched, one to the next, all the evenings of Mac's life.

> But in the last days it shall come to pass ...
> and they shall beat their swords into plowshares,
> and their spears into pruning hooks ...
> neither shall they learn war any more.

Pa closed the Bible. In the quiet that followed, each person mulled private thoughts. Mac, staring at the brightly braided rug at his feet, heard the echo of the words silently shouted from six hurting hearts. *If only it could be so.*

***

That fall, William Dennison, the Republican candidate for Ohio governor, was elected in a close vote. His inaugural address in January 1860 denounced secessionist movements and opposed slavery extension into the Western Territories. In May, at the Republican convention in Chicago, Ohio swung to Abraham Lincoln on the fourth ballot.

In November, Abraham Lincoln was elected president. But, contrary to the optimistic views of many that, once he took office, the South would accept it and let the furor die down, the situation worsened. In early 1861, Ohio's National Road, cutting east to west through Zanesville, Columbus, and Springfield, became a figurative Mason-Dixon Line as tensions steadily increased.

On a Saturday afternoon in April, Mac was in the office, holding a basin ready for Doc to pull Ezra Beard's abscessed tooth. Ezra was groaning and cussing. Doc, fitting the hook of his tooth pulling instrument around the offending molar, had told him curtly to quit squirming or he might just pull the wrong tooth, when pandemonium exploded outside. Horses tearing down the usually quiet street, boots pounding along the sidewalk, and high pitched voices unmistakably indicated trouble.

They weren't kept wondering for long. Obadiah Beldane, of the erstwhile black eye, burst into the office. "They've done it! I told you they would. The South's fired on us at some place called Fort Sumter. They're demandin' the fort be surrendered immediately or else they'll starve out the troops holdin' it."

"Shut the door," Doc growled. "Can't you see I'm operating? Hold still, Ezra," he added sharply.

Ezra's reply, around Doc's fingers, was incoherent.

"But Doc," Obadiah blurted, "this means war."

"Well, it'll just have to wait until I pull Ezra's tooth. If they can keep their trigger fingers still that long." As he spoke, he yanked. Ezra yelled a comment, audible this time, and the tooth hung from the turnkey. "Give me some of those lint scraps, Boy." When the scraps didn't come with his pupil's usual alacrity, he glanced over in surprise.

Mac stood rigid, eyes dilated with shock and fear. "My Pa," he blurted. "I got to go home."

Doc's stomach lurched as sharply as if he'd been kicked. Slowly, he laid down his turnkey, Ezra's tooth dangling from the hook. Still with that reduced speed motion, he reached for the towel to wipe his hands. "You're right, Boy. Maybe you better get on home."

Mac whirled, veering around Obadiah still standing in the doorway. Before he could flee, Doc's voice halted him. "Mac." It flew through his mind how few times Doc had called him by actual name. He ducked his head to hide his tears.

In the sharp stillness, Doc's boots rang against the wood floor as he walked over and laid his big hand on the boy's shoulder. "Come back when you can." Mac nodded blindly and bolted out the door. He watched him tear down the street, pushing heedlessly through the pack of yelling, swearing, cheering men. Turning back to the office and the patiently waiting Ezra, Doc threw his towel aside viciously and brought his fists violently down on the table. "Damn!"

Mac, stumbling out the east road toward home, was finally free to let loose his tears. But somewhere between the office and the farm, the tears turned to an ice lump lodged in his throat, threatening to strangle him with each indrawn breath. By the time he tore past the cornfield that only yesterday he and Pa had plowed as if there were no limit to all the tomorrows, the ice in his throat had spread to the pit of his stomach. Coming abreast of the well, he heard a muffled sob. Skidding to a halt, chest heaving, he peered around the curb and saw Rose huddled against the stones. The ice-knot hurt his throat so much he could scarcely force the words out. "Rose, he's going, isn't he." Stated as fact, not question.

She jumped. "Mac, our Pa's going to war." He stared at his little sister huddled against the well stones, blue eyes so like his own, dark with the misery of knowledge, cheeks streaked with dirt and tears. With a gesture beyond his years he reached his hand, silently squeezed her shoulder, even as Doc had earlier offered him such wordless comfort. Raising his eyes to the house, he took hold of her hand. He pushed open the door and the muffled voices merged into stark clarity.

"… no need we both go straight off. Makes sense for me to be the one." Zane broke off pacing, and his earnest argument, as the children edged into the sitting room.

In a fragmented whirl, Mac saw his father's determination, Ethan Michaels' protest, and his mother's face. She was as white as the flour he and Pa had ground at the Saxon and Cassill Steam Grist Mill.

Ethan glanced at Mac, hesitated, and decided to take advantage of Zane's silence. "It don't make sense you should be the one. You got far more to give up than me." Even in his dullness, Mac's mind registered how deeply agitated Charity's Pa was. He had dropped all his fancy words and precise grammar, something Mac had never heard him do.

Ethan rushed on, heedless of the battering he was inflicting on his beloved language. "You got the farm. Your family." His eyes included Mac, standing so rigid by the door, and Rose, crowded close behind her brother, peering fearfully past his shoulder. Finally his eyes briefly—so briefly—brushed Larissa's frightened face as she sat in her rocker, hands clutching the forgotten shirt she had been mending when Zane and Ethan burst in with their news.

Ethan swallowed, hurried on as Zane still held silent. "Your crops. Have you thought about the raisin' of them? Who'll tend your fields? Mac is becomin' a right smart hand, but you can't expect him to do it all. And crops'll be needed. Don't fool yourself they won't. It just makes sense for me to go." He finished on a note of desperation, for Zane, brown eyes looking deeply into Larissa's blue ones, was slowly shaking his head.

"I have my family, just like you say, but what about Charity? You're all she has, Ethan. You willing to chance taking that away from her?"

Ethan's shoulders sagged as suddenly as if Zane had driven a clenched fist into his belly. The one argument he had no defense against. His child. The living affirmation his love and Nettie's had been and still was so. His last promise to her. To rear Charity with the love and guidance that would bring her to womanhood as fine as Nettie's own. Where did his loyalty now lie? With his daughter? If he should be killed, she had no other living relative in the world. With his country? If he didn't fight for it in its hour of need, it might cease to exist. With a deathbed promise to the wife who was life itself to him, to whom he had never lied or failed to keep his word?

He scrubbed his hand across his eyes in sudden weariness. For he knew, instantly and totally, what his decision must be. "All right." His voice came harsh as he kept his gaze pinned on Zane because he could not bear to look at Larissa. "I'll stay and push a plow. You go and do the fighting for both of us." The harshness abruptly faded as, in spite of himself, for a fractional moment, his gaze touched Larissa's tortured face. "I pray it'll be over soon. God help us all if it isn't." Pushing past Mac and Rose, he strode out.

Zane dropped to his knees beside Larissa's chair. She had remained in that frozen position all during Ethan's argument. Now, heedless of the staring children, she simply, silently leaned forward and put her head against Zane's chest as his arms enfolded her.

Rose, in a high, thin voice said plaintively, "Pa?"

Only then he looked around to glimpse the stunned faces of his two children. Keeping his left arm tightly about Larissa, he reached out with his right. The children needed no further urging. Two suddenly uncoiled springs, they shot to the protection of his strong arm. They huddled thus for several precious minutes, once more a united family shutting out the rest of the world, with no way of knowing whether they should ever be so again.

When Mac and Rose went back outside because Pa said he needed to talk with Ma, they found Charity standing by the budding lilac. Her face had lost its terrified expression and glowed as though someone had lit a candle inside her.

"Pa's not going," she proclaimed joyfully. At sight of their stricken faces, the candle quenched. "But your Pa is," she whispered and reached a small hand to touch each of their arms. She said nothing more. What more was there to be said?

CHAPTER FIVE

Sunday, April 14, 1861 dawned blue-sky clear and fragrant with the scent of blossoming springtime. The Edwards family rose early to complete the every morning chores before church. Gathered around the breakfast table, their strained faces conveyed the fear they would not voice. Mac's flame-burnished hair lent one spot of brightness, but, Zane noted bitterly, his expression was more sober than any twelve-year-old should wear. Rose, too, looked far older than her seven years. And this was only the beginning.

In spite of her surface serenity, the purple smudges under Larissa's eyes bespoke their own tale. Zane knew she had lain sleepless much of the night. Fully awake himself, every time he stirred, with a wordless murmur protesting any distance between them, she had arched her slender figure against him, abandoning all except the fierce need of the warmth and comfort of her body curved to his work muscled length. He'd held her, her head nestled against his shoulder, hand resting on his chest, breath light and soft against his neck. Thus, they had slept during all the nights of fourteen years of marriage. The question had hung in the blackness above him. *How many more nights will we be given?* With bleakness he had never known, the answer had intruded. *Not many. Dear God, not many.*

Now, their hands joined around the table, Zane began the morning prayer. "Father, thank You for this day, for this food, for all the blessings …" Suddenly, totally, the words strangled in his throat. *How can this ripping apart of our country, our lives, be labeled a blessing?* Floundering in a tide of blackness, he heard Larissa, softly but firmly. "… You have bestowed upon us. Help us to be worthy of Your goodness. Amen."

His eyes, dull with despair, met hers, alight with love and tenderness. He felt her courage filling his emptiness, knew with certainty that, whatever her fears of the night before, and of all the nights to come, their love was a solid shield no outside force could breach. His eyes still holding hers, his voice suddenly returned. "Amen," he said clearly.

***

Breakfast finished, Zane harnessed Pegasus and Andromeda to the surrey. The matched bays were named, as were all their horses, from the constellations in Zane's beloved mythology books. The animals were the symbol of all they hoped to achieve in the raising and marketing of fine horseflesh. He knew when the family rode to church this morning, it would be with heads high, their grief firmly tucked away from the eyes of the world. He had determined only the best would fit such an occasion, and in spite of his heavy heart, his mouth twitched. *Rissa's "hyacinths for the soul" sometimes bloom in odd places.*

The early sun danced off the burnished coats of the bays. He reflected wryly he was not the only one who found solace in working with such fine animals. Those shining coats were direct evidence that Ethan Michaels, caught in his own hell last night, had found personal easement in currying the pair until they gleamed.

Larissa and the children emerged from the house, and he knew he had predicted correctly. She wore her special occasion dress. The deep blue matched her eyes, making them even wider and darker than usual. Rose's soft pink dress brought color to her cheeks so that she bloomed very much like the rose of her Christmas Day birth. And Mac. Zane's heart swelled with pride. He had added inches to his length these past months, so that Larissa had made him a new suit from Zane's old one, with room to let out coat sleeves and trouser legs. *He's grown in other ways, too. Has working with Doc Rawley given him added maturity? Or is it the threat of the destruction of all we, as a family, hold most dear?* As the youngsters scrambled into the backseat and he assisted Larissa into the front, a shiver skittered through him and he felt cold, in spite of the warmth of the day.

The yard of the white painted church, two blocks from the public square, was crowded that morning. Zane finally found a spot to tie the horses across from the Fairvale *Tribune* office. As he stepped from the surrey, Charlotte Sullivan, the schoolteacher, emerged from the boarding house where she roomed. She waved and they waited for her to join them.

In front of the third-floor newspaper office, a knot of men spilled down the stairway, across the sidewalk and into the street. Miss Sullivan eyed the clump uneasily. "They've been there since first light, waiting for information about Fort Sumter. At last word, Major Robert Anderson still refused to surrender, so the Confederates are continuing to fire on the fort. One report said the Confederates shot the Union flag flying over the fort off its staff. One of the sergeants inside grabbed it, climbed the pole, and nailed it back up in spite of all the shooting going on around him." Her solemnity lighted briefly, proudly, in tribute to the unknown soldier's courage, but she quickly sobered. "There's no hope Major Anderson can hold out. The reports say the men inside the fort have hardly any food or water." She pressed her lips together. "God help them all."

They entered the church, and silence surrounded them, a tense, heavy silence so unlike the usual pre-service quiet. As if pulled by a single string, all heads turned toward the squeak of the opening door, twisted back toward the pulpit when they were seen to have no news. Zane found places near the front. Another family entered and the head-turning process was repeated.

Reverend Gallaway stepped to the pulpit and gazed silently out over his congregation. Nearing fifty, with the accompanying graying and thinning of once thick brown hair, and the inevitable lining of cheeks and forehead, with his still broad shoulders and height of six feet, he remained a compelling force in his church community. Shawn Gallaway had never completely lost the rich accent of the Welch village of his birth. His brown eyes, undimmed by the coal dust of his ancestors, frequently held a twinkle lurking just beneath the surface. Today, the spark of light had flickered out.

"I planned," he began slowly, "to speak to you today from Luke 1:79. *'To give light to them that sit in darkness and in the shadow of death, to guide our feet into the way of peace.'* Now," his voice slowed still more, "I'm not so sure I can do it, that I can speak with authority of light, and dark, and death, and peace. *'Thou shalt not kill.'*

"Many of you have come to me since yesterday, seeking answers to the future of your souls. As a man of God, I should stand here and tell you peace is the only way to salvation." He smiled, and the smile held infinite sadness. "Unfortunately, I am not only a man of God, I am a man of human parents, with human frailties. The only answer I know is not original, but I believe, from the bottom of my heart, it is the true one: *'Man's goings are of the Lord: how can a man then understand his own —'*" He broke off as a sudden pounding of feet and a thump against the outside door caused all heads once again to swing to the back of the church.

The door thrust open and Obadiah Beldane, the town blacksmith, rushed in. "It's done," he blurted in a cracked voice. "Major Anderson surrendered Fort Sumter to the Confederates yesterday." Belatedly seeing the stunned faces, and finally realizing he was standing in church, Obadiah gulped to a stop and removed his hat. A heartbeat of deathly silence held everyone motionless, before the room erupted.

Zane surged to his feet with the other men, but Larissa's hand on his arm halted him. He looked into her stricken face and slowly sank down beside her. Reverend Gallaway's voice hurtled through the room, overpowering the tumult of shouted questions and pushing bodies.

"Everyone sit down. Now!" The thundering authority in his voice broke through the hubbub, jolting them to dumfounded silence. "We are still in a house of God," he roared. "It behooves us to act like it!" He gazed out over his stunned parishioners and lowered his voice a notch. *"'Beloved, think it not strange concerning the fiery trial which is to try you …'"* He raised his arms in blessing, his voice now infinitely tender. *"'And the peace of God, which passeth all understanding, shall keep your hearts and minds.'"* He walked slowly down the aisle and paused by the doorway, his eyes sweeping his flock for the last time. "God go with you."

The congregation filed quietly past him, but once out on the street, bedlam exploded again.

No one looked back at Reverend Gallaway standing on the top step, the fresh April breeze tugging at his coattails. Silently he stood, his grief darkened eyes following them, before he re-entered the church and slowly shut the white painted door. Alone with his God, he sank to his knees and buried his face in his shaking hands.

For a long while, as the tumult in the street swelled, his lips moved in silent prayer.

***

Never in his life had Mac seen so many people gathered at one time. He doubted Ma had, either, for she called to Pa, "Maybe we should go back into the church until it calms down."

Pa shook his head. "It's going to get worse, not better. I can't see anything important happening today, no real news or plans before tomorrow at the earliest. But there's no telling what these worked up minds will do. I'd feel much better if we could get home quick as possible."

With the crowd thrusting roughly against them, Pa gripped Ma's arm tightly and bent so Mac and Rose could hear him. "Mac, stand behind me. Hang on to my coat so we don't get separated. Rose, stand in front of Mac and hold on to his arms so you stay right with him. All right?"

Rose, small face drained of all bloom, blue eyes wide with terror, grabbed Mac's arms and held on for dear life as the wave of people knocked her off her feet. Head bent over his little sister, shielding her, Mac clutched Pa's coattails and clung like the most stubborn leech in Doc Rawley's collection. Buffered by his father's muscled frame, they waded into the chaos. Head down, Mac couldn't tell their direction. An eternity later the surging crowd thinned, no longer shoving so heedlessly against him.

"All right, son. You can let go. I'll take Rose."

Mac had never heard more welcome words. His fingers were so cramped with gripping they refused to relax. Pa twisted backward to inspect his coattail. Catching sight of the deep creases, Mac felt quick shame about hanging on so forcefully. *Skittery as a tadpole in Mill Creek glimpsing its own shadow.* But at least Pa didn't look mad.

"A burr couldn't have stuck better, son. By jingo, you did good. Rose, too." His smile suddenly became a full fledged grin. "Just don't hang on that tight when you milk Clover. She might not appreciate it."

"Zane!"

Pa winked, grandly ignoring Ma's aghast disapproval.

Behind her indignation, Mac saw Ma stifling a giggle, and a sudden chuckle hiccupped from him. In spite of all the tension and grimness, as the surrey rolled toward home, the world, for a few wonderful moments, brightened again.

The lighthearted feeling didn't last long.

***

Monday morning after the Fort Sumter news broke, instead of eating breakfast and heading to the cornfield as on the thousand other spring days of his life, Zane dressed to go to town and sign up for going to war. He planned to walk with Mac and Rose on their way to school. He could ensure there was no trouble in town, and that the youngsters wouldn't come to harm. He tried to make light of it all and of his ultimate reason for going. As he combed his wet-down brown hair, he joked, "The last time I remember dressing this carefully was the evening we got married, Rissa." Glimpsing her stricken eyes in the mirror, his voice trailed off.

Turning slowly, he faced her. Ignoring the fact Mac and Rose were watching, he reached to touch Larissa's soft chestnut hair. She caught his hand in both of hers and held it to her lips. "You were a sight to make my heart race that night, Zane Edwards. And never once since then has it slowed down." A smile tugged at the corners of her mouth. "Just in case that fact slipped your notice these fourteen years."

He brushed her lips with his thumb. "It didn't, Rissa-love. Be sure, it didn't." For another long moment he looked deep into her eyes. Love and glowing pride had replaced the stricken look. Pride in him, he realized with the same awe he always experienced, even after all the years. He turned to the silent children and Rose slipped her hand into his. "Ready, pupils? We don't want Miss Sullivan to mark you late. I wonder if she's wearing the same whale-boned corset she wore when I was a student? Talk about an unbending personality." As he intended, Rose giggled and Mac hid a coughing chuckle at such wicked talk.

At the door, under cover of their amusement, he bent to Larissa's ear. "I'll be home soon as I can."

She lifted her hand, and in spite of the heart heaviness he full well knew she was concealing, she gave him a glowing smile that made his toes curl. "I'll be waiting."

***

As always, after Zane left, enough household tasks reared their pesky heads to keep Larissa busy until midnight. She set up her washtub outdoors and determinedly put her hands to sorting laundry, but her mind jumped from one thought to another. She stooped to pick up Mac's plowing shirt, and the gold coin she wore on a chain around her neck slipped from under her collar and banged her on the nose. Catching it in mid swing, she started to replace it, but hesitated. Brushing her fingertips across the raised marks, she wondered whimsically that she hadn't rubbed them completely away by now.

Zane had given her the quarter eagle pendant before they married. Walking by Mill Creek one summer Sunday, they had stopped to watch the antics of two bear cubs in the meadow across the water. She made a low-voiced, laughing remark about how vigorously the pair was pummeling each other, only to realize Zane hadn't responded. Surprised, she glanced up to find him studying her intently. His expression held such mixed hope and distress her teasing question died unspoken.

He dug into the pocket of his ill fitting Sunday suit coat. Inhaling deeply, he pressed his palm against her white-gloved hand. "This is for you," he gulped.

Distracted by his sudden utter discomfort, she carefully lifted the gleaming scrap and discovered a small gold coin dangling from a delicately wrought gold chain. Sunlight, catching the gold, shot twinkling sparks off the surfaces of chain and coin. She gasped in utter delight. "Zane, it's beautiful. But however did you get the money?" She stopped, now as confused as he. She knew he had little cash, hired out as he was on a room and board basis at the McKelvey farm east of town.

"I dug Hiram Hill's well, and he paid me cash money." Having once begun his explanation, he rolled on, as if not daring to quit for fear he'd never get it said. "I know you're going to say I shouldn't spend my money that way. I know that's what your folks'd say. But I wanted to give you something nice. I made the hole through the coin, you see, by using a nail head. That's why it's square. I can't tell you the rest. It's a secret, passed down by my Pa to me from his Pa. I hope you like it." He ran down as suddenly as he had started, and watched her anxiously as she studied the Liberty head and coronet on one side of the coin and the eagle on the other.

Finally she raised her eyes to his and her lashes were wet. "Zane, it's beautiful. I can't think of anything nicer you could give me. Thank you."

He slipped it over her head. "I promise, the money I earn from now on, I'll not spend lightly. But I did so want you to have something to keep me in your thoughts."

Bending over her washtub in the spring sunshine fourteen years later, gently stroking the now-worn Liberty head and coronet, Larissa mused that, to the rest of the world, the quarter eagle was worth $2.50. To her it was priceless.

She had been so deep in thought that, ready to plunge the soiled laundry into the tub of hot water, she realized she had mixed Zane's and Mac's plowing clothes, heavy with dirt from the fields, into the pile with Rose's good dress and lacy white petticoats. She gave herself a sharp shake at such carelessness, but as she removed them to the proper stack, her fingers lingered over Zane's dirt stiffened socks. *How many socks have I scrubbed for him in our fourteen years?* The whimsical response came so readily that she put her hands to her back to ease the remembered ache of stooping. *Enough washtubs full to stretch from here to the barn and back, no doubt.* Silly as the thought was, she knew there was another, far from frivolous question she dared not ask, let alone answer, even in the most secret depths of her soul.

How many more, in life's pattern, are left for me to wash?

Hours passed. Only shortly before Rose was due home—Mac would, at Zane's insistence, stay to help Doc Rawley as he did each Monday afternoon—Larissa, in the kitchen, heard Zane calling her name from the front door. Dropping her soup ladle, she hurried to the sitting room.

She glimpsed his strained, taut face before he drew her tightly to him. "Rissa-love." That was all, but no other words were necessary. He kissed her slowly and deeply, and she felt his breath sigh out. "Thought of that's the only thing that kept me going, today." He smiled ruefully.

Bone deep weariness clouded his eyes. Taking his hand, she led him to his leather chair beside the fireplace, where he sank gratefully. She dropped to her knees beside him, still keeping her clasp on his hand. "Tell me, Zane," she said softly.

Gently loosening her hand, he drew her onto his lap, cradling her head against his shoulder. "That's better." He held her thus for several long moments before he spoke again. "I've never seen anything like what was going on in town today. Men pouring in from all around the countryside and from smaller towns without sign up stations. We ran across Ethan walking Charity to school. He was as uneasy about his daughter out in all that crowd as we were about ours. He'll get them after school, take Rose to the hotel with Charity, and bring her home this evening in time for chores." He grinned at her relieved expression. "She's taken care of and it gives us a couple of hours to ourselves. Ethan's one good friend. He doesn't say much, sometimes, but by jingo, he sure has dandy ideas."

"Zane!" The sudden light in Larissa's eyes belied her stern reproof as his arms tightened about her. During that long day, out of uncounted chaotic thoughts, she had vowed not to let her fears destroy the time remaining. Forcefully, she pushed aside the heart-bumping realization that "the time remaining" was *now*, not hours and days and years after Zane's return from war. *I will cherish each moment*. His work-roughened hands gently loosened the pins from her shimmering chestnut hair, and she felt a wild, unashamed rush of joy.

***

They were sitting decorously at the kitchen table, holding hands and talking, when Rose and Mac burst through the doorway, Charity and Ethan following behind. He apologized for bringing the children home so late. "The hotel's just jumping with business. We're doubling, even tripling them in the rooms, but no one seems to mind." He removed his hat. "For certain, I've not seen its like anywhere."

Rose tugged on Zane's sleeve. "You going to war tonight, Pa?"

"Rose!" Mac reproached her sharply.

Zane felt Larissa's involuntary jolt. Clasping her hand firmly another moment before slowly releasing it, he turned to his daughter. Her blue eyes, already wide with apprehension, filled with tears at Mac's rebuke. Reaching down, Zane lifted her onto his knee. Mac stood stiffly, his anger at his sister unable to mask the fact his eyes held as much anxiety as hers.

Zane circled his arm about the boy's shoulders, drawing him closer. Swallowing hard, he laughed. "Whoa, there. You two trying to get rid of me? One thing certain about the Army, it doesn't move that fast. You're just going to have to put up with me for a few more days."

Rose nestled against his shoulder. "I'm glad."

Some of the fear left Mac's eyes. "Me, too."

"Me, three," Larissa chimed in on a singsong note, so that they all laughed.

Ethan had listened quietly to the give and take. Now, with a gesture to his lagging behind daughter to follow him, he turned to leave.

"Ethan, wait," Zane called to his retreating back.

Ethan fumbled with the doorknob. "You and your family have private matters to consider. Charity and I'll head back to town. You and I can discuss details later."

"We will be planning, but not only as family. You and Charity are tangled in all this, too." He looked at Larissa, retying the red ribbon holding back Charity's blond curls. "Maybe more so."

Charity gazed pleadingly up at Ethan. He searched their faces carefully before, with a wry smile, he laid aside his hat. "You make it difficult to follow the polite rules of society." He sank into the chair beside Zane. "But you do make it comfortable."

Zane smiled briefly. "I'd like to tell all of you what happened today. That way we'll have a straight story, and won't have to worry about rumors and scare tales. That's going to be mighty important these next days—sifting facts and not jumping to conclusions over 'maybes.'" He regarded Mac intently. "This is especially important for you, son. A lot of weight's going to be put on your shoulders. That's plain fact. It's also plain fact I know I can trust you. That makes me downright proud."

Concern, confidence, and caring stamped Zane's face, but Mac couldn't detect the slightest fear. For the first time since yesterday, the future held something besides terror.

Rose still perched on his knee, and Zane tickled her nose with the end of her light brown braid. "And you, young Sprite," he said with mock sternness, "are getting so expert in the knitting department, I'm putting in my order for as many pairs of socks as you can make me. That way, when I go off to war, my feet will be toasty warm, all because of you."

Rose straightened her shoulders proudly, unaware Zane had just put his departure into a nonthreatening light. "I promise, Pa. I'll make you stacks and stacks of them."

Charity giggled. "You sound like your Pa's going to be wearing pancakes on his feet."

Ethan stared in wonder. He hadn't heard his daughter make a teasing remark like that since Nettie's death. Caught between laughter and a sudden blur of tears, he turned to Larissa. "Thank you," he said simply. She smiled, and he turned hastily back to Zane. "Now, my friend, tell us of your grand adventures in town."

Thus quietly reinforced in his efforts to remove some of his children's fears about his leaving for the unknown, Zane set about sidetracking them further. After leaving Mac and Rose at school, he had headed for the courthouse, figuring that signup stations would be set up there. It was only two streets away, but, "By the time I got there, I felt as if I'd already fought the whole war. Men were pouring into town from all sides, and every one of 'em was headed toward the public square. I tell you I didn't even have to walk. I just studied the crowd until I spotted one fellow at least seven feet tall, walking beside a man weighing at least two hundred fifty pounds. I slipped between them and the crowd promptly squeezed us together so close I simply lifted my feet off the ground and was carried along by these two accommodating gentlemen." Zane's eyes touched each of the attentive faces.

"I came back to earth rather abruptly, I'll admit, when Beanpole went one direction and Atlas the other and I landed flat on my—"

"Zane!" Larissa's outrage sounded strangely laughter choked.

"—feet," he finished, gazing innocently at her. Over the children's shouts of glee, he winked. She stuck her nose in the air and turned her head away. But not before he confirmed his suspicion. She was sputtering with amusement.

"Then what, Pa?" Rose's eyes were bright with curiosity.

"I, as the saying goes, 'got right back up on my horse' and joined the men already in line to register. While we all stood there waiting to inch ahead, fellows around me talked nonstop. News and rumors both, so it's a tad hard to sort out, but I'll take a crack at it. They gave Major Robert Anderson at Fort Sumter in Charleston Harbor, South Carolina, the chance to surrender before they ever fired on the fort. He thought about it and told the gentlemen who so graciously presented the offer that he declined. He also told them he would probably be starved out in a few days anyway, if the Confederates didn't blow the fort to pieces first. For all the shots fired, no one on either side was hurt. Anderson signed the surrender and they agreed to let him fire a fifty-gun salute to the American flag. Of all the ironies possible, when they fired the salute, a lighted ember fell into a gunpowder barrel. The barrel exploded, killing one private and wounding five other Union soldiers, giving them the dubious honor of being the first casualties of this war."

Larissa's eyes darkened in pain, but she made no sound. Zane continued rapidly, "The good news I heard, and near as I can tell, it's fact, not rumor, is that no man can enlist for more than ninety days. Seems there's actually a Federal law prohibiting it. So it appears I'll no more than be out from under your feet than I'll be home again. Which sounds mighty fine to me."

"Me, too." Rose clapped in delight and leaned around Zane. "How long's ninety days?" she hissed in Mac's ear.

Zane heard. "Well, Sprite, ninety days is the time that, if I plant corn now, near Easter time, it'll be knee-high by the Fourth of July, and just a few more days beyond that." Rose smiled, satisfied. Unlike all this strange war talk, Easter and Fairvale's eagerly awaited Fourth of July celebrations were comforting realities in her world.

"I also heard something about Senator Stephen Douglas. You young ones remember those debates we talked about?" Mac dimly remembered. Obviously Charity and Rose did not. "Well, Senator Douglas offered his support to President Lincoln in spite of their political differences. Quite a nice way of burying the hatchet, I'd say."

Rose and Charity still looked blank, but the words burst from Mac, startling all of them. "I wish all the hatchets in the world could be buried!"

Zane's jaw stiffened. "You and me, both, son. Anyway," he hurried on, "it took a while, but with all the stories and gossip, I finally reached the table set up on the courthouse lawn. They put my name in the book and asked some questions."

"Then what?" Mac, Rose, and Charity asked together as he paused maddeningly.

"Then," he intoned dramatically, "they told me I'll be in the Ohio Cavalry."

Three sets of puzzled blue eyes blinked at him.

"It means he gets to ride a horse instead of walk everywhere," Ethan stage whispered.

"Oh-h-h." The children, now suitably impressed, nodded wisely. Horses they understood.

"Apparently, they need men with experience caring for horses, not just riding them. When I explained about our stables here, I guess they figured I qualified on that score." He turned to Larissa. "It appears our horse raising venture will take us farther than we ever dreamed."

Or wished. She barely managed not to blurt it out.

"Then what?" Rose asked impatiently.

"Then," Zane paused for his most dramatic effect yet, "I signed my name on about a million papers, and they sent me home."

The children stared, bewildered by the flat ending to his glorious tale. Mac stirred first. "I'm glad they sent you home."

Zane smiled at his son. "I'm glad, too."

Under cover of the children's murmuring to each other, Ethan asked, "How long?" Larissa stiffened. Her hand reached instinctively for her husband's.

"They'll send for me. By the end of the week, for sure."

Zane said it quietly, but Mac heard, and the brightness in his face dulled. As he looked from one adult expression to the other, his childhood vanished.

CHAPTER SIX

The following days crowded past in erratic jerks. Mac came to terms with the dreaded plowing because it meant spending time with Pa. Ethan relinquished his hotel management to Walter McKandlass in preparation for moving to the Edwards farm. Larissa, face white and lips set, went the round of her work, preparing the old, first cabin for the new inhabitants.

Tuesday following Zane's sign up, Mac and Rose trudged to school because Pa insisted their education not be interrupted for war. In town, throngs of men smoking pipes, talking and gesturing excitedly, settled all issues. No women appeared, anywhere. Scraps of discussion floated from all sides.

"I heard Major Anderson surrendered the fort with no human casualties either side. The only fatality was one horse. Confederate, at that."

"… seventeen Southern ships seized in New York. Didn't have the right clearances."

To Mac's secret relief, the gossipers were so busy with their own concerns, they paid no heed to the two wide eyed youngsters threading their way along the sidewalk. Usually, by the time they arrived at the school grounds, several students were nosily jumping rope, playing ante over or shooting marbles. This morning the yard was deserted.

Rose's hand crept into Mac's. "Do you think they've all gone to war?"

He managed a weak laugh. "'Course not. No one our age goes to war."

For some reason, his scorn reassured her. "What should we do?" she asked, confident of his older brother ability to solve any problem that popped up.

He squared his shoulders. "We better go inside and see if anyone's here."

In spite of her renewed assurance, Rose stayed close beside Mac instead of skipping ahead as she usually did. They ascended the four steps, their shoes, striking against the wood, ringing in the stillness.

Mac pushed open the door just as it was pulled from the other side so that he and Rose almost fell into the building. Rose squealed as a hand reached out to catch them, and even Mac's heart did a wild bump before he recognized Miss Sullivan. In the semi-gloom of the cloakroom, her black dress blended so well with the background, he had to blink twice to reassure himself she really was their teacher and not a ghostly presence out of Sleepy Hollow.

"Goodness, you startled me!" Miss Sullivan offered no explanation for her abrupt appearance on the other side of the door, but in spite of her no nonsense attitude, her hand lingered a moment on Rose's shoulder, then Mac's. "Take your seats. I'll give you work while we wait for the others."

Five pupils sat, backs to the center of the room, at the desks fastened to the sawmill planed oak walls. Normally, nineteen students attended. Charity waved to Rose from her bench, but ducked back around to her *McGuffey's* before Teacher could reprimand her. Mac looked questioningly at Miss Sullivan, who narrowed her eyes and shook her head. Accepting her unspoken instructions, he settled in his seat and took out his arithmetic book.

Except for Ian Hollister and Bruiser Damon, who had foregone bringing snakes to class after Charity's memorable first day of school, Mac was the oldest pupil that day. Miss Sullivan held them to their lessons as firmly as usual. Watching her closely, he did not have any sense she was afraid. Somehow he could not picture Miss Sullivan fearing anything. But he realized she was exercising extreme care. They visited the outhouse only in pairs. She allowed them to go into the yard for recess and at lunchtime, but they had to stay fully in her sight from where she sat on the top step, correcting spelling papers.

Even Bruiser and Ian, however reluctantly, obeyed. Mac, eating his lunch under the oak that towered high enough to support two swings, heard the boys talking over their own slices of cornbread and side meat. He had no interest in their conversation, but Ian's voice carried to him anyway.

"My Pa says he's goin' soon as they tell him, and no two ways about it."

Bruiser, eyes on the chunk of meat in his hand, nodded. "Mine, too. Says he can't wait to do his patriotic duty."

Ian, head down, crumbled his cornbread between his fingers. "'Patriotic duty.' That's a good one. Least ways your Pa's givin' an excuse." Bitterness harshened his young voice. "My Pa's just goin' to get away and don't care who knows it."

Mac, thinking of the soon to end pleasant evenings at home with Pa and Ma and Rose, shivered involuntarily as Bruiser continued. "I know one thing. Soon as Pa's gone, I'm done with school. Comin's been easier than gettin' strapped for skippin', but soon as he lights a shuck, I'm out 'a here."

"What about your Ma?"

Bruiser shrugged. "Nothin' she can do. She don't strap hard enough to stun a flea. Pa's the one for that. I'll just tell her I'm through and if she don't like it, why, I'll hit the road, too."

"Then she won't have nobody to work the farm," Ian said slowly, eyes raising to his friend's face. "All the others are too little."

"That's right." Bruiser gave a hard chuckle. "What do you think her choice'll be?"

Admiration shone in Ian's eyes as he, too, snickered. "I like your way of thinkin'. I surely do. Comes to that, my Ma don't hit hard enough to stun a flea, neither." He clapped his friend on the shoulder and they sauntered away, their crude laughter floating back to Mac, still sitting unnoticed beneath the tree.

Miss Sullivan, not one to let a reduced class size or the imminence of war keep her from her teaching duties, dismissed school at the usual time. She did, however, refuse to allow Patrick Ord and Helen Olsen, the two young town children whose parents had not personally come for them, to leave by themselves. She assured them she would see them safely home. Mac, hearing as he waited for Rose to put on her bonnet, felt a swift shudder of sympathy for the luckless individual who could possibly be dumb enough to attempt to sway Miss Sullivan from her self-appointed duty.

He headed down the steps with Rose and Charity, but Miss Sullivan, standing on the top step, called him back. He looked up questioningly. The April breeze flared her black skirt and tugged the tendrils of graying hair around her ears. "Mac, your father will be leaving soon, too, won't he?"

The now always present lump in Mac's throat swelled, so that he had difficulty getting the words out. "Yes, ma'am. By the end of the week, he thinks."

Miss Sullivan, in her stark black dress, framed by the white doorway, seemed to shrink into herself, to become as old and gray as Old Man Tucker, who bragged that after ninety years he still had all his own teeth. She gripped the wooden rail as if unable to stand without support. "They're going. My children from all the years of my teaching. My children are going to war." For a long, motionless moment they stood so, the young boy whose father was going to war, and the spinster schoolteacher whose children, the results of her labor of a lifetime in this schoolhouse, were going, too. Then she stirred, caught herself, and became once more the imposing teacher. "You and the girls better get on, Mac. You don't want your folks worrying about you."

"Yes, ma'am."

"Mac." Again he stopped. "If I don't see your father before he leaves, please tell him good bye for me."

"Yes, ma'am. I will."

Standing firmly above him, the indomitable teacher of all his school years, she smiled and lifted her hand in farewell. Long after the youngsters trudged away, Charlotte Sullivan stood on the top step, staunch and stern as always.

Only her eyes betrayed her unbearable grief.

***

Wednesday afternoon, Mac dropped Rose and Charity at the hotel where Ethan Michaels would continue working until Zane's actual departure. Afterward, he pushed through the still noisy streets to Doc Rawley's office. Again, no one paid any attention as he dodged gesturing arms and carelessly aimed streams of tobacco juice. No women were visible this time, either. Hurrying, he caught snatches of conversation.

"I heard North Carolina and Kentucky are refusing to supply troops."

"… said he'd 'fight the Secessionist leaders till Hell froze over, and then fight them on the ice.'"

"Seventy five thousand volunteers for three months …"

Mac reached the office and slipped inside with a sigh of relief. Doc, already wearing his rumpled black frock coat, was standing at the glass fronted medicine cabinet, busily restocking his bag with calomel and laudanum. He turned at the sound of the door. "Here you are. Was hoping you'd get here quick. We've got a call to the Damon place. Miz Damon's time has come. Should be fairly easy, though. This is seven or eight. I've lost track." He broke off at his pupil's stunned expression. "Something wrong, Boy?"

Mac, hands gripped behind his back, leaned against the closed door. "No, sir. I just didn't know Mrs. Damon was expecting a baby."

Doc grunted. "I didn't either. I never do until word comes by one of the young ones that it's time." He snapped his battered black bag shut, reached for his hat and fairly pushed Mac out the back door where Bella was already hitched to the buggy. Once on the east road, heading toward the Damon place and seeming totally unaware of Mac's reluctance, Doc discussed the procedure they would follow. "If she's not already birthed it by the time we get there, like last time. I don't think you were with me for that one. She tends to be taken in the wee hours of the morning, so this is a new hitch of the rope for her. You think maybe she just wanted to do something different with her life?"

When Mac didn't answer, his pupil's distraction finally sank in on Doc, who probed him with surprise sharpened eyes. "What's the matter, Boy? You've been on deliveries with me before and know the process, now. It's not like it's your first time."

Mac hesitated.

"Come on. Spit it out. If there's a problem, tell me before we get into this call. I can't have you going green on me." Doc hid his concern behind grumpiness. *The boy has seen some pretty raw things, true, but he's always held up his end of the job. So what the devil is going on?*

Mac knew he deserved Doc's irritation. It was the first lesson the older man had instilled in him. If there was a problem, speak up. Doc had neither time nor patience for vagueness. He gulped. "It's just that I heard something yesterday, and I guess I better tell you."

Doc glared at him. "I guess you better."

Haltingly, Mac explained the conversation between Ian and Bruiser. "Mr. Damon'll be leaving her with a new baby and all those little kids. How can he do that?" His going-on-thirteen voice cracked in his earnestness and he reddened, but continued doggedly. "How'll she get along?"

Doc, after a startled moment of absorbing Mac's report, flicked Bella's reins. "Somehow it doesn't blow my haystack over. It sounds just like Theo. What's a little responsibility to his own family when a chance like this comes along to dump them all like yesterday's barn straw?"

"What'll happen to them?"

Doc's mouth tightened. "Sounds like Bruiser's right about quitting school. For now, anyway. Much as I hate to give him credit for anything. He's young, but if, and I stress *if*, he sticks with it, they should manage. They won't eat fancy, but they'll eat. Especially if some anonymous individual occasionally happens to drop a sack of eatables off at their house." He raised his eyebrows at his pupil.

Mac stared at him. "Doc! You're the one. The Widow Anders and Old Man Tucker never have been able to figure out who's been leaving all that food outside their doors." Wide eyed, he stuttered to a stop.

Doc glared at him. "And you haven't figured it out, either." Embarrassment at being caught out harshened his voice. "Just remember, all doctoring doesn't have to do with handing out pills. Sometimes it's a sack of apples or some side meat or fresh eggs. Given so the givee doesn't ever have to feel beholden."

Mac sputtered with laughter. "Widow Anders is certain it's an angel come down from the clouds of Heaven doing it. The way she tells it, you can see Gabriel himself, halo tipped over one eye, floating down with a sack of potatoes flung over his shoulder between his wings. Maybe," he said slowly, no longer laughing, "she isn't so far wrong at that."

A loud snort was Doc's gracious response to this compliment. "Got no use for wings and haloes, Boy. Nor time, either. Just you see this conversation don't go no farther. Only you and me know, so if I hear anyone else talking about it, I'll know where they heard it. You'll be taking the Hippocratic Oath one of these days. 'Whatever, in connection with my professional practice, or not in connection with it, I may see or hear in the lives of men which should not be spoken abroad I will not divulge, as reckoning that all such should be kept secret.' This food business, now, folks find out about it, the ones who need help the most won't take it. Understand?"

Now completely solemn, Mac lifted his chin. "I understand. And I promise."

Doc's fierceness relaxed. "Lots of things a doctor has to be shut mouthed about. Just consider this one more to add to the list." He looked out over Bella's ears. "We'll be at the Damon place shortly. I'm glad you told me about Bruiser's Pa. It'll more'n likely make a difference in the way Miz Damon delivers. If she's all torn up emotionally, it'll make the birthing that much more difficult. Of course," he cocked a speculative eye at his pupil, "with it being Theo Damon taking a hike, she just might take it into her head to make this one her easiest ever."

For a shocked moment, Mac could only stare at Doc, who stared right back. "Rough as it sounds, Boy, it is a fact of life. I don't expect it to be as such, though, this time. She knows right well while Theo isn't much to brag on, at least he makes a show of providing. Without him and his dubious help, she's going to have one mighty rough row to hoe with all those young ones." He paused for a thoughtful moment to guide Bella onto the rutted road fronting the Damon house. "Too bad Widow Anders' angel can't fly down with some kindling to build a fire under Bruiser. I'm afraid he's not going to make much more effort at providing than his Pa."

As they stepped to the ground, Mac's thoughts whirled so fast he felt an ominous quiver in his stomach. He gritted his teeth and swallowed. *Don't go green, now.* For a moment his fierceness matched Doc's best effort. If the older man saw his turmoil, he didn't comment. His heart slowed its racing. Doc's grumpiness was one thing, his full fledged wrath another, and Mac had absolutely no desire to tempt it. A full grown, reared back, she-grizzly would be more pleasant to face.

The unpainted front door of the sagging farmhouse opened to Doc's knock. Bruiser, pale faced, stood there, a whole flock of barefooted little Damons clustered around him like chicks to a mother hen. "About time you got here. She's whining right smart."

Entering the small, crudely furnished room that obviously served as sitting room, cooking, eating, and sleeping area, Doc laid his hat on the square wooden table holding a pile of dirty laundry and a candle stub stuck to a cracked saucer. "We got here as soon as we could. Now we need some warm water to wash up, and some clean towels."

Bruiser hesitated, glowering at Mac. "Nobody asked him to come. We don't want him here gaping at Ma."

Doc took off his coat and pushed up his sleeves. "Mac's with me, Bruiser. He stays. I suggest you get that water ready." His voice was dead level calm, but whatever Bruiser saw in the older man's eyes made him rethink his position.

With a final glare at Mac, Bruiser turned to obey as a long, low groan floated from the doorway across from them. The smallest child, wearing a sack dress, black hair falling in its eyes, let out a whimper, promptly squelched by Bruiser's snarl for it to "Hush yourself. Now!" As the child flinched, Mac guessed it was a girl, but it was hard to tell since the uncombed hair wasn't parted down the middle like a girl or to the side like a boy.

Doc leaped into action, scattering Mac's thoughts like windblown leaves. "Let's get to it, Mac."

While they scrubbed their hands at the tin basin in the corner, Doc glanced casually over his shoulder. "Bruiser, I suggest you take all the young ones out to the barn. We'll call if we need anything."

Even in the seriousness of the moment, Mac felt unholy glee at Doc's pointed support in using his name and in his "we" declaration. *For sure, Doc wasn't snoozing behind the door when smart was handed out.*

Openly resentful at being ordered around, with much more impatience than tact, Bruiser rounded up the flock of children and shoved them out the door, slamming it behind him.

Doc rolled his eyes.

Mac's answering chuckle snapped off as another moan trickled from the bedroom. Tossing aside the towel he was using to dry his hands, Doc motioned with his head toward the closed door. "Bring the bag, and a couple of those towels we brought. I don't remember a dresser or table for the instruments." Once before it had happened, and Doc had Mac lay out the implements on a clean cloth on the floor. Grasping the bag and towels, he followed Doc into the dimly lit room.

"We'll need more light. See what you can find." Doc bent to the woman writhing on the rumpled bed. "It's Doc Rawley, Elsie." His usually harsh voice was low and soothing as he took the stricken woman's hand. "We're here, now, to help you." Another moan, with a distinct undertone of relief, answered him.

Mac, failing to find a suitable surface for the bag, put it on a towel on the floor and hurried out to find more candles. He marveled, not for the first time, how Doc's personality changed when he tended the sick. The gruffness disappeared, and he became infinite gentleness itself.

Through the next hours, the time came and passed that Mrs. Damon should have delivered, and Mac caught on to Doc's concern, even though the older man gave no hint of it to the laboring woman. He was in the outer room, making a pot of coffee from the ground beans Doc had brought, having learned long ago to carry his own supply, when the doctor came out from the other room, carefully closing the door behind him.

"You better see if you can scare up something for those young ones to eat. I imagine Bruiser has his hands full enough, without them all yammering about being starved to death, too."

Mac hid a grin at the thought of a hassled Bruiser attempting to fend off a hoard of hungry little Damons, but sobered quickly enough. *Poor young ones can't possibly understand.* They'd looked hungry several hours ago. Mac suspected it revealed a usual condition with them, and it didn't make it any easier realizing this present state was probably mild compared to the future. Quick anger fueled in him at Theo Damon, the absent cause of all this, who hadn't even put in an appearance the past three hours. *But maybe that counts as an advantage after all.*

Doc's voice recalled him to the shabby little room. "Doesn't look like much in the way of eatables here. There's a sack of potatoes in the buggy. Go get 'em, Boy. They'll boil up quick and provide some hot nourishment for those young stomachs." Doc grinned briefly. "You know the saying, 'When you reach the end of your rope, tie a knot at the end and hang on.' I reckon Bruiser must be hanging on to the piece of rope below the end of the knot, by now. Guess we better take pity on him, and on those young ones."

A short time later, Doc's hunch proved right as usual. The little Damons clustered around the table and sniffed audibly at the bowl of steaming potatoes. Before Mac could help them to a serving, they descended upon the food like ravenous puppies and began gnawing at the potatoes, skins and all. Mac worried they would burn themselves, but they seemed oblivious to that danger as they filled their little bellies. Even Bruiser, who at first stood back with defiant stubbornness, caved in and grabbed a potato. Mac thought he had fixed enough for at least two meals, but the hot food vanished like puddles in the summer sun after a rainstorm.

Doc intended to banish them to the barn again, but with full stomachs and the lingering warmth of the hot food, they crept, one by one, into corners and out of the way spots and fell asleep. Mac found the smallest one curled up under the table, thumb in mouth, potato skin clenched in its little fist, and dead to the world.

He motioned for Doc to take a look. Doc smiled, but quickly sobered. "I'd rather they'd gone back to the barn, but there's no help for it now, I guess. They'll just have to bear with it, no pun intended."

Mac's uneasiness deepened. "Shouldn't she be finishing up, pretty soon?"

Doc pressed his fingers to his tired eyes. "She should be. It's not a breech or anything. Just a whopping big baby she's going to have to push out. Nothing we can do but let Nature do its work."

It took Mrs. Damon and Nature three more grueling hours. With a final, despairing howl, she went limp, scarcely rousing as the baby announced its arrival with a shrill yell. Mac felt silly with relief, and Doc's grin stretched from ear to ear. "A boy. Thirteen pounds if he's an ounce, I'd say. You did a fine job, Elsie."

Mrs. Damon smiled wanly at Doc's praise. "A boy for sure? After all that passel of girls after Theodore, it just doesn't seem hardly possible."

"Not only possible, but definite. See for yourself." He poked the baby's business end at the mother, and, exhausted as she was, she managed a blush and a chuckle.

"Land sakes, Doc, I wasn't doubting your word. Can I see the top side, now?" With a grin, Doc turned the baby's other end up, and Mrs. Damon stared in wonder. "This makes nine, but every time, it's the same, seeing them fresh from the hand of God." Suddenly, as if she had literally borne all she could, her face crumpled and she began to sob bitterly.

Doc thrust the baby at Mac, who had been standing back quietly. "Tend him, Boy. I have my hands full here."

Mac grabbed on to the slippery infant, and, startled by his weight, clutched harder to keep from dropping him on his still damp head. *Wouldn't that be a nice welcome into the world? As if you don't have enough troubles already. And all of four minutes old.*

Mac had done for newborns before, but not without supervision. Now, however, Doc obviously had no time to devote to the baby. He had already turned back to Mrs. Damon and was talking reassuringly to her. With the first finger of panic flicking in his stomach, Doc's voice sounded sternly in Mac's mind, so clearly he looked to where he bent over Mrs. Damon, completely unaware of his pupil's predicament. *"You do what you have to do, Boy, right when it needs doing. You can fall apart later, if you're determined to. But with doctoring, it's your responsibility to get the job done first, no matter what it is."* He clenched his jaw, took a firmer grip on the squalling baby, and turned to the wash basin.

By the time they climbed into the buggy for the return trip, Mac sagged with weariness. Bella knew the way, thankfully, for he suspected Doc's exhaustion topped his. He slumped into his corner. He'd close his eyes just a minute, then they'd talk like always. Summing up, Doc called it ....

A hand shaking his shoulder roused him. "Come on, son. Let's get in the house. Can't leave you here all night. Although I suspect you wouldn't care." The last was said with a muffled chuckle. Mac opened his eyes to Pa urging him from the buggy.

"I'm sure sorry about keeping him so late." That was Doc. "I had no idea it'd take so long. But he was a real help. I couldn't have tended Miz Damon and the baby, both. As it was, I had my hands full with her for a right smart time."

Mac lost the rest of the explanation as he entered the house and slogged up the stairs to his room. He sat on his bed to take off his shoes....

He opened his eyes to sunlight shining through the window. He lay, groggy with sleep, for several moments before he realized. He was under the covers. Horrible suspicion filled him. He peeked beneath the sheet. In his nightshirt. *Ma wouldn't have.* A deep flush stained his cheeks. *Would she?*

He had felt so grown up and responsible last night, helping with the birth. Then he'd acted like such a greenling, falling asleep in the buggy instead of talking to Doc about the case. And having to be put to bed like a diaper drooping baby. *"You do what you have to do."* Doc's voice came unsympathetically. *"You fall apart later, if you're determined to."*

Rose's Sunday School Bible verse from a few weeks ago popped into his head. She had hopped around the house, sing-songing *Proverbs 16* until he knew the words as well as she did, and he'd wanted to bop her over the head with her Bible to keep her quiet. Pa and Ma, of course, wouldn't let him. The verse rang in his ears, clear as if Rose were still chanting it. *Pride goeth before destruction and an haughty spirit before a fall.*

When the Good Lord handed out comeuppances, He handed out dandy ones, for sure. Could there be anything less prideful than being almost thirteen and being tucked into your nightshirt and your bed by your Ma?

With a heartfelt groan, he flopped back onto the pillow and yanked the covers over his head, feeling very young in spite of every one of those almost thirteen years.

CHAPTER SEVEN

A still crisp red gingham apron tied about her waist, Larissa, dusting the cherry whatnot in the sitting room, heard Mac stirring upstairs and glanced at the Seth Thomas clock on the mantle. Seven a.m. He hadn't really overslept in spite of the late hour he had come home with Doc last night.

She managed a small smile, one of the few to slip out in her private moments these past days. She touched her cheek in wonderment that her face hadn't frozen into permanent cheerfulness. She knew Zane saw through her surface serenity as easily as she saw through his unruffled calm. He sensed her emotions so well that hiding anything proved nearly impossible. Even through her fretting, her heart insisted flatly this was as it should be. Nevertheless, just this once, when she wanted so intensely to be brave for him, she wished it were otherwise. *You wish a lot of things were otherwise.* Chiding herself fiercely, she swished her dust cloth haphazardly over the back of her rocking chair. There was too much to do, and too little time to do it, to waste in negatives of any kind.

How many hours were left to them? This was Thursday and Zane had been certain they would call for him by the end of the week. Today ... tomorrow ... Her cloth slowed over the arm of Zane's chair. Time had hurtled past since the news broke Sunday morning. Yet each of the moments with Zane lingered, forever etched into her awareness.

"Morning, Ma. Guess I overslept."

Her thoughts shied off as Mac, hair tousled, eyes still heavy with sleep, descended the stairs.

"Not really." She managed another famous smile. "It's only a bit after seven. I thought you'd sleep longer after last night." A dark flush spread over his face before he ducked his head. "Mac?" She couldn't keep the surprise from her voice.

He wouldn't look at her, but mumbled, "Guess I better get going or I'll be really late for school."

He so obviously didn't want to talk about whatever troubled him, she hesitated to question further. Again, the need for open communication battled, as it had a few times during the past year or so, with the necessity to respect his privacy and his emerging adulthood. He had always been direct with Zane and her, she was sure, had always been able to come to them with his problems. But since working with Doc Rawley, there had been times he'd gone his quiet way, usually down to Mill Creek and a flat rock that overhung the water, providing a "sitting seat" where he could sort out his thoughts.

She and Zane had talked to Doc Rawley in their concern Mac might be carrying burdens too large for his young years. Never one at a loss for words, Doc had hesitated as if choosing his answer with utmost care. "Doctoring demands the last ounce we have to give, sometimes, and then we have to reach down inside and come up with more. Mac's finding this out. There are times, even now, I wonder why I ever decided to practice medicine. He's young, to be sure." He eyed them with open frankness. "That's the main reason I was reluctant to take him on at the start. I didn't know if he'd have the ability or the grit to get through some of the things he'd be called on to see and do. That's why I started him out easy, let him work up to some of the more unpleasant situations."

He'd tugged thoughtfully at his beard, still choosing his words carefully. "Everything I threw at him, he caught and not a word of complaint. Even Pa Packer and his beloved mule." His eyes held an unholy twinkle for a few seconds before he sobered again. "From the start, I made sure we talked about whatever case we'd just handled. I thought it would be part of his lesson. But a funny thing happened." His expression turned quizzical. "By discussing with him, *I* started feeling better. I didn't realize how much I'd stored up in myself through the years. Now it just seems natural to talk things over."

He'd looked straight at them. "I've watched him these past months. I'd say, let him keep on. Even if fancy medical ethics won't let him talk to you, he knows he can talk to me—that I expect him to." Doc grinned openly. "You're just his parents." He tapped a finger on his chest. "I'm his boss. I'll make him talk." He walked with them to the office door. "One thing else you should know," he put in as Zane's hand closed around the knob. They'd turned back to him, their expressions once more swiftly anxious.

"He's got a feel for doctoring itself and for the people he tends that no amount of teaching can give him. He may be young now, but in a few years, he's going to be one damn fine doctor." Offering no apology to Larissa for his crude speech, before they could more than grasp his praise, he'd shoved them out the door, shutting it on their expressions of gratitude.

Remembering Doc's words now as she followed Mac to the kitchen, Larissa faced one of those not knowing if she was right or not, but the decision must be made instantaneously, judgments that inevitably confronts every parent. She decided to allow Mac his privacy and hoped that he would speak to Zane. Once again knowledge of time fleeing too swiftly enveloped her. *How can I ever manage without Zane, without his steadiness and strength and common sense?* Thus, her morning thoughts chased themselves full circle. *You will manage.* She scolded herself fiercely as she whacked hot oatmeal into a bowl. *Because you're going to have to.*

***

Hearing scraping sounds, Mac, strapped schoolbooks slung over his shoulder, stopped in the barn doorway. Zane was raking the last of the old straw from Clover's stall. Seeing Mac, he paused and leaned on the rake handle. "On your way already, son? You sure didn't take advantage and oversleep this morning. Must be some of the farmer lurking inside you along with all that doctoring skill, after all." His grin assured Mac he was teasing. "I swear I have a built in rooster. Never able to snore past four a.m., summer or winter. Sometimes I think Clover and her ancestors wish I would, especially when my hands are cold."

Mac's chuckle joined Zane's hearty laugh before he said apologetically, "Sorry I didn't do my chores, Pa." He gestured guiltily to the pile of odiferous straw and dropped his books. "I can do them now."

Zane hefted the rake. "I'm almost finished, and you don't want to be any later for school. Besides, tell you the truth, I'm glad I got the chance to do 'em." Seeing Mac's skeptical look, he laughed. "Makes me realize I'm really lucky I don't have to do them every morning." He cleared his throat as Mac reached for his books. "I don't want to keep you from your learning or doctoring duties, but I sure would like it if you'd come right home from school this afternoon. I spoke with Doc last night, and he says it's fine with him. It'd mean a lot to me."

Mac tried twice before he got the words out around that dratted lump. "Sure, Pa." He managed a feeble smile. "I already asked Doc yesterday, and he told me to go ahead, today and tomorrow, too, if I want."

Ignoring his own moist eyes, Zane said gruffly, "I don't want you shirking your duty. A man gives his word, he needs to keep it. But in this one case, since Doc's agreed, twice at that, by jingo, I'm glad." He rested his hand on Mac's shoulder. "I also want to say, I'm powerful proud of you."

Mac ducked his head.

"Something troubling you?"

Mac looked up, hesitated, then blurted, "I've been wanting to ask you something for a long time, and now you're going away."

Zane's hand tightened on his shoulder. "You know you can come to me no matter what. Let's sit. I think school can wait a few more minutes." He led Mac over to an old flour barrel now used for storing odds and ends of farm machinery parts and motioned for him to sit on the lid. He eased himself down on a neighboring barrel, the rake forgotten in his hand. "Sometimes it's hard to talk about things. But your Ma and I have found that usually the more difficult something is to bring up, the more important it is to actually get it out in the open."

Mac plunged in before his courage deserted him. "I wanted to ask you about duty, and about going to war. Everybody's giving reasons, and they all seem to be different."

For just an instant, the far-away look came into Zane's eyes, and Mac flinched. But even as he did so, Zane recovered himself and faced Mac directly. "God gives a man a lot of things in this life. Some are pleasant, some not so appealing. Some can go both ways. Duty is one of those things. Sometimes it can be downright satisfying to carry out one's duty, as in a man tending his crops or knowing he's provided well for his family. Other times it's definitely less than pleasant, as in going to war. But it's those very times, having received so much, he has to give back. To do less is to fail himself as a man. And not just himself, but God, and his family, too."

Zane fell silent. Mac studied the patterns the rake tines had made in the straw dust on the floor. "You mean if he just sat back and let someone else do the work for him, it would be stealing because he didn't pay for what he took, like at the mercantile?"

Zane thought a moment, then smiled. "I never considered it just that way, but yes. That's a really good example. Everything has a cost, and when the time comes, a man has to be willing to pay his debt. You might say that's the price of being a man." His smile deepened. "It sure goes in a circle, doesn't it?"

Mac wrinkled his nose. "It sure does."

"You understand, then, what I'm talking about?"

Mac's pleasure in finally comprehending the puzzle collapsed. "It's an awful high price sometimes, isn't it, Pa?"

Zane reached his long arm about Mac to draw him close to his shoulder. "Yes, son," he said simply. Mac, face buried in Zane's shirtfront, did not see the utter despair that flashed across his father's features as he murmured the words.

Even then, Zane pulled Mac to face him. "Now, young man, that brings us to the other side of the coin. Your Ma and I try hard to respect your right to your personal thoughts. But, strange as it seems, we're regular people, and when we think we've done something to hurt another person, we worry. Especially when that person doesn't let us know our thoughts are wrong, that it's something else entirely causing the behavior."

Mac looked blank.

"This morning with your Ma," Zane nudged gently.

Mac remembered and red flooded his face once more.

"It must be a humdinger," Zane observed wryly. "I'm not prying, but if it's not your Ma's doing, it's only common courtesy to let her know that much."

"Pa," the words tumbled out, "last night I fell asleep. I woke up under the covers. Did Ma put me in my nightshirt?"

Even as he felt a relieved chuckle building that the problem was not more drastic, the beseeching look in his son's eyes raised a hen's egg sized lump in Zane's throat. Choking on the laugh, and the lump, he said matter of factly, "I put you to bed, son."

Relief so intense he felt ridiculous filled Mac. "Oh."

"Your Ma said I should be the one, now you're getting older."

"Oh."

He reached a big hand to Mac's hair. "Sometimes it's hard for parents to admit their little ones are getting older. We still tend to see you before you were housebroken, tottering around in short dresses. She wanted to respect your privacy."

Mac bit his lip. "I guess I better apologize."

"I guess you better. But how about this afternoon when you come home, and you get on to school now? Your Ma thinks you're already halfway there. She'd boil me for lard if she realized I kept you this long."

Mac couldn't resist. "You going to do your duty and tell her?" he asked innocently.

Zane pushed him off the barrel. "Yes, I'll tell her. You get along, now, before I 'duty' you."

Once more hefting his books, Mac paused in the sunlit doorway. "Ma told you, didn't she?"

"She was worried about you."

Mac's chin lifted. "I'm glad she did." He scurried away before Zane could react.

***

That mid afternoon Zane, trudging behind Buck and Bob at the plowing, saw Larissa working her way toward him. He halted the team and reached for his blue bandana to wipe dust and sweat from his forehead. Watching her progress over the lumpy field, he grinned. In her brown dress, starched red apron covering her front, head down as she navigated the furrows, she strongly resembled a perky robin hopping toward him while it pecked for worms. With difficulty, he stifled his amusement. Undoubtedly, she would not appreciate the comparison.

Nearing him, she smiled and held out the jug she carried on her hip. "Thought a busy plowing man could use a spot of refreshment."

He took the cool, sweat beaded jug and set it on the ground. "A busy plowing man certainly could." Slipping his arms around her, he bent his mouth down to hers. As ever, the joy of her response made his heart beat faster. He held her close a long moment, face buried in her hair as he breathed in her scent of cinnamon and yeast and a hint of wood smoke from her kitchen fire. Kissing the top of her head, he released her and stooped to pick up the jug. "I like this idea, too," he assured her with a grin. He pulled out the stopper and sniffed. "Buttermilk. You must have been reading my mind."

"At times, your mind isn't too difficult to read." She tried to be nonchalant, but failed miserably as a smile tugged at the corners of her mouth.

Jug raised, he paused. "Are you sorry, Rissa-love?"

She slowly shook her head, the brightness in her eyes giving its own answer.

"Good. For I shouldn't ever want you to be sorry about anything between us."

This time she took the jug from him, carefully corked it, and set it on the ground. Just as deliberately, she stepped close to him, slid her arms about his neck and drew his head down to hers. As her lips sought and clung to his, she raised on tiptoe to bring herself closer yet to him. There in the blowing dust of the cornfield, with the afternoon sun pouring down upon them, his arms circled her tightly.

The searing heat of her lips on his, and her total awareness of his ardent response prevented either of them from hearing the thrum of approaching hoofbeats.

Neither saw Ethan, riding headlong from town on his favorite horse from the livery stable, rein Buckeye to a skidding halt as he caught sight of them in the cornfield. For one instant, he witnessed them clasped in an embrace of such glowing passion his breath strangled in his throat.

Only a flash of time before he instinctively dropped his eyes, pulled his mount around to the direction he had just come hell bent for leather, and guided him quietly back toward town.

Only an instant that had become eternity.

CHAPTER EIGHT

Ignoring the vital news he needed to give Zane, Ethan rode slowly back toward town. Not once, in spite of the urgency of his message, did he consider bursting in upon Zane and Larissa as he had left them. All week they had existed in a world threatening to topple at any second. Knowledge he'd been the one elected to give the final, fatal push hurt deeply enough. He would not shove wildly and, like a thief, rob them of their snatched moment of pleasure. *Aren't you the noble one?* But his scathing sarcasm didn't erase the picture of Larissa standing on tiptoe, melted into Zane's arms. The strangling in his throat increased so, his stomach roiled. *That's right. Be sick all over the road. Folks'll really appreciate that.*

Reaching the waters of Cowbell Swamp, he dismounted and tied Buckeye to a nearby oak. Leaving him happily chomping the lush grass, Ethan wandered along the edge of the shimmering expanse, remembering Charity's story from Mac how it came to be so named. He stood, listening. No ghostly cowbell clanking this sunlit day. It was just as well. In his present state, he'd probably try to catch and milk the critter, just to keep his mind off—

He dropped onto a fallen log and buried his head in his hands. It was no use. *Better to face it here, alone, and get it over with.* So, to the shimmering water and whispering breeze and waving meadow grasses, he gave voice to what he had not, even in the depths of his heart, admitted. "I love her," he said simply.

Of course it was not so simple. He understood that with bone numbing clarity. Having now unshackled his feelings, he must deal with them instead of play acting they didn't exist. For, with his admission came swift, sure perception his love was deep, and it was true.

Having known Nettie's love, he had not expected to experience another such relationship, and so had had no enthusiasm for making an attempt. Not even for Charity. He recalled all the suggestions, subtle from male friends, outright from mothers of eligible daughters, that "for his own good" and "for Charity's sake" he must remarry. He had resisted them all. Not out of fear of dishonoring Nettie's memory. Nor out of any deathbed vow "to remain true to her alone forever" as the minister put it so dolefully during the funeral eulogy.

Ethan well knew Nettie would be the first one to pester him into initiating such an endeavor. He simply had no wish to settle for a lesser relationship. So how had he landed in this present predicament? For he was in trouble, full chisel and no doubt about it. From the first, he had entertained deep respect for Larissa. *And for Zane.* Guilt's bullying voice insisted on butting in. Observing them together, he had swiftly recognized they shared what he and Nettie had known.

His first sense of aloneness, the renewal of the never answered *why* his time with Nettie had been so brief, and his empathy for Zane and Larissa in finding a joyful relationship, changed with frightening rapidity. Initially, he'd simply admired Larissa's easy ability, in contrast to his own awkward struggles, as she managed her household and family, as she took Charity into her heart along with her own children. He'd soon realized, however, how inadequately "admiration" described his feelings.

"I never intended to violate the cornerstone of Zane's friendship," he protested to the indifferent water at his feet.

But you did. Guilt promptly responded with a jeer. *Words won't change it. Or forgive it.*

Taking utmost care not to let Larissa or Zane suspect the truth, he had, apparently, succeeded admirably. They'd continued to give freely of their trust to him, and of their hearts to his daughter. *For such generosity, I repaid them with betrayal.*

Retribution, however, already gleefully beckoned with a bony finger.

Because he was to live, now, not in the safe haven of the hotel in town, but near Larissa where he must continue to show her only friendship. To let a hint of his true feelings escape would be fatal, for all of them. Zane was going off to war, committing his family to his trusted friend's solemn promise that Ethan would see them safely through until Zane returned home.

If he comes home.

He shook his head violently. Knowing the agony of loss so well, he could not conceive for Larissa such pain past bearing.

Pulling out his pocket watch, he studied the hands as if, somehow, they would change the length of time he had sat on the fallen log attempting to make some sense of his life. One hour and thirty minutes had ticked by. Ninety minutes his heart and his soul had grappled for his moral integrity. Which had won? *God alone knows.* He returned the watch to his pocket and rose wearily to his feet. *At least I hope God knows. I certainly don't.*

He had done his best for Larissa and Zane by giving them these last, precious minutes. Now he would rip their world apart.

He mounted the sorrel, temptation to turn the gelding west, back to town, so overwhelming he actually drew on the reins. Castigating himself for such cowardice, he veered the horse's head east, toward the Edwards farm, toward his future. Settling Buckeye into an easy lope, he tried to shape the sentences he would shortly be compelled to use.

No phrases softened the words.

Arriving at the cornfield for the second time, he gusted a breath of relief to see Zane plowing. *At least I won't interrupt them.* Jaw clenched, he forced himself to let the thought trail off. Urging the sorrel into a more rapid pace that caused his hoofs to thud against the dirt packed roadway, he thus loudly announced his approach.

Zane swiveled sharply. Identifying horse and rider, he halted the oxen and shed the lines. Leaving the animals standing in the unfinished furrow, with slow tread he crossed the bumpy ground. Ethan pulled up Buckeye where the plowed dirt met the roadway. Dismounting, he wrapped the reins around a young mustard shoot and, as if in a trance, moved toward his friend.

The two men met midway. After all his anxious fumbling, he found no words were necessary.

Zane studied his face and, putting his hands on Ethan's shoulders, said quietly, "It's time, then."

"Yes."

"When?"

"Tomorrow morning. The public square at eight o'clock."

Zane's eyes searched Ethan's a moment more as if confirming by sight what his ears had just heard. Then, with a final squeeze of his friend's shoulders and a wordless nod, he turned away and raised his face to the cloudless April sky, studied the sweep of woodlot and creek, barn and house, so peaceful under the cloudless April sky. Closing his eyes, he inhaled deeply. "Strange, isn't it, how much a part of him a man's land gets to be, how he comes to know his own just by the smell and feel of it. Put me down on any inch of this place on a starless midnight, and I'd know right where I was standing." His indrawn breath sighed out. "I better go to Rissa now."

They turned toward the house and saw Larissa maneuvering across the rough plowed ground. Eyes locked with hers, Zane started forward. They met, unaware they had stopped so close to Ethan he clearly saw Larissa's features as she searched her husband's face.

Fragments pelted Ethan's mind, ricocheted. *Blue eyes almost black. Face white as the quartz Charity found in the creek a few days ago and bore proudly home.* Once more finding himself an unwitting watcher, he turned his head away.

Larissa's hands cupped Zane's arms. She tried to ask *When?* No words came.

"Tomorrow morning," he said softly and drew her against his shoulder.

She buried her face against his chest, tears burning her fiercely shut eyes. *There'll be plenty of time later for that. Don't you dare waste it now.* So admonishing herself, she raised her head and smiled. "A man fixing to travel the world needs his socks mended and a hearty supper. The socks are done, thank goodness, so I better get cooking."

He curved his palm to her cheek. "Rissa-love." No other words would come.

She put her hand over his and gently pressed. No other words were necessary.

He released her and she started back to the house. Turning, he saw Ethan grasping the plow handles. Startled, for he had totally forgotten his friend's presence, he said apologetically, "You don't have to do that. You're not dressed for it. It'll keep."

Ethan shook his head and snapped the lines. "Yes, I do," he said in an odd voice as the oxen leaned into the pull. "You go do whatever you have to," he continued in that smothered tone. "There must be a stack of things waiting. I'll tend to this."

After another moment of hesitation, Zane nodded. "Thanks. I know Larissa wants you to stay to supper."

He strode away before Ethan could protest that his staying to supper probably ranked low on the list of Larissa's priorities right about now. But time enough later to argue. He turned away as Zane caught up to Larissa at the edge of the field. Gruffly, he urged the oxen forward. He was still plowing when the three children arrived home from school. Seeing her father behind the plow, Charity called and waved to him. He lifted a hand in response and motioned for her to come to him.

Mac had been teasing Rose about Garth Van Ellis pulling her braids at school, but spotting Ethan in the field instead of Zane, his voice broke off. His eyes went from Ethan to the house and back. Ethan nodded. Mac went rigid for one long second before he eased his stiffness and reached for Rose's hand. "We better go inside," he said in a voice too old for his years.

Startled, Rose stared at him. Comprehension dawned and all the animation drained from her face. She held tightly to his fingers as they crossed the porch to the kitchen.

Charity started after them, but Ethan's call halted her. Sweaty and dirty as he was from the plowing, he crossed the furrows and scooped her into his arms. "That's no place for us right now."

She twisted in his arms to look at the house, and her eyes filled with tears. Turning back to him, she flung her arms fiercely about his neck.

***

Mac pushed open the back door. Ma and Pa sat at the table, holding hands, as he had seen them a hundred times before. This time, however, they were not talking animatedly, as a hundred times before. They simply sat at the table, holding hands. They looked up as he and Rose, still clutching his fingers, came in. Parents and children gazed at one another in silence so loud the ticking of the clock in the sitting room came faintly to them. Rose flew to Zane, his free hand already stretched out to her. As his strong hug enfolded her, Mac crossed the floor to stand beside Larissa. She put the hand not entwined with Zane's fingers on Mac's arm. Zane perched Rose on his knee and reached his arm around her to Mac. They remained thus, connected by touch each to the other, their family circle complete, as the clock in the sitting room ticked.

Zane broke the stillness. "Word came this afternoon."

"When?" Mac's throat was too tight to squeeze out more than the lone syllable.

"Tomorrow morning. I'm to be at the public square by eight."

Eight o'clock. On an ordinary day, Mac and Rose would be trooping up the steps of the brick schoolhouse with the other children as Miss Sullivan in her white waist shirt and black skirt stood at the top and pulled on the bell rope. But tomorrow would not be an ordinary day. Pa would go to war at eight o'clock tomorrow morning.

Zane cleared his throat. "I have a most important decision to make, and I need your help, Mac."

Seems like the most important decision's been made. What else can possibly matter? Mac's skittering thought broke off as Pa solemnly continued.

"It appears volunteering in the Ohio Cavalry requires special equipment. I'm to take my own horse with me. Thus, the puzzlement. Which one? Ma and I have been discussing it. We'd like your opinion, son."

Mac looked to Ma, who gave him a funny little smile. "Pa explained he needs a horse that can go the distance and not fold up on him. One whose rations stick to him between feeding up times. Which one do you think?" Her voice sounded everyday normal, but her funny little smile clung firmly in place.

Pa regarded him gravely. "We'd value your thoughts."

Rose, from the safety of Pa's knee, white face pinched with misery, stared at Mac. He saw her shiver.

"Can we go look them over?" he asked hesitantly.

Ma's funny little smile became a true one. Pa grinned. "We sure can. A man shouldn't make such an important decision without inspecting the merchandise pretty closely."

Entering the barn, they found Ethan wiping the ox yoke clean before hanging it on its pegs. Charity, nearby, scooped grain from the bin. Ethan, visibly uneasy, glanced over his shoulder before concentrating on his exacting task. "Charity and I were going to do up the chores and head for town. We'll be out from under your feet as soon as we can."

"We expect you to stay to supper," Zane said mildly.

"No. We'll not do that tonight." His voice rock solemn, refusing argument, Ethan looked directly at Larissa. "But we thank you." He saw the flicker of gratitude in her eyes, a response so faint he would have missed it had he not been focused so fully upon her. With effort, he turned to Zane and clapped him on the shoulder. "We will, however, expect to be invited to supper to celebrate, when you come back."

The eyes of the two friends met. Zane tipped his head once in acknowledgment. "We'll put it on the calendar." He squared his shoulders and dropped his hands to his hips. "Now, for the important spot of the evening. Mac, here, is going to help select a horse for me to take, courtesy of Army Rule Number 3,617BCZ. 'Horses will be provided to all cavalry units except the Volunteer Cavalry that signed up in Fairvale, Ohio, this date. Those men shall provide their own mounts.' Actually, I prefer it that way, knowing my horse's mind works like I do in a tight spot. So what do you think, son?"

Mac began his careful inspection, and they all walked along with him, offering comments, even teasing a little, much lightening the solemn moment. Cygnus ... Pegasus ... Orion. Aware of them watching, conscious of the deep importance of the occasion, Mac studied the horses, who studied him back with mild curiosity. Finally, "Deneb." His voice came out squeaky, so that everyone looked as startled as he felt. But, "Deneb," he said again, and this time his voice came firmly.

Pa and Ma exchanged one of those between-parents glances he couldn't read. Pa cleared his throat. "Why Deneb?"

Mac lifted his chin. "He's not a quitter. He'll go the distance and not burn all the hay in sight doing it. Remember how you read to us about the constellations? Deneb is the brightest star in the Cygnus constellation, and he's out of Cygnus over there." All eyes swiveled to the black Morgan placidly munching hay in his stall.

Now it was Pa's turn to get an odd little smile on his face. After exchanging another one of those looks with Ma, he put a big hand on Mac's shoulder. "You've made a fine choice. Your Ma and me kind of had him in mind before you got home. We're pleased as can be we all figure it the same way." Mac saw the pride and love on Pa's face, and his heart swelled so he was afraid it would burst out of him right there.

Ma put her hand on his other shoulder, her smile genuinely bright for the first time in days. "We always knew you were a horseman, Mac. From the first day Pa swung you up on old Molly. You couldn't even walk yet, but you grabbed onto her mane with both fists and let out a squeal we were sure they could hear in town. The only problem came when Pa tried to lift you off. You didn't want to have anything to do with getting down. You'd probably be up on her yet if Pa hadn't finally won the argument and carted you off to the house, with you kicking and squawking and reaching back for Molly all the way." Mac turned bright red as Mr. Michaels and Charity joined the laughter.

Too soon, however, Zane reached for the pitchfork, and the warmth and laughter faded. Larissa bit her lip and hurried to the house, Rose trailing her. Charity looked questioningly to Ethan, who picked up the rake, glanced at Mac, and put it aside again.

"Zane, I think Charity and I will head for town now. You have all the help you need right here." He put his arm around Charity's shoulders and walked with her to the door, where Zane's voice stopped them.

"You'll be here tomorrow morning?"

Ethan's shoulders hunched as at a blow. "We'll be here."

Zane was silent a long moment after they left. Then he turned to Mac. "It appears it's you and me tonight, son. And you know, I like it that way."

Mac swallowed around the pesky lump. "Can I do up Deneb?"

Zane silently handed him the currycomb and brush. Safely in Deneb's stall, Mac leaned his head against the horse's mane, the tears he could no longer control soaking into the gleaming black coat.

***

Now all the "last times" began, each one a hammer on chisel blow to Larissa's self-imposed determination. The last time to look up from stove or oven at Zane's entrance from evening chores. The last time to set out warm water and clean towels for his pre-supper washing up. The last evening meal together, the four of them seated at the table, heads bowed and hands clasped. The last time to gather in the sitting room and listen to Zane read from his beloved mythology book, tonight about Daedalus and Icarus. His deep voice and accompanying gestures caught the children's interest so they paid close attention. Hugging the moment to her heart, Larrisa watched and listened. This last time.

"'To escape from Crete, Daedalus made a pair of wings for his son Icarus and a pair for himself. He fastened the feathers together with thread and wax. He warned Icarus not to fly too high because the sun would melt the wax. In the joy of flying, however, Icarus disobeyed, and soared toward the sun. The wax melted. Icarus fell into the sea and drowned, so that Daedalus found only scattered feathers floating on the waves below.'" Zane closed the book and smiled at his young ones. "Now, you'd best put on your wings and soar upstairs to bed. Morning's going to come right early."

He bent his head to Rose's kiss and hug, and Larissa saw her momentary brightness fade. He put his hands on Mac's shoulders and studied him intently before, wordlessly, he pulled his son into a strong hug. The last time.

The children disappeared up the stairs. Zane stood and stretched his arms over his head. "Think I'll go out and look at the stars," he said as he had on a thousand other nights. She puttered about the kitchen, banking the stove, setting out the side meat for breakfast, as she had on a thousand other nights. As she had expected to do for a thousand more.

Zane, smelling of the freshness of the evening air, came in as she was quenching the candle flames in the sitting room. "Looks to be a fair day tomorrow. Good harrowing weather." His voice faltered as he remembered that he would not be there to harrow tomorrow or any other day for a long while.

She pinched the last flame and, in the faint glow from the banked fireplace, made her way to his side. She said nothing in words because words were of no use against his stark recognition. Instead, she took his hand and led him to the stairs. He slipped his arm about her waist, drawing her close as they made their way up the steps. As they had a thousand times. As the clock ticked. *The last time ... The last time ... The last* ....

***

In the pre-dawn blackness, Larissa felt Zane stir and his arms tighten about her. They had spoken little during the night, and she'd hoped the stillness of his body meant he had dropped off to sleep at last while she stared into the darkness overhead. His deep voice against her ear dispelled any such wishfulness. "You awake, Rissa?" At the feel of her chin tipping into his chest, he sighed. "My interior rooster is crowing. Guess he didn't sleep, either."

They dressed, Larissa's cold fingers fumbling against her skirt buttons. She looked into the mirror to put her hair up, and for a startled instant failed to recognize the pale face and enormous eyes staring back at her. She glimpsed Zane reflected behind her, watching, and made a face at her image.

He chuckled. "A thousand ways to remember my wife, and which one is going to be sharpest in my head? She's sticking her tongue out at herself."

Suddenly, she too laughed, a genuine laugh. "Just my special way of making sure you do remember me."

"Oh, I'll not soon forget you, Rissa-love."

"Just to make sure, I want you to take this with you." She reached into the neck of her bodice and pulled out her coin pendant on its gold chain. Lifting it off over her head, she cupped it in her hands. "Remember when you gave this to me?"

He nodded wordlessly.

"You gave it to me even before you asked Pa if we could marry. You said," her voice became gruff as his did in moments of deepest emotion, 'No matter what his answer is, I want you to have something that will keep me in your thoughts.'"

Zane found his voice. "I had two coins to my name to rub together. One I used to make that, and the one I used to buy the chain. I was so sure your Pa would say 'No, and stay away from my daughter.'"

"But he didn't," she said softly. "It wouldn't have made any difference if he had. He knew that. I think he also knew you weren't going to be coinless very long. He had confidence in you. I suspect he was always disappointed after he hired you that you didn't stay on at the livery, working with him."

"Were you disappointed, Rissa?" He watched her closely.

Her eyes held his. "You've never disappointed me. I don't think you'd know how."

He smiled faintly and touched the coin nestled in her palm. "I've never seen you take this off, not since the day I put it on you. How young we were." His voice trailed away.

"I promised you then I'd not casually take it off, and I haven't. Now, I want you to wear it as something to keep me in your thoughts." She stood on tiptoe to slip the chain over his head before she once more held the coin tightly. She pressed it to her lips and tucked it inside the neck of his dress shirt. "Keep it safe," she whispered. "Please."

***

Time suddenly moved in wild jumps as the ticking of the clock seemed to pick up speed. Breakfast. The four of them together. Zane's deep voice, "We thank You for this day." Larissa's carefully prepared food dry as uncooked cornmeal in her mouth. Forcing herself to take small bites. Zane eating heartily. "Might be a time before I get to enjoy a feast like this again. I'm sure going to make the most of it, now."

Breakfast over ... For the first time Larissa could remember, leaving the dishes piled in the wooden sink ... Following Zane upstairs, trailed by the children, so he could put his shaving things in the old carpetbag, reassuring himself Rose's knitted stockings were tucked safely in the corner ... Downstairs and out the front door to Deneb tied to the railing, saddled and bridled, coat gleaming like satin ... Zane bending to Mac and Rose in one last fierce hug ... Straightening, turning, his arms reaching to her ...

Clarity, returning with a jolt so sharp her heart jerked in protest at the abruptness of it, washing through her with pain so intense her knees nearly buckled.

Zane's arms around her, his head bending to hers. His lips finding her mouth, murmuring against it, "In my thoughts, always, Rissa-love." Her arms circling his neck to draw him close to her heart one last, precious instant. He was drawing away, releasing her. Picking up the battered carpetbag. A final good-bye to the children. Swinging up on Deneb. Riding away from her down the springtime road. Pulling up, turning back at the curve to raise his hand in farewell. She smiling ... smiling, her own arm lifted in response.

And he was gone to war down the springtime road.

She pressed her morning crisp, white apron to her lips where Zane's pulsing kiss, warm and comforting, still lay. A broken sob pushed into her awareness. She looked down at Mac and Rose. Tears rolling down Rose's cheeks. Mac's shoulders shaking with his effort not to let his own tears flow.

Larissa knelt to her children's level, standing them off a bit so she could see their faces. "Aren't we the fine ones?" She managed a weak laugh. "Standing here with lower lips drooping down to our knees when there's so much to do." Taking the edge of her apron, she busily blotted Rose's damp cheeks, all the while talking against the dreadful emptiness of her own heart.

"You know what Pa would do if he could see us?" Rose sniffled and shook her head, while Mac swiped at his own face with his shirt sleeve. Offering him a dry corner of her apron, Larissa kept her voice light. "Why, he'd say," and her voice went deep and gruff, 'Where's the spilled milk?' and we'd say, 'What spilled milk, Pa?' You know what he'd say, then?" Rose, her attention caught, shook her head.

"He'd say," she made her voice deep once more so that Rose managed a small giggle. "'The spilt milk you're crying over, of course. There must be enough tears here to float Noah's ark.' You know what we'd have to say, then?" Mac's head moved in negation with Rose's. "We'd have to say, 'No spilt milk, Pa. We're just crying to see which one of us can produce the reddest eyes and the drippiest noses.' You know what he'd say then?" Again their denial.

"He'd say," her voice dropped to its deepest yet, "'Near as I can see, it's a three-way tie. You're all winners in my book!' And you know what I'd say?" Another giggle of anticipation from Rose, a little bigger smile from Mac. "I'd say, 'We must be winners. No matter how far away one of us might be, we have each other, in our hearts, all the time, and that's what counts.'"

With a final blot to Rose's cheeks, Larissa stood briskly and smiled at them in turn. Cupping a hand about each of their faces, she said softly, "Your Pa wouldn't be going if he didn't absolutely have to. He loves you both very much. And so do I." She made her voice deep and gruff one more time. "And if you don't get off to school right now, you'll be late and Miss Sullivan will 'love' you right into staying after for at least an hour. So go!" Rose giggled outright this time and Mac's chuckle was music to Larissa's ears.

They scrambled off but Rose turned back, buried her face in Larissa's apron for a quick hug and dashed off after Mac.

She watched them go, smiling ... waving ... until they passed the curve in the road and were lost to her sight.

Only then she closed her eyes and sank to her knees as the last ounce of strength drained from her.

CHAPTER NINE

Safely out of Larissa's sight, Zane's ramrod stiff spine sagged and his proudly held shoulders drooped. Impatiently he sleeved at the tears blurring his vision. *Won't do a tinker's damn worth of good sniveling like a young one whose candy's been taken away.* Larissa sure hadn't been weeping and wailing all week, while the whole time he'd wanted to cut loose and howl. *Like a pointy nosed wolf squalling at the moon.*

For a full quarter mile, his thoughts on Larissa and the farm world behind him, he let Deneb set his own pace. Feeling Larissa's chain scratching at his neck, he withdrew the quarter eagle. Closing his fist around it, he thought of the day he'd given it to her and how deeply important it had been to him that she like it and understand why he'd made it for her. "All my worldly goods," he murmured. And he would do it again, this moment if he could. *Just to be with her once more, and not be riding off to—*

"Morning, Zane."

Submerged in his thoughts, the approaching horse and two riders astride its back caught him off guard. The greeting punched him upright. Hastily, he stuffed coin and chain inside his shirt. After a last furtive swipe at his eyes, he identified Ethan riding Buckeye, with Charity perched in front of the saddle. His voice squawking like a rusty gate the first time he tried, he made a second attempt to greet them. "Ethan. Miss Charity." With superhuman effort, he smiled at the little girl, touching his hat brim as though she were full grown.

Her usual gratification at this grownup elegance failed to light her face as she gazed at him worriedly. Ethan swung down and lifted her to the ground. "We didn't see Rose and Mac, so I suspect they're someplace behind Mr. Edwards. Why don't you walk that way, Charity, and find them?"

She looked up into her father's face. "Pa, he's crying," she whispered.

Ethan hugged her and murmured in her ear, "I know. It'll be all right. You go to Mac and Rose, now."

Obediently, she started around Zane sitting on Deneb, but suddenly halted, reached out, and gently touched the toe of his boot in the stirrup. Her eyes caught his for a split second before, circling away from Deneb's hooves as she had been taught, she trotted down the road to find Mac and Rose.

The men watched her out of sight before Zane swung down and draped Deneb's reins over his arm. Swallowing hard, he muttered, "Think I'll walk a while."

Ethan tugged at Buckeye's reins and fell into step beside his friend. The horses touched noses, then settled into a contented following of the two men. Several moments passed before Ethan said quietly, "I apologize for Charity's behavior. Since Nettie died, Charity's been extra sensitive about folks feeling—" he hesitated over his choice of words "—sad." He stopped and faced Zane. "She saw me crying more than once those first months. I didn't want to purposely upset her. But she needed to learn there's no shame in tears, from a woman or a man, if the reason's valid. I'd say your reason's pretty damn valid." Ethan turned to study the grassy path. Zane shook his head and raised his gaze to the top of a buckeye tree whose leaves swayed gently in the morning breeze.

Ethan nudged at a pebble with the toe of his boot. "I'll not say *I know exactly how you feel*. People kept telling me that after Nettie—when I was grieving so hard I couldn't see straight. They meant well, but—" he gave Zane a twisted smile "—to me they were just empty words. They *didn't* know. They *couldn't* know because they weren't me. I vowed then I would never do that to anyone. That's why I can tell you in all honesty that I don't know exactly how you feel, but I can tell you I have understanding of your pain. God knows, I have understanding." His voice trailed off.

Zane remained silent as they resumed walking, the only sounds the swishing of the grass beneath their feet, an occasional whuff from one of the horses, and all the springtime sounds of life carrying on around them. Finally, he straightened his sagging shoulders. "Thanks, Ethan. I needed to hear that. I'm not fool enough, at least I don't think so, to believe I'm the only man in the world feeling this way. But a good reminder never hurts. This war won't last forever. Larissa will be home, waiting for me, when it's over."

The other man's eyes darkened as Zane, unaware of the double-edged blow he had just dealt his friend, said hurriedly, "Now I apologize! That was a cruel thing to say."

Ethan forced a weak smile. "No apology necessary for the simple truth. She will be waiting for you."

Again they fell silent, until Zane said hesitantly, "I know I've already put an unfair burden on you, asking you to watch over Larissa and the young ones. Now I'm going to ask more."

Ethan's instinctive response was sharp protest. *What more can Zane ask than for me to live with her day after day, forbidden to show my emotions?* Somehow, he kept his face friendship concerned as he said quietly, "Anything, Zane. You know you only need name it."

Zane bit his lip. "Neither of us has family close by, now her folks are gone. Mine died not long after they moved here. Her only kin is a sister, married and living in Vermont. If I get—" he stumbled over the words

"—if something happens and I don't come back, I'd appreciate you seeing she gets to her sister. I expect there'd be lots of confusion, a time like that. A capable hand would sure help."

Ethan had wondered what more Zane could ask. Now he knew. *To assist her going hundreds of miles away and out of my life.* "Of course. If it comes to that." He shoved out a small laugh. "For sure it's not necessary yet. I for one don't expect it to be. You'll come back full of tales of adventure, and farm your place until you have a gray beard down to your knees. Just like Old Man Tucker. You'll have to keep all your teeth, though, to really rival him."

Memory of the old man's offer to show any disbelievers that he still possessed all his teeth, made even Zane's mouth twitch. But only for a moment before he said soberly, "You promise then. Anything happens, you'll be there for her?"

Ethan, now equally sober, said roughly, "I give you my word. I'll be there."

Crossing the little bridge over Mill Creek on the outskirts of town, they saw dozens of men, some in uniform and some not, hurrying to and fro as if on life and death errands. Maybe they were at that, Zane mused, maybe they were.

The men halted on the other side of the bridge. "It'd probably be best if I let you go your own way from here," Ethan said reluctantly. "If they see me with you, they're liable to sign me up first and ask questions later."

"Thanks for walking with me and, well, for everything."

"The best of luck to you. We'll, all of us, be waiting for you when you come home."

Zane grinned. "When I get back, I expect to see a corn crop that will make every other farmer in Sanilac County, Michigan, and in Union County, Ohio, green with envy."

"I'll make you a bargain. You come back and it'll be here waiting for you to harvest with your own hands."

"I'll be looking forward to it."

Their half-bantering broke off abruptly as each man reached out and their hands met in a strong grasp.

"Take care, my friend," Ethan murmured. "Take care."

Zane tightened his hand around Ethan's in a last, firm grip, and with no further word, turned away into the crowd of men hurrying toward the public square.

Ethan watched until Zane and Deneb had disappeared into the mass of would-be soldiers. "Take very good care." Mounting the sorrel, he crossed the bridge before he glimpsed Charity, Mac, and Rose approaching. Dismounting, he kept a firm hold on the reins as Buckeye, unaccustomed to the noisy bustle all around, backed a little. "Hello, youngsters. I see you found one another."

"Yes, sir," Mac blurted. "Where's Pa?"

"He's gone to the square." To Ethan's ears, the words sounded so inadequate, but he could add nothing meaningful. Taking in Mac's and Rose's forlorn expressions, he said as matter of factly as he could, "It's almost school time. How about Charity and Rose riding Buckeye here, and you and I leading, Mac? With this crowd, you might have a rough time getting through."

At the boy's listless, "Yes, sir," he lifted the girls onto the sorrel. Leading out, he unobtrusively matched his stride to Mac's. Talk was impossible in the shouting tumult, so they proceeded silently to the schoolhouse. Miss Sullivan broke off ringing the bell as they approached. She ushered the last pupil inside before turning back to the little group.

Ethan halted Buckeye and swung Charity and Rose down. Hugging his daughter, he tipped his hat in departure to their teacher. The two girls safely through the doorway and out of hearing, Miss Sullivan, one hand still grasping the bell rope, reached to stop Mac. He paused obediently and she said softly, "Is he going?"

Unable to form the words, Mac ducked his chin. Miss Sullivan gently pressed his shoulder. Looking up, then, he saw reflected in her eyes a grief as large as his own. Only a moment, and he, too, was through the doorway, with Miss Sullivan following and calling to the class to be seated so they could begin the day's work. The same as a hundred other days. And yet, so very different because nothing would ever again be the same.

***

Riding back to the farm, Ethan's emotions swirled so violently he found it impossible to hold any one thought. Raw pain for Zane's departure. Torturing uncertainty of his friend's future in the face of war, of all their futures and the nation's, too, in the coming months. Guilt he was not to serve his country in her time of need. Charity's whispered, "Pa, he's crying," relentlessly stabbing him. Knowledge he was, shortly, to be alone with Larissa for the first time since he'd met her. Fear because he did not know if he was strong enough to give her the space and freedom that were her right, and which he had absolutely no right to violate.

He reached the outer acreage. Smoke from Larissa's kitchen stove pipe wisped into the air. Out in the pasture one of the sheep blatted and another answered. Spring sunshine, soft and warm, reached into all the corners. All was serene in spite of the pulsing forces that threatened from without. In sharp awareness, he realized that the earth carried an inviolable goodness, in spite of the actions of the human beings who tilled it.

He nudged the sorrel with his heels, and horse and rider paced forward to meet the future.

***

He decided to tend Buckeye before going to the house to tell Larissa about meeting up with Zane. *Surely, she'll welcome any information I can report.* He was determined to give her any scraps of comfort he could. So thinking, he led Buckeye to the barn, unsaddled and rubbed him down before leading him to the pasture. Turned loose, the horse promptly rolled, obviously getting an itch off his back, and Ethan grinned. "Buckeye, I think I can honestly say, '*I know exactly how you feel.*' Nothing worse than an itch that can't be reached." Righting himself, the sorrel began grazing with a look that spoke plainly of silly contentment.

With a final chuckle, Ethan strode toward the kitchen door, since it was closer than the front. He wasn't making any particular effort to be quiet, but climbing the steps, he heard a half-sound that halted him in mid stride. Setting his feet carefully, he crossed the porch. Hand raised to knock on the door, he froze. The sound came again, unmistakable this time. The heartbroken sobs of a woman battling a deep and unchangeable torment.

So had he heard Nettie cry the day their son died. His own grief, and a husband's right, had allowed him to go to her in a mutual reaching of comfort.

He had no such right with Larissa.

To intrude upon this profoundly private moment would be the worst kind of betrayal of her trust and Zane's.

She must be in the kitchen, obviously with no idea he lurked anywhere within miles. Clenching his fists so tightly the nails cut his palms, he once more set his feet carefully as he stepped off the porch. Turning toward the cabin Larissa had prepared for Charity and him, he knew he would not, now or ever, tell her of his meeting with Zane.

He had thought it would be comforting to her.

He knew now that knowledge of Zane's deep and unchangeable torment would be no comfort at all.

***

Changing slowly into his work clothes, he hoped the oftentimes done movements would somehow restore him to a semblance of reality. The little cabin, not yet possessing a sense of lived in, we belong here familiarity, did nothing to lighten his pain. He supposed in time, with days and nights of living soaked into the walls and furniture, it would feel like home.

He noted vaguely the small touches Larissa had added to the simple furnishings. A plant he thought might be a begonia, because a woman guest had commented admiringly upon a similar one in the hotel lobby, sat on a walnut stand in front of the south window. A vase of bluebells graced the table that held a cut-glass lamp and would be their working and eating surface. Intricately stitched quilts covered the beds tucked into opposite corners. The curtains that could be pulled to hide the beds, like the quilts, were of bright fabric that dispelled the semi-gloom of the room.

A woman's hand. He tried so hard for Charity's sake to provide the sense of comfort Nettie had produced with seeming ease. He had learned many lessons these past four years, including one that the more effortless a completed task about the house appeared, the more work had, invariably, gone into it. Vesta, Roman goddess of the home, had, apparently, decided to thrust another lesson or two at him to study. No matter how hard a man tried to do, a woman did. No matter how hard a man pretended such female things were of no consequence, a woman, with a few deft touches, proved they did, indeed, make all the difference.

Leaving the cabin for the bright outdoors, a sudden chill shook him to his toes.

***

He and the harrow were listlessly plodding behind the oxen on the far side of the cornfield when he heard a melodic clanging. Startled, he looked toward the house to see Larissa pulling energetically on the rope of the bell that was sounded only at mealtimes or in dire emergency. He glanced at the sun, straight overhead. The morning couldn't be spent, but her signal confirmed it.

Arm held high, hat in hand, he swung it to let her know he understood. Across the stretch of field, he saw her responding wave before she disappeared into the house. Unhitching the team from the harrow, he led the oxen toward the creek where they drank stolidly, then just as calmly lumbered into the pasture where they began grazing as if they had no other plans for the rest of the day.

Ethan, feeling hopelessly dirty and sweaty, started for the cabin to clean up. He passed the back porch as Larissa appeared, pan in hand, towel flung over her shoulder. She set the pan on the bench beside the door. "Here's warm water and soap for you. And a towel." She held out the cloth.

Taking off his hat, he ran grimy fingers through his sweat plastered hair. "I was planning to go to the cabin. I sure don't mean to put you to extra trouble."

"It's no trouble. Be more so for you to have to fuss with the cabin fireplace for hot water and food, when I'm doing it over here, anyway." Again, she offered the towel.

After another second of hesitation, he mounted the porch steps and took the cloth from her. "Thanks. I'll admit, I am a tad ripe." His rueful admission failed to bring an answering spark to her eyes.

"It's to be expected. You're working hard."

His slight smile disappeared. "I'll try to remedy that expectation right now."

Without answering, she retreated to the kitchen. The door shut behind her and he let out a depressed sigh. His gaze fixed for a long moment on the closed panel before he flipped the towel over his shoulder and bent to the washbowl.

Minutes later, rinsed-out hair combed, and short brown beard and mustache as dirt free as he could manage, he brushed at his shirt and pants. The uneasy sensation persisted that he was not clean enough to enter the house, in spite of feeling several pounds lighter than when he started the washing process. Now, however, he faced a new dilemma. Standing before the kitchen door, he wondered suddenly what to do next. Knock before entering, as if he were a guest? Or just walk on in as if he owned the farm? The last thing either of them needed right now was the assumption he was taking Zane's place. Even if, for all practical purposes, he was doing exactly that. *All practical purposes.* His brain waved the words tauntingly. Abruptly, he raised his hand to knock and almost batted Larissa on the nose as she suddenly pulled open the door. Which of them looked more startled, it would be difficult to win a bet. She recovered first and backed up a little. Yanking his fist down, he too retreated a pace. "Larissa, I'm sorry. I didn't mean to attack you."

"Of course you didn't." Still no spark in her eyes. "I realized I'd shut the door on you. I apologize. It was rude, and there's never an excuse for that."

Yes, there is. His mind mouthed the words he could not speak aloud. *If ever an excuse existed, you have it in spades.*

Unaware of the run of his mind, she gestured to the table, set with two places. A soup tureen, holding thick pieces of meat and vegetables in gravy, steamed appetizingly. A platter of cornbread and a pitcher of milk flanked it. A vase of violets the blue of Larissa's eyes graced the center of the table. Taking the chair she indicated, waiting for her to be seated, he gestured to the delicate blooms. "The flowers are really pretty, Larissa," he said in an attempt to break the silence stretching between them. She sat down, but to his consternation, she stared at the flowers, then abruptly shoved back her chair and lurched to her feet.

"Please excuse me," she said faintly. "I have something to do. You go ahead and eat." Flinging the last words over her shoulder, she fled the room.

A swift glimpse of her face changed his consternation to horror. *What did I say to trigger such misery?* He started to rise, with some wild idea of following her, but hearing her feet stumbling up the stairway, he slowly sank back.

Bitterness filled him. He, who would not ever deliberately cause her pain, had just brought her unbearable anguish. He buried his head in his hands. He'd thought he could help in the day to day work, with her none the wiser about his true feelings. But he hadn't been in her presence two minutes before causing her grief. *So much grief she fled my sight.*

She'd said to go ahead and eat. He stared at the still steaming meat and gravy and his stomach turned over in flat protest. Food was the last thing he wanted now, even though, moments earlier, his belly had growled with hunger. His hotel breakfast had long since faded. Besides walking with Zane, he'd put in a full morning at the harrowing, in spite of his late start. He knew he should eat if he expected to turn out even half a job of work this afternoon.

He started to dip a bowlful of stew, and let ladle and contents fall back into the tureen. In spite of trying to distract himself with banal thoughts, he heard a door shut upstairs. Now, ears sharpened by agitation, he detected another sound, faint but undeniable. Racking sobs.

That did it. He rose from the table, all thought of food forgotten, and strode out the door.

***

He was once more tramping sluggishly behind the oxen when he heard his name called. Jolted out of his reverie, he caught sight of Larissa making her way over the now smooth field. She carried a jug on one hip, and in the other hand, a napkin covered egg basket. She waited until she was close enough to speak without shouting. "You're really coming along with this. I'm impressed."

His eyes followed hers across the harrowed sweep of land. He was startled to realize how much he had accomplished while walking in such a fog.

"Here's some dinner." She held out the egg basket and jug. Mechanically, he reached out, then stood clutching them clumsily, keenly aware of the wet coolness of the jug soaking into his shirtfront, chilling the work-heated skin beneath.

Again, no spark lighted her eyes, but the corners of her mouth formed into the smallest of rueful smiles. "You must be perishing of hunger. I saw the table and realized you hadn't eaten, and that you were back out here working." Her voice muted an instant before she continued more strongly. "I apologize for my behavior. I'm so ashamed you had to suffer because of my silliness."

He finally found words. "No. Don't be sorry on my account. God knows, you have a right to your feelings. I only regret my clumsiness caused you pain."

"You didn't know. How could you?" At his still totally blank expression, she said softly, "What you said about the flowers." Her voice wavered. "Zane said the same thing, almost exactly your words, a hundred times. It just got to me." Before he could speak, she hurried on as if afraid her courage would fail if she stopped. "I spent the last hour doing more than bawling my head off. I did lots of thinking, too. I suspect there'll be many occasions, for both of us, when something triggers a memory. That's only natural. It's important we be honest with each other and not pretend happiness we don't feel at the moment."

For the first time, the faintest glimmer sparked her eyes. "Although I don't recommend flying off the handle quite so drastically as I did a while ago." The twinkle faded. "I'll not do that again. I've already promised myself, and I promise you, too. At least by speaking up, instead of stumbling around awkwardly, we'll know each other's short reins and be able to respect them. What do you think?"

She could not know, and he could not tell her, that the combination of the glow in her eyes, however brief, and her words, embarrassed but honest, swept him like a cleansing breeze. His error was just that, then, a simple blunder of a most unfortunate choice of words. Relief leaping through him, he said heartily, "That's a fine idea. Nettie and I found, even if it came hard to bring something up, after we discussed it, we felt stronger toward each other for it." He was totally unaware of Larissa's realization that, for the first time since she had known him, he spoke matter-of-factly of Nettie.

"It's like that between Zane and me, too. I'm glad we each have understanding of it. I'm afraid I've been truly spoiled along that line."

"May we both continue to be so." He lifted the milk jug in a toasting gesture.

The motion abruptly recalled her to their present state. "Merciful Heavens, I'm keeping you from eating. It's a wonder you've not keeled over while I've babbled on." She indicated the jug and basket. "You eat before the milk gets warm and the bread stale. It isn't fancy, but it'll fill the empty spaces until suppertime."

"Smells like a king's banquet to me." He gestured to the shade at the edge of the field. "I'll just mosey over there and enjoy it to the full."

"I'll leave you in peace. I expect to see you at supper. No excuses," she said so firmly his protest died unspoken.

He watched her cross the field. While she was still within hearing range, he called, "Larissa." She turned, questioningly, and he gestured with the basket and jug. "Thanks."

She tipped her head, once, and followed her path back to the house.

CHAPTER TEN

After leaving Ethan, Zane, leading Deneb, shouldered his way through the crowds of soldiers to-be. Heading toward the brick courthouse on the northeast corner of the public square, he realized the tumult had become a roaring hum. Pushing through a last barrier of men, he discovered why.

The entire expanse of the square was filled with clusters of men assembled in roughshod order, spilling over into the outskirts of town and the wooded area beyond.

The smell from several hundred close packed bodies made his eyes water.

Deneb snorted in protest. In that first shocked instant, Zane muttered, "Easy, boy. Although I couldn't agree with you more." Passing slowly among the clumps of sitting, standing, reclining men, he exercised extreme caution that Deneb, already skittish enough, didn't shy and strike someone with a hoof. The other danger from the Morgan, of course, was more down to earth, and more than a few salty remarks and explicit suggestions from the men sprawled eye level with Deneb's belly followed in their wake. Fortunately for all concerned, he refrained from raining on anyone's parade as Zane continued toward the courthouse. He had the rough idea that, because it was where the recruiters had been, they would again be there to direct the men they had signed up. Before reaching his goal, however, above the insistent buzzing he heard his name shouted.

"Zane Edwards? This way!"

Searching the crowd, he spotted Obadiah Beldane gesturing him forward. Zane waved his free arm to show he understood and paced Deneb up to the grinning blacksmith, who slapped him on the shoulder. Deneb snorted at the sudden movement and sharp noise, and Obadiah immediately eased off, although his grin remained. "Sorry, Zane. Should of thought about him being nervous in all this confusion. But it's sure good to see you. I take it bringing your horse here means you signed on with the cavalry. I didn't know, since I haven't seen you since it all busted loose on Sunday. We're along this way," he added, gesturing toward the grove of oaks that edged the town.

Zane glimpsed another knot of men, with a line of horses picketed to a long rope stretched between several of the oaks. "You're cavalry, too?" was all he could think to say.

Obadiah chuckled. "Took me by surprise more'n it does you. When they found out I have a horse, and can ride, and know which part of the critter to nail the shoe to, they up and plunked me and Esau right in the middle of the 6th Ohio Volunteer Cavalry." At Zane's bemused expression, he chuckled again. "Guess all those horse races Esau and me have won over the years might've had something to do with it."

Zane laughed knowingly. Obadiah and Esau had been the bane of every racehorse rider at the annual Fairvale Fourth of July picnic for the last ten years. Dingily gray of coat, bleary of eye, deceptively saggy jointed and harmless looking, Esau, when presented with a starting line and opening gunshot, literally leaped into action. Mind and hooves once set upon the course, heaven itself couldn't hold him back until he crossed the finish line, invariably well ahead of any other contenders. Each year, the committee optimistically staged a race, because a few die hards who knew better persisted in believing that this time they could pull off a win.

When asked how he did it, Obadiah said solemnly, "I guess nobody ever told Esau, 'You can't win 'em all.' So he does." This observation, accompanied by a wink and a peal of laughter, effectively cut off any further pesty questions.

Obadiah led them toward a clump of trees near the creek. "It appears, as cavalry, we're luckier'n some of the other fellows as to our assigned roosting spot. We're picketed near the creek so our horses'll have plenty of water. The high ups aren't so concerned about the men who'll be the pieces in their fancy checker game. But our animals are valuable and rate good care."

Zane would have laughed at the irony of Obadiah's observation, except for a sudden uneasy feeling there might be more truth in it than he yet suspected.

"I'll show you the watering area that's been marked off. I was about to take Esau over, anyway." Obadiah untied his sleepy eyed horse and led him down creek. "After we're done, I'll give you a guided tour of our palatial quarters."

They followed a trampled path along the creek bank to a roped off area redolent with horse droppings. As both animals drank gustily, Zane studied his companion more closely. He'd known Obadiah for years, although neither considered the other a close friend. Since Zane, shoeing his own horses, didn't frequent the blacksmith shop, and Obadiah didn't frequent the church, theirs tended more toward a casual, nodding acquaintance. Quiet mouthed himself, Zane tended to shy away from Obadiah's garrulous never met a stranger friendliness. Of a height and age with Zane, with black hair and eyes, the farrier's blocky figure and impressively muscled arms deterred even the most confident bully spoiling for a fight from approaching him with anything but wary respect. True to form, Obadiah rattled on while the horses drank.

Pursuing his thoughts, Zane only half listened, but came back to awareness at the words "… physical examination before the train leaves."

"They're going to examine all those men?"

Obadiah, gratified at his disbelief, struck his idea of a military pose, saluting sharply with the wrong hand. "'Yes *sir*! Before the steam cars leave tonight, *sir*.'" His laugh rolled out. "As I live and breathe, one of 'em promised that just before you came along."

"They better have a whole hospital full of doctors on hand, if they expect to go through all those men in one day."

"Don't know about a whole hospital, but I saw Doc Rawley nosing around a while ago. He didn't look real pleased. But then he never does, come to think of it. I suppose they didn't give him much choice in the matter."

"Probably not." Zane remembered Mac telling about Doc's opinion of the war, men shooting bits of metal at each other and messing up what he'd spent most of his life trying to fix. Now they'd dragged him into it, too. Kicking and cussing, Zane wagered. He couldn't suppress a grin at the image of crusty Doc and the Army big bugs batting heads. For himself, he'd place his bets on Doc.

They had, by this time, strolled back to the rope where they secured the horses and Obadiah began his guided tour. They stopped first near a rather harassed gentleman in uniform, wearing captain's bars. Since he was surrounded by several other men who all appeared to be asking questions at the same time, it took a while before Zane and Obadiah worked their way up to him.

He evidently recognized Obadiah, for his features became a little more strained. "I already told you—" he began, but Obadiah pushed Zane forward.

"Another recruit, capt'n. This is Zane Edwards. Zane, Capt'n Norton."

The captain's hassled expression eased a little as he took in Zane's height and breadth of shoulders, and the fact he wasn't spilling words out of his mouth like water over a falls. "Edwards. You're a friend of his, I take it?" He gestured with his chin toward Obadiah.

"We've known each other for years," Zane replied carefully.

The captain looked at him with unmistakable pity. "If you ever find the one responsible for winding him up, for God's sake, take the key away from him."

In spite of himself, a chuckle escaped Zane. "Yes, sir," he said solemnly. "I'll do my best."

The hint of a twinkle in the captain's eyes faded as he once more became all Army. "You've picketed your horse? Good. Physical examinations today for all the men in the company, before the train leaves tonight. You'll be issued a uniform when we get to Columbus.

Don't leave this area." He threw this last, an obvious order, at Zane and Obadiah as a new cluster of men, flinging questions, surrounded him.

"Columbus," Zane repeated as they moved aside. So now he knew his destination.

***

That day had to qualify as the longest in Zane's experience, he decided ruefully as they waited, and waited some more, for something to happen. Even the eternal hours before the births of Mac and Rose hadn't dragged this much. Used to physical activity, the endless sitting, doing nothing, took its toll. Accustomed to his solitude and the peace of the farm, the presence of so many other bodies bore down oppressingly.

Making a genuine effort, he listened to the war news he figured could be factual, trying to get caught up on what was happening before it happened to him. Cutting through the babble, some voices spoke with the unerring ring of truth.

"The way I heard it, Kentucky's refusing to supply any troops for the Union. Interesting, that being the state where President Lincoln was born."

"Governor of Missouri sounded so impressive, I wrote it down. Got it right here. He said Lincoln's call for troops was 'illegal, unconstitutional, revolutionary, inhuman, diabolical and cannot be complied with.' All in one breath. So, fellas, what does that make us as is complying? Tell you what it makes me. Fighting mad!"

As the day wore on, the clatter of voices blended so that Zane was unable to distinguish real from unreal. Obadiah spouted off with the best of them, causing Zane to wonder where the farrier had accumulated so many "facts" in such a short time. He felt disinclined to ask, however. He suspected Obadiah would happily tell him, in detail. Eventually, he retrieved Deneb and wandered down to the watering area where the buzz of voices remained audible, but a muted hum, not a full fledged roar. He feared his ears had picked up a permanent ringing.

In no hurry to return, he picketed Deneb in a patch of clean grass and stretched out full length near him, his back to one of the massive oaks. Uneasiness pricked him, and he figured he'd better have it out right now. *You made your choice. You knew it wouldn't be all ten-foot-high cornrows and sunshine. So quit yammering. Accept it.*

It wasn't the thought of war itself, and battle. That'd sort itself out when the time came. He didn't consider himself any kind of hero. He'd be brave as some and maybe not so brave as others. That, too, would take care of itself. What he didn't know was if he could abide the unavoidable nearness of several thousand men until this war finished up.

If this morning held any indication, that was the real battle he would have to fight. *Only a few hours, and already you're jumpy as any youngling frog in Mill Pond.*

All his life he'd survived bad times by doing what must be done, whether hiring himself out as a farmhand at thirteen after his Ma and Pa died and their place went back to the bank, or leaving Larissa this morning. He had tried to instill it in Mac and Rose, a stored up defense against bad times that would, inevitably, interlace their lives.

So take your own advice. Accept it, and quit fussing like some old grandpa moaning about his aching knees. You told Ethan this morning this war'll be over eventually and you'll be coming home. Fine words to spout. Now you damned well better live them.

Leading Deneb back to the other horses, he knew he hadn't solved his problem, but at least he had a grip on it. How many times he had counseled Mac and Rose to start someplace, any place, but by jingo, start. He guessed being a parent meant taking an occasional hearty slug of your own medicine, no matter how foul tasting.

With Deneb once more secured to the picket rope, Zane strolled aimlessly on the outskirts of the crowd of cavalrymen-to-be. Not surprisingly, he didn't see anyone else he knew. He wasn't precisely sure what he was doing here, himself. If he took heart from anything, it was knowing he'd be caring for the company horses. Provided, of course, the Army kept its word. Horses, at least, he liked and understood.

"Zane?"

Wheeling at sound of his name being called over the hubbub, he spotted Obadiah working his way toward him. The imaginative oaths and sour looks following in the blacksmith's wake testified he wasn't especially careful where his heels and elbows landed as he pushed through. "Been looking for you. They're wanting us to line up for our physicals. The closer to the front of the line we are, the sooner we'll be done with the pesty business."

Zane saw now the formless crowd merging into lines of men all pointed creekward. Following Obadiah, he joined a queue for the next cycle of waiting. *If today's any indication, we're now on speaking terms with at least one specialty of the Army. Get there quick, then wait.* It took a while, but eventually Obadiah, in front of Zane, faced Doc Rawley. If Doc hadn't appeared real pleased earlier that morning with his "voluntary" assignment, he now showed even markedly less enthusiasm. His usual crabby expression had taken on a strong resemblance to a man discovering half a worm in the apple he'd just bitten into.

Zane listened carefully as Doc shot questions at Obadiah, then ordered him to remove his shirt for a series of pokes and jabs to his midsection. Finally, with a scowl that would have done credit to an angry two-year-old, Doc snapped, "You're fit. Just try not to talk the ears off every other man in the company before this foolishness is done."

Obadiah grinned. "Thanks, Doc. Say, why don't you come join us? Be a great adventure."

"I just pronounced you able. Maybe I better recheck your head to see if your Ma dropped you on it."

Obadiah's grin widened. "I hear you. But you'll miss the excitement of a lifetime." He broke off his words, dodged out of reach of Doc's grasp at his ears, and joined the next line to prove he knew which end of an 1855 Springfield rifle musket was the business one.

Stepping up to Doc, Zane did his best to control his mirth. No use setting off a medical man who had all the by your leave in the world to prod and pinch your anatomy.

Doc, however, saw the tail end of his smile. "Blame fool presumption he's going for a picnic in the park." He sighed. "Guess he should hang on to his notions a while. For sure, he won't have 'em very long." Zane remembered, then, how back in 1836, following the battle of the Alamo down in Texas, Doc rode with Sam Houston's army to the bloodbath at San Jacinto. Before he could comment, Doc waved his hand impatiently. "Strip off your shirt and let's get started."

Zane complied while Doc asked him questions about his teeth and hearing, whether he was a drunkard or had convulsions, and whether he had any infectious disorders. Receiving all negative replies, Doc fitted his "Doctor Skinner's Double Flexible Stethoscope" in his ears and listened to Zane's heart and lungs. "All clear," he pronounced finally.

"Thanks." He started toward the next line, but Doc's hand on his arm halted him. His grim expression startled Zane. *What could be wrong?* "Doc?"

"I've pronounced you healthy, Zane Edwards. Now, by God, you stay that way. I can give orders just as well as the next one in this man's Army. And in the Army, orders are orders. You see you follow them. Understood?"

Zane, seeing the doctor's unwonted glint of concern, nodded soberly. "I understand. I'll do my best to obey you."

"See that you do. You've a fine family who needs you a hell of a lot more than the Army needs cannon fodder."

Zane scared up a laugh. "Such a delicate way of putting it. For sure, I'll remember."

"Go on, then. I've got more fodder, I mean more examinations. I don't have time to stand jawing with you."

Zane retreated to the next line, but his thoughts remained upon Doc Rawley. What a combination of bluff, bluster and heart deep caring. Fairvale certainly rated high in blessings bestowed. *Without doubt, he's teaching Mac things he could never learn from anyone else.*

***

Having successfully proved he knew which end of the single shot Springfield rifle musket fired bullets, thereby confirming that little danger existed of shooting off his own foot, Zane retreated to a shady spot away from the worst of the confusion. Sitting with his back propped against the trunk of a stately maple, he opened the sack Larissa had pressed into his hands that morning. "A little something to keep you going in case they forget to feed you come dinnertime."

Upon inspection, the little something proved to be enough to feed a small army. It hadn't occurred to him they wouldn't provide some kind of eatables, but Larissa'd obviously been a furlong ahead of him. Again. The only problem, he wasn't sure he could choke it down for thinking of her fixing it.

"Zane?"

For the first time that day, Zane actually felt grateful to hear Obadiah hollering, relieved to see him come loping among the trees. "Here you are. Been looking for you quite a while. I got worried maybe you'd up and lit out." Obadiah's laugh took any sting out of the words.

"Nope. Just sitting here, enjoying the quiet."

Obadiah, completely oblivious to the barb, continued his lament. "Yeah, it is noisy over that way. Times today, I've been hard put to hear myself think, what with all those other know-it-alls adding their penny's worth every time I tried to tell them something important." He squatted down and peered at the sack on Zane's lap. "What you got there? Victuals? Well, now, if that isn't something. Guess there are more'n one or two advantages to married life. Never quite made it to that state myself, but I came close on a couple of occasions, wondering if I should throw my hat into the ring. Guess this makes another one." He winked. "Came to tell you they've put out kettles of soup, but this appears a good bit more appetizing. What'd she fix?"

Obviously, he would have been thoroughly amazed if Zane mentioned he hadn't offered to share his dinner. He suspected that, in Obadiah's mind at least, they were now fast friends. Two against the world, who would share all the trials and tribulations of the coming warfare, including any foodstuffs wandering their way.

Zane wasn't persuaded such a state exemplified his personal fondest wish, but one thing about the blacksmith. If a body needed information, Obadiah was the man to acquire it. If it wasn't forthcoming quickly enough, he'd just keep pestering until, like slapping an annoying gnat, they'd tell him just to get rid of him. Besides which, he decided as he brought out the bread and meat Larissa had packed, with Obadiah around, a man's mind couldn't remain unclogged long enough for a lot of depressing thoughts to roost. *Which just might be a high recommendation.*

***

Late that afternoon, another stir coiled through the waiting men. Word passed like wind riffling a ripening wheat field. The steam cars would soon chug into the Big Four Railway's station on the far side of the village. The stir increased, became confusion as the men gathered scattered possessions and looked to their horses, readying them for boarding.

Captain Norton herded his flock of embryonic cavalrymen together, giving them explicit instructions about loading the animals on the stock cars. Spying Zane, he gestured to him and a couple of other men. "Edwards. Cooper. Waterman. You three'll ride in the cars with the horses. See they don't come to any harm. Each of you'll be in a car. Pick a man to help you, but you're in charge."

Zane knew instantly who his helper would be, if not precisely by his personal choosing. In this instance, he acknowledged wryly, Obadiah's knowledge of horses would be worth his weight in gold. If only he'd stop talking and not spook the animals already nervous from the unaccustomed commotion.

Between Zane and Obadiah, the loading went amazingly smooth. All the animals aboard, the two men swung up and the doors slid shut. As the train began to move, the horses skittered so that Zane moved quietly among them, murmuring, soothing them into the long ride ahead. Surprised and gratified, he saw Obadiah doing the same thing, handling them with the expertise of long habit.

By the time he took stock of his surroundings, the train had left behind the old blockhouse, built in haste during Fairvale's youngest days and never even used for protection against Indian attack. No faintest reverberation stirred the air from the courthouse bell faithfully tolling the evening hour. Main Street's bridge spanning Mill Creek slid into the foliage as they chugged west to where their little branch line joined the first of the two main lines that would take them to Columbus.

With a rush of thankfulness, he realized the actual departure he'd dreaded all day had come and gone. He'd just been too busy to be aware of it.

CHAPTER ELEVEN

When the children arrived home from school late that afternoon, Ethan hailed them from the cornfield. Charity started toward the house with the other two, but halted at a warning whoop from her father. Turning, she saw him waving his hat for her to come. "I have to see what Pa wants," she told Rose. "I'll ask if we can work on our stories together. If he says yes, I'll come back."

"Why wouldn't he?" Rose asked practically.

Charity shrugged. "He still gets mad sometimes, but not like he used to." Her expression turned wistful as Mac, already on the driveway, gave no sign of hearing. Her father called again and she waved to him in acknowledgment. "See you later," she threw over her shoulder to Rose and started running across the field.

"Hi, Pa. May Rose and I work on our essays together?"

Ethan put his arm around her shoulders in a swift hug. "Not this afternoon."

"But Pa, Miss Sullivan said we could work together."

"Not this afternoon, Charity."

At his sternness, she pulled back warily.

"With Mr. Edwards going away, Mrs. Edwards, Rose and Mac feel really sad. We need to leave them alone for a while."

"If they're sad, shouldn't we be with them? When I'm that way, I feel better if you or Mrs. Edwards or Rose comes and talks to me."

"That works, sometimes. Other times, like now, they need to be alone, without anyone outside their family around." She still didn't look convinced. He said firmly, "This is one of those times you'll just have to believe what I say."

"I believe you, Pa. I just wish that Rose was my for real sister. Then I could be with her and help her be happy again."

***

Mac, trailed by Rose, entered the kitchen to find his mother stooping to take a loaf of bread from the oven. The yeasty aroma filling the room made his stomach grumble.

Larissa glanced up as her hands continued her work. "You're home? Where has the afternoon gone?" Using two snowy dishtowels to hold the pan, she lifted the loaf to her worktable and tipped it out beside the one already steaming there. "I gave all the bread to Pa this morning to take with him. I figured I'd better make more because I just might have two hungry mice wanting to nibble some." She smiled and held out her arms. "Did I figure right?"

Rose flung herself toward her mother. "You sure did, Ma. May we have some now?"

Larissa hugged her, a little more tightly than usual, and released her just as on so many other after school homecomings. "It does smell good, doesn't it? All right. One piece each and then change your clothes and out to your chores." She reached for the butter crock even as she spoke. Pausing, knife in hand, she looked at her son. "Mac?"

He hesitated. Maybe it was Doc's training getting into him, teaching him to always be observant. Flushed cheeks in her otherwise pale face could have been from stooping over the hot oven, but her eyes were swollen as if with weeping. Her expression held the smallest of warnings as she glanced at Rose and shook her head ever so slightly. Slinging his strapped books onto a chair, he inhaled an exaggerated breath of the warm fragrance. "Cut me a big piece, Ma?" he pleaded.

She immediately relaxed a little and held the knife over the loaf for a generous slice. "This big?"

He indicated the other end of the loaf. "This big?" he asked with wide eyed hopefulness.

"Mac!" Her effort to appear scandalized failed as his name ended on a catch of breath, but Rose, reaching into the cupboard for plates, laughed at their clowning.

"A plate for me too, please, Rose. I'll have some, if we can manage to keep it away from Mac." By the time Rose turned with the plates, Larissa was busily cutting slices and Mac was pointing hopefully for her to make them wider while she tried to shoo his hands away.

A few minutes later, as the children left the room to change into their chore clothes, Larissa said softly, "Mac." He turned and she smiled. "Thank you, son." He started to speak, but ducked his head and followed Rose to the stairs.

"Why'd she thank you?"

"Because I was big hearted and didn't eat all her bread, slow poke. Now get upstairs before I run you over."

She squealed and scurried up the remaining steps, so she didn't see Larissa standing in the doorway, watching and smiling. Nor did she see her mother's face, all the cheerfulness drained away except for that bright smile.

But Mac did.

***

Entering the barn the following morning to help with Saturday's chores, the children found Charity busily collecting horse blankets for airing in the spring sunshine. Ethan and Larissa had discussed it the night before. He'd told her firmly he expected Charity to help out around the place, just as the others did. She must have her assigned tasks to complete without any parental prodding.

Larissa had protested he was already doing more than necessary. His daughter certainly didn't have to be a farm hand too.

"She won't be, any more than your two are. But right is right. Rose and Mac are learning responsibility and work ethics. I want the same for her. Since this is where we are, this is where she'll have to learn them. Right, Charity?"

She bobbed her head. "I don't mind helping. Honest. It's fun, doing things with Rose. And Mac."

Mac reached for the milk pitcher. "She does good, for a girl. And she'd keep Rose out of my hair while I'm trying to get my work done." This last with a face at his sister, who promptly stuck her tongue out at him.

"All right, you two. That's enough," Larissa said sternly. "If this is a sample, I'm not so sure you'll want Charity learning my children's work ethics," she added ruefully to Ethan, who suddenly had a remarkably hard time swallowing his coffee.

"It really would help, Ma," Mac pointed out. "Doc says it's important to manage as much time as I can with him."

Rose, not to be outdone, put in, "We can do anything Mac can do. Can't we, Charity?"

Charity had looked a little dubious at this sweeping guarantee, but chimed in loyally, "Of course we can."

Larissa studied their hopeful faces.

"Looks like you're outvoted," Ethan observed solemnly. "Right, young ones?"

Three heads dipped enthusiastically in the affirmative, causing Larissa to raise her hands and let them fall into her aproned lap. "Some day a woman's vote will count," she predicted darkly, "but until then I guess I'll just have to accept majority rule. Charity, welcome to our work ethics."

The children had clapped. Ethan had looked ridiculously relieved. *Remind me never to place a bet on winning a skirmish with her.*

So this bright morning, the children scurried to finish their assigned tasks before the noon dinner hour. Afterward, Mac left to assist Doc in town, and Rose and Charity helped Larissa with the work in both the cabin and the house.

Ethan's second discussion with Larissa had concerned Charity's housecleaning the cabin. But this time he lost soundly.

"I will not allow that child to work hard in my house and then expect her to drudge away all by herself keeping your place clean."

She glared at him with fire in her eyes, daring him to oppose her, and he had the good sense to know when he was outclassed. "Yes, ma'am," he said meekly.

"That's settled, then," she said crisply.

He managed, however, to get in a parting shot. "Thought I heard some talk about women not having any vote. I must have been mistaken." Mournfully, he tugged at his beard. "They not only vote, they get the opposing candidate to vote for them, too, instead of himself."

"Go on with you. You're tracking up my clean steps." Larissa flapped her apron at him and he swiftly retreated. But not before he heard her say softly to his back, "Thank you, Ethan."

***

On his way into town that afternoon, Mac's mind raced while his feet dragged along the path. He had a problem and didn't know who to ask. He wished he could talk with Pa. *That's a good one. Your problem is about Pa, but you can't talk to him because he isn't here, and him not being here is your problem.* He tried to grin at his around-in-a-circle predicament, but couldn't make it stick.

It would be disloyal to Pa to take his uncertainty to Mr. Michaels. He couldn't talk to Ma. It would hurt her too much. Rose and Charity he dismissed with a shrug. When Charity told him her problems, he didn't mind listening, and even offering advice. But important as they loomed to her, they were only little girl worries, and her Pa hadn't gone to war.

Opening the office door, he found Doc sitting at the cluttered desk, writing in his journal. Doc had impressed upon him, straight off, the importance of keeping track of each treatment given to which patient. "You might think you'll remember forever, and some you do, but writing down what you've done helps when you have to treat someone in the future. It also gives you reference for what works and what doesn't from one patient to another. It's a pain in the *gluteus maximus* –got to keep you learning all those fancy Latin phrases, Boy—but I've found it a real lifesaver in every sense of the word, more than once."

Because Doc found Mac wrote a clearer hand than himself, and because he found this chore time consuming, he fell into letting Mac do the writing, while he dictated as he mixed medicines and rolled pills, thus enabling both of them to benefit. So when Mac found him scribbling away, he was surprised enough to forget his own problems for the moment.

"Glad you're here. I've written down some of my impressions of yesterday, giving all those examinations. Had to reject a few, and decided I better record why. A chance to get an eagle's eye view, so to speak, of the folks I never see 'cause they're off charming some other doctor with their pains. I just now finished about your Pa. You'll be pleased to know he passed in fine fettle. A good example of what a healthy soldier should be."

When Mac failed to respond to this high praise, Doc frowned. "Something biting at you, Boy?"

He hadn't intended to tell Doc about his worry, but suddenly the words came tumbling out. "It's my Ma. I know she's really sad about Pa leaving, but I don't know what to do to make her feel better. I should be doing something. I know she's depending on me to take Pa's place and be strong and help Rose not be afraid, and I don't know how to do that. I'm scared, too." Horrified, he stumbled to a stop. He hadn't meant anyone to know how frightened he was. He wished he could take back the words, but he'd heard Pa say more than once, if wishes were horses, beggars could ride.

Doc took a moment to recover from the surprise of his pupil's outburst, before he said slowly, "Come sit down. There's some things I think you ought to know."

Mac sank onto the chair beside the desk, eyes glued to the floor, hearing his heart thumping and feeling his face going red with mortification over his babbling.

"Mac, look at me." His voice brooked no argument, so Mac raised his head to meet Doc's grim expression.

"I saw your Pa yesterday. I examined him. I would have given a year's worth of medical supplies to find something wrong so I could reject him from going. I know what your Pa's giving up to go fight in this dumb-fool war. I gave it up once, myself, a long time ago." For a split second, Doc's eyes grew dim with remembering, before he continued harshly. "It's part of being a man, making a decision and sticking with it. Your Pa understands that. Your Ma does, too. I'm willing to bet my bottom dollar that all this past week, before your Pa left, your Ma was smiling and cheerful around him. Am I right?"

Mac remembered the funny little smile Ma had worn all week and mumbled, "Yes, sir."

"All right. She did her best to send him off without any more regrets than he needed to have. Your Ma's one damned brave woman. Don't you forget that. So, for my money, she's entitled to a day or two of feeling low and not putting on a fearless face. And she's entitled to know she has the complete support of her daughter and her son. She's not asking you to take your Pa's place. Face it. You couldn't do that, anyway. She just needs you to give back some of the love and caring she's lavished on you for thirteen years. Do you understand what I'm saying?"

Brain reeling from the unexpected onslaught, Mac nodded and felt the crushing weight slip from his heart.

"All right, then. Just see you remember it. These coming times won't be easy for anyone. No use making them harder than they need to be. I want you to go out back and get a drink of cold water. Splash some on your face and come back in. We have a sight of calls to make this afternoon."

Mac hastened to obey, but Doc's voice halted him. "It's always best you talk to your Ma. But any time you have a worry you just can't discuss with her, you come to me. Hear?"

Mac, face now shining with the relief of it all, turned back to the crusty doctor. "I will."

Before he could step outside, Doc's voice halted him once again. "I've told you before, doctoring is more than just taking care of the body. Sometimes we doctors forget we have to take care of ourselves, as well as our patients. And that closes your lesson for today, Mac."

Out on the back step, Mac beamed at Bella, already hitched to the buggy for the afternoon round of calls. She stared back at him, not the least bit interested in his emotions. Nor did she show any enthusiasm when he said aloud, "He called me 'Mac' and he said 'we doctors.'" She did, however, snort disgustedly as the doctor-to-be turned an exuberant cartwheel and almost landed under her nose.

***

A little later, directing the buggy toward their first house call, Doc aired his impressions of the day before. Mac, medical student dignity restored, listened intently. "Some fellas, unfortunately, get rejected at other recruiting spots, but keep making the rounds until some doctor, through laziness, hurry, or just plain incompetency, passes them. Let that be a lesson. Never get so rushed you throw over everything you know to be right, just so you can claim you finished the job. You do it wrong in your turn, others down the line'll pay for your foolishness, some with their lives."

Mac, picturing Pa standing before Doc, certified healthy so he could go face the body-threatening dangers of war, shivered. "You mean, if someone unfit gets passed, my Pa, who's healthy, could get sick because of the first person?"

"You've got it. Though you may never know about it, ultimately the responsibility is on your head. One day, some way, you'll have to answer for it."

Doc never professed to be a church-going man, the perceptions of the afterlife commonly accepted by his contemporaries and his own knowledge of science clashing at times. But Mac had, on more than one moonlit night, seen him halt Bella while homeward bound after the successful completion of a difficult case. Climbing stiffly from the buggy, Doc always removed his hat and stood quietly, gazing upward at the light of a million stars. Without a word, he then climbed back into the buggy and motioned Bella forward.

He never tried to dissuade Mac from the beliefs Zane and Larissa were instilling in him. He merely told his student to examine the case carefully, draw his own conclusions, and apply the treatment he felt best suited the situation.

Now, with this rare-hinted reference to an afterlife, Mac sat straighter. "You mean 'my brother's keeper'?"

Doc's lips twitched, but he said solemnly, "Something along those lines."

Mac thought for several seconds. "Maybe it wouldn't be impossible for that sick person to make someone else sick, who would then infect someone else, and on around in a circle, until it comes back to you."

"Stranger things happen in doctoring."

"What if they're sick and you honestly don't see it and pass them and then they make someone else sick?"

Doc scratched his bushy jaw. "No doctor can spot everything, every time. For that, we'd need to see inside a person to verify what his interior parts are thinking. Maybe someday they'll have a fancy machine to do that. Sure would be something, wouldn't it?"

Mac looked so skeptical Doc laughed. "Sound farfetched? Just remember what they've done with stethoscopes, and now these microscopes they touted in the last medical journal. Some doctors insist they're inventions of the devil and 'real' doctors shouldn't have anything to do with them. I suspect, in a few years, these same doctors won't want to get along without them. And until we have that fancy machine to let us peek at our inward goings on, we'll just keep relying on our hands, brains, and judgment."

Reaching a fork in the road, Doc turned the buggy south. "Speaking of inward parts, we'll stop at the Horton place. Thursday morning they brought in young Gideon with a knot on his head. Apparently he walked the corral fence on a dare and fell off. Knocked himself clean out. I think he's fine, but I instructed them to keep him quiet for a day or so, just to be sure. Told them I'd check on him when I next came by."

"He wasn't in school yesterday. His little brother Abe said he'd thumped himself good and got a dandy black eye. Abe sure sounded envious."

"He probably didn't mention Gid also earned a whopping headache,"

Doc said dryly. "Reckon he wasn't envious enough of that little fact to report it."

He confirmed that no permanent harm would come to the young dare taker, admired the multi-hued shiner, and admonished the wearer to be more cautious around corral fences. Accepting a crock of fresh churned butter in payment, he refused a cup of coffee, and got himself and Mac back on the road in short order. "Need to remember where the dish came from so I can return it. Sometimes I feel like a blasted peddler, distributing my kitchen goods."

Mac, with intense interest, studied a woodpecker in a tree out his side of the buggy, until Doc quit grumbling. "Our next call is on Mrs. Damon. I didn't tell you, but I rejected Theo yesterday." At Mac's start of surprise, he said roughly, "Yes, Theo, and that no account Kell Hollister, too. Both of them have weak sounding chests and neither one could puff up a decent amount of breath. I figured I'd do the Army and their families a favor and refuse to pass them, but you know what that low down Theo did?"

Without waiting for Mac's response, Doc growled, "He had the gall to tell me I better approve him because if I didn't, he'd find a doctor who would. Said he was going one way or another, and no way could I stop him, so I might as well get the agreeing over with." His face reddened at the memory.

"Did you pass him?" Mac asked breathlessly.

Doc glared at him. "Of course not. Never a man yet could bribe me out of doing my job, and I sure as fire didn't aim for Theo Damon to be the first."

"What'd you do?"

He snorted. "I refused to approve either one of them, just like I'd said. Then those chuckle heads slithered off together. Thought I was well rid of them until they showed up in my line again, smirking to high heaven. I told 'em I'd already rejected them and to quit wasting my time. They absolutely howled with laughter. Then each of them showed me a paper saying he'd been passed by another doctor. I was so mad I could've spit nails. I made them point out which doctor and they followed me, grinning and nudging each other, when I stomped over and demanded to know what idiot would approve those two.

"He turned out to be a weasely looking little thing, and he assured me huffily that they were, indeed, physically fit. I tried to tell him about their bad lungs, but he wouldn't listen. He merely said that he'd heard lots worse.

"I told him they'd be leaving families behind needing them more'n the Army did, that Theo'd be deserting a wife and a brood of youngsters, one only a few days old. He got downright oozy then. Started this fine speech about families making noble sacrifices for their country in its time of jeopardy. I knew if I didn't get away fast, I'd stuff his jeopardy down his throat. So I left him still raving on about 'for the good of the many.'" Once more Doc fell silent.

"So they stayed passed?"

Doc nodded glumly. "He'd approved 'em. I couldn't uncertify them at that point. Only he could. And he obviously had no intention of doing so. That's what I was talking about earlier. Rejected ones sneaking from one doctor to another until they're approved. And doctors more interested in numbers in their favor than in right."

"Now they're on their way to war," Mac said slowly, "supposed to fight alongside my Pa and others like him, who might someday have to depend on them for their lives." His words trailed off.

"God help them all," Doc muttered, "and God help their families."

CHAPTER TWELVE

Doc turned to Mac as they reached the Damon house. "I want you to listen to me." His voice was as harsh as Mac had ever heard. "No matter what your personal feelings about Theo, I expect you to treat his family with all the care and concern you'd normally give. Even more, comes to that. They need all the help they can get. And right at this moment, it's you and me been elected to give it to them. Understand?"

Mac swallowed, thought about Pa riding away from them down the road to war, remembered the baby asleep under the table with the potato skin clutched in its grimy little fist, and lifted his chin. "Yes, sir. I understand."

A rare smile creased Doc's face. "You have your Pa's sand. He's got what it takes to be a good soldier. You've got what it takes to be a good doctor." He knocked before Mac could catch his breath to respond.

Mrs. Damon opened the door.

"Elsie!" Mac had never heard Doc's voice so dismayed. "I expressly told you to stay in bed for a few days."

Mrs. Damon stood aside to let them in, and said wanly, "I know, Doc. But I couldn't lay there and let the little ones go untended. I reckon you know my man's gone off." The last words were a thread as she swayed.

Doc caught her before she hit the floor and swung her up into his arms. "I was afraid of this. Let's get her to bed."

Mac pushed open the door, revealing several small bodies curled up like puppies in their mother's bed. Wordlessly, he lifted them aside so Doc could put Mrs. Damon down. While he began his examination, Mac found a ragged quilt and spread it on the floor, then began removing the little ones from the mattress to the quilt. He looked up to see another flock of them standing wide eyed at the bedroom door.

Doc glanced around from counting Mrs. Damon's pulse. "Take them outside. I hope to God Bruiser's around. Find him so he can watch them, then come back in. I'll need your help."

Obediently, Mac shepherded the brood away from the door. Picking the one he thought was oldest, he asked, "Do you know where Bruiser is?"

The child nodded. Mac waited, but no other response came forth.

"Where?" he asked finally.

Large black eyes stared at him. "Outside."

"Do you know where outside?"

A nod.

Mac sighed. "Where outside?"

"In the yard."

"Can you show me where?"

Another wordless nod.

He thought he had it now. "Show me where Bruiser is out in the yard."

"Yes, sir." The child walked to the door, followed by the duckling brood, and pointed.

He suppressed a triumphant chuckle. Ask a literal question, and receive a literal response. "Let's go where Bruiser is out in the yard."

"Yes, sir." With Mac bringing up the rear, the covey of children followed the leader into the sunshine and queued over to Bruiser, who was hanging diapers on a line strung between two trees whose branches had been lopped off.

Bruiser, already looking none too happy with his task, scowled more fiercely at sight of the ragged children. Glimpsing Mac, however, his face turned beet red, and his scowl became a lip curling snarl. "What're you doing here?"

Wanting to be as far away from you as possible sprang to Mac's mind. But remembering Doc's command, he said mildly, "Doc's tending your Ma. He wants you to watch the children."

Bruiser's face paled a little under the red, and Mac wondered if it was out of concern for his mother or concern he might be stuck permanently with the little ones. "I been watchin' 'em. You get on back to the house, now." Mac started away, but Bruiser hissed his name and he turned to face the older boy once more.

"You tell anyone you saw me doin' this," he gestured with the wet diaper in his hand, "and I'll fix your flint. You understand?" The menace in his voice made the littlest one bury its face in the sack dress front of the oldest child, who put thin arms around it protectively.

"Saw you doing what, Bruiser? I didn't see a thing." Mac shrugged innocently as he again turned toward the house.

"Just see you remember it."

Remember to forget? He choked down a rueful chuckle. Sure he'd do just that. As Mac entered the house, however, all his impulse to laugh faded when Doc began issuing orders. Late that afternoon, he finally felt easy enough to leave Mrs. Damon. He told her he'd stop in at the Ford place, her nearest neighbor, and have them come over to lend a hand. Bruiser scowled, but Mac saw the relief that flooded his face. He didn't blame him a bit.

Their stop at the Ford farm completed, their ears ringing with the assurances of the elderly Fords they would go right over to help Mrs. Damon, Doc headed the buggy back toward town.

"You think she'll be all right?" All those children swarmed in Mac's mind.

"I think so. The Fords'll take some burden off her for a time, anyway. We'll have to see from there." Doc glanced at his pupil's pale face. "I meant to tell you something else about those examinations yesterday." He went on to discuss in detail what he'd looked for and what he found, until Mac's interest perked up again. Doc, seeing, allowed the side of his bushy mouth away from the boy to quirk upward as he continued briskly. "We think things have changed fast in the last twenty-five years, medical wise. Not many people realize this war'll make changes we haven't even dreamed about." At Mac's puzzled expression, he continued grimly. "I saw it happen before, in Texas. I'd never in this world say war is good. It's hell—pure hell—and in the end, no one really wins except the buzzards." Mac flinched.

Doc, noticing, amended hastily, "Sorry, Boy. I know you're thinking of your Pa. But put your mind on this. If any good at all can come of it, we'll be seeing operations and techniques unheard of right now. Necessity'll force medicine to expand its limits. Maybe even to getting that highfalutin' picture taking machine we were talking about earlier...."

***

That evening at the supper table, Mac reported his adventures of the afternoon. He'd been late getting home, and the others were almost finished eating. "Sorry, Ma." He slid into his place. "The last call took longer than Doc thought it would, then Bella started limping like she'd picked up a stone. We couldn't find one, but Doc didn't want to push her, so we were really slow getting back to the office. Then Mr. Wrade wasn't at the livery, and we had to find him so I could get a horse and not have to walk home." He stopped for air.

Larissa dished up a steaming bowl of bean soup and placed it in front of him. "Sounds like you had more adventures than three people, today."

Remembering his discussion with Doc earlier that afternoon, Mac detected none of yesterday's grieving in her expression. Merely concern that he had run into difficulties. *Should I mention what Doc said about seeing Pa?* If someone else had news, he would want to know.

"Is the livery horse in the corral?"

Mr. Michaels' practical voice startled him from his silent dilemma. "He's in Deneb's space. I rubbed him down and grained him." Realizing he'd mentioned Deneb's empty stall, he turned anxiously. "Was that all right, Ma?"

Her face became very still. "Of course. Thank you for tending him even before coming in to eat."

"Good work, Mac." Mr. Michaels' quiet voice once more drew his attention. "Your Ma and Pa are obviously raising a fine horseman."

Ma's features held love and pride. *What should I do?*

"Mac, do you want to talk about something?"

Fairly caught by Ma's question, eyes on the bread he was crumbling into his soup, he tried to untangle the words in his mind before he spoke.

"Mac?" Her voice contained a certain firmness indicating he'd better answer, fast.

"Doc talked about Pa today." He raised his head. Charity and Rose stared at him. Mr. Michaels looked grave.

Very carefully, Ma set down her spoon. "What did he say?"

In it now, he tried not to babble. "He examined Pa yesterday to make certain he was medically fit. He said Pa passed with flying colors. That he hunted for a reason to reject him, but couldn't find one." He looked imploringly at his mother.

She pressed her lips tightly together and placed her napkin carefully on the table. Then she smiled. Not a pinned on smile, but a gentle one that lit her eyes. "I'm glad you told me, Mac. Hearing it gives me comfort." She looked around the table. "Leave it to Doc to try to find an out. That old scalawag has a heart soft as custard for all his blustering."

The tension released, Rose and Charity giggled over Doc wearing a dish of pudding where his heart was supposed to be.

Ethan studied Zane's son and the thankfulness written plain upon those young features. His gaze touched Zane's wife, saw quiet pride lift her chin and light her eyes. Light he would bequeath a fortune in gold to put there.

Larissa caught the uneasiness already replacing Mac's relief. "Is there more you want to talk about?"

"No, Ma. It's something Doc and I discussed today." Swift shame flooded him. He knew perfectly well when he gave her that particular explanation, she immediately backed off from questioning further. He had never before deliberately taken advantage of this refuge, and felt blood rising hotly to his cheeks for doing so now. *But it was something we discussed this afternoon. That wasn't a lie.* So why did he feel so miserable about it?

Predictably, Ma immediately put her hand on his arm. "All right, Mac. If it's between you and Doc, we'll respect that. As always, though, if you need to talk, it won't go any further than you and me."

He knew that, too. He had never unburdened himself to either Ma or Pa, remembering Doc's confidentiality decree, but he was well aware if he said something, it literally would go no further, not even between his parents. He could trust them, totally. He squirmed, feeling like a three-year-old caught with his fist in the sugar bowl.

Ma's fingers tightened reassuringly before she withdrew her hand.

"So did Bella pick up a stone in her shoe?"

"Mr. Wrade couldn't find one, either. He thinks maybe she just stepped on one in the road and bruised herself a little." His throat was so dry the words stuck. He choked down his bean soup, unable to remember ever feeling so miserable.

Supper finally ended. Ethan drained his coffee cup and pushed back his chair. "Think I'll go take a look at Mac's horse. See what the livery stable's offering in choice traveling accommodations these days. We'll be going back to the cabin in about half an hour, Charity." His eyes twinkled. "Just long enough for you to help with the dishes."

He opened the back door and scooted out as Charity said plaintively, "But Pa—"

The door swung open again and Ethan stuck his head around the edge. "A fine supper, Larissa. My Ma used to make a bean soup I was especially fond of. Yours reminds me of hers." His head disappeared and the door shut firmly.

Larissa stared at the closed panel for a startled second before she remembered the children watching her curiously. Giving herself a little shake, she reached for Ethan's empty bowl. "My goodness, Charity, isn't your father the flatterer tonight? I suspect he just wanted to get out of doing any dishes himself," she said in a conspiratorial tone, so that the two girls chimed in their laughing agreement.

Mac set down his empty milk glass. "May I please be excused? I want to go help Mr. Michaels." He escaped out the door before Larissa could think of a reason to stop him.

He crossed the porch as light flared in the barn, where Ethan had lighted the candle in a tin lamp. Mac trudged that way, not sure whether talking to Charity's father was disloyal to Pa, and wondering what he would say if he did talk. He watched from the doorway as Mr. Michaels, finished with a quick inspection of the barn and animals, set the lantern on the workbench and approached the roan in Deneb's stall. "Mr. Wrade said he's sixteen hands."

Mr. Michaels looked over his shoulder, but didn't appear surprised to see Mac standing there. He ran his hand over the gelding's flank and stroked his muzzle. "I'd be willing to wager he's every bit of sixteen. With those legs and deep chest, he'll give a run for the money, you can be sure. Think I'll give him just a bit of currying here. Make him feel at home."

"Or like he's in seventh heaven," Mac joked.

"You're right. We treat him too good, he'll think twice about going back to the livery stable. I think I'll spoil him just a little, anyway. Seems I think on my feet better when my hands are busy. Is it that way with you?"

Mac picked up the brush and reached for the roan's mane. "Sometimes."

They combed and brushed in silence for several moments during which Mac argued ferociously with himself. Pa had told him to help Ma. Doc had practically ordered him to discuss his problem with her, saying he couldn't help her if he didn't talk to her and let her know what the trouble was. Another of those dratted circling around doubts. *Like a turkey buzzard with his eye on a hapless mouse.* When it came to problems, there sure didn't seem to be any other kind, the way they kept making his shoulders their favored roosting spot.

In order to obey Pa, he'd have to obey Doc, too. Part of him whimpered that he had talked to her. *Wasn't that enough?*

His other part answered with disgusting promptness. *You know it wasn't. You know you didn't tell the whole story.*

Ethan, watching the play of emotions across the boy's face, felt deep sympathy. Times without number he had disagreed with himself, as Mac was obviously disagreeing now. The problem was, no matter how good your argument, one of you always lost. Should he offer assistance? Keep his mouth shut? He didn't think he could stand silent much longer and watch that painful struggle.

He took a breath, but before he could speak, Mac blurted, "Mr. Michaels?"

"Yes?" The calmness of his own voice amazed him.

"Have you ever done something that wasn't really wrong but it wasn't right, either?"

"You mean something such as taking the larger piece of pie and leaving the smaller for your sister?"

Mac's eyes widened. "I didn't know you saw that." The words spilled out before he saw amusement lurking behind Mr. Michaels' beard. "Yes," he said sheepishly. "Kind of. Or like saying something that's truth, not lying, but you mean it different from what you actually say?"

Mr. Michaels contemplated that one. "I think everyone does that at one time or another. I admit I have. The big question in addition to lie or truth is whether it hurt someone else."

"But what if it would hurt the person more to say it as truth?"

Mr. Michaels studied the comb in his hand. "I can't speak for the rest of the world. I've a hard enough time making sure my own boots are scraped clean. But I've always held truth gets a man a lot further than covering up with lies. Cover up lies, even with the best of intentions, have a way of snowballing." He lifted his shoulders. "One thing about the truth. A person doesn't have to remember what story he told and fret about whether the next installment fits that story." He looked over at Mac who was pulling the brush through the roan's already brushed mane. "Is this connected with that second question your Ma asked at dinner about something bothering you?"

In for a penny, in for a pound. Mac ducked his head. Disloyal to Pa or not, he had no way now to evade finishing this discussion. He hoped he wasn't breaking Doc's confidentiality code, but Doc had told him flat out to discuss it. His spurt of confidence ebbed as he searched for words to make Mr. Michaels see how it had been.

"Doc Rawley said he examined Mr. Hollister and Mr. Damon yesterday and rejected them because they weren't fit, but they got another doctor to pass them. He also certified Pa was healthy. Now Mr. Damon and Mr. Hollister are going to fight in the war, and so is Pa. What if they do something stupid and Pa gets hurt because of it? If Doc hadn't passed him, if he'd found something wrong, Pa wouldn't have had to go." Mac raised his head and the pain in the boy's eyes jarred Ethan.

"I couldn't tell Ma how much I wished that Doc'd found something wrong. Then Pa would still be here, not going off to get—to get—"

Truth gets a man a lot further than cover up lies. That fine speech of only minutes before smote Ethan like a cackling bird of prey. Words so confidently said were already smothering him with huge black wings. How could he even begin to justify one man's carelessness against another man's life?

"Mac." The word came out so thinly that Ethan had to clear his throat and start again. "We all have duties and responsibilities in life. Your Pa had a duty to sign up to go to war. Doc had a responsibility to pass him if he was physically capable of going. Just as much as we all have duties and responsibilities, we all have places in the wider scheme of things. Mr. Damon and Mr. Hollister, too, even if we don't know or agree with where those places might be." Mac's eyes were riveted on him as if he were seeing into Ethan's very soul. Where he found the words to continue, he was never after entirely sure.

"During my time, I've seen many things happen, heart hurting things with no justifiable reason. I've also seen wondrous things, and there didn't seem to be any justifiable reason for them, either. Somehow, it all works out. No matter how bad they are at the time, there is a reason and a purpose for everything." He put his hand on Mac's shoulder. "I can't pretend I understand it all. But I do know that I believe it."

Mac's eyes glittered with unshed tears. "I just hope the reason and the purpose for those two men going isn't something bad happening to Pa."

Ethan had no light words to answer him. "I hope so, too. I have found that while I'm waiting for something to happen, time passes faster if I'm busy." He studied the boy. "I believe you have a duty to perform now, too."

"Yes, sir," he said dully.

"Would you like me to go with you?"

Mac scrubbed his fist across his eyes. "Yes, sir. But I think Pa would tell me I have to do it on my own." Putting the brush on the bench, he walked slowly to the entryway. Pausing there, he looked back at Ethan for a long second. Then he squared his shoulders and ducked out the door.

Ethan dropped limply onto the flour barrel seat Zane had used only a few days before. *Dear God.* Had he said and done right? Where were all his fine strength and courage and wisdom when he so badly needed them? Right now he felt as wrung out as yesterday's sweat soaked work shirt.

And he still had to collect Charity from the kitchen. The half-hour he had indicated to her was long gone. He didn't figure she'd mind the extended time, but going to the house meant facing Mac's distress. And Larissa's. He wasn't entirely certain his wobbly knees wouldn't betray him, like a just-dropped colt with its stick legs going every which way as it tried to stand. In spite of himself, his lips quirked a little at the picture, but he quickly sobered. *If you can send a boy to do his duty, you'd better be man enough to do yours as well without whining.*

He returned to the house.

Letting himself in the kitchen door, he found the girls seated at the table, Rose knitting a stocking for Zane while Charity read aloud. She broke off her sentence as he entered. "Hi, Pa. We found a good story in our reading book."

"That's fine, Charity, but you'll have to finish it another time. We need to go, now."

His expression warned Charity not to argue. She closed the reader and slid off the chair. "See you tomorrow, Rose."

"Please don't go yet." At the unexpected sound of Larissa's voice, Ethan, his back to the room, had only a split second to regain control of his expression before he turned. "I'm glad you're still here. I wanted to ask if you'll be going to church with us tomorrow."

Her voice was so normal, and the question so far from what he expected, it took him another moment to quell the pleasure he felt sure she could see jumping from him. His daughter looked up at him hopefully. "We'd like that, wouldn't we, Charity?"

"Oh, yes, Pa."

Ethan held his hat to his chest and sketched a sweeping bow. "We would be most pleased to accompany you, ma'am."

Larissa tipped her head in gracious acceptance and waved an invisible fan beneath her nose. "Very good, kind sir. We would like to leave about eight. After breakfast, of course."

"Your carriage shall await, my lady, and the young princess and I will be ready."

Rose's yarn and needles dropped forgotten into her lap as she and Charity clapped their hands in delight at their elders' play acting. Ethan bowed so sweepingly his nose almost hit the floor. Larissa curtsied, holding imaginary skirts a yard wide on each side.

"Come along, Young Princess." He reached for the doorknob as Charity glided grandly across the floor. He opened the door for her, but hesitated as she swept past him. The world and its troubles, forgotten for those few lighthearted moments, enfolded them once more. "Larissa, is everything all right now, with Mac?"

She didn't pretend puzzlement. "Yes," she said simply. "Everything is, now. He explained, and I want to thank you."

"No need for thanks. I'm glad it's straightened out."

"He was able to talk to you. That's so very important to me, and to him. I've worried about that part of Zane's leaving, that Mac would no longer have him to discuss things with. I know it's asking a lot more than we have a right to expect of a farm hand." A spark touched her eyes and winked out in a breath. *But it was there.*

The rest of her words flowed past his ears so that he scarcely knew what she was saying. He was dimly aware of Charity edging back into the room.

"I won't let him be a bother, I assure you."

He gathered his whirling wits enough to say with some coherence, "Don't you fret about his being a bother, any more than Charity is to you."

She moved around the table, then, to stand before him. Putting her hand lightly on his arm, she said softly, "Thank you. More than words can say."

He knew he had to get out fast. Murmuring, "Good night," practically dragging a bewildered Charity with him, he escaped onto the porch, where he stood a moment with his back to the closed door, breathing deeply of the cool night air.

"Pa?"

His daughter's voice jolted him to reality, and he came back to earth with a thump. Looking down, he saw her staring at him in amazement.

CHAPTER THIRTEEN

The train carried them west through the springtime dusk, then southwest under the star-speckled night. Zane and Obadiah alternated between tending the horses and sitting, doing nothing except talking, on Obadiah's part, and uttering, he hoped, appropriate responses on Zane's part. He knew the distance between Fairvale and Columbus wasn't great in actual miles, but by rail they needed to travel around Paddy's barn to get there. After steaming south to Xenia, they'd double back up north and east to Columbus. *Maybe someday lines will head directly to folks' destinations, but right now, someday is as useless as spitting to douse a fire in a haystack.*

The candle burning in the tin lantern gave them a rough idea of the passage of time as the train stopped several times to take on wood, water and, Zane surmised from the sounds, new passengers. Each time, the horses, lulled by the rocking of the car, came alert and restive at the jerking halt, so that the two men walked among them, soothing, murmuring nothing-words of comfort, and missing out on their chance to get off the train and stretch their muscles.

Sometime toward morning Zane, rousing from a half-doze, realized the train was again slowing. He sighed. The boxcar did not come equipped with any of the comforts of home. His blanket, spread across the wooden slats at his back and the board floor beneath, did little to soften the unyielding solidity. *I'm heading to be inflexible as these blasted planks if I don't get a chance soon to work the kinks out with a real walk. Talk about stiff as a board.*

He pushed to his feet just as the train jerked violently. The horses shifted restlessly, the beginnings of panic nudging them. With difficulty, Zane righted himself from the corner where he had been pitched. His first thought was the candle, and whether the lantern had fallen over. *A rousing fire would certainly complete the evening's entertainment.*

The lantern had tipped in spite of the nail fastening it to the wall shelf, but not toppled. His thanks, though fleeting, were deep and sincere. Neither one wanted the candle lit, but they had no choice. If the horses required instantaneous action, they couldn't afford fumbling in the dark, seeking the candle and Lucifer to light it, while a miffed horse kicked the wall down. Zane's next look was for Obadiah. The blacksmith's imaginative curses while picking himself up from the floor where the jolt had thrust him full length, proved only his pride had suffered damage. Certainly not his tongue, Zane thought ruefully.

The stirring among the horses quickened. For the twentieth or perhaps the hundredth time, he eased among the agitated animals, stroking, soothing, murmuring. Coming out around Deneb, he encountered Obadiah, who gave him a crooked grin before disappearing around Esau's backside. They finally soothed the jangled nerves of their charges. Unfortunately, their own remained frayed.

The boxcar door slid open. The accompanying gush of fresh air into their horse apple and ammonia laden atmosphere made Zane's head spin. In the dim candle glow, someone hoisted up into the car, but not until the figure spoke, did he recognize Captain Norton.

"Beldane. Edwards, how're things going?"

Zane actually spoke before Obadiah. "No problems, captain. They're restless when we stop, of course, but otherwise handling it well."

"That's good to hear. The first car had trouble. The horses didn't take kindly to being jolted and one bit Waterman when he bent over. I suspect he'll not sit down to eat any time soon." Captain Norton's face remained serious, but a tremor in his voice betrayed him.

Laughter rippled Zane's midsection, but he managed to say solemnly, "What about sitting a saddle?"

The captain choked and coughed. "He'll be sitting a saddle, even if he does it lopsided. The cavalry must go on."

Obadiah's hoot of laughter caused the horses to stir once more. Norton quickly returned to business. "Came to tell you we've halted in Xenia for an hour to let the horses out, before we head to Columbus. Your orders are to take advantage of the stop to clean up your quarters."

"Yes, sir. Gladly," Zane added under his breath.

Captain Norton, preparing to jump from the car, heard and paused. "Kind of a shame." He tipped his head toward Obadiah. "The aroma seems to have stopped his tongue from wagging at both ends." He hopped down and melted into the growing crowd of men on the station platform before Zane or Obadiah could answer.

Not that Zane had any intention of speaking. He was enjoying the silence far and away too much to mar it with unnecessary sound.

***

The second Saturday in May, Ethan hitched up the buckboard to take Charity and Rose shopping in town, and to drop Mac off at Doc's for his afternoon stint. Ethan tried to persuade Larissa to join them, but she declined. "I've a sight of work. Without everyone underfoot, I can scrub the kitchen floor. Enough mud's been tracked in this week to plant a flower garden. Not just anywhere, mind you. But right there in that corner." She gestured to the floor beside the stove with such an exaggeratedly pained expression Rose and Charity burst into laughter.

Ethan's lips twitched. "You sure? It's a beautiful day. Be good for you to get out."

Her fleeting lightness faded. "I'm sure. I'll do the floor, then while it's drying, I'll take a walk down by the creek and commune with nature. Besides, I can depend on Rose and Charity to take the eggs in and do the shopping. With such good assistants, I really don't need to go."

"We have the list, Pa." Charity waved it as proof.

"I have the eggs." Rose pretended to wave the basket and gleefully watched the adults instinctively lurch toward it.

"You little sprite!" Unconcealed amusement belied the threat in Larissa's tone as she unthinkingly used the nickname Zane had given their daughter years before. He'd caught her in baby mischief, making white handprints on the wall, and equally white footprints on the floor, with flour filched from the barrel in the pantry. Looking up at him, she had explained she was helping Mama bake. Her big blue eyes were so full of innocence that he was unable to discipline her properly, and turned her over to her mother for parental consequences.

"Elusive little sprite, isn't she?" he'd said brightly against Larissa's sputtering chagrin over the child escaping her vigilance and his failure, as witness to the misconduct, to promptly administer the required justice. "She looked at me with your eyes," he said simply, and made good his escape to the barn, leaving her with a flour-covered child, wall, and floor—and a melted heart.

Strange, how little things come back to us. Rose obviously saw nothing unusual in the use of her nickname.

In her relief, Larissa did not see Ethan's deep concern.

***

The kitchen floor scrubbed, Larissa tossed the last of the rinse water onto her flowerbed by the back porch and, for the first time, heeded the sun-bright day. Taking a whimsical notion, she set the pan on the bottom step and turned in the direction of Mill Creek. Wandering past the barn and the pond, with no particular destination in mind, she let the springtime laden breeze lead her where it would. Eventually she reached the creek. She stood for long moments gazing out over the busily flowing water before she inspected her surroundings furtively, even though common sense insisted no one lurked in the shadows for miles around.

Plopping herself onto Mac's sitting seat, a large, flat shelf of rock overhanging the water, she hiked up her skirts and removed her shoes and stockings, carefully placing them well away from the sloping edge. She slowly pulled the pins from her hair, shook her head to loose the neat coil, and felt it cascade about her, reaching nearly to her waist. For the space of several heartbeats, she remained motionless, eyes closed, the breeze lifting stray tendrils about her face. Wriggling her bare toes in luxurious freedom, the sun casting its heat on her bare legs below her still pulled up skirts, she leaned back on her arms and lifted her face to the warmth of the endlessly blue sky.

For a long while she sat, thinking how, in those young days of their marriage, before Mac was born, she and Zane used to come down here so he could bathe in the creek after a hot day working in the fields. The first time she came with him, she had slipped the pins from her hair, shaking it free to spill over her shoulders. Then she'd taken off her shoes and stockings and wiggled her toes, and he'd teased her to come in the water and really get cooled off.

"But I'm a mature, married woman," she protested. "I don't want you to think of me as a child wading in a creek."

His eyes went to her bare toes, to her sun-touched hair gently lifting and falling in the evening breeze, and to her blue eyes, dark with worry. "For sure, Rissa," he said slowly, "if there's one thing I know, it's that you're not a child. But I also know I'd never want you to do anything you don't want to do."

Anxiety overcame thought of self. "You're sure? It sounds so small and silly, saying it out loud."

"You're you. There's nothing silly about that, believe me. I'm just glad you wanted to come here with me."

Her eyes lost their dark worry and became once more joy filled. "I always want to be with you." Joy became swift mischief. "Even when you've been working hard all day and don't exactly remind me of a fresh-bloomed lilac."

"'For better or for worse,'" he quoted in the sonorous tones of the minister who'd married them two weeks before. "Seems to me it also said in there somewhere, 'In smelly times and good, until death do us part.' Since I'm not intending to die any time soon, I better get scrubbing."

Their amusement at the thought of either of them ever being old enough to die, warmed the short space between them.

"Maybe one of these times I'll surprise you, Zane," she said seriously, "and wade in the creek with you."

He chuckled. "Some day, Rissa-love. Some day."

But she never had.

She opened her eyes now, so many years later, and stared out over the water flowing merrily past. "Come home, Zane," she murmured. "Please come home safe, and I promise I'll wade in the water for you."

"Ma?"

The past shattered, became the present as she heard Rose calling frantically. "Ma, where are you?"

Her heart gave one wild bound of fear. *Zane.*

She jumped up. "I'm here, Rose, at the sitting seat." Sliding down the rock, she landed in an untidy heap. Heedless of her unbound hair whipping across her face and getting tangled in her eyelashes, and equally heedless of the stones bruising her bare feet, she started running toward her daughter's voice.

"What's happened?" she gasped as Rose darted into sight, waving something white.

"Ma, a letter. A letter from Pa!"

The abrupt switch from worried to death to supreme happiness was so swift Larissa stopped in her tracks as the world tipped. Only an instant as Rose veered in her direction. "A letter from Pa," she repeated and thrust it into her hands.

She stared at her name and address written in Zane's careful script, as careful as every task he carried out in his daily routine about the farm. Her wool gathering thought brought her up sharply. She smiled down at Rose's expectant face. "Let's read it at the sitting seat."

"May I carry it, Ma? Please?"

Unable to bear the thought of it out of her hands even a few moments, she said swiftly, "Let's each carry half." She offered the edge to Rose, who accepted her portion with a skip of delight, then carefully matched her steps to her mother's until they reached the creek.

Sitting on the rock Larissa had abandoned moments earlier, they hunted for the hairpins she had scattered when she jumped up. With a squeal of triumph, Rose handed her one and watched as she used it to carefully slit the envelope. Tucked under her mother's arm, each one held an edge of the letter Larissa had unfolded. "My, it's a long one, Rose. Look at all these pages." She snuggled closer as Larissa began reading.

"Dearest Family,

"On this Sunday, April 21, I take my pencil in hand to let you know I am well, and to tell you a little of the events of these days I have been gone from you. I am, at this writing, still in Ohio, in Columbus, with several thousand other men from our State. Doc Rawley assured me he would tell you the main events of last Friday while we waited for the train. So I will begin the tale of my great adventure with news Doc probably didn't pass on to you. I am now the proud possessor of two extra lower limbs, a pair of hands, a pair of eyes, and a pair of ears. Also one very voluble tongue. I can picture each one of you now, particularly Mac with all his medical training, wondering how this marvel could have been wrought."

Rose's giggle at picturing Pa with extra hands and feet interrupted Larissa, who joined in her daughter's merriment.

"Especially you, my Rissa, disbelieving that I now possess one extra very voluble tongue when my original was often so silent and awkward at expressing itself. I am certain you cannot guess my secret, so I will tell you in two words. Obadiah Beldane."

Mother and daughter exchanged a puzzled stare.

"Obadiah, Fairvale's erstwhile farrier, has attached himself to me like one of Mill Pond's leeches. It is a bit inconvenient, clumping around on four feet instead of two. I now have much more sympathy for Buck and Bob at the plowing. But it has moments of usefulness. When I need information such as What Is Happening Around Here? Obadiah, by a mysterious force, with his long, pointy nose to the ground like a coonhound's, finds the answer.

"Thus, I can tell you with near total certainty what has occurred since we arrived here yesterday about dinnertime. It has only been nine days since President Lincoln called for seventy-five thousand volunteers to defend our Union, with thirteen thousand of those to come from our own Ohio.

"According to Obadiah, that number has already come to Columbus and more are arriving hourly. Men are at this moment crowding the streets, wandering throughout the city, and massing on the grounds of the capitol. Our overwhelmed Governor Dennison has not yet decided what to do with us, in terms of feeding and sheltering. The hotels are overflowing."

Larissa stopped to catch her breath. "Where could so many men come from?" At Rose's awed shake of the head, she continued.

"Obadiah and I, in charge of our quota of horses, have fared better than many others. Quartered with our charges in a barn the Army 'borrowed' from a local farmer, we are housed, for the present, quite comfortably. Not all recently recruited cavalry units required their men to supply their own horses. Apparently, the government will provide them when the time comes. Somehow, in the mix up of orders, we were directed to do so. But this might well be a double blessing in disguise, because I am able to rely on Deneb, who understands me even better than I understand him. Also, because of the horses, whose need for shelter and care comes before the similar needs of fifteen thousand men, Obadiah and I are ensconced in this regular palace of a warm, dry, clean barn. So many other men are jammed into temporary shelters or just plain out on the street."

"Pa has to live in a barn?" Rose interjected worriedly. "I hope they have lots of cats to keep the rats away." Of all the realities of farm life, the one Rose had never been able to come to terms with was rats. Even now, sitting in the warm sunlight, she couldn't suppress a shiver.

Larissa didn't much blame her. Hiding her own misgivings, she responded with all the cheerfulness she could muster. "I'm sure they have great big cats that'll lead those old rats a merry chase. Pa's certainly having a real adventure, isn't he? The stories he'll tell when he comes home. What does he say next? Oh, he's talking about Deneb.

"Deneb is also faring well in his new surroundings. I have received nothing but kind words and, I must admit, from a few personages looks of envy concerning my fine mount. When I tell them proudly Deneb was my son's choice from our stable, they cluck their tongues in amazement at your expertise, Mac. When they spy Esau, Obadiah's horse as you remember, I'm afraid the looks and comments aren't quite so complimentary. None of it fazes Obadiah, however. He just grins at one and all. I fear they're beginning to think him light in the head, especially when he mentions horseracing.

"You may have surmised, this letter is written in bits and pieces as Obadiah and I hustle from one place to another, only to find ourselves behind yet another long line of men. I am rapidly learning that 'get there on the double in order to wait, and wait, and wait some more' is the Army's true motto. During one of those wait some more sessions, Obadiah and I stood for a traveling photographer. Those sessions have also given me time to visit with you, so it is not all bad.

"I am given to understand, courtesy of Obadiah's sleuthing, a camp called 'Jackson' will be set up beyond the railroad depot. There we will receive uniforms and weapons and begin training. (Even Obadiah's expertise can't determine the precise cut of our outfits.) He says word is passing about they are Federal blue with cavalry insignia to distinguish us from the others. With rifle and saber, won't I be the dashing one?

"Dear Family, I close by assuring you I am well. I miss you all deeply, but know in my heart assisting in this cause is right and necessary. God be with each of you, as you are with me. My Christmas Rose, whose socks are keeping my feet and my heart warm as toast because I know the love knit into each stitch. Mac, my horseflesh knowledgeable son, whose expertise swells my heart with pride and gladdens my stay here. And you, my Rissa, you who are in my thoughts always, from my first moments of waking to glad awareness of you close beside me, to the soft embracing night ever lit by the glow of your gloriously given love. Always, always I am with you. So many 'something to remember' times you have given me, Rissa-love. So very many.

"Your loving Husband and Father,

"Zane Edwards."

Larissa drew a long, shaky breath and, under her arm, Rose moved closer yet to her. "I'm glad he's all right, Ma, even if he does have to live in a barn."

Hearing the quaver in her voice, Larissa closed her eyes to banish the threatening tears and laid her cheek against the child's silky hair. "I'm glad, too. But you know what?" She backed Rose off a bit to see her face. "He's well and he's doing his duty. We're well and we must do our duty. Just as he expects us to. We can't let him down. Do you know what part of our duty is?"

Rose, gaze intent on her mother, shook her head.

She touched the end of her daughter's nose with the tip of one finger. "Part of our duty is being cheerful, not wearing sa-a-a-d-d-d faces." She drew out the word so mournfully, like a lamb bleating, that Rose laughed.

"I know, Ma. I'll smile if you will."

Larissa hugged her tightly. "I certainly can't pass up a bargain like that." She replaced the precious letter in the envelope and absently pushed her hair back off her face. Suddenly remembering her shoeless, stockingless, and pinless appearance, she gasped. "My word! Please look for my hairpins, Rose, while I put on my stockings and shoes. What if someone sees me in this state?"

Rose obediently scrabbled around for the missing pins. "I think it looks pretty, down that way."

"Pretty, maybe, but highly inconvenient," Larissa returned as she yanked on her stockings and shoes.

Rose bounced back up on the rock. "I found three pins. Is that enough?"

"Besides this one we opened the envelope with, it'll have to do." Larissa set her fingers to twisting a knot at the nape of her neck and secured it with the rescued pins. "There, do I look presentable?"

"You look beautiful." Rose flung her arms around her mother, almost knocking them both backward off the rock, so that by the time they righted themselves, they were slightly rumpled but laughing at their shared plight.

Returning to the house, Zane's words etched on her heart, Larissa allowed Rose, chatting nonstop, to carry the letter. "Wait till Mac hears all Pa's news. You think he'll be impressed 'cause Pa's getting a uniform and saber?"

"I'm sure he will be. Men and boys, your brother included, in spite of his doctoring tendencies, seem to be wildly impressed with such things."

Nearing the house, Larissa spotted Ethan standing beside the back step. He came slowly toward her, his eyes dark with anxiety. "Are you all right, Larissa?"

"Yes, we're fine. Truly."

He studied her dubiously. The pale weariness of the morning had vanished. Her cheeks were faintly flushed and her eyes held a warm softness. Tendrils of hair escaped the bun usually knotted tidily at the back of her neck. He swiftly averted his gaze to the letter still clutched in

Rose's hand. "Everything is all right with Zane?"

"Yes. He's good. He's in Columbus."

"The state capital. That makes sense."

She hesitated. "We'll share the letter with you. As his friend, I know you'll want to hear it. It's just that I'd like Mac to hear it first, since he couldn't be here, now."

"I don't want to intrude on your privacy."

"You won't be intruding, I assure you. Zane has lots to tell about these past days."

"I'd like to hear it," he said gravely. She stooped to pick up the pan she had earlier left on the step. "Larissa."

She turned, waiting for him to continue.

"Nothing," he murmured. "I just wanted to say how glad I am for him, and you, that he's all right."

"Thank you, Ethan," she said softly. "That means a lot to me." She turned and, followed by Rose, ascended the steps.

Her back was to him so she did not see the flicker of pain in his eyes, before he sternly quenched it.

CHAPTER FOURTEEN

Larissa, Ethan, and the girls had started eating supper when they heard Doc's buggy wheels, bringing Mac home. Before Larissa could collect her thoughts, Rose jumped up to stand beside her chair. "Please, Ma, may I be excused to go tell Mac we have a letter?"

Her young face held so much joy and anticipation after the days of sorrow, Larissa never even considered refusing the request. "Yes, you may. And hurry, before you burst." Rose skimmed out the door before Larissa even finished her sentence.

Ethan lifted one eyebrow. "I don't think her feet touched the floor."

"It's wonderful to see her animated again after being quiet for so many days."

Amen. Ethan's silent, heartfelt agreement did not concern Rose.

"She's really sad about her Pa leaving," Charity contributed. "I would be, too, if you left, Pa." She could not suppress a tremor.

With painful clarity Ethan beheld the deep anxiety haunting his child. *Not that I can blame her. Losing one parent is bad enough. The possibility of both doesn't even bear imagining.*

He touched the end of her braid. "I know, Charity. Just as I've promised you, though, that's not going to happen." Her undisguised relief made his eyes sting. Glancing up, he caught Larissa blinking rapidly.

"My goodness, Charity, whatever are we thinking?" Larissa's outburst successfully captured the little girl's attention. "We haven't invited Doc Rawley to stay to supper. Please run out and ask him before he leaves." She ran a practiced eye over the table. "Be sure to tell him we have plenty," she called to the girl's disappearing back.

Larissa handed a plate to Ethan to set next to Mac's place while she poured warm water into the washbasin. Doc, surrounded by the three youngsters, came in and Ethan turned, hospitably and naturally, to greet him with a warm handshake.

Removing his hat, Doc said apologetically, "Thanks for the invitation. I hope I'm not intruding."

Larissa set the washbowl on the bench beside the door. "You never intrude, Doc. Don't you know that by now?"

"You feed me so often my stomach thinks it lives here. Thanks." He took the soap bar and towel Ethan proffered and bent to the basin.

"Rose says we got a letter from Pa," Mac burst out. "Where is he? What's he doing?"

Larissa pulled the envelope from her apron pocket. "You wash up and I'll read while you're eating. He mentions several things you'll be interested in, too, Doc."

Shaking out the towel, Doc paused. "I don't want to pry into your private doings."

"Nonsense. If you aren't family by now, I for sure don't know who is," she said so sternly his hazel eyes widened and he tugged at his beard to cover his twitching lips.

"Yes, ma'am," he said meekly. "I have some news too, after this young man's curiosity is satisfied."

Their plates filled, Larissa slipped into her chair and carefully unfolded the letter. Mac interspersed her reading with several excited comments and looked down at his plate in embarrassed pleasure at the news of Deneb.

Doc, listening and eating, fixed his attention on Larissa as much as her words. To his guarded inquiries all week, Mac had responded simply that his mother looked peaked and was more quiet than usual, but keeping as busy as ever. He now noted with satisfaction the joy in her face and voice as she bent her head over the pages. She was one to go the extra mile with, for sure. Zane Edwards was one damned lucky man. Doc gave him full credit for knowing it, too. Unlike the brash young jackass he himself had been. If he hadn't been so convinced of his own God handed out right, maybe Marilla would have … He pulled his meandering thoughts up sharply. Long ago he had schooled himself not to travel that road under any circumstances. More as a distraction than anything else, he glanced at Ethan, sitting to his right.

Doc's grizzled eyebrows drew together and his lips, behind the bushy beard, pursed in surprise. He skimmed a glance at the others. The children, including Charity, had their attention fixed on Larissa. Head bent over the letter, she was recounting Zane's speculation about the uniforms.

He risked another look at Ethan sitting quietly, watching her. As seconds earlier, his expression conveyed absolutely nothing untoward. His eyes lightened, darkened, lightened in response to Zane's news. Doc mentally shook himself. *Just my cussed overactive imagination enticing me to read more into an expression of friendly concern than the situation warrants.* Of course Ethan had regard for Larissa. He wouldn't have taken over the farm work, otherwise.

Unfortunately, a strong misgiving bickered with Doc's reasoning. He trusted his instincts, even when no visible evidence indicated he should. More than once through the years, such trust had paid off in attending his patients. That same instinct now poked him in the midsection with a very active elbow.

Rose's lilting voice returned him to abrupt awareness of the others.

"Ma, you didn't read the last part Pa said about you. It was so pretty," she added innocently.

Larissa turned scarlet. "Oh, Rose," she murmured and then floundered.

Under his eyebrows, Doc watched Ethan. The faintest flicker showed in his eyes, vanished without Doc even able to swear he'd seen it, before Ethan responded with the same calm assurance he normally gave Charity. "Sometimes conversations between people, whether written or spoken, are very special. They aren't meant for anyone else to hear."

Rose puckered her forehead. "You mean like Charity and me telling each other secrets, and even when Mac threatens to dunk us in the horse trough, we don't tell him?"

"Exactly. That's an excellent example. Isn't it, Mac?"

Mac squirmed. "Yes, sir."

Having given Larissa time to regain her composure, Ethan turned to her. "A fine letter. Hearing about all those men staggers the imagination."

With the same instinct that had kicked in over Ethan, Doc's eyes probed Larissa. There was little he hadn't seen in three decades of medical practice, including unfaithful spouse disease. Whatever Ethan's feelings, they weren't reciprocated. He'd bet his prized stethoscope the farthest thing from her mind right now was fancy stepping Zane.

"Have you learned something new, Doc?"

Larissa's innocent question triggered a sudden severe coughing fit before Doc repeated the conversation with Zane that earlier Friday, adroitly omitting all references to cannon fodder. Before they could pelt him with questions, he tugged at his beard. "If I don't leave soon, Bella'll get disgusted and go home on her own. I swear she's part mountain lion, the way she trots along in the dark. Unfortunately, I'm not so well equipped. And it's a longer walk back than I care to make tonight if she decides to leave without me."

The conversation successfully turned, Doc bid them goodnight, then had a sudden thought. "Ethan, I know it's not the best time, but could you check my buggy wheel? It squeaks. I'd sure appreciate knowing if it's going to fall off."

Ethan looked surprised, but said agreeably, "Sure, Doc. I'll get the lantern."

"It's the rear one on the off side," Doc explained as they descended the steps.

With a reassuring word to Bella, Ethan bent to examine the axle. "Needs a little grease, but otherwise looks fine. Let's roll it to the shed. I'll put enough on to get you home, and you can get it fixed tomorrow."

"It's not going to come off, then. I was afraid of getting stranded somewhere mighty inconvenient."

In the shed, Ethan picked up the bucket of axle grease. "If you'll hold the lantern, this'll only take a minute."

Obediently shining the light, Doc told Ethan's back, "I'm glad Zane wrote so soon. Larissa was plenty excited."

Ethan kept his eyes on his task. Bent down that way, his voice was muffled. "She surely was. She's been low all week."

"Does she seem all right to you otherwise?"

Ethan glanced up, then back to his hands. "What do you mean? With her husband gone off to God only knows what fate, I don't expect she exactly feels like dancing on the roof."

"I don't expect she does, either," Doc said mildly. "It's just I promised Zane I'd keep an eye on her, professionally speaking, of course. It has to be a big help to her, you being here for the heavy work and all."

Ethan stood. "That should hold it for now." He walked to the workbench and picked up a rag to wipe his hands. He kept his back to Doc for a long moment before he turned. "Sorry. I didn't mean to snap. I've been fighting a few demons myself this week, but that's no reason to take it out on you." He inhaled deeply and looked Doc square in the eye. "It's this being with a woman again, sharing meals and conversation after I thought I'd grown used to not living that way."

"That's understandable. This whole situation must be awkward for you."

Bitterness tinged Ethan's laugh. "That's a polite way of putting it."

"Why don't you leave?" Doc asked curiously.

"I've considered it. But, like you, I gave Zane my word, and I'll not walk away from it."

"No," Doc said slowly. "Zane trusts you. So does she."

Ethan's shoulders slumped. "In the end, it all comes down to trust. There's really nothing left to say. Or do."

***

On the way to town, Doc let Bella have her head while he sat back slackly, replaying his conversation with Ethan. Diagnosing emotional ailments didn't often stump him. Unlike physical illness that could assume a variety of shades, heart hurts checked out mostly black and white, with a smidgen of gray thrown in, resulting from refusal, for whatever reason, of one or both parties to cooperate.

He had to admit, though, Ethan's predicament had him treed. He didn't doubt for a minute it was a predicament, although Ethan hadn't come straight out with it. "How could he?" he jeered to the unconcerned Bella. "I guess the poor cuss was supposed to admit flat out, 'By the way,

I'm in love with another man's wife. He's gone off to war and left me to fill his boots, taking charge of his farm and watching out for his family, so I know he won't mind this extra little item.'"

The only good point Doc could manufacture was Larissa's apparent unawareness of Ethan's plight. However deep his feelings ran, he had kept them from her. *So far.* Doc was a fact facer. He could not share the optimism of his fellow countrymen, on either side, who called this war a mere escapade to be over and done in three months.

Could Ethan continue to conceal his emotions?

Doc had felt a bond the first time they met, had intuitively liked his firm handshake and direct gaze. If Larissa was a woman to go the extra mile with, Ethan was the man to stake your gold on. *Exactly what Zane had done.*

He jerked the reins. Bella, startled, looked back as if stopping on the dark, empty road clearly indicated his cough syrup lacked a major ingredient. Clambering from the buggy, he paced a few steps and removed his hat. Raising his eyes, he contemplated the vast sea of stars. "Even though You and I disagree at times, we work mighty well together. Over the years, I've found difficulties have a way of coming right in the end, no matter how tangled they seem at the beginning. At this stage of my life, I'll not boss You around with my notions of how You should fix this one. I just want to ask You to be gentle with them while You're straightening it out."

He bowed his head and let the silence enfold him before retracing his steps. Climbing back in the buggy, settling his hat more firmly, he flipped the reins. Bella exhaled loudly, leaving no doubt of her opinion of the proceedings, before once more starting for town.

The unanswered question rode beside him in the starlit-drenched night, kept pace with the turning wheels.

How long can Ethan conceal his emotions?

***

Completely unaware of Doc's concern, Ethan tossed in bed, trying not to pitch around too much and disturb Charity sleeping peacefully across the room. What a fool he'd been, thinking he could carry on this deception. Barely into the subterfuge, he was already flailing beyond his depth. *What did you expect, a bumper corn crop and no cutworms? Grow up, face life as it is, not as you'd like it to be.* Behind her curtain, Charity stirred and sighed. He tensed, but heard no other sound. *Furthermore, what about your daughter? What are you doing to her?*

A chill tickled down his spine as he remembered that Saturday evening a couple of weeks ago. Fleeing onto the porch after his and

Larissa's play acting of a royal family, he'd thought his feelings were safely hidden. He completely forgot Charity standing beside him. Her first startled exclamation jolted him back to earth. Her second made him wish the porch floor would open and dump him through.

"Pa, you used to look at Mama like that. I remember. You'd look at her and she'd smile at you." She stumbled on as he stared at her. "I don't remember very much now, but I remember that because I always felt warm and glad inside." Tears shimmered in her eyes. "Mrs. Edwards seems almost like my Mama. Sometimes I pretend she is. I thought I was bad to do that. But it's all right, isn't it, 'cause you like her too, just like you did Mama." Tears of relief slid down her cheeks at finally revealing her secret.

Ethan tried to speak, but failed. He held out his arms and she burrowed against him. He finally managed to murmur, "Let's go home." Obediently, she loosened her hold but gripped his hand tightly on the short walk to the cabin. Once there he used a clean handkerchief and gently wiped away her tears. Standing her beside his knee, he said quietly, "Charity, I assure you there's nothing bad in pretending Mrs. Edwards is your Mama. Mrs. Edwards cares about you very much. Even in Heaven, I should say especially in Heaven, I know Mama understands and is glad you've found someone who makes you feel that way." The relief on his child's face was so enormous that once again the tightness in his throat prevented speech.

She threw her arms joyously around his neck, further hampering his articulating abilities. "I'm so glad. I didn't want to make you and Mama sad."

"You haven't made either Mama or me sad, I promise you." He hated to dull the glow in her eyes, but had no choice. "You must listen carefully." He chose his words as if he were selecting the finest wheat seeds for planting. "I like Mrs. Edwards, and she likes me. We're friends. The same as you and Mac and Rose. When you share friendship with someone, you're sad when they're sad, and you're happy when they're happy. When Mrs. Edwards and I play acted, she was happy. I was glad because she's been sad, just like Rose and Mac. When she smiled, it was like making Mama happy and gave me the same kind of good feeling, so I looked the same way I used to look with Mama. Do you understand?"

She studied him so intently he feared she was peering into his very soul, and his heart skipped a beat. "Yes. Just like you understand about me pretending she's Mama. I'm glad she's our friend." Again she threw herself into his arms in a joyful hug, and thus failed to see relief flash across his features, relief so intense that, had he not already been sitting, his knees would have buckled.

***

Staring up now at the darkness shrouded ceiling, Ethan felt reasonably assured Charity had accepted his "innocence." He had prevailed upon her not to discuss their conversation with Larissa, Mac or Rose, because it was between the two of them about their secret efforts to help Mrs. Edwards be happy. Talking about it would spoil doing something for her "just because." He fervently hoped she wouldn't unknowingly slip. *I'll just have to take that chance.*

His veering thoughts slid to his discussion with Doc that evening. Once more he flopped restlessly. *What had Doc seen?* He felt certain he hadn't revealed anything. After that harrowing exchange with Charity, he'd put a double watch upon himself. Maybe it all lined up just as it appeared, Doc simply looking out for Larissa's welfare as he had promised Zane.

Why couldn't Ethan believe that?

The town's pill peddler was as hard boiled as they came, on the outside, anyway. Ethan, however, had seen Doc interacting with Mac and his unconcealed dedication in dispensing medical knowledge to his pupil. He had also heard the townspeople relating Doc's efforts in their behalf. Because of his stubborn refusal to give up hope, even when all logical hope turned its back in a huff, more than one citizen was living, hale and hearty, when that individual by all rights should be residing under a buckeye tree in the churchyard. Doc's explanation was simple.

"I listened to my Interior Boss," he'd say, then turn prickly and, if pressed further, downright grouchy.

Had his Interior Boss nosed out Ethan's feelings? He wouldn't put it past the old curmudgeon. But if Doc harbored suspicions based on mere intuition, what would he think if he had observed Ethan this afternoon?

He had, through wrenching effort, kept memory at bay for many hours. Now, tossing tense and restless in the smothering blackness, his face burned at remembrance of what he had witnessed and what he could no longer deny. He had certainly received a dose of life as it is this afternoon. Rose and Charity had skipped into the post office sandwiched between the candlemaker and the cooper. Ethan hadn't had the heart to dissuade Rose's hoping for a letter by telling her it was too soon to receive one. Waiting, he'd studied the barrels displayed in front of the cooper's. *I really should unpack the last of our belongings from the barrels still sitting in the cabin.*

The post office door had burst open, scattering his thoughts. Rose, with Charity close behind, flew out, clutching an envelope. Her ecstatic expression rendered her singing words unnecessary. "Look, Mr. Michaels. We did get a letter from Pa."

Assisting the girls into the buckboard allowed him, momentarily, to ignore the thump in his stomach. Fortunately, they had completed their errands and could return home immediately. He suspected Rose wouldn't have survived a longer wait. As it was, she sat with the letter clutched in both hands and her slender frame straining forward, wordlessly willing the horses to go faster.

Once at the farm, barely waiting for Ethan to halt the buckboard, she scrambled out and darted into the house. An instant later, she burst onto the back porch, her expression frantic. "Mr. Michaels, I can't find Ma!"

Halfway to the buggy shed, he heard her wail. Halting the team, he handed Charity out and jumped to the ground. Rose, near tears, ran to him. "Where is she?"

"She can't be far. Does she have a special place she likes to go?"

Rose's face screwed into concentration. "The creek. She likes to go to the sitting seat."

"Good. We'll look for her there."

Following as Rose, calling her mother, raced past the springhouse, he became an inadvertent witness to their meeting. Neither one heard his sharp intake of breath at sight of Larissa, bare legs and ankles visible beneath her pulled up skirts as she ran to her daughter. Her unbound hair, shot through with sunlight, streamed about her face, floating down her back to her waist.

Neither were they aware he stood rooted to the ground as Larissa's expression changed from abject terror to total joy.

Neither one saw his face as cold reality slapped him to awareness and he backed out of sight around the corner of the springhouse.

Now, all these hours later, he tossed and twisted in the darkness at memory of her breathtaking beauty and her sweet vulnerability and her complete unconsciousness of either. All too sharply aware, himself, he turned and twisted and wondered.

What had Zane written to make her blush so?

CHAPTER FIFTEEN

On a Sunday morning in late May, Ethan and Charity knocked and entered the kitchen to find Mac with his head in the washbasin, Larissa openly exasperated, and Rose pleading anxiously. "But Ma, it's been so many days already. Isn't it almost time for Pa to come home?"

Larissa, trying to finish cooking breakfast, was having a difficult time of it. Intent on her questioning, Rose kept tagging after her mother so closely that each time Larissa turned or reached for something, the child was in danger of being stepped on or swatted in the eye with an elbow.

"Rose." Larissa's hard held patience slipped another notch.

"Good morning," Charity and Ethan chorused across Larissa's reply to her daughter. Reinforcements having finally arrived, Mac withdrew his head from the basin and stood well back, listening in drippy silence.

Quick relief flitted across Larissa's face at the timely interruption of father and daughter. "Breakfast will be a few minutes. Rose, please set the table."

"But Ma—"

"Right now."

Belatedly catching the *I'll stand for no more nonsense, young lady* of her mother's tone, Rose turned with drooping shoulders to the dish cupboard.

Charity joined her and reached for the silverware. Ethan turned to Larissa. "Are you all right?"

"Yes. No. Frustrated. You're here and breakfast isn't ready." Realizing the absurdity of her response, she smiled ruefully. "I'm sorry. Good morning. Welcome to our happy family gathering."

Such sarcasm was so out of character that Ethan frowned. "Can I help?"

Returning to the stove, she waved the pepper box. "Not unless you know a simple answer to an impossible question."

"I'm not guaranteeing success, but I'm willing to make an attempt. What question?"

"Rose asks me every morning when Zane's three months are up, if today is the last day, and will he be coming home. I keep telling her no, not today, and every morning it's harder to do. I know she doesn't understand. I'm trying to be patient." Her voice caught.

Ethan, seeing Rose's eyes widen with apprehension as her mother remonstrated, winked and grinned. Her swift answering smile rewarded him before he turned to Larissa who, her back to them, had missed this exchange. He instinctively reached a comforting hand to her shoulder but caught himself, stopped and swiftly crossed his arms over his chest.

"That's a stumper." He eyed Rose admiringly, so that she covered her mouth to stifle a giggle. "Sometimes I think young ones lie awake all night devising quandaries they hope can't possibly have answers."

"I pray this one does," Larissa said wearily.

The pain in her voice intensified his knife sharp awareness of her meaning. He leaned close so the listening children wouldn't hear. "Larissa, you must keep assurance."

His sternness so startled her that she stared blankly before dropping her gaze to the stove. "Yes." He nearly missed her faint reply. She contemplated the frying eggs for a long second. "Thank you." She lifted her head with a determination that, negating all his vows to himself as completely as if they'd never existed, made his heart swell with pride.

He hit earth with a decisive thud as she said smoothly, "What's your proposal for an answer to this particular quandary?" Arms folded across her apron front, she waited as calmly for his answer as if she were willing to wait forever.

Fairly caught, he shuffled his feet. "A calendar?" he suggested hopefully.

She blinked. "A what?"

"A calendar. You've seen them. Paper with squares for—" Her unmistakable outrage cut off his further explanation. "It was just a suggestion," he said humbly.

"Ethan, that's wonderful. Why didn't I think of it?"

"You likely had a few other thoughts claiming priority."

She wrinkled her nose at him and turned to Rose. "Making one will be your project, Sprite. Each morning you can mark off another day and count for yourself how long is left."

Rose, all fearfulness forgotten, bounced up and down. "Can Charity—? *May* Charity help me?" she amended dutifully. "May we start on it right now?"

Larissa laughed, a joyous sound to Ethan's ears. "No," she said firmly. "First you will finish setting the table. Then we will eat breakfast. Then we will go to church." A flicker of doubt crossed her features. "I'm not sure this is a project for a Sunday."

Rose looked so crestfallen that Ethan unthinkingly violated one of his and Larissa's rules concerning the children and, unasked, broached his opinion. "Thinking about it, it could be considered the Lord's work." Realizing he had just interfered with her discipline, he broke off. The sudden grimness on Larissa's face was not reassuring. "Sorry," he said guiltily.

"Ethan Michaels," she burst out, "are you going to tell us why or keep us in suspense, for Heaven's sake?"

He eyed her cautiously and decided it was not only safe, but prudent, to proceed. "I just wanted to suggest that in undertaking this project, Rose will help preserve your sanity. Isn't that one of David's requests in the Psalms?" he asked innocently. "*'O Lord, heal me; for my bones are vexed.'*"

Larissa attempted to speak and failed. Rose and Charity, with shaking shoulders, became very busy setting the table while avoiding each other's eyes. Mac's head abruptly disappeared under his towel. Ethan, with supremely unconcerned calm, waited while she sputtered again. "All right," she finally choked, "Rose, you have my permission to begin this project after we get home today. But unless you want to see how vexed my bones can really be, you'd better get that table set so we can eat. At this rate, we'll get to church about the time services are over."

She stooped to remove the pan of biscuits from the oven, and Ethan's words came back. "'Keep assurance,'" she murmured. *I'm working so hard to do that, Zane. I promise you I'll not give up.* If only the realities of life didn't keep stepping in and making such a tangled mess of all her efforts.

***

Unlike Larissa, Zane had no one to whom he could voice his doubts, no one to reassure him. He talked with the other men of his company, shared meals and jokes, camp duties and drills, but never progressed beyond surface acquaintance. He recognized it as his limitation, not theirs. After all the years with Larissa as confidante and advisor, he found himself unable to make the emotional switch necessary to achieve a deeper status of friendship with his fellow soldiers.

The past weeks, unlikely as it had appeared in the beginning, Obadiah was the closest he came to kindling a friendship. Less reticent with him than any of the other men, Zane nevertheless kept his deeper, personal thoughts and emotions well beneath his surface amiability. Listening to the other men talk freely of wives and sweethearts waiting at home, he pondered why this should be. He concluded that because Obadiah had never married, he could not understand the emotional bleakness of leaving one's spouse behind. As far as Zane knew, the farrier had never entertained serious thoughts about any one woman. If he had, Fairvale's good citizens would have detected it. *Leave it to a small town to nose out your activities before you're even aware you've planned them.*

He looked down, his grip tightening on the letter he'd just finished writing to Larissa. *How many days before she receives it and learns what I've known only a few hours?*

***

On a warm morning, Ethan drove the buckboard to town to have the sights checked on his hunting rifle. He emerged from the gunsmith's and saw Will Anderson hailing him from the post office. "Letter for Miz Edwards. Thought you might want to take it to her." He pulled at his salt and pepper handlebar mustache and his kindly brown eyes twinkled. "Be a shame to make her wait until the youngsters are out of school and home before she gets it." He handed the envelope to Ethan and winked. "Now I just have to think of something to tell those young ones when they come in this afternoon. They know the mail schedule better than I do."

Ethan glanced at Zane's handwriting, and the postmark in the upper corner caught his eye. Mumbling what he hoped were appropriate thanks, he guided the bays out of town at the most sedate clip he could manage. Once across the rattling bridge and out of sight of curious eyes, he urged Andromeda and Pegasus to a more rapid pace. With each passing rod, the portent of the letter on the seat beside him burned more deeply into his awareness.

Nearing the farm, he struggled to compose his features into something resembling normal casualness, before pulling up to the back door where Larissa could see him out the kitchen window. Knocking briskly, then entering without making her answer the door, his personal settlement of the hired hand dilemma of his first day there, he found her busily paring potatoes for dinner.

"My, you're back soon." She glanced over her shoulder with a smile. "That didn't take long." Her voice trailed away as he extended the letter. Potato and knife clattered forgotten to the table as she wiped her hands on her apron. She reached for the envelope, completely unaware of the mixture of pleasure, pain, and hope flitting in rapid succession across her features. He read only too plainly the joy that lit her eyes. "Cincinnati?" She stared bewildered at the postmark, then laughed at her absurdity in being surprised. "My common sense side knew he wouldn't stay in Columbus forever. I've pictured him there, everything he's been doing, and he's been someplace else entirely." She bit her lip.

Ethan's jaw clenched, so his words came a little stiffly. "Why don't you read it and find out what's happening? From the thickness, he has much to report." She was already pulling a pin from her hair to slit the envelope and didn't look up as he turned on his heel. "I'll go tend the team," he explained vaguely, doubting, as he pulled the door shut, that she had even heard him.

He set his hands to unharnessing the bays. Giving this letter to her should have been simple. *No sight of unbound hair and bare toes to haunt my nights and days.* He pulled fiercely at the strap he'd worked loose. Only the knowledge that all his hard fought efforts these past long weeks to bury such remembrances had gone into nothing.

All afternoon he endeavored to prepare himself for Larissa's reading aloud the letter at supper, one side wanting very much to hear Zane's news, the other steeling itself for the sight of her caught up in unabashed joy. That evening, as he had surmised, she pulled the envelope from her apron pocket the moment they finished the blessing. Mac and Rose, Charity, too, waited with hard restrained patience. Ethan, mentally braced to watch her read, became rigid as he detected ... what? Fear? Uncertainty? She masked it so well, the children obviously saw nothing but pleasure and excitement while she unfolded the closely written pages. Ethan, years removed from childhood, felt suddenly cold in spite of the warmth of that candlelit room.

"My Dear Family,

"I take my pencil in hand to tell you I am well and to catch you up on events since I last wrote. I received your envelope and have no words to tell you the gladness it brought me. Unsealing it was like opening Aladdin's magic cave. Then I actually felt sorry for him. He found only rare jewels and coins in his treasure trove. I, on the other hand, discovered the richness of three letters in one because each of you wrote me. Trade places with Mr. Aladdin? Don't even try to make me.

"You can see from the postmark I no longer reside in Columbus, but Cincinnati. How that came about is a long story I shall do my best to make brief. One thing I learned right off about Army life, whatever you count on the big bugs to do, their gift lies in doing just the opposite. I'm not sure whether they were born with this skill or have worked hard to achieve it. I suspect the latter.

"At any rate, Camp Jackson, which was laid out beyond the Columbus railroad depot in an area combined of trees and pastureland, proved to be a dismal failure. Soup lines, makeshift shelters, and long trenches dug by the recruits oversaw our basic needs while we waited for someone to issue uniforms and weapons and organize us into something resembling a real army. The biggest problem was that more men kept arriving. The newspapers latched onto the story right off, and decided in their infinite wisdom that the whole kit and caboodle of us should be sent immediately to Washington City, supposedly to fight the entire Southern army and win the war in one glorious battle.

"Their confidence in us was quite uplifting. At least they proposed a plan, which was more than we had before. They deserve credit for that. Naturally, however, the Army took the opposite track and, abandoning Camp Jackson to the previous bovine owners, set up camp beside the Little Miami River, just northeast of Cincinnati.

"Unfortunately, no Aladdin appeared at the proper moment to rub his magic lamp, so transferring to the new Camp Dennison, named for our Ohio governor, was a tedious process. Such pouring rain greeted us that some jokester immediately rechristened the place 'Swamp Dennison' and it's living up to the honor.

"We are here, officially, to 'provide protection for Cincinnati,' under threat from the rebellious gentlemen across the river. Of course the rebellious gentlemen don't appreciate this high praise. Neither, at first, did our own troops still struggling with mud, rain, and lack of proper uniforms and weapons.

"Unreal as it first seemed, chaos has actually evolved into order. Uniforms and weapons have arrived and been distributed, and the officers gleefully introduced us to drill. Not just 'drill' I assure you, but D-R-R-I-L-L-L. It's the first word to roll from the tongues of the officers in the morning. The last word from their throats at night. And very nearly every word in between those times. Initially, I must admit, our efforts were both pathetic and clumsy. Now, however, I think we have mastered pathetic and are furiously concentrating on clumsy.

"This is not the sneer it sounds. At first, the mud was pig-wallowing deep and clung to our boots while we shouldered fifty-pound packs of necessities for travel. Pathetic is an extremely polite description of the men struggling to maintain straight lines forward and back, as well as side to side while the officers called out marching commands such as left, right, left. Unfortunately, that created yet another problem. A few men with no inkling of right or left foot put forth the wrong member, succeeding in royally snarling up the whole works. Did that stop our officers? Most assuredly not. Captain Armstrong, and aptly named he is, devised a brilliant plan. He had each of these unenlightened gentlemen put a piece of straw in his left boot and a piece of hay in his right boot. The drill instructor then called out, 'Strawfoot, Hayfoot!' and we proceeded in much more orderly fashion. The upshot is these recruits no longer have Christian names. They are now, firmly and forever, 'Strawfoot' and 'Hayfoot.'

"Seems strange, doesn't it, for cavalry enlistees to drill on foot? The officers maintain that if we don't know our way around on the ground, we'll never make it anywhere following orders in the saddle. In this, I must agree with them.

"And now, Dear Family, the news that I have framed a thousand different ways to tell you since I learned of it this morning."

Throughout this reading, Larissa's voice held amusement and lightheartedness as she chuckled with the children about the absurdities of camp life. Now, however, she faltered, gripping the paper so tightly it crumpled.

Not realizing he'd moved, Ethan rose to his feet. Catching his intention, she shook her head, a barely perceptible movement, but one that made him sink back in his chair as surely as if she had commanded him aloud.

Puzzled looks crossed the children's faces at their mother's indecision. She wet her lips.

"This is the part I've wanted you to hear." To Rose and Charity, the higher pitch of her voice indicated only excitement and a mischievous teasing. The shadow of uncertainty hovering on Mac's face crept into his eyes as she continued. "I just can't wait any longer to tell you."

"What, Ma?" Rose was bouncing in her chair.

"Pa's going to Virginia. Maybe he's already there."

Charity stared at Rose. "Who's Virginia?"

Mac laughed, a thin sound that startled him as much as it did the others. "Not *who*, Speck. *Where*. Virginia's the state to the south and east of us." He looked to his mother for confirmation.

"Very good, Mac. All that geography studying has paid off. Do you want to hear the rest of the letter?" Shushing the girls' affirmative duet, she continued.

"Rumors have been flying thicker than snow flakes in a December blizzard. But according to Obadiah and his uncanny nosing out of the truth, it transpires the loyal Union folks in western Virginia are almighty upset about the Confederates destroying railroad lines and burning bridges. Seems these Virginia unionists asked Washington for assistance, but everybody there is so busy defending the capital, they haven't time to listen to Virginia's problems. But help is on the way.

"Our Governor Dennison and Indiana's Governor Oliver Morton hatched a solution to two problems, Virginia's and ours. They'll send some of the overflow troops from our camp here in Cincinnati to aid the beleaguered Virginians. Obadiah and I, you guessed it, are among the chosen. Because we know horses? Because we know our left foot from our right, without the assistance of straw and hay? Whatever the reason, we will be under the command of someone named George McClellan, a major general who, I understand, graduated second in his class from West Point. It's comforting to realize we'll be under the direction of a man who knows his military tactics (and his left foot from his right!) Word is, we'll pull out in the next few hours.

"With that likelihood, I may not have opportunity to write you again as soon as I would wish. So I take these moments to visit with each of you in my heart. My Christmas Rose, I promise you the rats have great respect for me. Or rather for Deneb's hooves, if the truth be told, and keep a proper distance. Mac, I have indeed been issued a saber and a fine tool it is, too, for cutting up the meat we put into our stews and slicing the bulky loaves of bread put out by the commissary. Rissa, I assure you I have been and will continue taking every precaution to keep your pendant safe until I can return it to you. Until then I remain,

"Your loving Husband and Father,

"Zane Edwards."

Silence followed Larissa's finishing the letter. Rose's quivering sigh and Mac's furtive swipe at his eyes were their only response until Larissa said softly, "He has his health, and he's meeting their expectations of a good soldier."

"What do you mean, Ma?" Mac's already shaky voice gave an adolescent crack and he turned red.

Larissa looked to Ethan, who tipped his head soberly and, when she motioned him to speak, cleared his throat roughly. "Your Ma knows because your Pa's been named to go on this adventure. The commanding officers have their choice of men, the cream of the crop you might say. Out of those thousands of soldiers, they selected your Pa. They wouldn't have unless he's one of the very best. He's received a high honor, and you can be proud of him." Larissa nodded her affirmation as she folded the letter.

Rose startled them all by hurtling herself toward her mother. Burying her face in Larissa's aproned lap, she spoke, but her voice emerged too muffled to understand. Larissa gently raised her head, and she said defiantly, "I'm proud of Pa wherever he is."

"Me, too," Larissa assured her staunchly.

"Me, three." Mac's voice cracked again, but this time he didn't flush. He raised his chin and met his mother's eyes.

Watching Mac repeat the familiar punchline, Ethan felt his own swift thrill of pride.

Later, lying in bed, Ethan silently addressed the darkness above him. *Whatever the future, my friend, the "cream of the crop" hasn't all been ordered to Virginia.*

CHAPTER SIXTEEN

On a drearily wet morning the last of May, Zane's company huddled in a thicket of scrub oak a short distance from the Baltimore and Ohio railroad junction at Grafton, Virginia. The men had idled in the drizzle since dawn. Initially, they had concealed themselves in the deeper protection of the foliage. The last thirty minutes, they had stood at the ready, waiting the command to move out against the Confederate detachment holding the railway station.

Deneb's bridle in hand, Zane hunched in his waterproofed slicker, trying in vain to keep the clammy rivulets from sliding down his neck. In spite of the hours they'd already waited, he glumly suspected they might be in for several more. The Morgan stirred uneasily and he reached a steadying hand to him. They had been warned to absolute quiet, lest their presence be discovered and the looming attack botched before it started. Deneb responded to his light touch, and Zane wondered wryly just how long the company of men and horses could avoid attracting attention. An arm's length east, Obadiah had one hand at Esau's bridle and was stroking the gelding's rain dampened muzzle with the other. *More specifically, how long can Obadiah hold silent without splitting a seam?* For the first time that miserable morning, Zane grinned. *I'd wager a cup of hot coffee that today alone he's already set a record.*

To their rear, a horse huffed and stamped, the hapless owner earning a withering glare from Captain Norton standing at the head of the soggy troop. As the offender guiltily quelled his restive mount, Zane reflected it was a lucky morning when, Fairvale's public square teeming with soldiers, Obadiah introduced him to the captain. Through all the vagaries of army dictates, he and Obadiah had remained under Norton's command, from Columbus and Cincinnati to this clump of trees outside Grafton. Without knowing for certain, he strongly suspected Captain Norton bore direct responsibility for the decision that had landed them in this forlorn spot in the wilds of Virginia. He for one wasn't about to squawk. Having worked under Norton over the past weeks, he could honestly say that he would trust him with his life ... Sudden stirring brought Zane's attention sharply back to the huddled men and horses. Scarcely more than a breath, the order swirled down the line. "Prepare to mount. Prepare to mount."

All morning, by strictest discipline, Zane had managed to keep his thoughts from lingering on Larissa, for even picturing her would openly invite the temptation to streak howling down the road to her, squalling like a scalded cat. Now, swinging into saddle, her pendant shifted beneath his blouse, and he knew he'd been completely wrong. She was not miles distant. She was right there with him as he guided Deneb away from the thicket, toward the railway station and the waiting Confederate troops.

***

On a humid July morning, Mac entered Doc's office and found him hunched over the desk. Hearing the door, Doc shifted to look over his shoulder, his normally grim expression strongly resembling one of the thunderheads rapidly building in the darkening sky. Simultaneously, Mac spotted the newspaper spread out on the cluttered desk. Sudden dryness in his throat forced him to try twice before the words came. "What's happened?"

Doc removed his reading glasses, his hand dropping to the newspaper. "I'm not sure. How long since your Ma heard from your Pa?"

"She had a letter the end of May. Nothing since. He said it might be a while before he could write again, but she didn't expect it to be this long." Mac forced his eyes from the ink smudged sheet to Doc's face. "Is something wrong?"

Doc gripped his glasses. "I'm not sure," he repeated. "Apparently, a battle took place more'n a month ago in Virginia. Must've taken the papers a while to get hold of it. I reckon the *State Journal* printed it because it's about Ohio troops."

In a haze of total unreality, Mac reached for the paper. Doc moved his chair so he could squeeze past. He bent over the newsprint, the headline fairly leaping at him.

Ohio Troops Battle The Foe

Word has been received that a force of valiant men from our glorious state of Ohio met the enemy at Grafton, Virginia, on the 29th day of May, and after furious struggle attained the goal. Federal troops, under the command of Col. R. F. Kelley, occupied the railroad junction, sixty miles south of Wheeling.

He looked to Doc, who shook his head. "I don't know any more, either. Just what's there."

Mac's gaze returned to the oddly blurred words.

Major General George McClellan ordered three regiments into western Virginia.

"Pa's last letter said he'd be under the command of a Major General McClellan. It must be the same one."

"Might be more'n one McClellan, but I can't think there'd be more than one a major general." Doc studied Mac. "Better read the rest."

He swallowed before pushing the words out.

"Colonel Kelly's troops marched in pouring rain to Philippi, just south of Grafton, where, on June 3, a planned attack on the Rebels failed. In spite of this unfortunate miscarriage of plans, the Confederates withdrew twenty-five miles southward to Beverly."

Glee pitched Mac's voice higher.

"The Rebels fled south with the Federals in hot pursuit and they're calling this chase the 'Philippi Races.'

"Doc, we skunked them. Pa fought a battle and won!" His face darkened as swiftly as it had glowed. "It doesn't say if—who might have been—"

"Ah, hell for breakfast," Doc said roughly to hide his own uncertainty. "If bad happened to your Pa, your Ma would have heard by now. This happened over a month ago. Remember, I've been in the Army. It takes them a year of Sundays getting the word out about good information, but they're prompt as tax collectors and sunrise on Monday morning passing on bad news."

Mac obviously wasn't fully convinced, but Doc noted some of the fear left the boy's face. "You'll want to tell your Ma as quick as possible. I planned see Mrs. Damon this afternoon. She's just not recovering like she should from the birth. I'll drop you at the farm on the way." He scooped up the paper. "Take this to your Ma." His voice brooked no argument.

As the buggy jounced over the bridge, Doc resumed his discussion of Mrs. Damon's difficulties. "It's mostly a matter of not getting enough rest and not giving herself time to heal, but I can't convince her to take it easier. I see her problem, having the sole responsibility of all those young ones, but she's not doing herself any good. It won't do them any good, either, if she collapses to the point she can't even get out of bed."

His next words were indistinct, but Mac caught a reference to her absent husband's ancestry. Still distracted in spite of Doc's efforts, the remark caused him to study his fingernails with intense interest.

At home, Mac scrambled from the buggy as Ethan, hearing their approach, appeared in the barn doorway. Doc flicked the reins. "I'll go on to Mrs. Damon, Boy, and stop for you on the way back."

Clutching the newspaper, Mac waited for Ethan to reach him. "I have to show this to Ma."

Ethan's smile of greeting faded as he skimmed the story. "Your Ma's in the house. I'll go with you." As Doc's voice had earlier, Ethan's tone left no room for argument.

Larissa wasn't in the kitchen, but when Mac called out, she answered from the sitting room. "You're home early. Wouldn't anyone cooperate and be sick today?" Her light teasing broke off as she entered the kitchen and saw their faces. "What's happened?"

Mac held out the now crumpled sheet as she looked from one to the other. "I wanted to show you this." Grasping the paper, she sank onto a chair. He became sharply aware of his own heart beating, and Mr. Michaels' hand on his shoulder, but didn't take his eyes from his mother.

She turned the paper over as if seeking more information. "It doesn't say what happened to the men," she burst out.

"Doc says—" Pitching his squeaky voice lower, Mac started over. "Doc says no news is good news. Since it's over a month and you haven't heard anything bad, that's good."

She blinked at this somewhat chaotic explanation and stared at the newsprint once more as if willing additional information to suddenly appear.

"Ma." He took a step toward her.

"No, Mac." Only a breath, the words uncompromisingly halted him. She raised her chin. "A very wise man once told me I have to keep assurance." Her eyes, so briefly, met Ethan's darkly anxious ones before she focused on her son. "That's just what I'm going to do until I hear anything different. You and Rose will do that, too. Agreed?"

He stared at the floor.

"MacCord." Her tone was one she had not used toward him for many months. "I asked you a question."

Plainly, her question did not involve a large choice of answers. Just as plainly, adolescent rebellion did not lead the list of options available at the moment, no matter how self-justified. "Agreed," he muttered sullenly.

"'Philippi Races'," she murmured, ignoring his sulking. "Can't you just picture it?"

Ethan chuckled. "Wouldn't surprise me if Obadiah Beldane didn't cause the whole rout. Put him at the front of the troops and start him talking, the Rebs'd have to turn and run to keep their ears from getting yakked off." As a humorous attempt, it was admittedly feeble, but at least the image pricked Mac's swelling bubble of resentment against Larissa's *you will obey me or else* dictate. Her smile finally showed light around the edges.

Having succeeded in distracting her from her worry, even if only for a few seconds, Ethan studied his dusty boots. In describing the Grafton battle, the paper had mentioned civilian casualties without naming the victims. When he and Nettie lived in Fredericksburg, Virginia, her closest childhood friend had traveled with her husband and infant daughter all the way from Grafton to visit them. Because Nettie couldn't do it herself, he sent up a swift prayer for the safety of the family who had meant so much to her.

***

News that month proved a mixed-bag assortment. As during the Fort Sumter siege, clumps of men gathered on the courthouse steps, around the telegraph office at the small railroad depot, outside the Weller Pottery Works, and in front of the *Tribune* office. Once more, speculation and rumor flew among the townspeople waiting with breathless impatience to hear something … anything. Information came in distressingly slow fragments, but gradually Fairvale's citizens pieced together a crude picture.

On June 21, George McClellan had arrived at Grafton to take personal command of the campaign. Fairvale inhabitants repeated his speech to the troops so frequently that soon one could not walk from one end of town to the other without hearing snatches.

"'Soldiers!'" he reportedly said, "'I have heard that there was danger here. I have come to place myself at your head and to share it with you. I fear now but one thing—that you will not find foemen worthy of your steel.'"

Doc naturally offered his opinion, mostly to the effect that, "Fancy words don't give a man someone to look to for leadership when he's in battle being fired on from all sides." He, personally, was "more interested in seeing McClellan's actions than in listening to his spouting off." Just as naturally, the townspeople ignored this pessimism, for wasn't he always throwing cold water on folks' enthusiasm?

Doc also suggested watching this Confederate Army recruit Robert Lee as a force to be reckoned with. Sure as green apples caused a bellyache, they'd be hearing more from that fellow. Again, Fairvale smiled and went its determined way.

In July, word came that McClellan had taken three brigades to launch a strike at Rich Mountain, Virginia. Using one brigade in a flank attack under George Rosecrans' leadership, McClellan stood by with the other two to capitalize on whatever success Rosecrans attained. Led along a narrow mountain track by a local resident loyal to the Union, Rosecrans' Ohio and Indiana regiments assaulted the Confederate flank on July 11. One hundred seventy of the one thousand, three hundred Rebels were killed, captured or wounded. The Union forces suffered about sixty casualties.

Unfortunately, McClellan, hearing the battle unfold, thought Rosecrans was losing and so did not engage in a follow up attack. Consequently, most of the Confederates escaped. Doc said plenty about it. However, since Rosecrans sent the Rebels into full fledged flight, eventually capturing over five hundred, again no one paid him any heed. Following the Union's successful July 13th attack at Corrick's Ford, McClellan became "the Young Napoleon."

Again, McClellan's words echoed through Fairvale. "'Soldiers of the

Army of the West! ... You have annihilated two armies ... taken five guns ... fifteen hundred stand of arms, one thousand prisoners ... I have confidence in you, and I trust you have learned to confide in me.'"

Doc snorted.

***

On an afternoon later that month, however, even Doc's impudence was stilled.

The day was hot. So hot that, "By the time Mac and I finished hoeing a row of corn, the stalks at the other end were a foot taller than when we started," Ethan related solemnly at the noon meal.

Charity looked skeptical, but Rose asked with solemnity equal to his, "Does corn grow that way in Sanilac County, Michigan, too, Mr. Michaels, or just here in Union County?"

Ethan looked justifiably startled by such a question from shy Rose. Mac dropped his napkin and ducked under the table to retrieve it. It took a long time, and while he was down there, a series of peculiar wheezing sounds floated up.

"Have I been extolling the virtues of Sanilac County, Michigan that much?" Ethan asked innocently. From around the table a three voice chorus in the affirmative and a fainter, but no less enthusiastic accompaniment drifting up from the region of Ethan's feet, led him to suspect he had.

By mid afternoon, the leaves of the maples hung listless in the shimmering heat and the humidity was as drenching damp as though they had just stepped out of Saturday night's tin bathing tub. Larissa and the girls prudently took their churning to the springhouse. In the welcome shade provided by one of the native oaks that Zane had refused to clear so many years before, Ethan and Mac sawed firewood in the lot beside the barn. Over the rasping of the bucksaw, they didn't hear the pounding of hooves along the road from town. Glimpsing a blurred figure on a black horse, Ethan squinted past Mac's shoulder. For one excruciating heartbeat, he thought Zane was returning on Deneb, before he recognized Jake Barton, Fairvale's male version of the insatiable gossip, on his stallion Midnight.

"Something's happened." Trailed closely by Mac, Ethan reached the road in time to catch Midnight by his bridle as Barton yanked him to a halt. Without dismounting, Jake shouted as though Mac and Ethan were still standing in the woodlot.

"Word just come in over the telegraph. Big battle yesterday in Virginia. Some place called Bull Run outside Washington City. We got whipped something awful. The Feds all hotfooted it back to Washington.

But it looks like the Rebs didn't follow." Jake stopped to draw breath and curb his prancing mount, allowing Ethan a swift question.

"Any word of individual men?"

"Nothing when I left town, but maybe by now. I'm letting folks know fast as I can. Better get to town yourself to find out more. I'm heading on over to the Ford place."

"Cool your horse a minute," Ethan advised. He gestured toward the barn. "Plenty of water in the trough. You look like you could use a drink yourself."

"Folks need to know the news. I'll cool him at Ford's." Jake swung Midnight's head away from Ethan's grasp on the bridle.

Ethan jumped back as horse and rider surged forward. "Too hot to treat good horseflesh that way," he muttered. "He'll run him right into the ground." Turning on his heel, he stepped on Mac, whose panicked look mirrored his own dread. "We'd best go find your Ma." Ethan looked up, straight at Larissa. The commotion had obviously brought her and the girls from the springhouse in time to hear Jake's rapid fire account.

For the first time in their relationship he reached, with a bone hard grip, to cover the fingers knotted against her apron front.

Her face crumpled. "Zane."

His iron grip tightened. "We don't know anything. Remember that."

She stared at him wildly. "But—"

"No. We don't know. We're going to keep our assurance in that." He shook her hands emphatically. "We both know Jake's claim to fame is blabbing first and asking for the truth later." She drew a shuddering breath and her mouth became a firm line.

"Good." Ethan proffered a twisted smile. "Zane would be proud." He freed her hands. "I'll go to town and see what's known. I'll be back as soon as I can."

Something flicked in her eyes. "I'm going with you."

"What?"

"I'm going too." The something became iron determination. "I will not stay here, tossing feed to the chickens, waiting while you go to town and back, with no telling how long in between."

He started to protest but gave up before the words formed. He might be a slow learner, but he recognized that expression.

"All right. It's liable to be a long wait. I'll hitch up the surrey. At least that way we'll have a little shade."

Rose tugged at her mother's sleeve. "May we go, Ma?"

Rose's face reflected all the confusion and terror of Larissa's own heart. She could no more refuse her daughter than Ethan had succeeded in denying her. "You may come. But as Mr. Michaels said, it might be a long wait before we hear anything. You will both have to be very patient."

"We will, Ma. We promise." Charity, uncertain until that moment whether the permission included her presence, nodded vigorously. Mac was already halfway to the buggy shed to help Ethan hitch up.

Larissa looked down at her apron, and those of the girls, stained from the churning they had completed just before Jake Barton's arrival. "My goodness. I think we're wearing enough buttermilk to give us the most beautiful complexions in three states. Let's go change while they bring the surrey around."

They reappeared shortly, wearing their saved for going to town outfits. In an attempt to ease the worry etched on their faces, Ethan removed his hat, nudged Mac, and let out a long whistle. "If these aren't the three best dressed ladies in Union County, I'll eat my hat. Not this one, mind you," he stage whispered to Mac, "but my Sunday one."

His reward was a faint blush tinting Larissa's too pale cheeks, and a look of open mouthed wonder from Rose, before Charity giggled. Still the elegant gentleman, hat pressed to his heart, he handed them gallantly into the surrey.

Mac scrambled into the back with Rose and Charity, pushing energetically to make them move enough to give him his rightful one-third share of the seat. Rose started to protest his older brother bossiness, but remembered where they were going and why, and silently slid over.

No one said much on that ride. Larissa's stillness caught them in its threads and silenced trivial chatter.

Even before entering Fairvale, they caught glimpses of figures in wagons and buggies and on foot, all hurrying somewhere. Most of them appeared headed toward the telegraph office housed in the railroad depot at the far end of town.

Larissa expected Ethan to turn that direction also, but he veered instead toward the southeast side of the public square. In her this can't really be happening state, she wanted to shriek with frustration at his meandering. Fists clenched, she bit down hard on her tongue to keep from lashing out at him. Coupled with the agony of uncertainty soaking into her very bones was knowledge that, if any sound at all escaped her, it would be a scream without end.

Ethan halted Pegasus and Andromeda in front of the newspaper office. "John Shearer may have news. Worth checking here first before facing the crowd at the depot." He disappeared up the stairs into the third-floor *Tribune* office. To the four waiting in the humid afternoon sunshine, time stretched interminably. In reality, only minutes ticked past before he reappeared. "No names, yet." He climbed into the surrey, his voice, filling the tense silence, harsh to his own ears. "John has a boy waiting at the telegraph office to bring him word. He's expecting it any time, now. The initial report came early this morning. Apparently there was a big battle yesterday, near a railroad center called Manassas Junction, not too far outside Washington City."

Larissa shuddered.

"It appears Jake had it fairly straight, for once. Our boys were trouncing the Rebels most enthusiastically up into the late afternoon, when one of the Confederate officers ordered a massive counterattack, and our fellows couldn't hold the line. We fell back, and next thing anyone knew, we were headed full bore back to Washington. For whatever reason, the Rebels didn't follow, or follow up their advantage. Guess the *why* of that'll come out eventually."

He finally turned and looked at her. Larissa continued to stare straight ahead. In the back seat, Rose moved closer to Mac and shivered. This time he didn't shove her away.

Ethan guided the surrey into the turn that brought the railroad depot into view. A muttered exclamation escaped him. Larissa bit her lip and the children strained forward.

Horses, buggies, wagons, and people filled the area around the depot. Some of the townsfolk wandered about in the limited space between the haphazardly parked rigs. Most simply sat in their vehicles, waiting. Waiting for—the half formed thought snapped off because Ethan refused to complete it. Wrenching his thoughts away, he realized why the scene held such an eerie quality. Even though fully four hundred people from town, the Pottery Works, and outlying farms had gathered, the area was silent. The stamp of a horse's hoof, a child's wail quickly shushed, a snort as an animal blew sounded loud in that stillness because the people were making no noise, no conversation. They were simply … waiting.

Larissa, Ethan and the children became part of that waiting.

Occasionally, a new horse and buggy or wagon with a woman and children appeared on the edge of the crowd and merged with it as they in turn gave way to the latest arrivals. Time lost all meaning for Larissa. She sensed only that at some point this gulf of nothingness would be filled and then she would know. Then, she would know.

A sudden ripple started from the cluster nearest the telegraph office door. Like a spring wind, it fanned outward, fluttering through the tightly packed crowd. As one, the five occupants of the surrey leaned forward, willing the information to be passed rapidly, to reach them without the delay that, after the patient waiting, had suddenly become intolerable.

The telegraph office door abruptly swung inward, dumping in a tangled heap those bodies pressed closest to the building. Just as the leaves of the sugar maple sigh when the spring breeze ripples them, a murmur fluttered through the crowd as Miles Painter appeared with a paper in his hand. "Only have one copy. I'll read it." His voice, although not shouting loud, carried to the farthest edges of the waiting townspeople. "Two Union County men dead. Three wounded. The dead—" involuntarily his eyes swept the crowd "—Ross Van Ellis and Brand Farley. The wounded—" A high pitched, keening wail interrupted him as Martha Van Ellis, come with her four young children from her small farm north of town, thus learned of her husband's death.

From the fringe of the crowd, a figure detached itself and pushed toward the now weeping woman. Doc Rawley. Mac stood. Ethan's hand closed around his arm in a viselike grip. "No, Mac. Not this time."

At the scarcely audible command, Mac sank back. His eyes followed Ethan's to his mother's white face as Miles Painter's voice continued in the distance. "The wounded are Hunter Cade, Lemuel Jorgenson, and Vincent Rourke."

"He's not on the list!" Larissa's outburst, her first words since leaving the farm, made the three youngsters jump. "Did you hear, children? Your Pa's not on the list." The sighed words were a prayer of thanksgiving from the depths of her soul. She reached back and Mac and Rose each put a hand over hers. They sat thus for a long, joyful moment. When she turned to face forward once more, her eyes met Ethan's.

"Thank God," he said simply.

CHAPTER SEVENTEEN

To Larissa, the next days rippled past in an unreal blur. Heart singing knowledge Zane had survived a battle of crushing defeat and staggering casualties for the Union was tempered by ice cold awareness that any day, a clash of the two armies could bring his death. Much as she tried to force the grim truth from her mind by rejoicing in *here, today, he has not come to harm*, the futility confronted her daily in Martha Van Ellis's haunted eyes and white face.

The women of the community visited the Van Ellis farm each day to do what they could to ease the young widow's uneasable grief. The men of the village rode over daily to tend the farm chores and crops. The town closed ranks about her, knowing too well their assurance that fields and stock and house were cared for could not give her what she wanted most in the world—her husband.

In the quiet time after supper, Ethan and Larissa discussed it. "What'll happen to her?"

She asked with such bitterness that Ethan had to clear his throat before he could answer with any measure of calm. "With everyone taking turns, we'll get her through harvest. After that—"

"After that she only has to get through the rest of her life. What about Brand Farley's parents? Should they feel comforted he wasn't married, that he didn't leave a widow and small children behind? Comforted that their farm can survive without him?" She stopped to draw a gasping breath that turned into a terrible sob. Before Ethan could react, she jumped up from the table and fled into the night. He started after her, but a soft wail spun him around.

Rose, eyes wide with horror, stood in the doorway separating the sitting room and kitchen. His numb brain registering that she had obviously heard Larissa's outburst, she catapulted into his arms. Tears streaming down her cheeks, she sobbed so hard he couldn't understand her words. Not once, in all the months past, had she thus turned to him. He held her, let her tears soak into his shirtfront, murmured nothing words against her braids, knew he could no more leave her with her grief than he could have left Charity.

All the while he tried to still his mind to Larissa, out in the darkness, battling her hell alone.

Finally, Rose's anguish eased into wavering hiccups and she lay drained in his arms. He smoothed her tear damp hair and hunted for his handkerchief. She blew her nose in a long, noisy, satisfying release. Folding the cloth neatly, she politely handed it back to him. He blinked, took it gingerly and used a clean corner to blot the remaining tears from her cheeks. "Better now?" She ducked her head in assent, but not before he glimpsed guilt skitter across her face. "Sometimes, no matter how courageous we are, we have to let go," he said gently. "There's no shame in that. It just shows how much we care when we're worried about someone."

"Ma said to be brave no matter how scared we are for Pa. I guess I'm not very brave." Tears welled again.

Shifting her against his arm, he looked directly at her. "You are a very brave young lady. Sometimes it takes just as much, if not more, courage to show our feelings when we think other folks won't approve. We have to be honest with ourselves, just as with other people. That's what you did, and it's nothing to be embarrassed about."

"Are you sure?" A glint of hope struggled with misery.

He smiled. "I'm sure. Your Ma is very proud of you. I know, because she told me herself."

She smiled shyly and sat up straight. He thought she'd slide off his lap, but she suddenly sagged against his arm again. "If it's always best to be honest, should I tell Pa when I write him tonight about being scared for him and crying? Ma said we're supposed to write happy things so he won't be sad we're sad he's not here."

Ethan took a moment to unsnarl that one. "Your Ma's right about happy news. You're also supposed to write things you really want to tell him. It's your choice to make," he said carefully. "You were honest with me, so you're not hiding anything. Remember that when you write your letter."

She solemnly searched his face, looking for he knew not what. Finally she bobbed her head once and wrapped her arms around his neck in a quick squeeze before scooting off his lap. She flew through the doorway to the sitting room. He heard Charity's questioning lilt but, already halfway across the room to go to Larissa, he missed Rose's response. Just as he pulled open the outer door, it swung inward. He promptly tripped over his feet.

Larissa, obviously as startled as he, backed up. "I'm sorry," she stammered.

Recovering, he essayed a grin. "We're going to have to quit meeting like this."

"At least I didn't try to punch you in the nose," she retorted. Her eyes were swollen. Her tone, in spite of a faint note of teasing, carried flat warning any questions would prove a large mistake. Biting back the words, he watched her cross to the sitting room doorway.

"Larissa."

"Yes?" The teasing note had vanished. Only the flat warning

remained.

"I've been thinking. Would you like to take the youngsters on a picnic after church Sunday?"

Whatever she had expected him to say, this, obviously, was not it. "Where were you thinking of going?"

"Up past the grist mill. Let the children go swimming, maybe get in a water fight. Mac can chase the girls with a frog. You know, the usual placid, Sunday afternoon doings."

It brought a smile, even if a small one. "Of course. Wet clothes, stubbed toes, possibly a bee sting or two. Do you want to be the bearer of this good news?"

"I don't think that'll be necessary." He gestured to the three faces peering eagerly from the doorway.

She sighed heavily. "I'm just not sure we should."

A three voiced clamor of pleading immediately drowned her out. Mac and Rose rushed her, and Charity clasped Ethan's arm in supplication.

"Wait. Wait." Larissa, laughing, raised her hands to fend them off. "Do I hear promises to help fix the food?" At their enthusiastic assent, she winked at Ethan. "In that case, I think a picnic is an excellent idea."

Rose muttered darkly to Charity, "I know just how Mac'll help. We'll cook everything and he'll taste test it to make sure it's right."

Mac, overhearing, gave her braid a yank. "With you and Speck helping cook, someone better test it first."

"If the doctor gets sick, is he patient with his patient?" Charity's grin was pure mischief.

Mac dived for her, only to be brought up short by Ethan's firm grip on his collar. "Charity, since I believe Mac has a point, I shall count to three, then I shall release him. I suggest you scoot for home. Now."

With a squeak, Charity raced for the door, Rose close behind. "Three." Ethan freed Mac's collar. The boy shot after the girls like a blast from a cannon.

"'Just the usual, placid Sunday afternoon doings,' I believe you said," Larissa murmured.

She escaped into the sitting room, but a few low voiced words drifted back to him that caused him to grin broadly and start his own hasty retreat after his fleeing daughter.

***

For a long time afterward, the picnic that Sunday afternoon stood for them as an oasis of calm in a world of grief and uncertainty. True to Larissa's prediction, they came home sunburned and exhausted, but fortunately minus any bee stings, their hair and clothes sticky damp, and lighter of voice and mood than for many days.

***

Mac, making the rounds with Doc Rawley, learned about a new kind of grief. In his fledgling days as Doc's assistant, he had witnessed Mrs. Theron's anguish for her dead baby and wondered how she could endure such loss. Later, he beheld Mrs. Damon's dry, hopeless pain over her husband's desertion just as one more mouth to feed and body to clothe joined the flock.

His mother's sorrow, he thought, was like Mrs. Damon's, yet not. Ma would give her crown in Heaven to have Pa safe home again. With Mrs. Damon, however, in spite of all the hardship created by Theo's absence, Mac wondered whether she wasn't secretly relieved he wasn't underfoot. He fretted for a time, debated whether to mention such heresy to Doc, and remembered his stern instructions to discuss matters regardless of how farfetched they appeared, in order to get a full perspective. He finally came out with it on their way to check a neighbor's report that Ian Hollister was complaining of fever and rash.

Doc listened silently to his pupil's summary. When he spoke, it was not the comment Mac expected. "How long have you had this feeling about her?"

"A few days. It's nothing I can put my finger on. It's just she seems, well, lighter, than she's ever been before. When we made our call last week, she was holding the baby in the rocking chair and singing to him. I've never seen her do that. It seems so strange," he pushed on lamely. "Before Pa left, Ma was always light and happy around him. Whenever I saw Mr. and Mrs. Damon together, she always looked sad and worried. Now Ma's quiet and never sings like she used to, and Mrs. Damon looks peaceful." Mac slanted a glance at Doc, who was studying the top of a large maple out the right side of the buggy. "Maybe I've got it all wrong," he finished awkwardly.

Doc took so long answering, Mac's heart sank with the realization that all that childish rambling had infuriated him. The older man finally turned his head. The boy had never seen the expression now stamped on his face. "Mac." Doc's tone held a peculiar rusty note. "How old are you, now?"

"I was thirteen last June ninth."

Doc ignored his pupil's puzzlement. "Thirteen." He shook his head. "How long have you been studying with me?"

"Two years this past April."

This time Doc nodded. "A few more years to put under your belt, then."

Mac could have sworn his voice held relief. *Why? Can my guessing be that wrong?* He slumped miserably in his corner, acutely aware of Doc's silence and not daring to break it.

Still with no words, they turned into the Hollister road to check on Ian. They'd had no reason before to visit here. "Disgustingly healthy," was Doc's ungracious diagnosis, and after the snake incident on Charity's first day of school, Ian never again urged Mac to stop by. He noted now, while more cared for in appearance than the Damon acres, this place too was sagging. For the first time he gave fleeting thought to Mr. Michaels' role around their own farm.

"Here we are, Boy." Doc's voice registered its normal grouch level. "We're told rash and fever. You've seen a sight of them and plenty of different kinds. You're to make the call on what it is, just as if I wasn't here. Understand?"

What Mac understood perfectly well was that he wasn't being given a choice. For that matter, neither was Ian. Had Doc forgotten the animosity between them? Knowing Doc, he was simply ignoring it. *Easy for him to do.* A finger of ice stirred Mac's stomach, but Doc was already knocking on the front door, so further panic wasn't a choice, either.

Ushering them into the sitting room, Mrs. Hollister gestured to a closed door. Mac noted the room was better furnished than the Damons' small, all in one living space, but remembered also that Ian had only one sister instead of a large flock of siblings. As Doc was fond of saying, *For sure, Nature has a strange way of working things out.*

Ian was moaning and thrashing around on his bed in the darkened room. Glimpsing Doc, he upped his groan level a notch or two, but when Doc raised the shade for light and Ian saw Mac rolling up his sleeves, his moans turned to a distinct hiss. "What are you doing here?"

Mac's panic abruptly subsided into wry amusement as he remembered Bruiser, beet red, wringing out all those soggy diapers, asking him the same question. *After two years of studying with Doc, what do they think I'm doing there, waiting for the train to Columbus?* Pushing down his glee, assuming his best bedside manner, he said sympathetically, "I'm here to see what's wrong with you. Soon as I wash my hands, I'll begin my examination."

If looks could have killed, Mac would have been the one in the bed. Ian, torn between his dramatic display of illness for his mother's benefit, and loathing that Mac should be the one to diagnose him, visibly fought a severe interior battle before he decided pathos would get him further than argument.

Aware Ian couldn't possibly object, Mac poked and prodded thoroughly. "You ever had the chicken pox?" he asked finally.

"The chicken pox? That's for kids."

Mrs. Hollister broke across her son's fury. "No, now you mention it, he hasn't. Is that what's the matter? My land. I never even thought of it."

For confirmation Mac turned to Doc, who nodded. "That's just what I'd say we have here—a case of good old-fashioned chicken pox. Now what's your recommendation, Mac?"

Mac strove to hide an unprofessional grin over what he'd like to recommend. Summoning up his most serious manner, he laid out a plan of nursing and medication. Once more looking to Doc, this time all business because he might not be correct, he waited for the older man's verdict. Doc looked down at Ian's wrath and said firmly, "That's exactly right. You follow those procedures for the next three weeks, Mrs. Hollister, and he'll be good as new."

Returning to the main room, Mrs. Hollister produced a bumpy sack. "Potatoes," she said apologetically. "I'm afraid I can't pay you cash."

"The potatoes are fine, Mrs. Hollister," Doc said smoothly. "We can always use potatoes, can't we, Mac?"

Remembering the horde of hungry Damons, Mac bobbed his head vigorously. "Yes, ma'am."

Mrs. Hollister's relief and gratitude followed them to the buggy. Back on the road, Mac waited for Doc to sum up as he always did after a case. Instead, Doc remained silent and the glee that had earlier sustained Mac faded. *Sure as green apples bring bellyaches, something is wrong.*

***

Doc held that peculiar silence until they turned into the farmyard. Finally he stirred. "I expect your Ma is in the house. I'd like to talk to her. In private."

Mac found her lighting candles in the sitting room. Trying not to let his misery show, he delivered Doc's message and ignored Charity's and Rose's shocked expressions as Larissa hurried out.

He thought they'd come into the kitchen, but they stood beside Doc's buggy for an interminable space of time. Ethan forcibly restrained Rose and Charity from peeking out the window and reporting over their shoulders to Mac, who was pretending to eat his supper.

Ethan, sitting across from him, thought of and discarded a hundred words of sympathy. *For what?* Mac obviously had no inkling, either.

They finally heard Doc's buggy rattle away and Larissa's steps on the porch. When she opened the door, Mac noticed her face held the same peculiar expression Doc's had earlier, when he asked Mac's age.

She sat at the table beside him. Fork forgotten on his plate, he waited for—whatever it was—to fall. "Mac," she said carefully, "Doc's been telling me about your adventures, among them that you correctly diagnosed Ian Hollister's chicken pox. He said he couldn't have done a better job himself." At the amazed relief in his eyes, she laughed. "He admitted he's 'not much of a praising man,' so he left it for me to tell you. He mentioned some other things he's observed. He says," her eyes grew misty, "you have a feel for doctoring like few he's ever met. Mac, he wants to pay your way to send you to medical school in Pennsylvania as soon as you're old enough to be accepted."

Mac's mouth fell open, but no words came. Larissa hugged him as Ethan and the girls stared speechless. Then Ethan reached to shake his hand, congratulating him jubilantly. Rose began prattling a mile a minute, unaware of the shadow that passed across Charity's features before she joined the chatter, neither girl listening to the other. Over their babbling, Larissa said softly, "I'm so very proud of you, son. And I know Pa will be too, when he hears."

Mac, pleading that he had to "go out back," finally fled to the barn, where he buried his face in Andromeda's mane. Still too dazed to really believe it, he murmured over and over, "Medical school. Real medical school. Just like Doc."

A sudden thought caused him to grin from ear to ear. *What I wouldn't give to see Ian's and Bruiser's faces when they hear the news.*

CHAPTER EIGHTEEN

Zane, seated on a stump beside his supper campfire, swished at the wafting smoke. Stacked beside these past months of hardship, such annoyance reckoned so small he gave no thought to either cause or gesture. Concentrating on Larissa's letter, he realized he knew it by heart, but wonderment rushed through him with each re-reading.

Mac's going to attend medical school. The words Larissa had written caused his heart to swell with such pride it seemed impossible for it to stay beating in his chest. With his own rudimentary education, realization his son would achieve knowledge he himself had thirsted for and been denied, fulfilled a long cherished dream. Uneasiness nudged him at that part about Doc Rawley financing Mac's schooling. *A man pays his own debts and obligations, doesn't pawn them off on someone else.* Squinting against a fresh puff of smoke, he studied Larissa's explanation.

"Doc contends the obligation is on his side, not ours or Mac's. He says Mac's been working for him over two years with no pay, and he'll likely be working another four before he'll be old enough to enroll at the Pennsylvania school where Doc went. He says six years deserves some compensation. Few men would work so long for nothing. He can't think of a better way to pay Mac.

"Doc insists it's selfishness on his part, so we're not to think he's 'just doing it for his chance to listen with his Doctor Skinner's Double Flexible Stethoscope to Saint Peter's heart thump.' He wants Mac to return to Fairvale after graduating and eventually take over Doc's practice. He stressed *eventually* and glared at me to make certain I understood."

With vast amusement Zane mulled Larissa's vivid portrayal. Of course Doc groused, to cover that inconveniently soft as the down on a duckling heart of his. Lowering the paper, he stared unseeing at the group of soldiers squatting in a circle a few feet away, rolling dice over a blanket. *It comes hard to a man, accepting from another.* Rawley, however, made it obvious where he felt the obligation lay, and Zane had yet to see the man or beast who argued with Doc and won. *Only Death has ever defeated him.*

The heaviness temporarily banished by Larissa's news whacked his heart. The never ceasing questions smote him. *How much to tell her? How much to spare her?* Against their long-ago promise to be honest with each other no matter what, he was at a loss. Glossing over facts warred with the integrity of the relationship they had built together. But sharing the horror of the truth stretched beyond his capability. For a long time, he stared at the men tossing dice on a blanket, heard as at a great distance their alternate cheers and curses. Rules strictly prohibited gambling in camp, but threat of consequences failed to faze the men.

Finally Zane stirred, folded Larissa's letter carefully, and reached inside his blouse for pencil stub and paper. Never had they treated each other as children to be shielded from the truth. He would not start now. So he wrote matter-of-factly how, since the Philippi Races and the fight at Corrick's Ford in July, McClellan had kept a running argument going with the Confederates who, it must be admitted, were not the most congenial of hosts here in western Virginia.

"In July, Jacob Cox and *our* Ohioans" —he carefully drew a heavy line under *our*—"chased a Confederate brigade all the way up the Kanawha River. Speaking of Kanawha, it seems folks living in this part of Virginia don't hold with eastern Virginia's doings. There's talk about splitting from the main piece and becoming their own state. Some're already arguing a state name. 'West Virginia' and 'Kanawha' momentarily lead the race. Obadiah, of course, is already placing bets on whether it will happen, when, and which name will win.

"It's said this fellow Robert Lee has command of all the Confederate forces in western Virginia, but I don't see he's doing such a great job. Under General Rosecrans, we stopped him cold at Carnifex Ferry in September. (Not bragging, you understand. Just pure fact!)"

With a start he realized his writing was barely visible in the swiftly descending dark. He looked to his surroundings. His campfire showed only a heap of red flickering coals. The soldiers had gathered their dice and blanket and departed on errands known only to them, leaving behind silence and a worn spot in the grass of the pasture in which they were camped.

Unable to finish his letter tonight, he stood, wondering where he would be when next he set pencil to paper to complete it by telling her that, in a repetition of July's military orders, his ninety days were extended once again.

***

On a frosty November Saturday, Larissa stood at the worktable in the pleasantly warm kitchen and kneaded bread dough. Rose and Charity, dusting the sitting room, were discussing Christmas and Rose's birthday. How far off the day seemed, they agreed, even though it was the very next month, only thirty-three days away, counting today, as proved by the faithfully x-ed out calendar Rose continued to keep for her father's return.

Larissa, hearing their chatter as she shaped her loaves, thought how very near the day seemed, what with the doubled work and fuss attached to it. Alone in the kitchen, no one saw or cared as her shoulders drooped. How could she face Christmas, and all the attendant merrymaking, when her heart ached with knowledge Zane would not, after all, be home by then? How could she find joy for Rose and the special celebration they always held in the afternoon, apart from Christmas, because it was her birthday, too?

"Ma!"

"Mrs. Edwards, look."

Her just shaped dough splatted onto the table in a sticky mass as she whirled at sound of the girls' frantic voices. "Look outside," they chorused as they tumbled out of the sitting room. "It's snowing." Blissfully unaware they had almost given Larissa a heart attack, they dragged her to the window and crowded on either side to gaze out into the fast whitening world. She slipped an arm about each of them, Charity unconsciously snuggling as close as Rose.

Larissa stared at the swirling snow and responded to the girls' delighted exclamations. But her thoughts drifted, aimless as the flakes. *Zane, I hope the Christmas package we sent reaches you in time. Mac and Rose, Charity, too, worked hard making gifts you can use in your travels. Your last letter said you were in winter quarters, that you're warm and safe, for a while anyway. Please God you stay that way. If you do, I'll make Christmas and Rose's birthday as joyous as I can. I promise.*

***

Those next busy weeks, Larissa's resolve was repeatedly tried as day followed day and no new letter came from Zane. She could force her outward self to be excited about Christmas, "and my birthday," Rose always amended mischievously, but how did one will the heart and spirit to follow suit when they lagged defiantly behind?

Added to her discouragement, she knew something was bothering Ethan. Courteous and accommodating as always, yet, in some subtle way, he had withdrawn from her. Since she could scarcely come right out and ask, "Why have you become so distant?" she spent long moments pondering the situation and finally decided the holidays must be as painful a reminder to him of Nettie's absence as they were to her of Zane's.

Unable to express her isolation to Ethan, unwilling to intrude upon his privacy, she held her silence.

***

Christmas Eve morning, a Tuesday, Larissa had everyone up and going early. Her plan included the children completing all their usual chores and then helping her with the everyday ones before Ethan took them to school in the buckboard on runners. Thus she would be free to devote more time to the many holiday tasks awaiting her. It was a good plan. The children, however, were so excited about only a half-day of lessons before the festivities, their assistance proved dubious at best. In exasperation, finally admitting defeat, she shooed them outside to Ethan, then lingered a moment in the doorway to view their antics.

Unfortunately for Ethan, his exuberance at the moment matched the children's and he threw a snowball at Mac as the boy started down the steps. It whizzed smoothly past its intended target and landed with a messy plop on the wall an inch from Larissa's ear.

Loud silence followed, except for the erstwhile snowball dripping noisily onto the porch floor. The children froze in position so completely they resembled ice statues. Ethan's face mingled disbelief, guilt, and panic in fairly equal parts as, in horrified fascination, he watched Larissa's mouth form a soundless, astonished *oh*.

He turned beet red and tried to stammer the beginnings of an apology. Larissa whirled back into the kitchen and slammed the door. Sinking onto the nearest chair, she doubled over, laughing so hard the tears streamed down her cheeks and soaked her apron front. Finally gaining a little control, she peeked out the window. Horses, buckboard, ice-statue children, and chagrined tosser of snowballs had deserted the battlefield and were, presumably, on the road to town.

Gurgling chuckles still intermittently escaping, she hurried upstairs to her room and gathered up the dresses she had not yet finished for Rose and Charity. She carried them down to the sitting room, where the brighter light allowed her to see more easily the minute stitches she was setting into each one. Firmly disciplining herself not to think about that ridiculous look on Ethan's face, another bubble of laughter promptly exploded her resolve. Needle flashing in and out of the material, she concentrated fiercely on a mental list of all she must accomplish today. Thank goodness Mac's and Ethan's gifts required only wrapping. Hopefully the children, and Ethan, would give more help this afternoon than they had contributed this morning. Unfortunately, the thought brought on another string of hiccupping chuckles.

She tied the last knot in Charity's hem and was biting off the thread when she heard the jingle of the bells Ethan had fastened to the horses' harness. Expecting him to head for the barn, his quick rap and the kitchen door opening startled her.

"Larissa?"

"In the sitting room. I didn't expect you back so soon." He poked his head around the doorframe and she saw he was still bundled in his coat and muffler. Quick alarm frizzed through her at his grave expression. "What's happened?"

"Nothing. I just wanted to apologize for this morning."

She now possessed shaky control of those infernal humor-spasms, which was fortunate for him, because he looked exactly like a small boy caught with his hand in the jam pot. "You startled me," she said reprovingly.

"Not nearly so much as I startled myself," he admitted ruefully. "I hope you can forgive me."

"You're forgiven. Just so it doesn't happen again."

"Word of honor." His relief was so unashamed she felt guilty teasing him. Before she could admit it, he brought his hand from behind his back. "Merry Christmas, Larissa."

She stared at the flat package, her heart skipping a beat as she recognized Zane's script.

"It just came today. Word of honor," he repeated against her questioning look. "I know how much you've been waiting for it, so I brought it as fast as I could." He doubted she even heard his last words as she examined the postmark. "I looked, too," he admitted. "He's still in Virginia."

"He thought he would be, at least for a while," she murmured, torn between opening it immediately and waiting for the children, for it obviously contained more than just a letter.

"If you want to open it, then seal it again, I won't tell," he whispered conspiratorially.

Reluctantly she shook her head. "No." She spoke so low he barely caught it. Then, with sudden firm decision, "No. It's for Christmas. I've been insisting poor Rose practice patience all these weeks. I guess I'm getting an extra-large dose of the castor oil I've handed out." She smiled. A bit twisted, it was the best she could do. "The important thing is, he's still all right. Knowing that, I can wait."

"You can wait. However, I sure wouldn't want to wager next year's wheat harvest that those young ones can."

***

Christmas morning, the children rose early. As a special treat, Charity was allowed to sleep over with Rose, and now the girls, Mac bringing up the rear, charged into Larissa's bedroom. "Merry Christmas!"

"And my birthday," Rose chanted.

Larissa groaned and attempted to pull the covers over her head, but the girls would have none of it. Tugging at the blankets, they pleaded with her to get up.

"You're never this eager to get up on school mornings," she pointed out grumpily.

"Oh, Ma, we know you're teasing. Please, may we go downstairs?"

"There might even be something for you down there, Mrs. Edwards," Charity added craftily.

"How can I possibly resist such reasoning?" Larissa laughed and scooped Charity toward her for an exuberant hug. Putting her other arm around Rose, she planted a kiss on her daughter's nose. "Happy Birthday, young lady. Eight years old. Where has the time gone?" With a smile for Mac, standing back scorning to join the little girl antics, she tumbled the children off the bed. "Get dressed, then you can go down as soon as Charity's Pa gets here." The thunder of feet in the hallway, Mac's included, echoed in answer as they raced for their clothes.

Admonishing the children to stay upstairs until she called them, Larissa went down to start the breakfast fire. She entered the kitchen just as Ethan, arms full of stove chunks, stepped through the woodshed door. Greeting her cheerfully, he cocked an ear toward the erratic thumps issuing from the ceiling. "I hope that's just a herd of eccentric elephants up there and not my Christmas present."

"You spoiled my surprise. I hoped you wouldn't guess!"

He dropped the wood into the box and chuckled. "I think we'd better rescue the eccentric elephants before they pound a hole in the ceiling."

Larissa watched the children's faces at their first glimpse of the decorations garlanding the sitting room. Ethan had fastened pine boughs, cones still attached, along the mantel and around the windows. She had woven crimson ribbon into the branches and tiny, glittering stars nestled among the greenery. The children's attention, however, immediately focused on the presents heaped on the walnut table. Looking ruefully at Ethan, she admitted defeat and they were soon lost in a swirl of paper and gifts.

Charity gave Larissa and Ethan handkerchiefs she had hemmed, with their initials embroidered in the corners. Rose had knitted slippers for Ethan and, using Larissa's finest-sized needles, a bookmark for her mother. Sputtering with amusement, they discovered Mac had given hair ribbons to Rose and Charity and that Rose and Charity had given hair ribbons to each other.

Together, the girls handed Mac his present because, Charity explained, "It's from your family and ours, too."

Mac tore into the wrapping. Anticipation changed to swift shock as he stared at the contents and finally lifted out a gold pocket watch and chain. "Holy cow!" His short speech wasn't majestic, but it was obviously heartfelt.

In chorus, Charity and Rose explained how the watch itself was from

Zane and Larissa, the gold chain Ethan's contribution, and the fob their work. Triumphantly they related how in the evenings, *right in front of him*, they had stitched the material and embroidered his initials without his ever suspecting what they were doing.

His dazed grin as he grasped the fob and clicked open the case provided full assurance he didn't mind the joke on him. "It even has words," he blurted. "'McCord Zane Edwards, December 25, 1861.'"

"I didn't know your middle name's 'Zane'," Charity interjected.

"Has been ever since I was born."

She stuck her tongue out at him. "Charity!" Ethan barked, aghast.

Larissa smoothly smothered his stunned disapproval. "Doc Rawley contributed the inscription. When we questioned him about what type watch would be best for you, he asked if he could join in on it and had the engraving done. Rose and Charity are right. It really is from all of us."

Ethan, outfoxed from disciplining his daughter, settled for a "We will discuss this later," look that caused her chin to dip sheepishly. He turned to Mac. "There might be a bit too much chain now, but I'm sure not for long. The way you're growing, we might even have to add links."

Mac beamed and did his best to look tall.

Larissa finally drew out the parcel from Zane. "We have one more package."

"From Pa!" Mac and Rose shouted in unison and dove for it. Larissa's cry of distress as she raised the parcel above her head halted their heedless rush.

"We wouldn't have hurt it, Ma. Honest. We were just teasing. Right, Rose?"

Rose's mutinous expression clearly indicated otherwise. Mac forestalled her already welling squawk of protest by punching his elbow vigorously into her ribs. She glared at him, and eyed his ready to poke her again elbow. "Oh." Her now-I-get-it tone suddenly became all injured innocence. "No, Ma. Not when it's from Pa." Fortunately for them, Larissa was too eager to open the package to press the issue.

Beneath layers of paper she discovered a tablet similar to those Zane used for his letters. A series of pencil sketches nestled inside. Larissa carefully lifted the top one. "This one has your name on it, Rose."

"A rose. Where did Pa get it?"

Larissa harbored strong suspicions but kept them to herself as she handed the next one to Mac. "Ma, it's a cavalry soldier. He has a saber. I think it's Mr. Beldane."

Larissa peered more closely. "I believe you're right. It looks like he's talking. His mouth's open, anyway. Here's one for Charity."

"Look, Pa, it's a squirrel running along a fence."

With a swift glance at Larissa, Ethan bent to study the drawing.

"That's wonderful, Charity. The little fellow truly looks lifelike. Be careful not to get too close, he'll chatter at you and scurry away."

"Ethan." Larissa was extending a sheet of paper to him.

"The barn, by jiminy. If I didn't know it was a picture, I'd try to stable Andromeda and Pegasus inside."

"What's yours, Ma?" Rose craned her neck to see inside the paper. "It's Mac. There I am. And that one's you, Ma. Oh!" She broke off, overcome at the final sketch.

"It's Pa," Mac breathed.

Larissa didn't know whether to burst into song or tears as she drank in the crudely rendered but undeniably lifelike drawing. Blinking rapidly, she dashed at her eyes with trembling hands.

"Where did he get them, Ma?"

She reached one arm to Rose and the other to Mac, pulling them close beside her. "He drew them," she said softly.

"Pa? I didn't know he could draw."

"As you see, he draws very well. He just didn't have opportunity to do it when he was growing up. Later, he felt he had been away from it for too long." Not for all the cash money from next year's corn crop would she tell Zane's children about the long-ago derision he had endured from his own father, now decades dead. Larissa wondered, not for the first time, if at the end the old man had regretted his harshness to his son. She doubted it. Before the children could pursue the astonishing revelation further, she removed a folded paper from the tablet.

"A letter." Rose clapped her hands in delight.

Ethan quickly stood. "Come, Charity. We'll let them read their news in private."

"You don't have to go," Larissa protested. "Zane's addressed it to us and 'Ethan and Miss Charity, too.'"

Ethan looked into his daughter's pleading eyes and slowly sat down again. Charity sighed in delight and leaned against his knee.

Larissa smoothed the letter carefully. "Dear Family, and Ethan and Miss Charity, too. Merry Christmas to each one of you from the bottommost corner of my heart."

"Merry Christmas to you, too, Pa," Rose whispered.

For the second time that day, Larissa had to blink a sudden mist from her eyes, before she could see the letter easily enough to continue reading.

"I am well. We are now settled into our winter quarters in the sixteen by twenty-foot huts we built, one for every sixteen men. Obadiah Beldane and I are deemed general assistants to the company blacksmiths and farriers, and are called on to help tend the horses any time of day or night, so our hut is built with access to the blacksmith shop and the corrals. The narrow south end of the shelter contains the doorway leading out onto the company street. The north end holds the fireplace with a chimney built of sticks and sealed with mud. Straw ticks on bunks along the walls comprise our sleeping arrangements.

"Luck, in the person of Obadiah, has smiled on me yet again. I mentioned before, when a body wants to know something, Obadiah noses it out. When one wishes to procure articles not provided by the sutler's shop, he noses them out, too. Thus, unlike some of the other cabins, we boast such refinements as a barrel table, and chairs made from hardtack crates.

"We will be posted here at least until late winter when the snow melts enough for us to be on the move again. In the meantime I am tolerably comfortable in my surroundings. I have even learned to sleep to the snoring of fifteen other men. Obadiah, of course, gets the grand prize in the freight train division of the snoring competition. Or is it only my imagination because he bunks next to me?

"Please take care, dear family. Know that I am with you in my heart this Christmas Day. It is my fervent prayer that next Christmas will see us all together once more.

"Your loving Husband and Father.

"P.S. Happy Birthday, my Christmas Rose. I carry you curled warm and close to my heart on this, your special day."

Silence followed Larissa's reading until Rose crept forward and leaned her head against her mother's knee. "The very best Christmas present of all. And birthday, too." Over her child's head, Larissa's eyes met Ethan's.

"For all of us, Rose, without a doubt," she murmured.

CHAPTER NINETEEN

Christmas afternoon they celebrated Rose's birthday. She was quite put out over Larissa insisting she stay inside and help bake her own birthday cake while Mac, Charity and Ethan frolicked in the snow. "Do you want a cake or not?" Even at the tender age of eight, Rose knew Ma was not asking a question. While the others romped outside, she helped beat twelve egg whites into pristine peaks for an angel cake. "I think singing helps the time pass faster. Shall we try it, Rose?"

Once again, Rose knew the question carried a one choice answer. "I guess so."

"Let's do *Pop Goes the Weasel*. I'll start. You come in."

All 'round the cobbler's bench,
the monkey chased the weasel ...

Rose reluctantly added her voice to make the round, but finally gained steam. Breathless and laughing, they reached the end. "May we do it again, Ma?"

"I've created a singing sensation," Larissa teased. "Look, we just finished the last egg white. How many verses can we sing before the batter is ready?"

Rose's face screwed into concentration. "Eight."

"I wonder why you picked that number? I say, five."

Under Larissa's holding her breath and smiling at the same time supervision, Rose slid the cake into the oven. "Ma, how did Pa draw his own picture?"

Jolted by the question from out of the blue, Larissa's wits fled. Only knowing Zane's writings by heart rescued her. "His very first letter, Pa said someone took his picture. Maybe he sketched from that."

"Drawing pictures is such fun. I never knew Pa likes it, too. I wish I was good at it like him," Rose said wistfully.

"You draw very well."

The woodshed door banged, cutting Larissa off and causing her to fear for the rising angel food cake. Charity stuck her head inside. "Mrs. Edwards, may Rose come play?"

Larissa sighed. Her heart could cope with one pleading face, but not two. "Yes. The cake has thirty more minutes." She brightened. "I'd like some fresh air, too."

Once they were bundled against the cold, Charity led them around the west corner of the barn. "We're playing here 'cause the wind isn't so bad."

Larissa, following, her eyes glued on Rose, saw her daughter's start of surprise and wonder at glimpsing the secret they'd kept so carefully from her.

"A snow castle! With towers and a moat and everything."

Charity burst out laughing that Rose hadn't guessed a thing.

Mac and Ethan, grinning foolishly, holding willow twig swords, stood stiffly at each side of the entrance gate, soldiers guarding the castle against uninvited fire breathing dragons, wicked toads and other such nuisances. At her approach, their crossed swords barred her path. "Speak your business, young miss," Mac commanded.

"I'm Princess Christmas Rose and this is my mother, Queen Victoria. We wish to enter our home."

"Enter, Princess Rose and Queen Victoria." Mac and Ethan bowed deeply, shouldered their swords and stepped back.

Speechless with delight, Rose examined the "rooms" in the castle, then went flying to Charity, Mac, and Ethan in turn with a hug as big as the joy on her face.

"So much work," Larissa marveled.

"I have sore muscles in places I didn't even know I had muscles," Ethan groaned.

***

Christmas Day evening Zane, momentarily alone in his hut, balanced on a hardtack crate and bent nearer the candle stub flickering on the flour barrel table. In the fitful light, he once again examined the muffler Rose had knitted. Her note said she'd wanted to use red yarn "to make you feel cheery but Ma said soldiers needed to make sure they didn't attrackt the other army's attention to themselves, so bright colors weren't good." It was, therefore, Union blue. She hoped "it'll keep you warm and inconspikus and that you will think of me when you wear it." Ignoring the fact he sat inside the reasonably warm hut, he wrapped the length about his neck.

He lifted Mac's gift, a new canteen. Zane'd mentioned in an earlier letter how the men had already learned to heat their army issue canteens over a fire to melt the solder seam. The container then became two pieces useful for cooking, eating and drinking. Mac said he wanted to be sure Pa could carry water with him on the march and not have to depend on stopping at a stream or creek. Zane smiled at his son's unconscious doctor reasoning and silently promised to keep the canteen as full as circumstances permitted.

Charity's bright red flannel stomacher caused him to grin unrestrainedly. She assured him wearing it around his waist, under his shirt so no one would see the color, would "prevent dishinterry as I've heard soldiers get." He tucked it under his blouse, the sting in his eyes not caused by the smoking candle.

Ethan had sent him a container of Frank Miller's Harness Soap, the saddle soap they used on the farm, so he could transport himself in memory whenever he wished. Inhaling the rich aroma, Zane closed his eyes. For a fleeting moment he stood back in the barn at home, the good animal and leather smells about him as Orion waited patiently to be saddled.

At last he cupped Larissa's gift in his hands. She had sent him a pebble in a small, flat can of dirt. "Not just any pebble, mind you, and not just any dirt. The stone is from Mill Creek and the earth is from the cornfield. The can is small so you won't have any difficulty packing it, and this way you aren't really away from the farm. You'll take it with you wherever you go."

However had she known how deeply he had felt the need to touch the good earth of the farm, that without it a vital part of himself was missing? Sudden memory enfolded him. Larissa bending over her sewing. He pacing and fretting about not paying Ethan for the farm work. Her voice, coming as plain as if she sat at the table with him. *"How would you feel if you lost this farm? It's your right arm. Take you off the land, you'd wither like a tree pulled up by its roots."*

An oft-repeated, rueful thought caused him to grin. *A furlong and a half ahead of me again. Will I ever catch up with her? Every time I pride myself on making progress, off she goes, leaving me in the dust. But would I have it any other way? No, by jingo.*

***

January proved disagreeable for the men stuck in winter quarters. The monotonous diet. The cramped, smoky huts and constant, inescapable nearness of so many other bodies in various states of odiferousness and lice. The inactivity and uncertainty of their futures come springtime, all fermented in the soldiers' souls. Daily fistfights, in spite of the officers' efforts and the harsh punishment, became the norm rather than the exception.

Zane kept to himself much as possible. Men in a fighting mood apparently retained enough sanity to measure his breadth and strength, and enough prudence to seek lesser targets. It suited him just fine.

On a gray, miserable day toward the middle of that month, the men huddled inside their huts, shivering in spite of the dubious warmth of the fireplaces. Zane lay on his bunk, arms locked behind his head, mentally planning the spring planting, ignoring the coughing, groaning, sneezing, spitting, and poker game going on about him.

The street door whooshed open, emitting a blast of cold air that sent the smoke swirling and added pithy curses to the general commotion. With his usual grace and tact, Obadiah, boots dripping snow, leaving a trail of slush and fresh curses in his wake, clumped over to Zane's bunk. Oblivious to everything except his errand, he motioned for them to go outside. Puzzled, Zane nevertheless grabbed his coat and Rose's muffler and followed the blacksmith out, to a fresh chorus of epithets as snow again blasted into the hut.

"You're not real well thought of in there about now." Zane jerked his thumb toward the hut.

Obadiah grinned. "You ain't neither, friend. Just wait till we wander back in."

Zane tipped his chin to the near blizzard conditions. "You bring me out here to discuss popularity contests?"

Obadiah's ready grin faded and Zane's belly twisted. "Something's happened. To my family?"

"No. Hell, Zane, I wouldn't do that to you. I'd come straight out with it and no wisecracks."

Zane, knowing that was true, relaxed slightly. If everyone was all right at home, he could take whatever Obadiah was about to dish out.

"Talk's been floating around. Heard it with my own ears, and it sounds mighty peculiar."

This, in itself, did not render Zane speechless. Obadiah's ears drew peculiar talk like dropped seed drew crows. "Word is that we ain't going to Missouri or Arkansas come spring."

Zane frowned. For weeks, the entire company had waited for orders to one state or the other. With western Virginia securely in Union hands, the 6th Ohio Volunteer Cavalry's work here was finished. The men chafed to get on with showing the South a thing or two. "Where, then?" He didn't argue with Obadiah. True, the man heard many reports, but he also possessed an uncanny knack of sorting the real from the washout. If Obadiah said they weren't going to Arkansas or Missouri come spring, bets were better than even they weren't going.

Odd for him, Obadiah stretched the silence by kicking at a clod of snow. "Nebraska Territory."

"Where?" Zane decided his ears must be failing.

"Nebraska Territory. Out west, t'other side of Ioway. A right smart piece off, and no wisecracks about that, either."

Zane shook his head as if to clear it. "The other side of Iowa? Not even a proper named state? What in God's name are we supposed to do out there?"

Obadiah's grin resurfaced. Sure as corn made whiskey, Zane was agitated. Obadiah couldn't ever recall him stringing that many words together at one time. "Fight Indians."

"Fight—Obadiah, most times your information's square as a beam. But I swear—"

"Just happening to be nearby, I heard Capt'n Norton himself talking to Colonel Collins."

"Standing with your ear stuck in the keyhole, more likely." Despite his shock, he couldn't resist the jab at Obadiah's methods.

"I never. I was looking for Capt'n Norton. Colonel Harris sent me with a message for him. Said if anybody could find him prompt like, it'd be me. I've even got the attention of the big bugs."

Zane suspected the attention wasn't flattering, but hadn't the heart to slop water on Obadiah's obvious pride at the accomplishment. "When we supposed to go?"

"Soon as word comes. I gather we're supposed to be in St. Louis by Feb'ary first, which means they better get cracking. All that distance, and this weather, getting there'll be more than just a Sunday stroll in the park. By the way, I forgot to mention that apparently Capt'n Norton's going with us."

In spite of everything, Zane felt a flick of relief. If Captain Norton was going to this God forsaken place, by jingo, he reckoned he could mosey along with him.

Obadiah's speculation squatted over their heads, unconfirmed, for another three long days. Zane spent the time alternately wishing word would come, just so the uncertain waiting would stop, and cursing Obadiah's rumor sniffing ability. At night, lying awake staring at the bunk above him, he mentally composed his letter to Larissa as though it were already unchangeable fact.

In the end, Captain Norton himself made the announcement at Sunday morning roll call. Whatever his personal doubts or regrets, the captain kept them to himself. The men listened in more or less stunned silence to the new orders and Norton's bare bones explanation of where they were going and why. Zane, so sure he was prepared after his own days of knowledge, felt as if he had been felled with a double bitted ax.

He must now write the letter to Larissa, that letter he had composed a thousand times in his mind, and of which he could not now recall a word.

***

Larissa, blue woolen shawl pinned over her head and shoulders, dishpan in hand, paused by the porch steps to fling out her sudsy water. Her eyes following the sparkling arc, she caught a glimpse of purple half buried in the snowy flowerbed. As she stooped to investigate, the jingle of harness bells warned her someone was coming. Straightening, she waved to Ethan returning from taking the children to school, and called him to come see her discovery. Obligingly, he alighted from the buckboard on runners and peered into the flowerbed but looked blank.

"Crocuses, Ethan. The first spring flowers. We made it through the winter."

"Isn't it too early? If we get another big storm, they'll be buried."

She couldn't resist a smile at his masculine anxiety. "It wouldn't hurt them. They get along fine in the cold."

Dubiously, he studied them. "The way you have with flowers, I'll take your word for it."

The unexpected compliment surprised and pleased her. "Why, thank you." Before she could say more, he handed her a white envelope, effectively capturing her attention. As always, her first glance went to the postmark. "He's still in Virginia." *Still in winter quarters, still safe for a little longer, Zane.*

She slit the envelope with a hairpin. Ethan turned to the buckboard and the neglected team edging toward the succulent green shoots of the courageous crocuses. Already absorbed in the letter, she walked slowly toward the porch steps. Ethan, reaching for Andromeda's halter, heard a thump. Whirling, he saw her, looking dazed, perched on the bottom step.

He ran to her. "Larissa, are you all right?"

Still staring at the letter, she nodded weakly. "I wasn't watching and tripped over the step. He's going to Nebraska Territory. I don't even know where that is."

Once assured she was shaken, not hurt, he focused on her words. "Nebraska Territory? I think it's part of a stretch of land called the Great American Desert. I know it's west of any of the platted states. Zane's being sent there? But why?" His bewilderment was, if possible, greater than hers.

In a haze of unreality, she smoothed the crumpled pages. "It's in the letter. He writes,

"My Dear Family,

"Life leads us down odd paths, ones we never dreamed we'd take. One of those odd paths now stretches before me. With western Virginia securely in Union hands, my company was to go to either Arkansas or Missouri. By the time you read this letter, I will be on my way to St. Louis, Missouri. Not, however, to fight against Confederates plaguing the area. Four companies from the 6th Ohio Volunteer Cavalry are ordered to Nebraska Territory, out beyond the state of Iowa. My company is one of them."

Her voice thinned, then picked up the thread as if expressing the words would make them more comprehensible.

"It seems the Indians in that region are attacking travelers, mail stages, and stage stations along the Oregon Trail, and the Washington powers that be are taking big exception to such highhanded tactics. Plans remain sketchy. Army Rule Number One, don't tell the man doing all the work what he will be doing or where he will be doing it. We are, at least, grudgingly informed we will go by rail and horseback to St. Louis to catch a steamboat up the Missouri River to Fort Leavenworth, Kansas. There we will join frontier guides who know the region and the Indian tribes inhabiting it. As I learn what the future holds, I will keep you informed. At the moment, I do not have more facts, but am certain of one thing. If it can be ascertained, Obadiah will do so, and I will pass it on to you.

"One piece of great fortune comes with this troop movement. Captain Norton, of whom I have written, will lead us. Under his capable guidance, I feel secure facing the unknown, doing the duty to which I have been called.

"No matter the distance between us, my heart remains with you.

"Your loving Husband and Father."

In the ensuing quiet, Pegasus shook his mane. The cheerful jingling of the bells Ethan had so blithely attached to his harness rang loud and unreal. Searching frantically for something intelligent to say that would help, not hurt her more, Ethan finally let his eyes rest on her. "When the young ones come home, we'll borrow their geography book. I'm sure it'll tell about the region. If it doesn't, we'll look until we find something. Miss Sullivan probably knows all about it." He had grave misgivings about the amount of reassurance this little speech offered. Were he the recipient, he'd probably punch the speaker right in the nose.

Her eyes, however, lost some of their glazed look and she stirred. "Those are good places to start."

"Are you all right, Larissa?" He didn't give a damn how plainly his concern showed.

"Yes. I have to be." She smiled wryly. "But wait until this war is over. I'm going to get it out of my system by throwing the biggest, wildest fit Union County or Sanilac County's ever witnessed." She paused in the kitchen doorway. "Thank you."

"Keep assurance," he murmured to her retreating back. "Keep assurance all the way."

***

The next months, news of Zane's movements came sketchily. The already irregular mail service from the West continued to be disrupted by attacks led by the Eastern Shoshoni Indians, resulting in burning of mail bags and, when they could pull it off, stage stations and coaches. As Larissa understood it, in addition to food, these warriors raided to obtain glory. Killing enemy whites and stealing horses brought them great honor within their tribe. Why anyone should be lauded for deliberate destruction of another's property, with cold-blooded killing thrown in to boot, was beyond Larissa's ken. Fortunately for Ethan, he understood that her irate, broody hen fussing and squawking created an outlet for the fear she wouldn't voice.

They learned Zane's company reached St. Louis without grave mishap and continued up the Missouri by steamboat to Fort Leavenworth. There they met their guides, one named Jim Bridger, a grizzled old bear of a mountain man. Mac broke off his reading of the letter. "Jim Bridger? We've studied about him. Why, he hunted and trapped in the Rocky Mountains ever so many years ago, and knows the territory like the back of his hand, Miss Sullivan told us."

"Did she tell you how long ago?" Ethan's voice held only curiosity and a deep desire to learn.

"Oh, ages ago. Twenty years at least."

Larissa, sewing, emitted a peculiar gurgling sound.

"Ma, you all right?"

"Yes," she gasped. "I was listening so closely I didn't pay attention to my sewing and stabbed my finger." She stuck the wounded digit between her lips. Around the tip of her finger, she smiled wickedly at Ethan, who was attacked by a sudden coughing fit.

"Mr. Bridger knows Pa. I want to hear more," Rose cut in.

"I want to hear more too," Ethan seconded.

Mac continued the letter in which Zane recounted that, besides the mountain men guides, Lieutenant Colonel William Collins led the four companies of soldiers. "Black bearded and tall, Collins possesses a soldierly bearing and boundless energy for leading his men. In his everyday life, he practices law and formerly served in our Ohio legislature. Captain Lot Smith, heading a company of Mormon troops sent to dissuade the Shoshoni, admires Collins because he refuses to kill Indians indiscriminately."

In a later letter, Zane related fishing in the Platte River before reaching Fort Laramie. Colonel Collins produced a twenty-five yard long net. Even Obadiah "scratched his head over its source." The men, turn about, threw out the net and hauled it in. "Caught a good mess of pike and divided it among all four companies. When we reached Fort Laramie, we found the magnificent sum of sixty soldiers posted there. James Craig, Union Brigadier General—how do you like that fancy title?—up to now has patrolled his whole region with only those few men. I'll tell you, those fellows were all-fired happy when three hundred forty-eight of us came wandering in."

They later learned, "We've been posted farther west. We're presently in charge of South Platte, a one hundred forty mile stretch between Upper Platte Bridge and the Utah Territory border."

Zane, however, neglected to mention one small item, how that particular piece of road was considered the most dangerous section of the entire mail route. He fervently hoped such specific information never reached Larissa. For, facing hard facts honestly, what use for her to know? He had so few ways to ease her worry. He would not needlessly add to it.

The summer, and the fighting, wore on. Daily, Larissa saw the small but undeniable changes wrought in her children. Rose, only eight, had already left her little girlhood behind. Her eyes held knowledge beyond her years, and she had not, for a long time now, asked when Zane was coming home. Mac, fourteen, had sprouted like a young oak, his chest and shoulders beginning to take on Zane's breadth. A little more hauntingly clear each day, Zane's image gazed at Larissa from her son's eyes. With a deep pang, she wondered whether her children's newfound maturity would have come so rapidly had the war not encompassed their lives like a smothering blanket.

Mac drove out with Doc almost every day. In spite of his youth and the never ceasing worry over Zane's safety, Mac was experiencing the deep contentment that comes with finding the work one is born to do. Doc, too, looked to Mac's future. Totally out of character, he spoke often and almost garrulously of the boy's attending the University and the wonders he would experience. He even went so far as to write the school and request the latest textbooks so that Mac "might not be a total lunkhead" concerning the newest techniques the first time he entered the University doors.

On a humid July day, with thunder muttering outside the office, Doc presented the books to Mac as "a birthday remembrance, regardless of the fact they're a little late," his voice more gruff than usual to hide his pride in his student's accomplishments. Mac, red faced, stuttered his thanks at the magnificence of the gift, and Doc promptly informed him he expected him to have them memorized by the time he left for the University.

The summer saw Ethan going about the farm work. In the fields he held fiercely to his promise Larissa should never learn his feelings. In the house, his resolve wavered like a breeze-touched candle flame as he sat across from her at meals or in the evenings. While she sewed or mended, he read from Dickens' *Tale of Two Cities*, her Christmas gift to him, with the children listening and studying at the table.

Wrapped in worry, Ethan failed to notice the effect on Charity of all the harshness grating at their daily lives. For the first time since their coming to Fairvale, she slipped into her cocoon of quiet. Only around Mac, her eyes lit with their old sparkle.

CHAPTER TWENTY

On a crisp October day, Larissa, hands idle in the dishpan, gazed out the kitchen window at the russet and gold morning. In the distance, a wedge shaped line of feathered commotion flew over the sugar maples, a black smudge above the butter yellow trees. Hands dripping, she ran to the door, yanking it open in time to catch the strident cries of the geese winging their way south. For long moments she stood, their raucous calls drifting to her ever more faintly until only silence echoed among the familiar farm sounds.

Why does fall affect me so deeply? During other seasons, the farm was her world. But come autumn, with leaves turning bronze and scarlet, ducks and geese filling the skies with hoarse calling, it was as though she became a different person. A strange restlessness welled, an age-old pull that, like the birds soaring overhead to their winter destination, she, too, should be going someplace and doing something.

But where? What? She knew it wasn't discontent. Come winter, the feeling curled contentedly within her, just as a cat, finishing a bowl of warm milk, stretches lazily and drowses in front of the crackling fire, unable to fathom any other life. From earliest memory, this sensation had come every autumn, the haunting cries of ducks and geese kindling that impulse of her heart.

Sliding her hands back into the now cooled dishwater, she dutifully picked up a plate and ran her cloth over its egg sticky surface. As she passed it through the rinse pan, the idea tickling the back of her mind jumped full blown into awareness. A smile that Zane, were he there to see it, would call her "pure mischief" grin, lightened her wistful expression. Resolve quickened her motions and, the dishes finished, she paused only long enough to draw off her blue calico apron before hurrying up the stairs to her room.

A bit later, she walked sedately along the road to town, any feelings of guilt at abandoning her work firmly squashed by the excuse she needed a spool of thread to finish Mac's new shirt in time for Sunday services. The children were in school. Ethan, out hunting, had told her not to expect him back before late afternoon. The sunshine filled morning at least was hers, and she was prepared to enjoy it to the brim.

Strolling leisurely, she feasted her eyes upon bright patches of flowers and molten gold leaves and an impudent squirrel, from the safe vantage of a towering oak chittering his annoyance at her intrusion of his territory. She eventually crossed the Mill Creek bridge.

Just past Morey's Furniture Store, a blue velvet bonnet in the millinery shop window caught her eye. Stopping, she deliberately took time to admire it wishfully. And once inside the drygoods store, she wandered among the displays, inspecting, mulling, and rejecting as it suited her fancy. Finally, responsibility, the drooping shouldered keeper of her conscience, stirred, stretched, and prodded her to the notions counter. Purchase completed, she turned and almost mowed down Martha Van Ellis, the young woman left widowed with four small children when her husband died at Bull Run.

The women, having avoided a collision, laughingly greeted each other. Larissa had not seen Martha since Sunday services. Noting how the faint color on her friend's cheeks of that last visit now bloomed in a glow that lit her eyes, she exclaimed with deep sincerity, "You're looking wonderful."

"I'm feeling good. It's taken a while, but I know now everything is really going to be all right."

Impulsively, Larissa hugged her. "I'm so glad."

A deep voice spoke beside them. "Good morning, Mrs. Edwards, Mrs. Van Ellis." Before they turned to the source of the voice, Larissa saw the pink in Martha's cheeks deepen. Reverend Gallaway removed his hat, smiled at Larissa, and turned to Martha. As he did so, a strong suspicion nudged Larissa that the two people standing beside her had, somehow, forgotten her very existence. They turned toward her with his apologies for interrupting their conversation, and her explanation of running into Larissa, very nearly literally, and how they were now catching up on all the news.

Tactfully, Larissa did not let her inward smile surface at their careful casualness, but listened to Reverend Gallaway recount the latest war news. "You know how rumors have been flying about President Lincoln's Emancipation Proclamation?" Martha nodded knowledgeably, and Larissa less so. Because such news did not directly bear on Zane or his activities, she didn't give it much heed. But thanks to Ethan's discussions at the dinner table, she at least knew what the Proclamation involved. She suddenly realized that while she was wool gathering, Reverend Gallaway had continued talking. "... were giving him a rough time that it wasn't a wise move. Way I heard, President Lincoln drew himself up to his full height, stood his ground and told them in that nasal tone, 'I can only trust in God I have made no mistake.' No doubt about it. The man puts a world of meaning into a few words."

Martha touched Larissa's arm. "How is Zane?"

Forcing herself to speak calmly, she related the latest Nebraska Territory news imparted *via* Zane's letters. "Apparently, the Indians attacking the mail and passenger stages have become even more bold and defiant. Lieutenant Colonel Collins, in charge of the troops Zane is with, decided to spread the soldiers along the Oregon Trail, a stretch of almost one hundred forty miles. Colonel Collins has posted men at every stage station between South Pass—that's near the border of Utah Territory—and Upper Platte Bridge. 'Pretty much in the middle of nowhere,' according to Zane." *Becoming quite the geography expert, aren't you?* Her mind, mocking her, sounded uncannily like the chittering squirrel earlier daring her to continue her trespass of his private property.

"With Indians forever plaguing the upper route," she continued hastily, "some brilliant soul decided to make a safer path for the stagecoaches by building a second road south of the Oregon Trail. With telegraph lines already strung along the first trail, the men now have to guard both roads. Those with authority to change the lines to the lower road refuse to do so, and wagon trains going west still use the upper one." She swallowed, trying to rid her throat of the bitterness welling within her at knowledge that, with the stretching thinner of the soldiers' line of defense, Zane was in twice as much danger as before. *Not that he's spelled it out, of course, but he's never been able to evade the truth without giving himself away.* Belatedly, she realized Martha and Reverend Gallaway were waiting for her to tell them more.

"His last news confirmed the men are building a new fort to protect the lower trail. He said they're calling it 'Fort Halleck' for some general named Henry Halleck. I sure hope this general appreciates what's being done for him." Unable to mask her distress, she trailed to a stop.

Taking Larissa's cold hands, Martha squeezed them hard. "I have no words of comfort. I can only say I'm here for you, any time of the day or night. Don't you forget that," she added sternly, enabling Larissa to summon a wavering smile.

Reverend Gallaway put his hand gently on her shoulder. "I'm the one who's supposed to have words of comfort," he said ruefully, "but somehow, I can't think of even one word better to say than what Mar—Mrs. Van Ellis has told you. I'm here for you, too, as pastor and friend."

Thanking them, Larissa sped for the door lest she bawl in front of them. Passing the millinery shop and the blue velvet bonnet without a sideward glance, crossing the little wooden bridge, she finally gained the shelter of the trees and the safety of the road home. She tried to concentrate on Martha Van Ellis's glowing expression when Reverend Gallaway appeared, but failed because the thought that had come to her earlier demanded utterance.

What are a few mailbags compared to the men's lives?

***

The autumn days swished past. Before they knew it, Christmas and

Rose's birthday were once more upon them. On Saturday before the big day, Rose and Charity helped prepare supper. Charity chatted animatedly to Larissa about the spelling match in school the day before, detailing the words, who had spelled what, and who had missed. It was some little time before Larissa noticed Rose's silence.

When Charity paused to taste her cherry pie filling before pouring it into the waiting crust, Larissa took advantage of the break in the descriptive flow. She watched as Rose, dutifully pressing the biscuit cutter into the floured dough, cut the same circle twice. "Rose, is something troubling you?"

The girl started and came back from whatever distant place she had been. She searched for words, then blurted, "Ma, you don't have to celebrate my birthday this year."

She couldn't hide her astonishment. "Why, of course we'll celebrate it. Whatever makes you think we wouldn't?"

Rose ducked her head so that Larissa had difficulty hearing her answer. "I was just thinking. We don't need to celebrate my birthday with presents and cake and everything. I already have the best present anyone could ever give me."

Puzzled as Larissa was, she waited patiently for her daughter to continue. Charity stared as if Rose were speaking a language she'd never heard before. Obviously, she was as much in the dark about this decision as Larissa. "Pa's all safe in winter quarters," Rose explained shyly. "I can't think of a nicer present than that, can you?" Her blue eyes pleaded for her mother's understanding.

Larissa choked and held out her arms. Rose moved on winged feet and buried her head in her mother's flour spattered apron front. When she raised her face, a worried frown puckered her forehead. "Is that all right?"

She touched a streak of flour on her daughter's chin. "Of course it's all right. That's a wonderful present. Pa will be very proud of you for thinking of it."

The pucker disappeared in a smile full of light. "Maybe next year, Pa will be home and we can celebrate together. Wouldn't you like that, Ma?"

This time Larissa's attempt at speech was a total failure. She held her daughter tightly and nodded against the golden brown braids beneath her cheek.

***

Christmas morning dawned cold and snowy. In spite of the family's disbelief she truly meant it, Rose stuck to her decision about not having a birthday celebration. Ethan and Charity, and finally even Mac, asked

Larissa if they were really supposed to ignore such a special day. As Ethan gruffly put it, "It just doesn't seem right."

Larissa, submerging her own disappointment in pride at her daughter's selflessness, understood their disillusionment. "But," she said firmly, "it's Rose's day and her decision. We have to respect that and not lessen what she's giving by acting disapproving." Mac got the general idea. Charity didn't understand very well but came under strict orders from Ethan to go along with Rose.

After much deep thought, Larissa came up with a way to take everyone's feelings into consideration.

Christmas Day afternoon, when they normally would be assisting Rose with innumerable helpful suggestions as she cut her cake, and bickering amiably about who should receive the biggest piece, they gathered quietly in the sitting room and listened to Ethan read *A Christmas Carol*.

Larissa had discovered, quite by accident, that reading this tale was one of the Christmas traditions he and Nettie had observed. She, Charity and Rose were in the sitting room one morning, hemming sheets and talking about, of all things, ghost stories, when Charity lifted her head from her work. "Pa used to read a story to me before we came here. I don't remember so much about it, now, but I know it had ghosts, bunches of them." She shivered. "And a mean old man and a little boy Pa always said was just my age. I sure wish he'd read it again," she finished pensively.

Larissa adroitly questioned Ethan until she learned "the mean old man" was Ebeneezer Scrooge and the little boy "just my age" was Tiny Tim. From there she schemed, and Charity, receiving a book for Christmas, was delighted to find her bunches of ghosts again.

While Ethan read aloud, Larissa slipped into the kitchen and reappeared bearing a thickly frosted cake from which a lone candle gleamed. "Look what I found." She saw the quick delight on the others' faces but concentrated on Rose, whose expression changed from puzzlement to dejected realization.

"Ma," she said in a small voice, "I'm not supposed to get a cake."

Larissa, suddenly torn between tears and laughter, decided she'd better laugh. "I know, but this cake isn't for you." Mac and Ethan stared at her, mirroring Rose's bewilderment. "It's Someone Else's birthday today, too, you remember. And I expect it's been a very long time since anyone made Him a cake. So, since we're not having your birthday, I thought it would be nice to acknowledge His."

Comprehension dawned, and the light that spread across her daughter's face made Larissa rethink her decision to laugh instead of cry. Ethan and Mac, who had not been in on the surprise, cheered. Charity, who had helped plot the Great Plan, grinned joyfully at Larissa.

In her room that night as she made ready for bed, Larissa carefully sorted the memories of that day and breathed a sigh of relief her birthday plan had worked. What if it hadn't? But that thought didn't even bear considering.

She loosed her bun from its confining pins and picked up her brush. Wandering to the window, she stood gazing out at the stillness of the night as she absently ran the bristles through her hair. The snow had stopped earlier and now a moon not yet to the first quarter cast its glow over the unbroken whiteness. Finally, she picked up Zane's letter.

"Dear Family,

"It seems strange, writing a Christmas letter in October. There is a notable lack of vegetation here, and so not many leaves or bushes to signal whether Mr. J. Frost has had his paint pots out. But I close my eyes and instantly picture the maples and oaks at home in all their before-winter glory.

"Lieutenant Colonel Collins warned us that although winter has not yet set in, when it comes, it will be with a vengeance. He strongly suggested that if we intended to send Christmas thoughts to our loved ones, we'd better do it now. Once the snow begins, mail travel will become extremely slow and totally uncertain (as if it isn't, now.)

"Hence, this 'Merry Christmas' to each of you, Ethan and Miss Charity included, of course, as I lounge beneath the lone scrub oak constituting foliage as far as the eye can see in any direction. But what a scrub oak. A veritable prince of its kind as bronze leaves rustle over my head and an occasional one drops *on* my head.

"The squabbling with the Indians goes apace. They harass us when we leave the fort for water or fuel or if a detail goes out on patrol. We then pursue them for miles. When we finally give up and turn fortward, empty handed and disgusted over our failure, they reappear and chase us back to within site of the fort. They're always careful to stay just out of rifle range of those soldiers awaiting our return. Thus it goes, day after day. Lieutenant Colonel Collins says this is our daily agenda until the cold and snow chill the Indians' spirits enough to keep them in their camps. Enough about all the fun I'm having. I certainly don't want to make you jealous!

"Since my last writing, another company of soldiers arrived from Ohio, with more to follow or so we're told. These men are to merge with us, and according to Obadiah's news sniffing nose, we will all become the 11th Ohio Volunteer Cavalry Regiment.

"I am now acquainted with two of the new fellows, Ben Clayton and Steve Jamison. Being friends, they signed up together in Marietta. Ben and his wife Anne have two young sons. He seems a likable sort. Steve's wife is named Amanda. Their son is just a few months old. Ben worked loading freight on the docks in Marietta before he signed up and got volunteered to this end of the world. His dream is to own a cattle ranch some day, be his own boss and not have to answer to anyone (except his wife, of course!) Steve doesn't say much. Ben talks enough for both of them and even gets a kick out of Obadiah. Never thought I'd see another man who could out-talk Obadiah, but Ben sure gives him a run for his money. Works out great for Steve and me. They talk, we snooze, and we're all in fine fettle.

"The enclosed page is my Christmas present to all of you. Anything even resembling a Christmas gift is scarcer around here than your peach pie, Rissa. A fellow from Company C was singing the other night, and when I heard him, right away I thought of you. I asked him the words afterward and wrote them all down as he said them. I'm sorry I can't include the tune in this letter, but I have to admit, it would make rather difficult sending. Maybe someday they'll invent a contraption to let you hear music coming from all the way across the country, while you're right in your own sitting room. Wouldn't that be something?

"Anyway, I hope these words will give you a sense of what I'm trying to say. Each of you is in my thoughts and heart, now and always.

"Your loving Husband and Father,

"Zane Edwards."

With trembling fingers, Larissa carefully unfolded the accompanying sheet of paper.

Words and Music by Mr. Stephen Foster
Jeanie with the Light Brown Hair
I dream of Jeanie with the light brown hair,
Borne, like a vapor, on the summer air;
I see her tripping where the bright streams play,
Happy as the daisies that dance on her way....
Oh! I dream of Jeanie with the light brown hair,
Floating, like a vapor, on the soft summer air.

I long for Jeanie with the day-dawn smile,
Radiant in gladness, warm with winning guile;
I hear her melodies like joys gone by,
Sighing round my heart o'er the fond hopes that die.
Oh! I dream of Jeanie with the light brown hair,
Floating, like a vapor, on the soft summer air.

A long time she sat and gazed at the words that gave her so much more than just a sense of what he was trying to say.

***

Zane wrote cheerfully to Larissa, filling her in on the amusing and ordinary, frustrating and unexpected day-to-day details about life in a frontier fort constantly under Indian surveillance. What he did not tell her was how, in the vast loneliness of the windswept plains, a man became insignificant. He didn't often feel small. He found it a strange sensation, not unlike standing at the barn door with darkness brushing softly around him and looking up to see a million stars glittering. At such times he acknowledged that, for all his size and strength, he fit as a mere fragment into the greater whole.

He wrote of the monotonous meals, "a diet of beans, potatoes, salt pork and bacon." He didn't mention that the monotony sprang from the fact that the fort might receive a generous shipment of potatoes but little else, so for weeks on end the men ate potatoes for breakfast, dinner and supper. The next shipment might consist solely of dried beans, so that by the time barrels of salt pork arrived, the men swore they'd never again willingly look a bowl of dried bean soup in the face. Hunting forays produced pronghorn, prairie chickens, and buffalo, but divided among so many men, such welcome fare, even the mammoth buffalo, vanished faster than ice in July.

He recounted Colonel Collins' and General James Craig's "revolving wheel" system of guarding the stage stations.

"Each of the men serves a week in one of the stage stations now dotting the plains with an ugly infestation of civilization. Ten to twenty men are deployed at the larger, home stations. The smaller stations make do with three to four soldiers. At week's end, each garrison moves to the next station in line for a week's guard duty there, while the former occupants take over the station ahead. Thus leapfrogging, eventually serving at all the outpost stations, we return to the fort and routine duties until the turning wheel draws us in line once again."

The four home stations boasted such refinements as a telegraph, crude eating and sleeping accommodations for travelers, a corral and horse barn. Duty in these stations was not so isolated or tedious as in the smaller posts, which generally consisted of one room and a rough shelter for the animals. The Indians, discovering fewer men guarding the smaller stations, quickly took advantage. Those less protected outposts suffered almost daily harassment, leaving the men on edge and inclined to be irritable.

Winter blasted down with a vengeance, just as Colonel Collins had warned. The Ohioans, certain they knew what a cold winter was, found themselves in the midst of icy winds that whirled and howled. Snowstorm upon snowstorm dumped down on them, isolating the men in the outpost stations more effectively than a deadly ring of arrows and rifles.

Just when the suffering soldiers thought things couldn't get worse, Nature and Lady Luck stepped in. Early in the new year of 1863, Ute and Shoshoni raiding parties increased their harassment of the beleaguered troopers. The main object, aside from pure devilment, was stealing as many horses as possible. Unfortunately, they proved themselves highly competent at the task.

Following roll call on a bitter cold morning in February, Colonel Collins, backed by Captain Norton, regarded the assembled men. As usual, he didn't mince words. "I need forty-four men to reinforce Fort Halleck just as soon as we can get there. We all know that getting there is going to be damned hard. It's been fifteen minutes since the last blizzard, so we're due for another one." The men shifted, bit their chapped lips and stiffened their shoulders to forestall any unmilitary chuckles of agreement that might land them in the guardhouse.

Collins eyed them speculatively. "Since this isn't a routine patrol, I'm asking for volunteers to come forward before I start naming names. Any man willing to tackle this assignment, step up now."

With the announcement, the men's laughter stilled. One or two troopers strode forward, and a few more followed. Zane looked at Obadiah who, tongue-tied for once in his life, simply nodded. Turning, he found Ben and Steve regarding him intently. As Obadiah had, Zane tipped his head. The decision made, Ben observed wryly, "Looks like we better get ourselves up there right quick and get this snake skinned. The way those idiots are pilin' 'round Collins, he'll have his forty-four all picked, and we'll be left out of the fun."

As they approached the colonel, Collins barked, "You four, stand over there."

Wondering uneasily what they'd done to merit singling out, they watched as Collins dispatched the other volunteers. Obadiah muttered out the side of his mouth, "Whose bright idea was this volunteering business, anyway?"

"Yours!" the other three hissed in unison, so that, for the moment at least, Obadiah was vanquished.

Finally, Captain Norton strode over to them. "Colonel Collins needs six men to accompany him personally on this mission. I suggested that you be four of them. I don't know Clayton and Jamison so well, but I know Edwards, and—" a weary sigh escaped him "—you, Beldane. I've noticed that, most times, a man tends to keep friends of a caliber similar to his own. That's why I'm putting my money on you four."

"Permission to speak, sir," Steve Jamison put in. "The colonel said six men."

"Trooper Kenney will be joining you. I'm the sixth one."

Keeping his face carefully bland, Zane nevertheless felt large relief.

Provisioned and assembled, the forty-four started toward Fort Halleck under the command of Major John O'Farrell, followed shortly after by Collins and his six troopers. Bitter cold as it was, they pushed forward and shortly caught up with the larger force. They saw no Indians or even a hint of one, so that distinct uneasiness nudged Zane. During his tenure in this godforsaken sea of grass and snow, he had noticed the men's hair was more likely to stay attached to their heads if they knew the whereabouts of their foes. He considered such knowledge infinitely preferable to wondering if the patrol would be attacked, in spite of the army scouts' vigilance, at the next hump in the road. With every man covertly and constantly scouring the terrain, the question hung large, and pounded with the crunch of packmule and horse hooves on snow. *Why don't the critters show themselves?*

They were not left wondering long.

The pewter sky hulked ever more sullen. A sharp breeze flitted across the plains. With a sudden howl, the wind leaped from the north, nearly blowing them off their saddles. On the heels of that blast came such a mass of snow that, within seconds, they could not see the gloves gripping their reins. Only the horses' instincts kept them moving forward. Seeming to take hours, in reality only minutes, the gale force assault finally eased a bit, permitting the officers to put their heads together to confer. The troops, ordered to dismount, stomped around to keep their blood flowing while the higher ups discussed the men's future existence. Obadiah took advantage of the occasion to mutter, "Least now we know why we ain't seen none of them wily fellas. They was smart enough to know this storm was comin' and to keep to home all nice and cozy in front of a cracklin' fire."

Ben groaned. "Don't mention fire. Bet I could get a part as an icicle in one of those play-acting theaters, and no one could tell the difference between me and a real one."

Decision reached, officers and men pressed on toward Fort Halleck. With maddening slowness, the animals' hooves bit off the white, frozen miles. All at once a shout sounded from the rear. Turning, Zane saw two soldiers sliding from their saddles, the nearest men grabbing hold before they hit the ground. A struggle ensued as the horses of the rescuers, nervous enough with the storm, shied at the sudden extra weight. For a long moment, the scene was one of grabbing men, backing mounts, shifting snow, and imaginative curses before the troopers were eased to the ground and the horses steadied.

It rapidly became apparent the two soldiers were too frozen to travel farther. After another quick huddle, the officers decreed Major O'Farrell should continue to the fort with the other troopers, while Colonel Collins stayed behind with the ailing ones. Captain Norton surveyed the knot of men awaiting orders and beckoned to Zane. Puzzled, he angled his way to the front of the cluster. "Trooper Edwards, Colonel Collins needs someone to stay with him to help tend those men. He requested you."

Puzzlement turned to astonishment even as he responded automatically. "Yessir."

After another quick talk fest among the three officers, Major O'Farrell and Colonel Collins stood back and watched solemnly as, once again, Captain Norton approached Zane. "We need you to make a decision. Army style, we can tell you what to do. As men, we feel you should have some choice in this particular matter. Colonel Collins is in charge here. Being straight up Army, he has official rules and regulations to guide him. But you—" His words broke off.

Zane, bewildered, waited for him to continue.

"Should we take your horses with us?"

An immediate, resounding "No!" exploded in Zane's head. He stared in astonishment that the officers could even dream up such an idiotic question. If the patrol took the animals, it would literally be a case of abandoning to the elements the four men remaining behind. But if the horses stayed, they would freeze to death out in the open, if they didn't run off first in search of shelter. Staying with the men, the animals' chances for survival were nil.

As he awaited Zane's decision, nothing in Captain Norton's face hinted at his personal feelings. Zane swallowed hard. Horses were his life's work. He couldn't deliberately subject them to a cruel death. Especially when they were of no use to the men staying behind. But for the troop to take their only possible means of escape—"Take 'em."

Captain Norton nodded with soldierly bearing, but his eyes showed deep sympathy. "I wanted to be the one to ask you," he said quietly. "I'll tell the others."

Colonel Collins and Zane watched the storm swallow the larger patrol, then set about trying to thaw out the two troopers without, in the process, becoming chunks of ice themselves. It proved very nearly impossible. Gusting wind and driving snow thwarted all their efforts to make and keep a fire going. Neither was a snow cave successful. The wind that caused huge drifts to pile up, just as swiftly blew them into nothing. At that point, they had one all or nothing chance of saving the stricken men and giving some odds to their own survival. The alternative was, after all, not particularly appealing.

They took the one road left open.

CHAPTER TWENTY-ONE

As soon as the storm blew itself out, a search party set out from the fort. Steve, Obadiah, and Ben insisted on joining the patrol, Obadiah warning flat out they'd mutiny or whatever it was soldiers did, unless they received permission to join the rescue effort.

The horses plodded across empty miles of glaring snow before the patrol reached the spot they'd left the men, only to be greeted with the same white expanse in all directions. "This is the spot, capt'n," Obadiah insisted.

Norton paced his horse in a widening circle. "Hope they didn't cut and run," he muttered. "They'd sure not get far."

The drift between Ben and Steve erupted as a snowy wraith clutching a flapping blanket surged upward and came to earth under the nose of Obadiah's justifiably startled horse. Esau shied so wildly he almost dumped his rider into Norton's lap.

"God in Heaven, you're alive!" Plunging into the swimming-deep snow, Ben and Steve grabbed Zane's arms as, blinking in the sunlight, he sagged to his knees.

"Collins?" Zane yelled. Wrenching his arms free, he began digging frantically at the snow hole he'd just abandoned. Scooping at top speed, the men reached the colonel and dragged him out. When he tried to stand, however, his lower body gave way. Laurenz, the post doctor, began a hasty examination as the troopers uncovered the other men.

"Laurenz!" At the urgency in O'Farrell's voice, the doctor whirled. One of the freed men was chattering with cold and Laurenz gave spitfire instructions even as he bent over the second man. Ear to the trooper's chest, he listened a long moment, then, shaking his head, slowly straightened.

At the doctor's verdict, Zane clenched his fists, guilt engulfing him. He had no time, however, to argue with himself that he should have done more. The doctor speedily loaded the survivors, including Zane, into the post ambulance, Zane protesting he could just as well sit a saddle. No one listened.

Jolting along, Laurenz questioned Collins, but could come to no conclusion except that he was suffering a paralysis of the lower limbs, apparently brought on by the intense cold. Whether he would recover, the doctor wasn't saying.

Over all Zane's protests he was fine and didn't need medical assistance, he, Collins, and Trooper Hewson were unceremoniously settled in the post hospital under strict orders to stay there until the doctor released them.

With Collins suffering intensely in the next bed as his lower body slowly awoke, Zane explained how, all other options exhausted, they had spread their ground sheets on the snow beneath the sick men. Collins on one side, Zane on the other, they had huddled close, covered all four of them, heads included, with their bedroll blankets and let the snow drift over them like a huge quilt. This, they'd hoped, would generate enough body warmth to keep them from freezing. Working to keep an airhole open took so much effort they'd lost track of time.

Grim as the cold was, Zane and Collins had known another, more deadly enemy stalked them. To stave off the sleep that kept enticing them to close their eyes for just one second, they talked of their lives before the war and their hopes for when it should finally be over. "The snow started vibrating around us. Took a minute to figure out it was horses coming. That's when I jumped up."

"Jumped up?" Obadiah hooted. "You came busting out of the snow like Lazarus comin' back from the dead and scared all of us into foaming fits. Don't ever do that again, you hear? And you sure ought to know better'n to go spookin' a man's horse like that. Now Esau's jumpier'n a jackrabbit on a hot griddle. I don't know as he'll ever settle down."

Zane grinned. The deeper Obadiah's emotion, the more cantankerous he became. Without doubt, he was at the moment crabbier than a grizzly bear just discovering his favorite honey tree is empty.

Out of consideration for his genuinely ill patients, and probably longing for peace and quiet, the doctor finally surrendered to Zane's railing and released him from the hospital. Obadiah drew guard duty that evening, but Steve and Ben discussed the unpredictable fate that allowed three men to live and one to die. Zane, having talked more that day than the rest of his life put together, said little.

"All this," Steve ventured, "it's made me think." He withdrew a gold pocket watch from his blouse. "My wife Amanda gave me this when we got married. She said the only excuse she'll stand for me letting it out of my sight is when I pass it on to our son some day. Matt was such a small piece of humankind when I left, it's hard to imagine him grown up and wearing my watch." He grinned, shamefaced at showing such emotion, then sobered. "If something happens, I'd like Ammie to know I kept this watch with me, just like I promised."

Ben reacted first. "I expect you're right. I sure wouldn't want Anne wonderin' about me. Tell you what. Anythin' comes up, I'll go tell Amanda myself and deliver the watch to her. You have my word."

Steve looked enormously relieved. "Same here. Anything you need done, I'll see to it."

Ben's glance swung to Zane. "That goes for you and your family, too." His voice held none of his usual bluster. "We'll get word to your wife, same as if it was Steve or me."

Zane smoothed the gold coin between his thumb and finger before holding up the pendant. "I'd like Larissa to get this. It'd mean an awful lot to her, and me."

"If it becomes necessary, consider it done."

Lying on his bunk a little later, Zane once more touched the coin. When describing their adventure earlier, he had admitted he and Collins talked in order to keep awake. He had seen no reason to inform his attentive audience that Collins had confessed he'd never been married, "except to the Army," as he put it, and that he wondered sometimes if maybe that wasn't a mistake. Zane didn't feel it any more necessary to admit that Larissa's gold-coin pendant, clutched in his fist, had been the only reality to tell him he must stay alive.

Unaware of events unfolding at home, he felt only deep gratitude that total catastrophe had been averted. He fervently hoped that such a situation should never again befall the men risking their lives that others might travel in safety and sleep comfortably at night.

***

Equally unaware of his father's brush with death, Mac was nonetheless worried. He had been uneasy for several weeks, debating how to discuss his observations with Doc Rawley. Remembering those early days and the older man's insistence his pupil talk over any troublesome matters, he'd faithfully followed orders. Up to now, anyway. But how could he tell Doc of his deep concern when it was Doc himself who was causing his fretting?

Nearly a month, now, off and on, Doc had been acting peculiar. For long periods, he stood at his office window staring out into the street and, Mac suspected, not seeing a thing. Sometimes Mac spoke two or three times before he gave a start, then answered as if returning from a distant dreamland.

At least his medical work didn't suffer any. Covertly observing, Mac found nothing to fault. He was, if anything, more meticulous than ever in caring for his patients, but he had started giving his pupil much more responsibility for checking out ailments and prescribing appropriate remedies. The last few days, he appeared to be in another world completely, except when he was with a patient. He had made no mention for at least three weeks of Mac's going to the University. And he had lost his grouchiness. He hadn't growled about any of the procedures he thought Mac should do more carefully or more efficiently.

Is Doc sick? If he is, why doesn't he talk about it? A chill tickled bony fingers down Mac's spine. *Is he dying?*

Mac spent a restless night kicking off his covers and pulling them back up. The preceding day in the office had been particularly unnerving. Doc had hunched over the desk, going through his journals and checking the information he had accumulated about each patient. Every few minutes, he mumbled to himself. Doc never mumbled. He was a firm, vocal believer in the notion if a body had something to say, he should speak loud and clear and no nonsense about it.

At the worktable, Mac had finished rolling pills and begun mixing cough syrup and sealing it in the bottles he had earlier washed, a chore he'd completed many times. In spite of all his practice, Doc always stood at his elbow making sure he was proceeding correctly. That morning, he bet Doc had forgotten not only his pupil's task, but also his presence.

When Doc emitted a particularly loud, "It will too work!" Mac jumped, almost dropping the bottle of syrup he was stoppering. He had turned, determined to speak, but Doc put that journal down and reached for another. This attitude had worsened through the day. By the time Mac left that evening, alarm bells were jangling all through him.

He wished fiercely he could talk to Pa, who would whittle this problem down to size in no time flat. Pa would understand he couldn't betray Doc without at least speaking to him first. But what could he say? *Hey, Doc, you going crazy?* Thus, his blanket tossing session through much of the night.

At breakfast he felt Ma's and Mr. Michaels' eyes upon him but concentrated diligently on emptying his oatmeal bowl. Her deep worry plain, Larissa reached her hand to him as he passed her chair on the way out. "Mac." He stopped obediently. "Remember, son, if you need to talk, you can come to me and be absolutely certain it will go no further."

He almost blabbed out his problem, but some instinct reminded him sharply to talk to Doc first. "I've been doing some figuring, Ma. I just hope it works." She caught his hand and held it tightly. He patted her shoulder awkwardly because she was his Ma and not just any old patient.

On the walk to town, he was glad he'd kept his worry to himself. Much as something pulled at him to speak, he still owed his first duty to Doc. Sometime toward morning of this past restless night, he had come to a decision. He fell asleep, then, and waking had not changed his resolve. His hand shook a little as he pushed open the office door, but he ignored both that and the sudden dryness in his throat.

Doc was still hunched over his journals, but he had recently made coffee. A fragrantly steaming cup sat at his elbow. He looked around at sound of the door opening, and his brows drew together in surprised questioning as Mac walked directly to him instead of pausing to hang up his coat and cap. "Doc, I need to talk to you."

The perplexity deepened at his pupil's seriousness, but he asked mildly enough, "What's troubling you?"

The dozen ways Mac had rehearsed the words fled like a fox pursued by yapping hounds, and he burst out, "I'm really worried about someone, and I don't know what to do about it."

"We don't have anyone sick enough right now who's cause for that much fretting. Who is it?"

His dry throat refused to work for a moment before he pushed the words out. "It's not a patient, Doc. It's you." Such enormous relief flooded him at finally having the truth out that his legs nearly gave way.

Astonishment swept away Doc's puzzlement. "Me? Whatever on earth for?"

Now started, Mac knew he'd better have a concise reason, and fast. "You've been acting different for three or four weeks now. Not at all the way you usually do."

"How 'different'?" Doc's tone was quiet and level.

At least he didn't blow his stack. Mac, taking that for a good sign, nevertheless chose his words carefully as he specified his observations. After the first few words, he felt as though they were discussing a patient's ailments, as they had so many times before. Doc listened intently. Only once his face registered consternation that was quickly gone. Finished, Mac braced for doom to swoop.

Doc eyed him keenly. "There's more, isn't there?"

The boy stiffened, now at a loss for words.

"Spit it out, Mac. Won't heal festering inside you."

"That's just it," he said miserably.

"What's 'just it'?"

He studied the floor, the books on the wall shelf, everything but Doc's face. "You've been calling me Mac. You don't call me Boy anymore."

Doc was silent for so long Mac finally took a chance and nervously turned his head to see what he was doing. He wasn't doing a thing but staring at his student in baffled amazement. Even as Mac studied him for signs of anger, a twinkle began to build in Doc's eyes. "Shed your jacket and cap and sit down. You are entirely right about it being past time for us to talk."

He slid into the other chair. "You're not mad?"

"No, I'm not mad, I assure you. I just keep forgetting how perceptive you are about other people's feelings. This ought to teach me to remember, if nothing else does."

He relaxed. If Doc wasn't angry, then whatever he had to say couldn't be so bad.

"You're right. I have been chewing something over for a spell now. I neglected to take the very advice I'm always hammering at you. Talk a problem out, then we'll figure how to go about solving it. I've been debating with myself the pros and cons of a certain action I may take. Every time I make up my mind for positive, negative comes along and throws a few more rocks in the bucket and splashes cold water on my decision. Mainly because I'm not the only one who'll be affected by it. You will be, too."

The questioning in Mac's eyes grew larger.

"I'm thinking about joining the Army."

Mac felt as though one of Doc's rocks had smacked him in the stomach. The breath whooshed out of his lungs and he couldn't seem to draw any back in. Doc waited patiently as he struggled to regain control. Finally he blurted, "Why?" and couldn't keep the panic from his voice.

Doc lifted his hands, the hands that had brought healing and peace to countless hurting bodies and souls, and let them drop into his lap. "You might not believe this, but that's one of the questions I've been wrestling with most. *Why?* I have a good practice with a lot of years of hard work backing it. I'd be leaving people who depend on me to see them through their miserable times. And leaving for what? A chance to slog along wet, muddy, dirty roads in rain or dust or snow so I can patch up men who, when they're well enough, will go right back to being cannon fodder.

"You don't have to tell me what a fool I am. I've told myself that enough times these past weeks. But," his voice softened, "our men, their men, are out there dying. They're dying needlessly because there's no doctor to help them live. If I can save even a small portion of those husbands and brothers and sons, on both sides of this war, then maybe I can feel I've done a tad to help straighten out this mess."

"But if you leave," Mac said in a small voice, "the people here won't have a doctor when they need one."

Doc's mouth twitched beneath his beard. "They will so."

"Who?"

"You." He calmly dropped his boulder in the bucket and sat back to watch the ensuing splash.

"Me?" The word came out a high pitched squeak.

"Yes, you. Why not?"

"I'm not a doctor. I've never done a thing without you watching and correcting me."

"Everyone has to start sometime. Actually, you started a long time ago. You've just never realized it."

Mac's brain reeled. "But I don't know enough."

Doc was unmoved by this logical rebuttal. "If I go and you don't take my place, there are sure to be folks who will die when you could have saved them. Give yourself some credit. You know a lot more than some so-called doctors do. Remember, I've taught you. I know what you can do."

"But what if I treat someone and they die anyway?"

"We've talked about that before, remember? Most will live, because we've helped them. Some will die no matter what you or me or anyone else does to try to save them. Those are the facts of the job. We can't stop helping the other ninety-nine people who come to us for assistance just because we couldn't save the one."

"What if people won't let me treat them because you're not there?"

"We can't make other people's choices. You can help with their illness or not. They can choose to let you help or not. The decision is theirs and we have to abide by it. I do know this." Doc's voice held unmistakable pride. "Folks around here are accepting the fact that you treat them. True, there was more'n a bit of skepticism in the beginning. That'd only be natural, young like you were. But the only comments I've heard for a long time are positive ones. They recognize your ability and aren't bashful about admitting it."

Doc's encouraging words did nothing to lessen Mac's panic. "If you go, when will it be?"

"Not today or tomorrow, for sure. I'd need time to wind up matters here. Also, I presume the big bugs have to agree to taking me on. It's entirely possible they won't want me."

Mac said surely, "They'll want you, Doc."

"Thanks for the voice of confidence, Boy."

Mac raised startled eyes and Doc gave a rusty laugh. "Guess I better start watching my language around you. I swear, you notice everything. Now you better get to mixing and fixing those medicines over there. And take care. Just because I'm not breathing down your neck doesn't mean I don't know every move you're making." Mac believed him.

He reached home that night with a bagful of mixed emotions. His first gladness was knowledge Doc wasn't dying. Or angry, either. He'd said at Mac's departure, "When I told you to observe and speak up if you felt something was out of kilter, I sure didn't mean me."

Relieved as he was on those two scores, full realization of Doc's expectations was sinking in. *How can I ever hope to fill Doc's shoes?* Disgust over feeling so young and uncertain, when he should be thrilled at the turn of events, made his feet drag as he entered the warm, candlelit kitchen where everyone was at the table.

"Mac, get washed and sit down. I'll have your supper in just a minute." Larissa, already rising from her place, glimpsed his expression. "Is it the same problem you had this morning?" she asked softly.

"Kind of, but not exactly."

At this cryptic response, she looked at Ethan, who was regarding him gravely. He shook his head and she picked up Mac's plate. Ethan cleared his throat. "Rough day?"

"Sort of. I guess I need to talk to you, Ma." Her fingers curled around the edge of the plate as if she were in sudden danger of dropping it.

Mac had already decided not to mention Doc's absentmindedness. He wasn't sure if it came under Hippocratic confidentiality, but decided not to risk it since the problem was solved. As he ate, he worked out what he would say, so he wouldn't flap around like a squawking hen with a new egg. "Doc and I talked today. He's thinking about joining the Army." Larissa gasped and Ethan's hands clenched his coffee cup. "He says there's a huge shortage of medical men, especially qualified ones."

"But at his age?"

"He probably considers it his duty," Ethan said slowly. "Especially if he can help in a positive way. I for one understand that." Larissa looked up at the odd note in his voice. His face held pain and faint but definite guilt.

As she started to speak, Mac said hesitantly, "There's more." He drew a deep breath. "He wants me to take over his practice while he's gone."

Total silence followed this revelation as Larissa and Ethan absorbed his words. Then, "Mac," she whispered. He saw plainly the incredulity in their faces, but searching carefully, detected no sign of scorn.

"He asked you to do this?" Ethan attempted to make sense of the astounding announcement.

"Yes, sir. People here will still need a doctor. Doc says sickness and birth go on, no matter what."

"What are your feelings, Mac?" The fleeting uncertainty on his face told Larissa she'd hit the nail on the head.

"It scares the socks off me," he blurted and immediately turned blazing red. "I don't know if I can do it all alone."

"Doc wouldn't suggest it if he had doubts," Ethan put in quietly. "It's obvious he has faith in you."

Mac still looked dazed.

"In ordinary times, you wouldn't be called on for something like this. But these aren't ordinary times by any stretch of the imagination. We're all having to do things we never dreamed we'd come up against."

"We aren't telling you what to do, Mac. We just want you to know that, whatever decision you make, we'll stand behind you."

Larissa looked to Ethan and the girls for confirmation and was answered by a chorus of, "Yes!"

He still looked unsure, but managed a wry smile. "Just do me a favor and don't any of you get sick. I'd sure feel strange, treating my own family."

CHAPTER TWENTY-TWO

Zane leaned against Stage Station Four's doorframe, sunlight touching Larissa's letter that he was reading for the third time since it had arrived that morning.

"Doc Rawley insists Mac is capable of handling the day to day crises a doctor confronts. He identifies fevers, prescribes instructions for care, splints broken limbs, and, should the occasion arise, can deliver a baby. Let's pray the last occasion doesn't come about any time soon! I questioned Doc about Mac's uncertainty over making correct decisions. Doc said he'd rather see him somewhat uncertain than too bigheaded, but that Mac must understand the importance of presenting an assured manner to his patients. If he does, the patient feels reassured. If he appears hesitant or timid, the patient invariably picks up on it and mirrors that attitude.

"Doc said he's discussed this with Doctor Ingemar over in Delaware County. Doctor Ingemar promised he'll be available should any situation arise Mac can't handle. After all, Mac'll relieve his burden by treating patients here, so he won't need to practice over two counties. Apparently, he's heard how Mac 'tends to folks' aches and pains and does a square job for all he is kind of young' and he's curious to meet him. Mac was distinctly relieved to learn a real doctor will back him up. I'm careful not to discourage him, but you'll understand completely if I say I can't blame him for feeling relieved about another doctor to talk to.

"Tomorrow is exactly two years since you left. Perhaps next year —"

"Edwards." At the shouting of his name, Zane raised his eyes from Larissa's handwriting. "Stage is coming."

Folding the letter, he stuck it inside his blouse and gripped his rifle. The routine was well set. They'd cleared the grass in a wide sweep around the station, and lookouts kept unbroken vigilance. When a stage arrived, all the troopers took positions where they could see across the horizon. Stagecoaches, sitting idle while teams were changed and food handed out, proved an irresistible temptation to marauding warriors, who would attack as much for the sport of it as for anything of value. A horse, naturally, they considered of value.

Rifle in the crook of his arm, Zane descended the porch steps, lifted a hand to the hostler bringing up the fresh team, and rounded the southeast corner of the station. Passing the log breastworks from behind which Obadiah had already taken up a firing position, they spoke over the clatter of the stage approaching from the east. Today, Zane was assigned the rear, north side of the building with an unlimited view of the plains. Ben covered the west wall and Steve the front.

The stage swept in with rattling trace chains and creaking leather. Halting the team, the driver clambered down, muttering about his "blamed stiffness." The shotgun retained his position, high up with a good view of the countryside. The driver opened the door and assisted three young women out, their husbands following. They reached the porch and the shotgun called, "All clear up here." He slammed forward off the seat and thumped to the ground, the shaft of an arrow protruding from his spine.

The driver shoved the women through the station doorway. "On the floor. Keep down!" Their husbands dove for cover as an arrow spranged into the door beside them.

"Indians! East quarter, eight and counting."

Zane, hearing the cry, ran to the northeast corner where the building's protruding logs gave cover. Shots sounded from the front as the Indians bore down on the station. Obadiah, from his position behind the breastworks, began firing and reloading, steadily but carefully. Zane drew a bead on the warrior fronting the pack, led him a bit, and fired. The Indian hit the ground like a sack of grain. Zane heard Obadiah's cheer but concentrated on tearing open a fresh paper cartridge with his teeth, pouring powder down the rifle barrel of the single-shot musket and pushing in a new bullet with his thumb. Dust and smoke, rising and mingling, made seeing a foot ahead impossible. He reached for his ramrod. Obadiah cursed and fired, then groaned.

"Obadiah?" Zane yelled.

He heard a faint, answering call. "I'm hit ... leg ..."

Keeping low, moving carefully against the east wall in the billowing gray cloud, Zane edged toward the barricade. The fighting had shifted to the southwest area and the smoke-dust haze lifted enough to reveal Obadiah sprawled behind the breastworks, its logs sprouting arrow quills like a miffed porcupine. Less than a dozen strides off, an Indian, face to the dirt, lay slack. Still edging forward cautiously, Zane reached the barrier and hunkered down as Obadiah, cursing, yanked an arrow from his thigh, snapped the shaft in two and, with another colorful epithet, flung it as far as he could.

"How bad is it?"

"I ain't the star guest at a turkey shoot yet, but he sure tried to make me one. 'Least I got him before he disattached my hair." Pain creased his voice. A steady scarlet trickle from the deep hole in his thigh stained his pants and pooled on the ground. Using Obadiah's bandana to try to staunch the flow of blood, Zane pulled out his own cloth and bound it tightly above the wound.

"You've got to get back around the corner. Think you can hang onto me?"

"I reckon I'll make certain to," Obadiah gritted. "I'm sure as sin not going to stay here and let them two-legged polecats use me for target practice."

Rifle in right hand, Zane reached his left arm to help Obadiah stand. Steadying him as best he could, watching for suspicious movement, they drew back around the northeast corner. The smokescreen was not quite so heavy here, and he eased the injured man to the ground. They jerked their heads up as a burst of gunfire and a hoarse scream sounded from around the west wall. Zane's heart plunged. *Steve and Ben.* "Obadiah, can you cover this corner?"

Obadiah gave him a rough shove. "Get goin' already. I'll keep watch here."

Zane put his hand on his friend's shoulder. "I'll be back quick as I can." He turned west, sprinted along the wall.

"Zane!" At Obadiah's shout, he whipped around. Saw three warriors, bows at the ready, slide around the northeast corner.

He started back. Saw Obadiah's rifle lifting. Saw smoke spurt from the barrel and the leader pitch to the dirt. Was already swinging his own rifle to bear. Steadied the sights on the fringed, beaded vest below a fierce, black-paint-striped face filled with hate and triumph. *Ease the trigger back, now.* The Indian slumped, face sliding below vision range. Zane reached for a paper cartridge to begin reloading and searing flame engulfed his chest.

The sun-bright day ... so black, now ... pain ... crushing ... like Obadiah'd dropped a hot anvil on him....

In that instant, he was no longer in the din and terror of battle, but standing in his newly sprouted cornfield with all the familiar farm sounds and odors around him, the early summer breeze fanning pleasantly against the back of his neck.

Standing on the good, rich earth of his young-growing cornfield, he reached to touch Larissa's light brown hair. As he cupped his palm gently against her cheek, the lilting tune drifted to him on the summer breeze.

"I dream of Jeanie with the light brown hair ..."

The love and trust in Larissa's eyes brought such a lump to his throat that he couldn't speak. Faintly, as from a great distance, the melody came to him.

"Sighing round my heart like the fond hopes that die...."

And was gone.

***

When the battle was over, Ben and Steve, hunting the missing men, found Obadiah bending over Zane, unashamed of the tears tracking down his dirt-stained cheeks.

***

Larissa, hanging out her just washed sheets on a bright morning early in May, stepped back to admire their pristine whiteness. A pillowcase, billowing in the sharpening breeze, promptly slapped her in the face. Untangling herself from the cold, clammy material, she heard Ethan call as he strode from the barn. His thundercloud expression startled her. "Ethan?"

Hearing her sharp anxiety, he silently berated himself for his unthinking action. It took so little these days to worry her. "Nothing important," he assured her quickly. "I planned to finish up the west field this morning while the good weather's holding, but I need to go to town."

She tilted her face to the brilliantly blue sky. "Do you think it'll rain? I hoped to give the sheets a little extra sunning time today."

"Can't say for positive, but this makes three clear days in a row. It can't hold forever."

"What do you need in town?"

His annoyance returned. "I've spent all morning digging out that oak stump in the north field. I put the oxen to pulling it, but the chain snapped. I tried to fix it, but no luck. Too many of the links are mangled. I'll have to go to town, get it straightened and welded properly."

"How ever did that happen?"

His annoyance became disgust, and obvious unwillingness to answer. "I fastened the chain around the stump and started the oxen pulling." His reluctance increased, and so did her curiosity. "I didn't see a bee land on Buck's backside and I slapped him on the hindquarters with the lines to get him moving."

Her sudden horrible suspicion of his next words caused a treacherous shiver of laughter to fizz up. He shuffled his feet. "Well, I whacked him on his rear and smacked right down on the bee, who didn't take kindly to that at all. He stung Buck, who jumped and bolted, dragging Bob with him. Next thing I knew, the oxen were tearing across the field with the stump bounding after them. They'd pulled it right out of the ground. But it kept bouncing against the chain. The stump and the chain got tangled. I took off after all of them and thought I'd never get them halted. The stump finally got wedged between two boulders down by the creek and Buck and Bob had to stop." At this point, he had to stop too. Larissa, hand over mouth, was emitting a series of choked squeaks and her shoulders were shaking so hard she could barely stand.

He stared at her indignantly as she tried, unsuccessfully, to gain control. "I don't see what's so funny," he said tersely.

Larissa sincerely attempted to speak, but only broken words about "Just see—you waving arms—yelling—chasing stump. Stump chasing—bee. Bee chasing oxen. All—of you running like mad—clear across—field." She gave it up and clutched her aching side.

His righteous wrath threatened to erupt. He'd expected sympathy, not laughter at his expense. He drew in breath for a surely regrettable reply. And suddenly saw the picture as she had so perfectly painted it. His anger evaporated into a reluctant chuckle.

"I'm sorry, Ethan, but picturing you—"

"I know," he said wryly, "you described it so vividly the first time, it really doesn't bear repeating. I'll just take your word for it."

She patted his arm, all laughter suddenly stilled. "I didn't mean to make you angry."

He closed his eyes, the touch of her hand heating his skin even through the cloth of his shirtsleeve. "I'm not angry. Guess it's a good joke on me, after all."

She bit her lips to keep them from quivering, and he put in swiftly before she should succumb again, "As I was saying, I have to go to town. Do you need anything while I'm there?"

"I can't think of anything."

"I won't be any longer than I can help. I really want to finish that field today." He bolted for the barn, lest he set her off again.

The wayward chain safely stowed in his saddlebag, he cantered Orion toward town. He scanned the sky, thinking he detected a gray smudge against the blue. The stiffening breeze fanned the leaves of the hickory, oaks and maples. Except for acute awareness of the weather, his mind was not on his surroundings. Hopefully he'd have the dratted chain repaired and be back on the farm before the storm hit.

Crossing the bridge into town, he slowed the black. *Quite a few folks around. More like a Saturday shopping day than Tuesday.* He nudged Orion north onto Walnut Street toward the blacksmith shop, now tended by Miles Painter's twin sons, Jacob and Jonas, since Obadiah Beldane's departure for war. As he navigated the intersection, out of the corner of his eye, he spotted a horse and rider a block south pounding hell bent in the direction he had just come.

He recognized Midnight, Jake Barton's horse, and Jake himself, Fairvale's uncontested "Worst Scandalmonger and Snoop" and wondered what the hurry was. *He'll kill that horse yet, running him that way.* Recalling Barton's treatment of Midnight that hot July day Jake had ridden to the farm, ablaze with eagerness to spread bad news of the Bull

Run battle, Ethan clenched his jaw. Jake had, so far, showed no inclination to join the Army, although he had no responsibilities except to himself. Ethan had caught a few muttered comments about Jake's aversion to defending his country, but kept his own opinions quiet.

You've a fine right to criticize anyone. These last two years, you haven't exactly been in the front ranks with the other men fighting this war, have you? His mind veered from the ever-present knowledge that, long ago, had became a steady ache in his soul.

Having dropped off the offending chain, with Jacob Painter's promise it would be ready in an hour, he headed toward the public square. Glimpsing a crowd near the *Tribune* building, uneasiness nudged him. Something must have happened. The paper came out Wednesday, not Tuesday. Rumors had sprouted of another battle brewing around Fredericksburg, Virginia, where he and Nettie once lived. *Did the fighting come to pass?*

He guided Orion that direction, swung down and tied him to the hitch rail, acutely aware that the men, ten or twelve of them, and no women, were silently watching his every move. He greeted a few, but the only responses were a dip of the head or a muttered, "Ethan." They parted as smoothly as the Red Sea as he passed among them and started up the stairs to the third-floor office.

Pulses now hammering, nerves jumpy as a mouse in a roomful of hungry cats, he forced himself to calmly step across the threshold. John Shearer, Fairvale *Tribune's* editor, was bent over his desk. He turned, saw Ethan and slowly straightened. At Shearer's sober expression, he felt something hard as a cannonball slam his insides. "What's happened?" His voice sounded peculiarly flat.

Shearer wore the look of a man who's just learned he's been voted town executioner. He picked up the paper he'd been studying. "More fighting. A big battle in Virginia, outside a town called Chancellorsville. Four Union County men are on the list."

"Killed?" Ethan's gut-tight fear eased. Zane couldn't be one. He was nowhere near Chancellorsville or Virginia.

"No, thank God. Wounded, but the report doesn't say how bad." Shearer hesitated visibly. "Ethan, there's more. It's Zane. Word came by telegraph not fifteen minutes ago. He was killed in an Indian fight last Thursday. Here's the message Miles Painter received." He held out the paper. Ethan saw his own hand reach to take it. That was odd because his whole body suddenly felt carved from wood. His eyes dropped to the sheet, but his vision blurred, curling the words into scarcely decipherable shapes.

"Regret ... inform ... Trooper Zane Edwards ... killed ... arrow ... Indian skirmish ... Thursday last ... sympathy ... Captain Randall T.

Norton."

The words jumped about on the page, refusing to stay pinned down long enough to make any sense. He dragged his eyes back up to John Shearer's stark grief.

"God, I'm sorry, Ethan. I'd give anything not to be the one to tell you. He was my friend, too. If there's anything I can do, I'm here for you."

Ethan swallowed hard. "No, John, nothing anyone can do. Thanks for being the one to tell me. Now I have to tell Larissa." Sustained only by that carved from wood sensation, he tucked the paper into the pocket of his red flannel shirt, stumbled outside, and pushed unaware through the Red Sea of onlookers. Mounting Orion, he started back to the farm—and Larissa.

***

After Ethan and Orion disappeared around the curve in the road, Larissa turned toward the chicken coop. An old hen was refusing to nest her just hatched brood and Larissa spent longer than she intended arguing with her about it. When she finally emerged from the henhouse, rolling clouds darkened the sky, thunder muttered, and the morning fresh breeze had become a full fledged wind. The linens she had hung on the clothesline were now whipping about as though at any moment they would rip from the pins to go sailing away. Retrieving her laundry basket from the porch, she unceremoniously dumped the sheets into it.

She started for the back porch with the full basket, but heard hooves thrumming along the drive beside the house and turned that way. *Ethan's back so soon?* Then, *He's coming awfully fast.* Her impression wisped away as the horse and rider rounded the corner of the house. Jake Barton. *If the town had a nickel for every gossiping tidbit he's spread, we'd all be rich.*

The rising wind whipped her pink skirt out, tugged at the tendrils of hair escaping the knot at the back of her neck, and riffled the linens in the basket clutched in her arms. Seeing her standing thus, Jake pulled Midnight to such a quick halt the animal skidded, raising chunks of dirt. "Miz Edwards, I wasn't sure I'd find you home, but I took a chance. I wanted to tell you how sorry I am."

The children. One of them must be hurt. "Sorry about what?"

"Why, ma'am, about your man. I thought you'd heard."

"Heard what?"

"Why, ma'am, you don't know, do you? I guess I shouldn't have come out here like this. I was just tryin' to be neighborly."

"Heard what?" She shrieked the words at him, but the wind whipped them away.

He pushed back his hat, cleared his throat, shifted in his saddle, but when she opened her mouth to screech at him again, he blurted out his news. "About your man Zane being killed in an Indian ruckus. I sure thought you knew or I never would of come busting in like this." The seconds ticked past as she stood and stared at him, did nothing, said nothing, just stood and stared at him.

This time, the nervous shifting in his saddle was genuine as he felt the impact of those eyes burning into him.

With a howl that rose from the depths of her being, Larissa hurled the clothesbasket at him. More by accident than design, the basket sailed through the gap separating them and smacked sharply against Midnight's muzzle. The panic-stricken horse reared, almost dumping his rider. As Jake fought to get him under control, that long wailing cry escaped her again. "Get out of here! Get *out!*"

By this time, Jake was only too happy to obey. Wheeling his mount, he touched his hat brim, mumbling indignantly, "I was only being neighborly." She stooped and grabbed a rock. He gave up all pretense of neighborliness and, slamming Midnight into a flat out run for the corner of the house, disappeared around it.

With a racking moan, she heaved the rock after him and sank to the ground as lightning flickered and thunder rolled and the first heavy drops of rain spattered down on her.

CHAPTER TWENTY-THREE

Ethan raced Orion out of town, his only coherent thought getting to Larissa. All else he shut out of his mind as one shuts a gate on a rampaging bull that it might not attack and overwhelm all defenses raised against it.

About a mile down the road, however, the all encompassing numbness receded. Reality slammed him with such brutal force the world went black and he swayed in the saddle. Orion, confused by the sudden slacking of reins, slowed.

The first raindrops spatted down, and almost with the next breath, became a deluge soaking him from head to foot. The lightning and thunder that had sounded far off began flashing and rolling almost simultaneously, leaving no doubt the storm was now directly overhead. Part of his brain registered this downpour as a real duck drowner. Somehow, he dredged up the effort necessary to stay in the saddle and keep Orion going. But now that the gate had swung open, feeling flooded him in an overwhelming tide of pain.

Trooper Edwards ... Shoshoni arrow ... killed Thursday last ... The words from the telegram whirled in his head until they were a spinning blur.

Trooper Edwards ... Zane. My friend.

At top speed, Orion rounded the curve to the farm before Ethan suddenly realized he couldn't go pounding up to the house like the devil approaching hell. Doing so would scare the wits out of Larissa, and very shortly he was going to hand her more grief and heart hurt than she ever before believed existed. He slowed the black's mad pace but kept him at a speed appropriate to a man dashing to get out of the rain.

He rounded the corner of the house, the downpour blurring his vision so that Orion stumbled as his hooves tangled in some ungainly object ground into the dirt of the drive. Hurriedly dismounting, Ethan hunkered beside what proved to be a rain soaked, mud smeared piece of material. Pulling it free of the muck, he recognized it as one of the sheets Larissa had hung to dry that morning.

Cold, rasping fingers clutched his throat, snaked a shudder through him from head to foot. "Larissa?" He sprang up, gaze frantically skimming the surrounding farmyard, but saw nothing of her. Glimpsing movement in the flowerbed by the porch steps, he dropped the grime stained sheet and lunged that direction. Her empty laundry basket, caught in the corner of the steps, swayed in the lash of the rain and wind.

"Larissa!" he yelled over the pounding torrent and knew the storm blew the word away even as he uttered it.

Sprinting up the steps and across the porch, he allowed himself the hope that he would find her in the house, safe and dry and laughing at him because, with his dripping hair and beard, he bore a remarkable resemblance to a water-dunked cat. Pushing open the kitchen door, he stuck his head in. "Larissa, are you here?"

Silence answered him.

On the wall above the woodbox, sewing pins secured Rose's "counting off the days until Pa's return" calendar. The blue gingham apron Larissa had worn at breakfast hung from a hook beside the stove, the only tangible evidence she had been here recently. Tracking mud and water across the floor on his way to the sitting room, he could just hear what she would have to say when she caught sight of him. *For sure, she'll scold me roundly for making such a mess.*

The sitting room was just-cleaned tidy—and empty.

Taking the stairs two at a time, he reached the top. To his left stretched a hallway with a door at the far east end and flanking doors on the north and south walls. He had never been up here, so picked a panel at random and found Mac's room. Above the desk hung a woodcut of a medical contraption he thought might be a microscope. Backing into the hall, he tried the door across the way. Rose's room. Dainty white curtains outlined the window. The flower Zane had sketched for her Christmas gift hung on the wall above the bed. Pulling that door shut, he sprinted to the end of the hall.

Hope and certainty battling, he pushed the panel open. Certainty won.

His eyes swept the room, took in the dresser with Larissa's comb and brush neatly arranged on top, and the sketch of Zane, now framed, on a table beside the four-poster bed. Hastily averting his eyes from the bed and the bright patchwork quilt covering it, he studied the crude drawing. Full realization of Zane's death clutched him viciously, so that he stood unmoving a long moment as pain, now undiluted by numbness, shot through him.

No. Think of Larissa. There'll be plenty of time later to mourn what should never have happened.

Shutting the door on the brush and comb and the now-framed picture of Zane, he hurried back downstairs.

Out the seldom used front door, circling the house, because she might be around the east corner.

She wasn't.

Dear God, Larissa. Why can't I find you?

Standing in the rear yard, he suddenly realized Orion had drifted to the barn and was now slouched, head sagging, under the roof overhang.

Had she been caught in the barn when the storm began? Judging by

Orion's drooping attitude, Ethan doubted it. Sloshing toward the black without bothering to veer around the puddles in his way, he felt the wind slackening.

Grasping Orion's reins, he wrenched open the barn door and the quiet lunged at him. As in the house earlier, the dusky room held the feeling of no one there. "Larissa?" No response except Orion's uneasy stirring. Back outside. *Think.* She went off visiting. *In this foul weather? Use common sense.* The sitting seat by the creek? *In a storm that would have had Noah himself cussing?* Disregarding common sense, he raced down the path past the springhouse and the sugar maples.

Nearing the creek, he saw a flicker of pink among the rocks. *She was wearing a pink skirt this morning.* "Larissa?" He circled a head high boulder, and she came into his full view. He halted in disbelief. "Larissa." This time it was only a breath.

Skirt and petticoats hiked above the water, she was wading barefoot in the creek. Her shoes and stockings lay in a sodden heap on the sitting seat. Her hair, free of the binding pins, clung to her face in water dark strands and fell over her shoulders in a tangled mass. She was so drenched, water ran off her in rivulets. Oblivious to her disheveled state, and to him, she was talking although no one else was around. The words came brokenly over the chattering creek.

"... promised you ... wade barefoot ... creek ... came home."

A spasm of fear knifed him. "Larissa!"

At the sound of her name, she turned. A glow so radiant it took his breath away transformed her wistful expression. "You've come back. I knew you would if I kept my promise to wade in the creek. Are you surprised, Zane?"

His stomach jolted as if she had punched him. He managed, somehow, to answer with a semblance of calm—and with perfect truth. "I am, more than you know. Larissa, it's time to come out of the water." Keeping his voice gentle, taking care not to startle her, he reached his hand to her.

"You were so right, Zane. This is fun. I'm sorry I didn't do it sooner for you."

"Don't be sorry. We all have to do things in our own time." All the while, stunned by this totally unforeseen circumstance, he moved closer. *One more step.* He clasped her outstretched hand, and she waded to shore willingly enough. He thanked God for that, unable at that moment to credit the true reason. How could he tell her he was not her husband when the truth might shatter her fragile hold between joyful confusion and screaming sanity?

He helped her up the sloping bank, intending to lead her to the sitting seat so she could put on her shoes. But as she came level with him, instead of releasing his hand, she grasped it in both of hers and brought it up to her cheek. "I'm so glad you're home. It seems as if it's been forever. Does it seem that way to you?"

"Yes. It seems ... that way to me, too."

"Isn't it incredible how we so often feel the same way?"

"Yes, it's incredible."

The glow in her eyes smote him, knowing as he did that it was not for him. "Larissa, come now. Let's get your shoes on. You need to get back to the house and into dry clothes."

"But I don't feel the least bit cold."

"Come along, anyway. It really is time to go back." He tugged at her hand, urging her over to the sitting seat. She pulled at her still dripping skirt, but the weight of it hampered her making the step to the top of the rock. Putting his hands at her waist, he boosted while she scrambled up.

Laughing, she sat and, settling her skirts, dangled her bare feet over the edge. "You come up and sit, too."

"Larissa," he said sternly as he could, "You have to get back to the house and into dry clothes. If you stay out here, you'll end up with lung fever."

She bent and touched his hair. "You've always worried too much about me, but I love you for it."

He couldn't have spoken then if his life depended on it. He picked up her stockings, but they were so water soaked he had a hard time sliding them onto her equally wet feet. They ended up crumpled around her ankles. Her shoes were in even worse shape. Soaked inside and out as they were, her toes wouldn't even go all the way in. She put her hand over her mouth to stifle her laughter at his clumsy efforts.

Finally, he gave up. "The stockings will protect your feet a little, anyway." She hopped obediently off the rock as he reached his hands to her, but winced as her feet hit the stony ground. "Can you make it?" he asked doubtfully.

"I can make it," she assured him. "I've done it before."

He couldn't tell her the glimpse of her running to meet Rose, the day Zane's first letter came, had lived with him ever since.

Through the still pelting rain, they made their slow way past the sugar maples and the springhouse. "I think I'll make an apple pie," she said suddenly. "Does that sound good for dessert tonight?"

Walking beside her, feeling the softness of her hand in his, listening to her lighthearted conversation, despair, guilt and anguish churned in him. Never had he seen her so joyous, so open about her feelings. This, then, was the Larissa Zane had known .... "Yes," he responded belatedly. "Apple pie sounds great."

The path divided. He started to take the west branch, back to the house, but she tugged at his hand. "Zane, where are you going?"

"To the house, so you can dry off."

"It's this way," she insisted. "Have you forgotten? You were away a long time." Her voice faded in confusion.

"All right. We'll go this way."

They took the east path to the cabin.

"See, I was right." Her tone held no triumph, only delight. Keeping hold of his hand, she drew him with her up the short walkway. Entering the cabin, she turned in a complete circle, viewing the furnishings. Faint puzzlement crept into her tone. "Maybe I've been away a long time, too. I don't remember the furniture being placed this way." Abruptly her expression changed once again. "Goodness, but you're wet. I know I'm wet because I was wading in the creek so you'd come home, and you did. But how did you get so drenched?"

Groping for the right explanation, he dumped her sodden shoes onto the hearth. *Charity thrust her damp shoes at me that long-ago day she fell into the mud puddle.* He set his hands rekindling the morning fire, sharply aware that, in Larissa's present state, a single wrong word or action could shatter her fragile peace of mind. *For her sake, you had to get her into a dry room without her balking and likely running off into the rain again. Fine. You did that, even if it is the cabin instead of the house. You're here, now, and the only rain is what you brought inside. You must tell her. It's cruelly unfair, continuing the fantasy she's weaving.* His frantic seeking brought him full circle. *Dear God, what will the truth do to her?*

He stood, brushing ash dust off his hands. "I came home and you weren't in the house. I guess it was raining harder than I realized when I went outside to look for you."

"You were worried about me?"

He dipped his head, unable to take his eyes from hers.

Her concern over his drenched state changed swiftly to tenderness. "I'm sorry I worried you, Zane. I would never do it deliberately. For some reason, I just felt I had to go wade in the creek." Her brows drew together in a frown of concentration. "I don't remember why, but it seemed so very important I go there. I guess I was hoping that if I did, you'd come home sooner." The tenderness returned in a dazzling flash of joy. "And it worked. Here you are." She slipped her arms about his neck, raising her face to his. "I'm so glad you're home."

"Larissa." His protest died as her lips met his. For one blinding instant of wonder, she clung to him. Even as his reeling senses comprehended what was happening, she drew back, uncertainty overshadowing her radiant joy.

"Not Zane."

Even as he tried to speak, to tell her the truth, uncertainty became bewilderment. "Ethan?"

"Larissa." Never in his life had he known that a single spoken word could hold so much relief, and so much pain.

Her fingers touched her lips where his mouth had so recently rested. Her eyes swept the room. "Why are we here?" Bewilderment became swift horror. "Zane," she breathed. "Oh, Zane." His name ended in a keening cry that would forever echo in Ethan's soul. Before he could catch her, she sank to the floor and curled herself into a tight ball, her face buried in her arms.

Frantically rolling her over, he expected resistance and was totally unprepared when she flopped face up. "Larissa?"

Her eyes were open, but she paid no heed to his panic stricken voice. "Can you hear me, Larissa?" Still no response as her wide open, deep blue eyes stared upward. He knew she wasn't hurt, physically, anyway. With no other idea what to do for her, he realized she was cold clear through from her prolonged exposure to the rain. "Larissa, can you hear me? You have to get out of these wet clothes."

Suddenly she began to shiver, a slight movement that rapidly turned into violent shaking. Afraid she was going into shock, he grabbed the wool blanket folded at the foot of his bed and wrapped it warmly about her. Dropping into a sitting position on the floor, he gathered her into his arms and leaned back against the footboard. Holding her close, murmuring nothing-phrases, he waited in vain for a response. The fierce trembling continued as her eyes stared at nothing.

He had hoped that holding her thus would make her warm enough, in spite of her wet clothing, to come back to awareness. But when he carefully brushed her cheek with his fingers, she still felt much too cold. He knew then what he must do, and steeled himself, because he had done it before, six years ago when Nettie was bitten by the rattlesnake. Feeling he was being thrust back into a terrible nightmare after he thought he had finally escaped, he tucked the damp strands of hair back from Larissa's face with an unsteady hand. "I'm sorry. I have no choice. I just hope you'll forgive me when you know."

Cradling her against his chest, he stood and carried her to his bed. Easing her onto the braided rug covering the floor alongside, he turned to the trunk beneath the window. Hands shaking, he pushed back the lid. Once again, he heard the finality of the clasps clicking into place as he shut it after Nettie's death. He gazed at the contents a long moment before he lifted out a lace-edged nightdress. Again memory flashed, but he thrust it grimly away. *Just do what you have to. Sniveling won't help.*

Armed with the nightdress and a towel from the washstand, he knelt beside her. Carefully pulling her tangled hair out from the blanket, he rubbed it gently with the towel until it no longer dripped water down her neck. She made no movement at all during this process. Uncertain whether to be concerned or relieved, he set his jaw for the next encounter. Unwrapping the blanket, he realized the wool cover had absorbed some water after all. He tried to unfasten her skirt waistband, but the soggy material resisted his efforts to push the button through the hole. Already clammy and damp when he started, he was sweating profusely by the time he finally worked it loose. And this was only the beginning of his task.

Trying fiercely, futilely, to dull his heart from recognition of what his hands were doing, he removed the rest of her waterlogged clothing, dried her carefully with the towel, and slipped the nightdress over her head. Lifting her into his arms once more, he slid her beneath the blankets and pulled them up snugly under her chin. During the entire unnerving process, her eyes stayed open. He tried to shut them by passing his hand over her face but, unblinking, they remained stubbornly wide. Although certain she was unaware of his movements, he could not banish the unsettling feeling she was staring directly at him.

Once he'd tucked her safely under the warm covers, he turned to the job of shedding his own wet clothing. He toweled briskly until his hair and beard were no longer sodden and warmth began to return to his chilled bones. Pulling on clean and blessedly dry pants and shirt, he glanced at Larissa and his heartbeat quickened. She had turned her face in his direction, but her eyes were now closed. Not sure whether this was good or bad, he moved quietly to the side of the bed. Putting his hand to her cheek, relief flooded him. She no longer felt chilled-to-the-bone cold and her breathing came soft and even, without any hint of the rasping that could so easily become lung fever.

Her hair spilled over the pillow, the damp darkened mass a soft chestnut where it had dried. Touching the silky strands with a suddenly trembling finger, he hesitated before once more turning to the trunk under the window. Taking out a comb and brush, he returned to the bed and began to work the brush through the tangles.

Sometime during the process, her eyes opened once more. Again he was not certain she heard him speak her name, but he began to talk soothingly, letting his voice flow over her as he smoothed the damp hair strands through his fingers. He wasn't, in the end, able to get all the snarls out without lifting her head, but he made a good start. He braided it as carefully as he braided Charity's hair in the morning before she left for school. *Amazing, the accomplishments that come to a man, that he never in an eternity would have seen himself doing.*

He was returning the comb and brush to the trunk when he heard a soft moan. Turning quickly, he saw her eyes were still open. Now, however, they held stark grief and pain. Before he could reach her, she pressed the back of her hand to her mouth as her cry of despair pierced the quiet room. Her face contorted and the tears she had not shed before streamed down her cheeks. She began writhing violently, as if seeking to escape that from which there was no fleeing.

Kneeling beside the bed, he captured her flailing hands. "Larissa," he said urgently, "can you hear me? I'm right here with you, holding your hands. Hold on to me if you want. Larissa, you're *not alone*. I'm here with you. I'll be here as long as you want me to be." He was not certain how much she heard or comprehended, but remembering his own black, plunging spiral of despair six years before, he was going to make damned sure his voice was there with her.

Broken cries, as of an animal in mortal pain, wracked her body and once more she began to shiver violently. He knew full well no human being could help her fight her ultimate battle, but that was the future. This was now, and not for all the pearls in the Heavenly Gates would he stand by and let her endure alone the heart-ripping anguish of first awareness. He lay down beside her and pulled her to him, not at all certain she would accept his embrace. As his arms touched and encircled her, she stiffened away from him. "Larissa," he murmured, "you've always trusted me before. You can trust me now. I'm not going to hurt you. Please trust me."

She remained rigid as his words hung between them. Then, with a shuddering breath, she drew near enough to bury her face against his chest. As he rested his cheek against her rain-washed hair and murmured soothing phrases, he knew the words themselves were not nearly so important as the gentle flow of his voice. Gradually, the harsh sobs and violent trembling eased, and she lay quiet against him. At last the soft, even rhythm of her breathing told him she had fallen asleep.

In a daze of unreality, he held her close. She was so fragile, so vulnerable as she slept in his arms, that awareness of her absolute trust filled him with wonderment.

Realization she would soon waken finally nudged him. Loving her as he did, he knew with certainty her grief would be compounded by dismay and embarrassment if she woke curled against him. He brushed a kiss against her hair before, wishing with all his soul that he didn't have to do so, he carefully eased her out of his arms. She stirred, sighed, but did not waken. He slid out of the bed, his arms feeling unutterably cold and empty.

He reached to tuck the quilt around her and her eyes blinked open. Suffused with sleep as she was, comprehension of his presence didn't sink in for a moment. Too soon, the haziness fled and sorrow shadowed her features once more.

"It's true, then. He's dead."

"Yes."

She rolled her head away from his unconcealed grief to stare out the window. When she turned back, the look in her eyes would haunt him for many days. This time, however, she shed no tears. "I'll have to tell Mac and Rose."

"Do you want me to?"

"No. They need to hear it from me."

"I'll do anything to help you, Larissa. You know that."

She raised her hands as if to ward off any compassion that would shatter her fragile control. "Don't." The word came out high pitched and urgent. She stopped and swallowed before continuing in a more normal tone. "I know you mean it, but *not now.*" At his answering silence, she dropped her hands to the quilt covering her.

Awareness she was lying in Ethan's bed, wearing a nightdress she had never seen before, slowly dawned. "You did this?"

"Yes. You were soaking wet. I was afraid you'd take a chill."

She nodded as if, with the greater grief, there was none to spare on such things as waking in his cabin, in his bed, wearing a nightdress she had never seen before.

"I seem to remember running in the rain."

He wanted fervently to ask her how she came to hear about Zane and knew he wouldn't. Not yet.

As if sensing the unspoken question, she closed her eyes a moment before looking directly at him. "I remember pulling the clean sheets off the line before the storm hit. I started toward the house with the full laundry basket. Jake Barton pounded up the drive on his horse. He shouted at me. I don't remember after that." Her eyes pierced his very soul. "You found me. Where?"

Ethan's thoughts lurched back to his arrival in town earlier that day. *Jake whipping his horse Midnight, barreling out of town this morning as I rode in.* His destination, the farm ... and Larissa. Giving no hint of the rage building in him at Jake Barton's unbelievable cruelty, he said simply, "Down by the creek." There would be time later for dealing with Jake. *I'll see to it personally.* "It was raining really hard by then and you were drenched. I brought you here to the cabin."

She touched the nightdress and the braid falling over her shoulder. "And took care of me?"

"Yes."

"Thank you."

He nodded, once, then hesitated. "The young ones will be home in a little while. You'd probably rather not have them see you this way."

"No, but ..." She gestured to the nightdress, to the wet pile of clothing.

He glanced out the window. "The storm's over. The easiest way, I expect, would be for you to wear the nightdress over to the house. You can wrap a blanket around you. No one will see you or know."

She looked at him, hearing what he had not said. "I believe I'll do that." She slipped from under the covers and took the blanket he offered.

"I'll take your wet clothes. You'll have enough to manage with the blanket and all."

In silence, they walked to the house through the rain-fresh afternoon.

He deposited her soiled clothes in the washtub in the wood shed. He started to leave, but paused. "Will you be all right here by yourself?"

"Yes. Thank you, Ethan. For everything."

With an infinitely gentle gesture, he reached to touch her cheek. "I'm just glad I was here to help."

He shut the door behind him and she stood in her kitchen, listening to the silence.

CHAPTER TWENTY-FOUR

Unknown to Larissa, Ethan gathered the grimy sheets from the driveway and stuffed them into the laundry basket. For the moment, he thrust the whole mess into the buggy shed and shut the door on it. Finally tending to Orion, he turned him, rubbed down and curried, into the corral and then stationed himself where he would see the children rounding the curve in the road. Following her wishes, he would not tell them of their father's death, but he wanted to head Charity off, so Mac and Rose would be alone with their mother when they learned the news.

His mind fiendishly blank of even a clue what to say, he waited. But now, standing idle, the white-hot coals of grief, wonder, and guilt he had smothered for Larissa's sake flared rebelliously. At last the children came into view. Mac strode along, ignoring the girlish antics of Rose and Charity, who skipped ahead, then darted to the side of the road to pick wildflowers.

Spotting her father, Charity ran toward him, waving her bouquet. "Hi, Pa. These are for you. Are you surprised?"

Taking the bouquet, he inhaled deeply. "Thank you. They smell good enough to eat."

She giggled at the absurdity of Pa munching on wildflowers like Clover the milk cow grazing in the pasture.

Rose held out a fistful of bedraggled blooms. "I picked these for Ma. Do you think she'll like them?"

"I'm sure she will. They'll really brighten her day."

Mac, behind Rose, heard the forced cheer behind the words. Searching Mr. Michaels' face, he saw that, for all the banter, something was wrong. Before he could speak, Mr. Michaels caught his eye and gestured ever so slightly to Rose. The implications had flown completely over her head. Not certain just what was happening, Mac reached for Rose's hand. "Let's go to the house."

She jerked back suspiciously. He never held her hand any more like he used to when she was little. Still uncomprehending, but belatedly recognizing his big brother sternness that brooked no obstinacy, she swallowed her taunting comment and obediently trotted beside him toward the house. "Is Ma mad with us?" she asked in a thin voice.

"'Course not. We did our chores this morning and we've been in school all day. How could she be mad?"

She looked skeptical. Mac was forever harping on how she had to do what he said just because he was older. But he wasn't always right. Clutching her flowers, she followed him into the kitchen. Ma sat at the table, a look on her face Rose had never seen before. Mac stiffened and Rose knew he saw it too. What she did not know was that he had seen that very expression on the faces of relatives just told by Doc Rawley that their loved one had died.

"Ma?" He formed the word but no sound came.

"Yes." Her voice came scarcely more audible than his.

Rose, now sensing something terribly wrong, stared wildly from her brother's face to her mother's. Young as she was, she knew only one thing to make either of them look that sad. "Pa?" Her voice shivered.

"Yes, Rose." Larissa held out her hands. Rose dropped her flowers and fled to the safety of those encircling arms. Mac, his fourteen years' dignity and his medical training abruptly non-existent, followed only a step behind.

***

Ethan watched Zane's children trudge up the steps, and memory slammed him, sending him back into the farmhouse in Michigan, to that moment of telling Charity her mother was dead. "Come, Charity, let's go home and put these flowers in water."

As Mac's tone with Rose, something in her father's voice bade her obey without argument. "Is something wrong?" she asked in a small voice.

"I'll explain when we get home."

Once inside, he drew her to his knee. Before he could speak, she asked in a quivering voice, "Did Rose's Pa die?"

Stunned at her perception, he blurted, "Why do you ask?"

"'Cause you look sad like when Mama died."

"You remember all that time ago?"

"Not much. I just remember you were sad for ever so long. Like now."

He'd no idea she would remember after six years. Or link her mother's death with Zane's. *The things our children teach us. She's definitely your daughter, Nettie. I'm so proud of that.* "Yes. Mrs. Edwards heard today that Mr. Edwards died last Thursday."

"Oh, Pa!" She threw her arms around him and held on tightly, her warm tears soaking his shirt. As with Larissa, he found no words of comfort, could only pat her braids and rock her until she raised her tear streaked face. "I liked Mr. Edwards. Why did it have to happen to him?"

The eternal question. If I could answer that one, I'd be rich as Croesus. "I don't know. No one does. Maybe, someday, we'll find out why."

"Rose and Mac will be so sad. Mrs. Edwards, too."

The voice of experience. And she's only ten. "Maybe you can help them be not quite so sad."

"How?"

"You and Rose like to do things together. Why do you think that is?"

"She's my friend, and I'm hers."

"That's exactly right. Now, more than ever, she'll need you to be her friend. Think you can do that?"

She gave him a watery smile. "You know I can."

"I know. I'm very proud of you, and Mama would be, too."

"Do you think Mama and Mr. Edwards will meet in Heaven and get to be friends?"

"I'm sure they will, if they haven't already. Mama's been there longer, so she can show Mr. Edwards around and explain how things are done."

"I like that. Do you think it would be all right if I tell Rose?"

"I think it would comfort her very much to hear it from her friend."

She hugged his neck tightly again, and his shoulder muffled her next words. "I'm glad you didn't go to war. Is that bad?"

She does realize it could have been me. He loosened her grip so that he could look directly at her. "No, Charity, it isn't bad. This is very sad, and we're all going to have mixed up feelings for a while, but we'll help each other get through it. Talking is an excellent way to do that. You can come to me with any thoughts or feelings you have. Just as you've always done. Will you remember that?"

"Yes, Pa."

"Good. Now go wash your hands and face and we'll go to the house."

With a final hug, she turned to the basin.

They started out the door, but she halted suddenly. "May I take some of the flowers I picked for you and give them to Mrs. Edwards? Would she like that?"

"I think she'd like that very much."

Crossing the back porch to the kitchen, he said quietly, "Let's knock. If they don't answer, we'll go back home so they can be alone a while longer."

He had scarcely rapped his knuckles against the door before it flew open. Rose, face and eyes swollen from weeping, stood there, Mac and Larissa just behind. Mac's eyes were red. He was biting his lower lip fiercely to stop the trembling. Larissa, head high, was not weeping or trembling. Only her eyes betrayed immeasurable grief. "We're so glad you came. We're feeling the need of the comfort of friends."

Her slight emphasis on the last word both thanked Ethan and put their actions that afternoon into the realm of *that was then, this is now,* blessedly freeing him from the awkwardness threatening to swamp him at first sight of her.

"I brought you these, Mrs. Edwards." Charity held out the flowers.

The young girl's compassionate gesture brought Larissa perilously near to breaking down.

"Why, Charity, how thoughtful. Thank you. Will you put them in a vase, please? Rose will show you which one."

Larissa thus occupied, Ethan's gaze traveled absently about the kitchen, coming to a sharp halt on a blank spot on the wall above the woodbox. Rose's calendar ... the calendar she had made so carefully and kept so faithfully, marking off the days until Zane should return ... was gone.

"I'll get to the chores now, Ma."

At Mac's words, Ethan, with wrenching effort, tore his gaze from the blank spot on the wall. "I'll go with you."

"No. I want to do them myself tonight." Mac fled without waiting for a response.

Larissa turned hurriedly to the stove. "Supper's almost ready. It's good you came when you did."

"You needn't go to trouble on our account."

Her shoulders bowed a moment, then straightened. "No trouble. I expect I feel the same as Mac. I need to do it."

Understanding totally, he knew no words to give her solace.

***

In bed that night, Ethan turned from back to side, only to find himself on his back once more, staring up into the blackness. *At least this time I won't disturb Charity with all my flopping.* She was spending the night with Rose, and couldn't be upset by his fish out of water restlessness. So much had come to pass the last few hours that only now, alone in the darkness, could he even begin sorting it out.

Zane is dead. Harsh grief clogged Ethan's throat. From their first meeting, they had shared a mutual understanding and respect that, if a man is very lucky, he might find once in a lifetime. He would miss him sorely.

Larissa. He ached to help her, but knew only too well even the best intentioned words held pitifully little consolation. Of all the well meaning condolences people had offered after Nettie's death, nothing anyone said or did came close to easing the anguish of loss. Recalling that first long night without Nettie, he could only pray for this night to go swiftly for Larissa.

In spite of his determination, his thoughts returned to those first seconds when she acknowledged awareness of Zane's death. She could not know, and he fervently hoped she would never know how, holding her tightly, compelling his own strength into her, in the space of a heartbeat, he had returned to that moment he knew Nettie was dead, when he had died, too.

"... it was the season of Light, it was the season of Darkness, it was the spring of hope, it was the winter of despair ..."

The words from Mr. Charles Dickens' *Tale of Two Cities* Larissa had given him for Christmas sidled out of the night, their accuracy mocking him. Lying in the bed where Larissa had so recently lain, he felt enmeshed in a net compounded of friendship and loyalty, love and loss, life and death. Remembrance of the rain-washed fragrance of her hair beneath his cheek, and the softness of her body curled trustingly against his, shot through him.

With all his frenzied searching, he found no way out of the season of darkness trapping him.

***

The next months blurred by. Out of necessity, Larissa performed the ever present tasks of cooking, cleaning, baking, and scrubbing. In later years, however, when the children mentioned an activity that took place, such as celebrating Mac's fifteenth birthday in June, she drew a total blank.

Somehow, the summer passed. Larissa, coping with her own grief, also had to be supportive of Mac and Rose. At times, accomplishing the combined effort seemed insurmountably hopeless. Through the surrounding grayness, her motherhood instincts, dulled by pain, were not entirely silenced. Rose became quieter as the weeks wore on. In spite of opportunities Larissa made for her child to talk as they worked at the household chores, Rose rarely responded. At night however, Larissa, lying wakeful would hear muffled weeping. Going to her daughter, she lay down beside her. It was then Rose lost the strength to keep her pain to herself. Invariably, without words, she crept into her mother's arms and sobbed until she fell asleep, unaware of the tears running down Larissa's cheeks.

During those endless weeks, out of everyone offering condolences, she found only two with any real perception of her struggle. Martha Van Ellis, having walked the path of torment Larissa was now negotiating, did not mouth sympathetic, empty phrases. To floundering Larissa, she offered much more. She listened to the broken words of grief without minimizing the agony as "something you'll get over, in time."

When Larissa apologized for dumping her sorrow into her friend's lap, Martha took hold of her hands and squeezed them hard. "You needn't ever apologize. After Ross died, well meaning people told me all kinds of things to cheer me up. Everything from, 'You're young, you'll soon find someone else,' to 'It was better for him to die than to live after being so horribly wounded.'"

Martha paused, assembling her next words into polite language. "The choicest bit by far came from a friend I hadn't seen for several weeks. We bumped into each other in the mercantile and she asked how I was doing. Because she asked, I answered that I had my good days and my not-so-good days, but was making progress. She stepped back and said in absolute amazement, 'You're still grieving? It's been four months. It's time to get on with your life.'"

At Larissa's aghast expression, she smiled grimly. "I got on with my life, all right. The first thing I did was eliminate her from my list of friends. I still talk to her because I absolutely refuse to give her the satisfaction of knowing she had power to hurt me." She sat quietly, then, giving Larissa time to absorb the impact of those words.

"Do you feel you're the same person you were, before?"

Martha considered. "On the outside, I suppose I'm more forceful. I have to be because everything around me, it's what my life is, now. One must cope or quit. I refuse to quit because of my children, Ross's children. Even more so, I refuse to quit for me. Inside, where no one can see, I still feel lost, lonely, and scared. But I get angry with myself, then, and that makes me even more determined to keep going." She laughed apologetically. "I know it doesn't make much sense. I just haven't said it aloud to anyone to realize how mixed up it'd sound."

"I don't think it sounds mixed up at all," Larissa said softly. "It makes perfect sense to me."

***

The other person who brought comfort to her shattered world was Ethan. Not only in words, for he didn't talk all that much, unless he really had something to say. For her, the consolation he imparted lay in his endless patience, listening to her without judging, minimizing or topping her troubles with a story of his own.

One conversation they shared remained etched in her memory.

Ethan approached her three mornings after they learned of Zane's death. She could not know he had spent much of the finally over with night sleepless. His promise to Zane that last morning they had walked to town, his vow to help Larissa move to her sister in Vermont "if something happens to me," had emerged from its hibernation hole, coiled to strike with venomous fangs. *Would I have promised so readily had I known I would be compelled to keep my word?* Unable to call back the past, he had no answer. Steeling himself, he proposed she and the children move to Vermont. Her outright rejection of the plan took him aback.

"This is my home. This is the home Zane and I built together for our children. He put sweat, sacrifice, and love into this ground. A very real part of him is here in the fields and trees he nurtured. I will not leave here."

She spoke with such flat finality that he, having no intention whatsoever of discouraging her decision, didn't press. He simply attempted, futilely, to quash his soul deep relief, even as his second question grinned at him spitefully.

"If you and the children plan to live here, do you want me to stay and continue working the farm?" She looked at him with such blank amazement, he realized she hadn't considered how Zane's death affected his and Charity's position here. Nor had she given thought to the possibility of their leaving. *Not that I blame her, under the circumstances.* Because he possessed no desire to move hundreds of miles away out of her life, he didn't argue or even mention it again. He simply, quietly kept his promise to stay and help her run the farm.

He did not speak to Larissa of those stolen hours the afternoon they had learned of Zane's death. She still possessed only the haziest recollections of that time, of Jake Barton galloping up on his horse, shouting. The impression of being as soaking wet as if she'd fallen headfirst into Mill Creek. Remembrance of cold so deep her bones had chilled. Although she knew it could only be her imagination, dredged up by futile yearning, a mist-blurred remembrance of kissing Zane persisted.

One event burned in her memory—waking in Ethan's bed. Obviously, his care had brought her there wearing Nettie's nightdress, but she could not ask how it came to be. Her hold on self-control still shattering fragile, she could not endure learning the full details of that terrible day. *Later on. But not yet.* Because Ethan never spoke of it, it lay between them, silent question on her part, grave knowledge on his.

As if Larissa's soul weren't already sorely tried, Mac began acting strangely. He left early each morning for Doc's office, sometimes returning long after dark. She fretted about him not getting enough sleep, but this problem paled beside a much greater concern. In the last year, quiet assurance and deep satisfaction of a job well done had emerged with his growing responsibilities and his new found maturity. Now, in neither his going out nor his coming in, could she find any trace of either assurance or satisfaction.

Concern goaded her into consulting Doc. His going to war orders had come through. He was to report to the medical commission in Washington City on September 1st to receive his assignment. Until then, he was putting every ounce of effort he possessed into caring for "his folks."

Now with none of his usual gruffness, he said, "I've noticed too. I wish I had an answer. His work's not suffering. On the contrary, he's putting even more care and attention to detail into his cases. I've tried to sniff out what's chewing at him. I thought maybe he was still worried about handling everything after I leave. But I don't think that's it. After finding out Dr. Ingemar'll help him with the really serious cases, he's appeared to accept it." He paused to frame his next words carefully.

"I've also wondered if it's Zane's death that's thrown him for a loop." He tossed the words at her and she didn't stumble. Only her eyes shadowed a deeper blue. "If that's the case, it's entirely understandable and he'll just need time to work it through. If that's not it either, I plain don't know. He's definitely got a whole nest of yellow jackets swarming around his head. Just remember, it's not the buzzing that's bad. That's the thinking time. It's when the noise stops that a body needs to be prepared."

CHAPTER TWENTY-FIVE

For Mac, the summer went by both too slowly and much too quickly. The new worry living with him day and night loomed impossibly high and black shadowed. Knowing he couldn't confide in anyone, that the problem was his alone to solve, added to the insupportable weight of uncertainty.

In July, Ohio residents experienced a small taste of what the war was like for those thousands of people living in counties and villages, and on farms and crossroads that became sites of relentlessly fought battles. Confederate leader John Hunt Morgan and twenty-five hundred of his "Morgan's Raiders" crossed the Indiana border into Cincinnati on July 13th, and Federal authorities declared martial law in that city. The raiders' rampaging, thievery, and murder of innocent civilians was so outrageous it turned the stomachs of the most hardened military leaders. For thirteen terrifying days, Ohioans followed Morgan's progress as his men fought a skirmish at Camp Dennison and headed east toward the Ohio River, intending to cross into Kentucky. Federal troops, militia, and gunboats foiled that attempt. Morgan suffered over eight hundred casualties. In desperation, the remaining raiders followed the Ohio north toward Pennsylvania, fighting again near Springfield. On Sunday, July 26th, Morgan and his remaining three hundred sixty-four men surrendered to Federal forces, leaving behind a swath of burned homes, destroyed crops, and death to mark their progress.

***

Bit by bit Larissa's memory returned. In piecing the scraps together, Jake Barton's unspeakable behavior emerged. With no possible doubt remaining of his guilt, Mac determined in Pa's stead to teach Jake the error of his ways. Certain his mother would attempt to dissuade him if she knew his mission, he simply mentioned he planned to ride to Doc's office after supper, as he did sometimes.

Because neither one mentioned such intentions, he was unaware that Ethan had come to a similar conclusion. Mac halted in the barn doorway at sight of Ethan saddling Orion. "You're going to town tonight." Statement, not question.

Ethan glanced up, his hands continuing their task of buckling the girth strap. "I need pipe tobacco."

"I forgot something at the office. I'll ride with you."

Their eyes met in mutual understanding. Ethan didn't need pipe tobacco, and Mac didn't need to go to the office.

He crossed to Cygnus and lifted down the saddle blanket.

"Mac."

"I'm going. She's my Ma and I won't see her treated that way." His voice held flat finality. "Pa would want—would expect—me to see it's set right."

Disconcerted, Ethan nevertheless recognized in the young voice determination equal to his own. "I'd be happy to ride along. Man traveling a dark road can never be sure just what kind of no account polecat he might encounter."

"I get first crack at any varmint we flush."

"If I know my critters, I expect there'll be enough of this particular skunk to go around."

Riding to town, they decided to check the livery barn first. Skel Wrade, the owner, kept a whiskey bottle hidden in the grain bin, handy to share with any crony dropping by. Jake, judging by the frequency of his visits, considered Skel to be his bosom friend. As Ethan and Mac approached the stable, the talk and raucous laughter spilling into the street covered any noise softer than a stampeding herd of buffalo.

In spite of his qualms, Ethan let Mac go in first, taking up his own stance immediately outside where he could see and hear but remain undetected. *Forgive me, Larissa, but he's right. He has to handle this for you, for Zane, for himself.*

He heard Mac call, "Jake Barton!" The livery stable abruptly became quieter than a cat sneaking up on an unsuspecting mouse meal.

"Yeah, what you want, kid?" Jake's voice was only slightly slurred. With relief, Ethan judged him drunk enough to be cocky, but sober enough to be cautious.

"I want to talk to you."

"So talk."

"You might rather step outside."

"What's this all about, kid?" Jake's tone held an undercurrent of amusement as he sauntered out the door with Mac on his heels. "We're outside. So talk."

"You came to see my Ma a few weeks ago."

"Your Ma? I never. Wait a minute. You're the Edwards kid, the one been running all over creation playing doctor. Sure, I wanted to give your Ma my sympathy on your old man getting his axle greased. She started acting like a crazy woman, screeching and throwing rocks. I thought she'd snapped her fishline for sure. I hightailed it out of there, I'll tell you. Some thanks I got for being neighborly."

"We don't need your neighborliness. Just stay away from my Ma and my family. You're not welcome at our place."

"Ain't you high and mighty? I go where I want, when I want, and no wet nosed kid tells me different."

Ethan had retreated around the side of the livery stable as the two walked outside. He took a step toward Jake's back, but halted at Mac's next words. "To you I'm a wet nosed kid running all over creation, but helping Doc Rawley, I hear things. Women who don't get out and visit much surely do like to talk. Medically speaking, it relieves their stress, you might say, and naturally they trust their doctor to know what's true and what isn't. So they ask him. Sometimes three or four ladies ask the same question the same day. A favorite topic is matchmaking." Mac shook his head dolefully at the whims of female patients before continuing in a high pitched tone.

"'Is this person really seeing that person?' And, 'Is that scandalous rumor true that's been spreading like fire *all over Union County*? About a certain man, who has a sweetheart, and such a nice young thing she is, too, being seen in the company of a *certain woman with shocking morals*? Whatever is this world coming to?' You know. That kind of talk. Right in front of a wet nosed kid, too."

Etched in the light spilling from the livery, Jake stiffened and swung his fists up. "You know that ain't true, you little weasel."

"What do you intend to do, Jake, beat me up? That's not a good idea." Jake looked confused by Mac's abrupt switch to earnestness. "The same ladies who are hungry for news think it's really fine, my taking to 'healing folks alongside Doc Rawley.' You beat me up, those nice ladies will wonder why. And it'll just make more gossip," he said sadly. "Comes to it, who will they believe, you or me? Tell you what." The sudden ice in Mac's voice plainly increased Jake's befuddlement. "You leave my Ma alone, *never come near her again*, leave all of us alone, and nothing will be said, to anyone. Deal?"

Jake finally gathered his tattered wits. "You conniving brat. Don't you ever come near me again, you hear? If I find out you're spreading rumors, I'll knock you into next Tuesday."

"Just remember, Jake, it works both ways. You leave us alone, and we'll leave you alone."

"You blackmailing little snake." Jake glared at him, turned on his heel, and stomped back into the livery stable, where a chorus of voices greeted his return. Mac slumped.

Ethan hurried to him. "You all right?"

He nodded weakly. Ethan grinned from ear to ear. "That was the finest piece of vocal artistry I've heard in many a day. Let's get out of here before he figures out what put the knot on his noggin." He chuckled. "The look on his face will cheer me up for many moons to come."

"You won't tell Ma?"

"No. I wish I could. Your Pa would be proud of you. Your Ma, too. I know I am."

***

September first arrived.

Ethan, standing in the now matured cornfield, inspected the plump ears stretching away in all directions on stalks that reached higher than his head. Satisfaction of a planting done well was tempered by memory of his last words to Zane. *The corn will be ready for you to harvest with your own hands when you come home.* The corn was ready, but Zane would not come home to harvest it, this season or ever.

With Doc scheduled to leave on the afternoon train, Mac reached the office earlier than usual. Those last weeks, Doc had increasingly handed diagnosis and treatment responsibility over to Mac until, toward the end, he simply stood and watched while his pupil took full charge of the varied situations their patients presented. Doc never faulted Mac's treatments while he was giving them. Afterward, riding in the buggy to the next call or back to the office, they talked over the various procedures, and Doc made suggestions for handling unusual situations, should they come up. During those last days, they had given all possible care to the current cases. Even so, as Mac entered the office that bright summer morning, he felt undeniably queasy.

Doc, coffeepot in hand, waited for him. "Hoped you'd get here early, Boy." He handed Mac a steaming cup and poured himself one as if they'd been doing so every morning for decades. "Remember we talked a while back about a fancy machine that could see right into a patient's innards and tell us what was wrong instead of having to rely on feel and instinct?" Doc chuckled. "I still have my money on that. The way things are progressing, it wouldn't surprise me a bit if it didn't show up in your lifetime, maybe even while you're still in practice." He'd meant the comment as a nonchalant, in the future possibility, but Mac's response startled him. The boy's face darkened with such a spasm of pain, Doc thought he'd keel over right there. All lightness gone, he stepped quickly to Mac's side. "Put your head down and breathe deep."

"It's not that kind of pain," Mac gritted.

"Then what is it? You've sure got the Spartan boy matched for keeping quiet while the fox chews on your insides. You've been festering for weeks. I'm leaving in a few hours. Don't you think it's time to spit out what's on your mind? I'm putting all my dependence on you to take care of things here. That means I've got to trust you'll take care of yourself. A doctor who won't tend his own needs isn't worth a hoot in hell when it comes to taking care of others."

"I don't know whether I want to be a doctor or not."

Doc's eyebrows shot up. "What do you mean 'want to or not'? You are a doctor. Nothing can change that now." His forcefulness softened slightly. "You'd better fill in the holes." He dropped back in his chair.

Mac's carefully reasoned reply took as sudden whirring flight as a barn pigeon at home when the cat skulked by. "I don't know if I can do it. Take care of people, heal them, and watch them ride away to war to be killed by a person who was healed by another doctor and sent off to war to kill someone else. What good is it all?"

Doc was silent a long time. "You're meaning someone like your Pa?" Mac, eyes glittering with unshed tears, shuddered.

Doc studied his fingernails. "I can't answer that question. No one can. War's god awful. No denying it. You, your Ma and Rose know it doesn't just touch the men fighting. It ripples out and swamps innocent people. Even the person least directly involved can't avoid being splashed by it." He raised his head and looked Mac hard in the face. "I told you before, we're healers. We can't avoid our calling or sidestep it any more than your Pa could avoid going to war, even knowing what the consequences could be."

"It just all seems so useless."

Doc rared back at that one. "Now, you just hold on. It's not up to us to decide what's useless and what's worthwhile. We've been handed a job, same as your Pa was. It's up to us to work at it the very best we can and leave the future to take care of itself. One thing I do know, hard as doctoring is sometimes with hurt and death and grief staring us in the face, there's also a lot of joy in it.

"You delivered Retta Hill's baby last week. Retta was hurting something fierce and before it was all over, I reckon she was wondering just why she'd thought it was such a good idea in the beginning. But when you plopped that red, squirming, wet, screaming with indignation bit of humanity on Retta's belly and she saw her daughter for the first time, the look in her eyes was as if you'd just introduced her to God. I know because I was watching her. No matter how poor the circumstances might be with a family or how many are already taking up space at the table. The mother's eyes flash that look of awe and wonder and joy every blessed time. That, my young friend, is why we do what we do. That's what makes it all worthwhile." Doc paused to draw breath.

Silence stretched between them. Finally, Mac said in a low voice, "I won't let you down. Whatever happens later, I'll do my best, now. I promise."

Doc glared. "Promises are easy made and hard kept."

Mac straightened his shoulders, his voice no longer barely audible, but strong and firm. "I give you my word." His eyes locked with Doc's.

Doc tugged at his beard and cleared his throat. "Your Pa was a man of his word, clean down the line. I reckon I can expect the same of his son."

"You can."

Doc shuffled his feet and tugged harder at his whiskers. "All right. No use grinding it into the ground. Now I have something I want to show you before I go." He disappeared through the doorway into his private living quarters, but reappeared almost immediately, bearing a large packing crate. He set it on the floor at Mac's feet.

At the boy's questioning look, he said gruffly, "Go on. It won't bite you." He then turned away to fiddle with the coffeepot and his empty cup, but out of the corner of his eye watched Mac raise the wooden lid and stir through the crumpled papers inside.

Mac gasped, turned white, then red as he lifted out a black medical bag. "Doc," he stuttered, eyes wide as silver dollars. Running his fingers over the MacCZE stamped near the handle, he smoothed the soft leather, and sniffed it.

"It's genuine. It better be, I tell you. Well, open it and see if there's enough room for all the equipment you'll need to carry."

Mac unlatched the strap and went totally white all over again as he caught sight of the gleaming instruments nestled inside. Speechless, he could only stare from the bag to Doc and back again.

"So, do you think it's stocked with enough fixings to get you through any calamity your patients might dream up?"

It took four tries to get his voice to work. "It's—It's—" Again words failed him. Doc guessed the shine in the boy's eyes would have outdone a hundred candles. "Thank you," Mac finally managed.

Doc cleared his throat again, noisily. "You had me going there for a minute with your 'it's useless' talk. It'd be a real chore to have to send all this back."

Mac grinned weakly. "I wondered how I was going to manage with you taking your bag and instruments."

"Think these will do you in a pinch?"

Mac's grin suddenly turned full strength. "Wow," was all he could manage.

***

A short time later, Mac accompanied Doc to the railway station at the west edge of town, where the community once waited to hear the news of the first battle of Bull Run. During the remaining minutes before the train huffed in, a thousand questions buzzed through Mac's mind, but he couldn't seem to frame any of them into intelligible form. For his part,

Doc talked casually until, in the distance, they heard the whistle wailing and he, too, suddenly seemed unable to frame his words into intelligible form. The train swept in with a hissing of steam and a clanking of wheels.

Walking toward the passenger car, Doc said roughly, "Keep up your journal. I expect to hear from you regular, keeping me posted on everything that happens, no matter how small seeming. We'll have lots to discuss when I come home." He swung away but, foot on the car step, suddenly turned and shook Mac's hand. "Good-bye, *Boy*." Mac caught the edge of the twinkle in Doc's eye as he mounted the steps and disappeared into the car. The train swept out with a clanking of wheels and a hissing of steam.

In a confusion of confidence and fear, uncertainty and determination, Mac returned to the office. He stepped into the room that, because of a strange mixture of war and loyalty, death and the choosing of one life path over another, had become his responsibility. The gleaming new medical bag sat on the corner of the desk in the place where, until now, Doc's had always perched. Awed, dazed, he lifted it.

"I'll do my best, Doc." His voice pushed back the newly acquired stillness of the room. "I give you my word."

CHAPTER TWENTY-SIX

The next weeks tripped over themselves as the days scurried past. Fall swept in with the accompanying cries of ducks and geese winging overhead. Again, that lifelong restlessness welled up in Larissa, the urge to go somewhere, do something. This time, however, in an awareness sharp as Ethan's that he should be doing more toward his part in the war, she knew exactly where she wanted to go and what her heart wanted to do. And even as with Ethan's recognition of impossibility, she knew her desire to see Zane's grave, to touch the plains grass covering him, would not be fulfilled.

On a crisp October evening, the family was just sitting down to the table when they heard the rhythmic beating of horse hooves on the drive. Mac, for once there to begin supper with them, hurried onto the porch. Cosimo Theron reined in his horse, shouting as if Mac were rods away instead of a few feet. "Young Doc, my wife. It's her time. Without Doc Rawley here, I came for you. It's happened quick."

"It'll be fine, Mr. Theron. You go on back to her. I'll get my horse and be right behind you." He turned to the kitchen and saw Larissa framed in the candlelight.

"Mac, I know you are completely competent to handle this." She visibly hesitated. "Would you like me to come along? Not to tell you what to do, but an extra pair of hands might be helpful at a time like this."

He grinned at her tact. "It sure would make it easier. I'll get my bag and hitch up the buggy."

"You go ahead. I'll bring your bag and a clean apron and be ready to go."

During the interval that followed at the Theron house, Larissa, although quick to follow Mac's instructions, stood back and, admittedly, watched her son going about his business more than she did Adelpha Theron's efforts.

Unaware of his mother's scrutiny, Mac concentrated fiercely on his work. Of all the medical emergencies he had known he would eventually encounter, the thought of childbirth had made him most nervous. This delivery was particularly unsettling because he remembered starkly that the Therons' year-old baby girl Ariadne was the first death he attended when starting his medical education with Doc. *How can the Therons stand it?* His own young voice echoed in his ears. Memory of Doc's stern answer also resonated. *Life has to—and will—go on. Just make damned sure what you gave was your best.* Strangely enough, as his hands performed each task, it seemed as though Doc were actually standing behind his shoulder, that gruff voice guiding each step, just as he had all the times before.

Cosimo Theron was right. Events "happened quick." Less than an hour passed before Adelpha Theron gave a final cry and pushed her child into the world. Mac abruptly became too busy to dwell on the past. He laid the screaming with indignation, red, squirming, wet bit of humanity on Adelpha's stomach before cutting the cord. "It's a girl," he informed her buoyantly. Watching closely then, he saw it. The look in her eyes was, indeed, as if he'd just introduced her to God.

He had totally forgotten Larissa standing in the background watching. She was glad he was unaware of the tears she tried to blink away. How could she begin to explain that they were compounded of pride, and memories of his own birth, and awe that the squalling infant of fifteen years before had become this strong young man?

When I look at him, Zane, I see you in our first years together. Our son. You'd be so proud of him.

***

Fall blew away in a swirl of russet and gold leaves, with winter upon them once more. Much as they strove to be cheerful, Christmas and Rose's birthday were subdued affairs. Last year's hopeful anticipation that, soon, Zane would be home, celebrating with them, became this year's never again certainty.

Springtime arrived, with Larissa's lilacs bursting into fragrant bloom, and swallows that had nested in the barn rafters teaching their young the finer details of swooping acrobatic maneuvers. For the first time in her life, however, Larissa dreaded the season's appearance. Spring, the planting time, with its promise of new life, and the richness of corn and wheat crops emerging from the sun warmed earth, had been Zane's favorite months. The potential inherent in newly planted seeds had never failed to move him deeply.

On a soft morning in May, Larissa walked to the creek and stood gazing into the water. A year ago today, she had learned of Zane's death. Had he lived, he'd be coming home soon. The government's initial fine promise of "no enlistment longer than ninety days" had, by adroit bureaucratic juggling, stretched into three years for those first recruits, and Zane's would have ended last month. A long time she stood, gazing into the water.

Turning to go back to the house, she glimpsed Ethan in the distance, inspecting the apple and cherry trees budding in the orchard. Standing well back from the creek, he had in no way intruded upon her privacy.

As she neared him, however, beneath his casualness she saw plainly the relief he could not hide. He too remembered....

"Ethan?"

"Larissa." His breath sighed out with her name. "Are you all right?"

"Yes. I was just ..." Her gesture back toward the creek said more than words ever could.

"I know. I've been thinking about him, too."

She looked up, but his hat brim shadowed his face. "We haven't talked about that day. I have fuzzy impressions, but I'd like to know, now, what happened."

He raised his head then, and his face was no longer shadowed, but deeply troubled. "You're sure?"

"Yes. Today, remembering so much else, the time has finally come. It's not so much wanting but needing to know."

His grave expression remained. "I'll tell you whatever you ask, as much as I know, anyway. Let's sit in the shade." He motioned to a newly leafed apple tree that offered a respectable shadow. "You don't mind sitting in the grass?"

"No. The orchard was so much a part of him, I still expect to see him come swinging along through the rows." Her voice trailed away.

"I know. I do, too." She looked up as his voice caught then strengthened again. "What do you want to know first?"

Panic touched her as she realized that after a year of uncertain wondering she was to have certain knowledge. *No more vagueness. You can't fight shadows, but no matter how bad it is, you can live with the truth.*

"It's so hazy. Just bits and pieces flashing. I remember the thunderstorm coming, hurrying to get the wash in off the line, and Jake Barton yapping. I threw something at him. The laundry basket, I think."

The vivid picture of a wrathful, five-foot-one-inch-tall Larissa heaving a full basket of clothes at her mounted adversary caused Ethan to lower his eyes and study a streak of mud on his left boot. His brief lightness vanished as she continued.

"My next clear thought is waking up and seeing you." Blushing furiously, she wouldn't look at him.

"Larissa," he said quietly, although his own heart was pounding so hard he was sure she could hear it. "It's very important to me that you know I would never intentionally cause you pain. As soon as I heard the news in town, I came back here as fast as I could. Then I couldn't find you. I probably shouldn't say this, but I promised to tell you everything. You were gone. It frightened the wits out of me. I'd no idea Jake had come here and told you. I only knew you wouldn't willingly leave the place. Not in such a pouring storm that even Noah's giraffes would have had to do some fancy neck stretching to stay above water. I searched in

227

the house and out and finally remembered you go to the creek whenever you're troubled." She raised her head at that, but he, staring off into the distance, didn't see.

"That's where I found you. Standing barefoot in the creek, talking. To Zane. About how he would come home if you waded in the water." A strange light came into her eyes, but having started, he plodded on. "You didn't realize you were soaked from head to foot and then some. You were so cold your teeth were chattering."

She waited for him to continue, but he remained silent. "You promised to tell me."

He looked at her, then, and his eyes pleaded with her to let it be.

"Tell me. I need to know all of it."

"You thought I was Zane, come home to you."

Her eyes darkened to so deep a blue they looked black. Her lips moved, soundlessly at first. "What did I say?"

"How glad you were that I was home safe, and that you planned to make an apple pie for dessert that night. I didn't know how to make you realize the truth without hurting you more, but I knew you needed to get warm and dry as soon as possible. You were so drenched and so chilled, I was afraid you'd come down with lung fever. I thought if I got you back to the house, maybe you'd come out of it."

"Then why was I in the cabin?"

"You insisted on it. Apparently, you thought you still lived there. It made more sense to go along with you than to stand in the rain arguing about it."

"So you took me there and tended me."

"There was no one else to do it," he said simply.

She sat silently, head bowed, for a long time. He had no idea what she was thinking. A foraging bee droned in the apple blossoms above their heads. Faintly, he could hear Mill Creek gurgling on its way. At last she raised her eyes to his. "I caused you so much trouble and worry, and I put you in a terrible position, thinking you were Zane."

"Larissa." It was the only word he could manage.

The often sensed, haze blurred memory of kissing Zane swept over her. Glimpsing Ethan's haggard expression, sudden, acute awareness of the truth shot through her, and she turned red from the roots of her hair to the collar of her blue calico dress. "It was you I kissed. Ethan, I'm so sorry."

By this time he was nearly as red as she was. "Don't," he said urgently. "You did nothing to be sorry about, I promise you. If it's any comfort, as soon as it happened, you pulled away, because you knew I wasn't Zane." She pressed her lips together and tilted her head back to study the sky. "I never thought I'd be saying this about another man," he added wryly, "but when you think about it, that's quite a tribute to him, and to you."

You can't fight shadows, but no matter how bad it is, you can live with the truth....

*****

A few weeks later, Larissa, returning from weeding the vegetable garden, heard the clatter of a rig approaching along the drive. Pausing beside the back steps, she waited for the horse and buggy to round the corner, and recognized Martha Van Ellis. Over raisin cakes and cups of fresh coffee, they were soon catching up on all the news. Martha, still better informed than Larissa, mentioned a big battle that had taken place in a wilderness area of Virginia earlier that month. Rumor had it that the Union lost more than twenty-two hundred killed and more than twelve thousand wounded. No one knew how many Confederates had died.

The friends sat quietly for a time, thinking of the grief even then being visited upon the wives and children of the soldiers killed. "When will it be over?"

Larissa had no answer to Martha's question. Although the struggle with the southern states had to end eventually, she suspected the fighting with the Indians in the western areas would continue for a much longer time. She didn't want to think about either conflict or about the deaths and heart hurt still to come for other families. "What did you think of Reverend Gallaway's homily about the loaves and fishes?"

At Larissa's question, not as innocent as it sounded, pink suffused her visitor's cheeks. "I thought it was very well done. Shawn—Reverend Gallaway—gives such wonderful sermons, don't you agree?"

"They are very thought provoking," Larissa admitted nonchalantly.

"Yes. We were talking afterward. I just had to ask Shawn—Reverend Gallaway—a question that puzzles me every time I hear that story."

"What question?"

"Jesus started with five loaves and two fishes and ended up with twelve baskets full of leftovers."

"Yes?"

"Where did the twelve baskets come from they put the leftovers in?"

It took Larissa a startled moment for the question to sink in. "Why, I never thought of that. They would have had a problem, wouldn't they?" Seeing the twinkle in her friend's eyes, she laughed, harder than she had in many days. Martha joined in, until they both needed to wipe their eyes. Finally regaining some composure, Larissa said encouragingly, "It sounds as though you and Reverend Gallaway have had some interesting talks."

"Oh, yes. We've had several discussions the last few months. About the Bible and other religious subjects, of course," Martha added hastily.

"Of course," Larissa murmured. "I must agree with you. He has a special way of making any subject interesting."

"Oh, Larissa, may I tell you? I haven't spoken to anyone else. I want so much to talk to someone who will understand."

She reached across the table to squeeze Martha's hand. "Certainly. I won't say anything to anyone else."

"I know. That's why I can tell you. I like him so much. And he feels the same about me. After Ross, I didn't think I could ever go through that again. But we talk and laugh. Is it wrong?"

"How does he feel about the children?"

"He's very good with them. And they like him."

"If it's right for the two of you, and your children, then it's good and it's no one else's business."

Martha beamed at Larissa's undisguised support. "Thank you. I thought so, but with him leading the church and all, I didn't know if I should feel this way."

"Don't you listen to anyone who tries to tell you it's not right. Anyone who says that is just a cackling old hen."

"A few have hinted. I didn't know what to say. Now I'll picture them squawking and have a hard time not laughing."

Larissa wished she could tell Ethan about it, but a promise was a promise. Besides, ever since their discussion in the orchard, she tended to shy away from such personal topics. *Not that I'm uncomfortable talking about it. It just seems more tactful to avoid such a subject.*

***

On a warm afternoon near the end of the month, Larissa bent to retrieve a peach pie, made with the last of her winter supply of canned fruit, from the oven. *Not apple,* she admitted wryly. Setting it on the worktable to cool, she heard a knocking at the front door, and frowned. Anyone visiting always came to the kitchen door. Checking her apron for spots and pushing back a bit of hair straying from its pin, she hurried to the sitting room as the knock sounded again.

Two strangers stood on the step. Unaccountably, at sight of their faded blue army uniforms, her heart beat faster.

The shorter, more heavy-set of the pair courteously removed his cavalry forage cap, revealing dark brown hair. "Miz Edwards?" She noticed, for all his seeming calm, his sunburned hands gripped the hat he had just taken off.

"Yes?" Something that might have been recognition flicked in his blue eyes and was gone before she could tell for sure.

"I'm Ben Clayton." He gestured to the tall, slender, dark-haired man beside him. "This is Steve Jamison." She stiffened, knowing now what he was going to say. "You're Zane Edwards' wife?"

"Yes." It was barely a breath.

"We served with Zane out in the Nebraska Territory. We'd like to tell you 'bout it."

With great effort, she managed to answer steadily. "Of course, please come in." She broke off and turned white as she stared behind them. They had shifted position, providing her a glimpse of their patiently waiting horses. She pressed the back of her hand hard against her mouth to keep from crying out. The men silently parted to let her pass.

As in a dream, she descended the steps and reached her hand to Deneb, the black Morgan horse that had been the pride of Zane's stable. She let him whiff her hand before touching him, and he tossed his head as if saying he remembered her too. Stroking his muzzle, with great effort she resisted the impulse to bury her face in his silky mane. "You brought him all this way home," she said in wonder.

"Yes, ma'am." Steve Jamison's deep gray eyes met hers without evasion. "We promised Zane. That's why we want to talk to you."

"Please come in. I have peach pie just out of the oven and hot coffee. Would you like some?"

The grown men exchanged boyish glances. "Yes, ma'am!" Steve's attempt to curb his enthusiasm failed miserably.

She gestured to the sitting room. "Please have a seat. I'll be right back."

Again the men exchanged a fleeting look and Ben spoke. "If you don't mind, Miz Edwards, we'd like to join you in the kitchen. We know it's not polite to ask. We've not lost all our manners in the army. But you see, it's been so long since we've even been in a real house. And smellin' that pie and after all the army food we've eaten, sittin' in a regular kitchen again would pleasure us fine."

Wordlessly, she led the way.

Two large pieces of pie each and several cups of coffee later, Ben sat back with a contented sigh. "Thank you. That's by far the finest we've eaten these three years."

They began, then, to tell her of Zane and the friendship they had formed with him and Obadiah Beldane. They spoke of the soldier's life as they had come to know it out in Nebraska Territory. They told of the adventure in the blizzard with Colonel Collins, and Zane's bursting out of the snow under the nose of Obadiah's horse Esau, scaring the daylights out of beast and man. They told her, finally, of Zane's death. She listened quietly, without interruption, until they finished, only her darkening eyes betraying her grief.

"Where is he buried?"

"At Fort Lar'mie. The buryin' place for the soldiers there is protected from bein' disturbed by anythin'. We made sure he had a proper ceremony and headstone and all." Ben was obviously phrasing his words as carefully as possible. "We tended his grave ourselves while we was there. When we left, Obadiah said he'd see to it."

"Obadiah's still there, then? I thought he'd be discharged last month, same as Zane would have been."

Steve answered. "It took Obadiah a while to get over his wound. When he was finally fit again, and the question of bein' discharged come up, he decided to stick with the Army f'r a while. He said the way things are goin', the West'll be openin' up after this war is finished and he might as well be part of it. I think what he didn't say is he couldn't face comin' back here after what happened to Zane."

She said nothing to that, for there was nothing to say.

"One more thing," Ben said gruffly. He reached inside his army blouse and pulled out a small, handkerchief-wrapped bundle. With awkward fingers he undid the knot and handed her an object that gleamed softly against her palm. She stared at it as the ever-present ache in her heart swelled and spread throughout her body until there was no place within her left untouched by pain. Her fingers closed over the gold coin pendant and chain she had given Zane that last morning before he rode away on Deneb. *Did I know, even then, he would not return to me?*

"Zane told us once that if somethin' happened, if he didn't make it home, he wanted this returned to you. We promised we'd see to it," Steve said simply.

If something happened. If he didn't make it home. The words whirled in her brain. *Had he known, even then, he would not return to me?*

"Thank you." With great effort she dragged the words out. "A small round tin. Did he have that with him when …?"

The men's eyes met. "He did," Ben said in a low voice. "We saw him a hundred times take it out of his pocket. Sometimes he'd open it. Sometimes he'd just hold it. Bein' curious-like, I finally asked him straight out once what it was. He showed me a bitty pebbly stone in it, sittin' in some dirt. That really got my curiosity up. F'r sure he wasn't one f'r talkin' much, but he said you'd sent it to him f'r Christmas. That his farm and his creek and all his crops past and future were in that little can. We found it inside his blouse that last day."

"Did you bring it back with you?"

"Matter of fact, we didn't. We talked 'bout it, Steve and me. Admittedly, we're not always sharp as steel traps, but even a blind man could see how important it was to him." Ben shuffled his feet. "So we saw to it that it was buried with him," he finished abruptly.

The men declined her offer to stay to supper. "You see, ma'am," Steve explained earnestly, "We're on our way to Marietta to join our own families, my wife and baby son, and Ben's wife and two little boys. Seein' where Zane lived, and meetin' you and sittin' in your kitchen, it's made us real impatient to get home."

Before leaving, at Larissa's urging they gave their horses an extra measure of grain, but when they offered to put up Deneb after his long trip, she confessed she wanted to tend him herself. When they were lost to sight down the road, she returned to Deneb, now settled in his old stall. She intended to clean his hooves and curry him until he gleamed. Instead, she leaned her head against his neck and cried.

An astounded Ethan found her there when he arrived home with a sack of freshly ground flour from the steam gristmill.

He agreed Deneb was in fine shape and none the worse for his three-year adventure. He listened gravely to her tell of her visitors and repeat what she had learned. He watched as her fingers caressed the gold coin hanging once again on its chain about her neck. He breathed a deep prayer of gratitude that, at long last, many of the questions tormenting her had been answered. He saw how the deep grief that had lived in her eyes for so long had begun to fade.

Of this last, he said nothing, for he knew of no words to convey what it meant to him.

***

Standing at her bedroom window that night, Larissa looked out upon the peaceful farmland. Once more her fingers touched the gold pendant. Once more Ben Clayton's words came back to her. *His farm and his creek and all his crops past and future were in that little can. So we saw to it that it was buried with him.*

She leaned her head against the window frame and gazed out upon the farmland Zane had tended and loved. *How glad I am I sent you the pebble from the creek and that small piece of your cornfield. You had to leave them behind when you left here. Now they'll be part of you forever.*

CHAPTER TWENTY-SEVEN

Unbelievably, the war that had ground on for so many days and months came to an end in the spring of 1865. Physical cost was high in terms of soldiers dead, wounded and maimed. In Union County, over one thousand soldiers were killed, died from disease and wounds or were taken prisoner. Destroyed property and livelihoods snatched away increased the price. Emotional cost reached higher still. Many of the wounded eventually recovered. Most of the maimed learned to live with their handicaps because they had to if they were to live at all. Destroyed property was restored. New work replaced old. But damaged hearts and minds and spirits took much longer to heal.

The weeks after peace was declared should have been joyful ones, devoted to returning to ordinary living after four years of taking nothing for granted, but President Lincoln's assassination plunged the country into mourning.

Ethan had the unnerving feeling he had been pitched into a new war directly on the heels of the old one. Charity, heretofore a sunny natured child, began having bouts of rebellion. She didn't go so far as to be rude or raise her voice to him. She knew only too well the consequences of those particular actions. But she mumbled the most minimal of answers when he spoke to her.

In addition to that contrariness, half the time she floated in a dream world of her own. He vividly remembered the first such time it happened. Bent over, his back to her, he'd been making his bed. "You about ready over there? The sooner we get to the barn, the sooner we'll be done with that top to toe cleaning we're giving it today." No answer. He turned, expecting to see her making her own bed. Instead, she stood totally still, pillow clutched in her arms, staring off into space. "Charity?"

She remained mesmerized. Totally baffled by such acute concentration, he actually turned his own gaze to the spot on the cabin wall where her eyes were fixed. No spiders, no cobwebs. Nothing there but the cabin wall. "Charity, what are you doing?"

His voice came sharper than he intended. She started violently. Instead of answering, she simply returned to her work without even glancing in his direction. He started to speak, frowned, and ruefully swatted a small wrinkle out of his quilt. That episode, unfortunately, didn't mark the end of her daydreaming or her odd behavior. Several times during the ensuing weeks, she burst into tears for no reason he could fathom.

Because she did not confide in him, Ethan could not know her changed attitude stemmed from awareness the time was fast approaching when Mac would leave for his medical schooling in Pennsylvania.

Try as she might, Charity couldn't picture her mother very well, any more. She had a blurred impression of Mama looking a lot like Mrs. Edwards, although she couldn't be sure. The one image remaining clear, even after so many years, was the warmth and peace enfolding her when she snuggled on Mama's lap, listening to her soft singing. She now felt that way inside whenever Mac was around. But he never acted like he felt that way about her. Actually, when he paid any mind to her at all, it was the same teasing-his-little-sister attention he showed Rose. No one in the whole world knew how she felt. Even Rose, her confidante in all things else, had no knowledge, because Charity had no words to tell her.

***

In late summer, Doc Rawley came home. Mac was in the office, rolling pills. The door opened and Doc stood there. He had aged noticeably. The once gray-specked hair and beard were snow white and his movements slower, as if he had walked too many miles down too many roads. His eyes, too, were old, as if he had seen too much death and too much suffering to ever again be young in spirit.

"Doc!" Mac's pill roller clattered to the table as he vaulted across the room. Suddenly remembering his dignity, he skidded to a halt and held out his hand.

Doc shook it solemnly and looked long into his pupil's face. "Mac," he said finally, and much of his old gruffness, too, was gone. "You've grown considerably. In height and heft. Guess I better watch who I'm calling 'Boy' now."

Mac grinned broadly, not the least embarrassed that, with Doc's words, every bit of restored dignity had taken flight out the window. "You can call me 'Boy' any time you want. I never heard anything that sounded better in my life. Come sit down. Want a cup of coffee?"

As if dazed to be back in the office where he had spent more than three decades of his life in serving others, Doc allowed Mac to lead him to his old chair in front of the desk. He sank down with a sigh as Mac poured him a steaming cup. He tasted it and made a face. "Something wrong with this. It tastes like coffee!"

For a long while they discussed the patients, new and old, under Mac's care. "I think I got most of your letters. Did you keep up the journal?" Mac showed him the carefully detailed pages. He flipped through them, pausing here and there to study a passage or ask a question.

Of his own experiences, Doc said little. "Maybe later on we'll talk about them. Right now, I just want to let knowledge sink into my bones that I'm in my office with no shooting and plenty of medical supplies around me. Most important, we have to talk about you going to the University."

Doc sat up a little straighter and a bit of the fire came back into his voice. "How old are you, anyway?"

"Seventeen, last June ninth."

"Seventeen." Doc sighed. "I was seventeen once, a couple of lifetimes ago. What I want to hear is if, in these last two years, you've made up your mind about doctoring being as useless as you once claimed." A spark of the old glare showed from under his shaggy brows as he waited for Mac's answer.

Mac rubbed his thumb over the handle of his empty coffee cup. "It's hard to put into words that don't sound as if I'm out to dramatically save the world from all its ills. I know now that can't be done by you or me or anyone else. Like you said that day you left, it's not up to us to decide if what we do is useless or worthwhile, but it is up to us to do our very best and then let the future take care of itself."

The spark in Doc's eyes sharpened. "You believe that now, do you? What brought about the transformation?"

Mac studied the wall beyond Doc's shoulder. "A lot of little things coming together. Mrs. Theron having another baby after her first little girl died, willing to take the risk that this one won't die too. Mrs. Damon, fighting with everything she's got to give her children a fair chance in life. Remember that night you delivered her last baby? I cooked so many potatoes I thought they'd last a week, but the young ones practically inhaled them. Then the littlest one fell asleep under the table holding on to a piece of potato skin and looking like she'd just been admitted to Heaven."

Doc smiled a little, remembering. "How about Bruiser? How's the world holding up under the weight of his feet?"

"He's really surprised folks. His Pa never did come back, but he's stuck it out helping his Ma with all the little ones. He still snarls a lot, but at least he puts food on the table while he's doing it."

"How about Ian? His Pa back, yet? Any hope for Ian becoming a member of the human race?"

"Nobody's heard from his Pa, either. Unfortunately, it's not looking likely for Ian. Remember how he used to pick on littler, more helpless kids when he was younger? He still starts fights, only now he manages to create full fledged brawls. He's been up before the town council and warned several times, but he just doesn't seem to get it. I only hope someone doesn't end up seriously hurt before he has some sense knocked into him."

"Sounds like he's good for business, if nothing else." Doc studied him intently. "So you're telling me, with all this round about, side stepping of the question, you think you might stick to doctoring after all?"

He grinned sheepishly. "To tell you the truth, I think it's stuck to me like a burr. It doesn't show any signs of letting go, either."

Doc grunted. "Glad to see you came to your senses. How's your Ma doing? Anybody courting her? And Rose. What's she up to these days?"

"Ma's doing better now. It took her quite a while after word came about Pa. A couple of fellows came shining around her, but they didn't show up more than once or twice."

Doc's snort was a ghost of his former ones, but it sounded good to Mac's ears. "What's the matter with the male population of this town? If I was a few years younger, I'd take on the job myself."

Mac shrugged. "You've got me. Rose'll be twelve come Christmas. Draws and sketches pictures every chance she gets. I have to admit, she's pretty good. She's always been quiet, but seems even more so since Pa died. Doesn't appear to be anything wrong with her. When she has something to say, she says it."

"Sounds smarter'n all the rest of us put together. I know a few people should take lessons from her. Is that Ethan Michaels fellow still helping out?" Doc asked casually, but his eyes peered sharply from under the snowy brows.

"He sure is. Doing a really good job, too, considering how uncertain everything's been for so long. He pulled the farm through when lots of other folks couldn't make a go of it. We sure would have had a hard time managing without him."

"He find anybody yet to marry and help him raise that little girl?"

Mac chuckled. "That little girl is twelve, now. Rose and Charity are still great friends. Maybe because Charity talks and Rose listens. Mr. Michaels hasn't come up with anyone yet as far as I know. He sticks pretty close to the farm." He started to add something, but stopped.

"What is it, Boy? I seem to recall a discussion we had once about you speaking up when something was on your mind."

"It's nothing I can pin down for sure, but a couple of times I've had the sense he really cares for Ma."

"Well, has she done anything about it?"

"Not far as I know. They talk about all kinds of things. She laughs with him. They've always seemed to have lots in common. As for it going any further, it's not up to me."

"So how would you feel about it if it did?"

Mac rubbed a bruise on his knuckle before raising his eyes to Doc. "When I was little, I never thought about Ma and Pa's relationship with each other. I just put it in terms of how loved and secure they always made me feel. Now that I've seen other marriages, I'm beginning to understand how rare theirs was. I don't know if Ma's even thinking in the direction of getting married again, but if she does, I can't come up with a better choice than Mr. Michaels." He grinned. "With all this round about, side stepping of your digging for information questions, my answer is that if they can find happiness together, I couldn't be happier for them."

"Glad you've got sense. Your Ma's a rare fine woman."

"Why don't you come to the farm with me for supper? That way you'll get to see everyone for yourself."

"I don't want to intrude."

"I recall Ma more than once saying you couldn't intrude if you tried. Besides, if I tell them you're back and you're not along, I'll be in such hot water, you could boil an egg."

The family was, as Mac had predicted, overjoyed to see Doc. Supper turned into one of the liveliest in a long while with everyone speaking at once to catch him up on two years of town news.

As Doc climbed into his buggy afterward, Mac asked hesitantly, "Do you want me to come to the office tomorrow?"

Doc stared at him in astonishment. "Good Lord, yes. And make dratted sure you're there early." He slapped the reins at Bella, who rolled her eyes and sighed as loudly as ever, before she started with a deliberate jerk.

***

Several months later, on a breezy June morning, Larissa headed to the springhouse to get a pound of butter for that night's chocolate cake dessert. Halfway there, however, she glimpsed Ethan coming from the orchard. She'd be going to town later, and wanted to ask if he needed anything. Figuring she might as well find out now, she followed the path toward the apple trees, but he suddenly veered toward the creek.

Probably wants to check out his favorite fishing hole. Or take a nap without getting caught. Amusement rippled through her but stilled as she again caught sight of him. He was not studying the creek for fish. Nor was he napping. He merely stood, staring at the water. Having no desire to interrupt his communing with nature, she turned back. Something in his posture, however, made her pause. Although he'd said nothing about it at breakfast, his slumped shoulders indicated deep dejection. He had listened to her problems so many times. She had no intention of leaving him now without offering whatever assistance she might render. "Ethan?"

He spun around and she saw his confusion.

"I'm sorry for interrupting. Are you all right?"

"I'm not sure about that, but I am glad you came by."

Reassured she wasn't intruding, she shifted course to the sitting seat and turned, expecting him to continue. His whole body had gone rigid. Desolation clouded his eyes. "Ethan?" Alarmed, she reached to him, but before she could put her hand on his arm, he drew back sharply.

"I'm all right."

"What is it?"

Hearing her panic, he shook his head as if to clear it and gave her the ghost of a smile. "Didn't mean to scare the stuffing out of you. Trying to be a mother to my daughter is really getting me down."

Although she strongly suspected he was not telling her the full cause of his gloominess, she waited for him to continue, promising herself she would find out the rest, even if she had to hold him down and sit ... She said hastily, "Trying to be a mother to a thirteen-year-old daughter would get anyone down. What's she been doing? Talking back to you? Or not talking at all when you want her to?"

His mouth opened in stupefaction. "How did you know?" Then sternly, "She's not discourteous to you, is she?"

"Not a bit more than Rose is to you."

"Rose? But she's always polite. I keep wishing some of it'd rub off on Charity."

She managed to keep her expression serious. "Around you, yes. Just as Charity is with me. But in private it's quite a different story."

"You mean you really feel like pulling your hair out, too?" His relief was so enormous, Larissa suddenly no longer felt like laughing.

"Only about ten times a day."

His sigh came from the bottom of his toes. "I must be doing something wrong, and I feel so guilty."

"Believe me, she's acting perfectly normal. I think there'd be a whole lot more to worry about if she weren't behaving like this. You have to remember," she said gently, "she's experiencing a whole range of changes and feelings she's never had before as she becomes a young woman."

He groaned. "I just wish she'd give me an advance hint once in a while." Then hopefully, "So I'm not doing anything wrong? It will improve?"

"You're not doing anything wrong, and it will improve." She hadn't the heart to tell him it would, without doubt, get much, much worse before it became better.

They stood quietly for a few minutes, he by the edge of the creek, moodily tossing pebbles into the water, she leaning against the sitting seat. Her standing so brought back to him vividly the day she had perched on that same rock, laughing at his awkwardness in attempting to slide her wet stockings and shoes onto her equally wet feet. It also ignited all the emotions he had experienced during those hours of caring for her physical needs. But most of all, it rekindled the soul deep certainty that never again would his love for her be confined to that dark, pretend it doesn't exist corner of his heart.

She, having no memory of those moments, totally unaware that she was the cause of his distress, wondered how to learn what was troubling him so deeply. *You want to know, just ask. He doesn't want to answer, he won't. What could be simpler?* "Ethan?"

He stiffened but didn't turn.

"You still seem troubled. Is there any way I can help?"

He flung another pebble across the creek.

"I don't want to meddle, but I've known for a long time now that something's troubling you. I have the distinct feeling it's more than just Charity's shenanigans. You've helped me so much. I wish I could help you."

He slowly turned toward her. The mixture of emotions on his face startled her. He opened his mouth to speak, but suddenly looked away and, in a gesture of obvious disgust, flung one last pebble to the ground. Keeping his distance from her, he blurted, "I've been wild, hoping a chance would open up so that I could talk to you, and now it has, and I don't know how to say it."

"I'll do my best to understand, I promise."

"I told Zane once what a lucky man he was, being married to you." He showed the trace of a smile. "Smart man that he was, he wholeheartedly agreed. I said I could tell what he had because I'd had it myself, with Nettie. She taught me about loving and being loved in marriage. Once you've learned that kind of love, you can't ever unlearn it. I couldn't, anyway, even though I was certain I'd never find it again. Finding it once in a lifetime is a wonder. Finding it twice is a miracle." He realized he was skimming perilously close to breaking his hard held vow to himself, and his silent, but equally binding vow to her. At the same time, his innate self-worth refused to be callously disregarded.

She gazed at him with awed perplexity. Still not touching her, he continued quietly, "It's not a one-sided situation in a marriage, that's for certain. If it doesn't go both ways, it can't exist at all. I'm saying this because with Zane having it, obviously you did too. I don't know whether, having experienced it, you'd ever be willing to chance it again." He stumbled to a stop.

"Ethan." He could barely hear her. "I don't know what to say. I've known a long time that you care for me." At his sudden guilty look, she reached up and gently brushed his bearded cheek with her fingers. "I've been so full of pain for so long, I just couldn't let myself see how it really was with you. All I knew was that you've been here for me, no matter what, with no questions asked. Even that day I learned about Zane, you were with me when you let me imagine, for just a little longer, that he'd finally come home to me. You gave me the time I needed to cope with the truth. But how terribly unfair it was to you. I know that, and I'm so sorry."

"You have nothing to be sorry for. I allowed it to happen. We both know now that what we have one day can literally be snatched away the next. I've asked myself whether I could ever risk going through it again."

Martha Van Ellis had used almost the same words when she had admitted her feelings for Shawn Gallaway. "Did yourself answer?"

He studied a patch of blue sky caught in the branches of the willow thicket across the creek. "He did."

Her heartbeat suddenly quickened. "Was it the answer you wanted?"

He lowered his gaze to her face. "It wasn't the answer I expected," he said simply. "Zane and I were talking once and I told him how after Nettie died, it seemed as if every woman in town had ideas about my future, either for herself or for her daughter. The best way I can describe it is that it felt like wearing a new pair of shoes that haven't been broken in, that aren't the shape of the old, comfortable ones. With each of those women, something just didn't fit, didn't feel right after the way it was with Nettie. When I felt absolutely nothing for any of them, even though some of them were, admittedly, attractive, I accepted it must have been meant to be that I spend the rest of my life alone. Not feeling sorry for myself," he put in hastily, "but simply being thankful for the time Nettie and I had together. My plans for my future worked well, for a while."

"What happened?"

His eyes holding hers, he said slowly, "Your son fished my daughter out of a mud puddle, and I met you."

She let out her breath, unaware she'd been holding it.

"I knew, then, why I had no interest in other women."

Her eyes filled with tears. "Ethan."

He touched her lips with a gentle finger. "It's not something that can be rushed. Nor should it be. And that's why I've waited for you to come to your own understanding."

Brushing at her eyes with the backs of her hands, she gave him a lopsided smile. "This is all so new to me. And yet it feels as if it's been this way for a very long time. That probably doesn't make much sense."

"It makes complete sense to me."

"I care for you, Ethan, very much. I guess I've just needed time to get adjusted to the fit of these new shoes."

His struggling self-reproach abruptly burrowed down, nose to paws, and went to sleep. The corners of his mouth twitched. "You don't feel any blisters coming on?"

She slowly shook her head. "Not even a twinge of one."

"I reckon it's been worth the wait, then. It's not every day a man gets to witness a miracle in the making."

"What should we tell the children?"

"Nothing." At her start of surprise, he said firmly, "We needn't say anything to them for the time being. A lot's going on, now, with Mac getting ready for the University. We won't have him here with us much longer. And we're both aware that when he leaves, the Mac we know now won't come back."

At the wistful look in her eyes, he continued gruffly, "New people, new places, new ideas. He can't help coming home expanded in mind and outlook. You need to be free to focus on him, to enjoy the time that's left. After that, when the time is right, *our time*, will you marry me?"

Soft as the brush of duckling down, steady as the beat of feathered wings in springtime returning migrating creatures home from a distant land, knowledge, blissful and abiding, curled within her, stilling the autumn cry of her heart.

"Yes, Ethan. Oh, yes." Her words were a joyful rush.

When the time is right ... In wondrous awareness that *this* time and this *now* were so very right, she slipped her arms about his neck and raised her face to his.

Startled by her movements, he nonetheless recovered with admirable speed. His arms encircled her, drew her to his heart as he returned her kiss that, this time, was for him.

EPILOGUE

Upon his return from war, Doc Rawley had lost none of his determination that Mac should go to the University. However, with unaccustomed humility, he asked Mac to stay on with the practice in town until he could get the hang of it again.

On a September day of russet and gold, Mac boarded the train for Pennsylvania. Everyone came to the station to see him off. Larissa, smiling, tears firmly hidden, hugged him tightly although she now must reach up to do so. He pulled Rose's braid, told her gruffly to write him all the town and farm news. "I'll send you sketches, too," she promised shyly.

Ethan put an affectionate hand on Mac's shoulder. "You do your Ma and Pa proud, achieving all this. They're mighty lucky, having you for a son."

Doc handed him the medical bag. "You write, Boy. I want to know everything they teach you at that school so I can at least try to keep up with you when you come home."

Mac had his foot on the bottom step when Charity edged out from behind the others. "Good-bye, Mac. I wanted to be the last one to tell you so I could give you this." She thrust a small object, wrapped in school tablet paper, into his hand and scooted behind Ethan before he could thank her.

As the train started, he found a window seat and waved until he could no longer see them. For a long time afterward, he stared out the window without noticing anything of the towns and countryside clicking past. Finally remembering Charity's contribution still clutched in his hand, he unwrapped it to reveal a shiny brown nut from a buckeye tree. He rubbed his thumb over the marks strongly resembling a deer's eye, and the wrapping started to slide off his lap. He grabbed it and saw she'd written a note on the paper.

"Dear Mac,

"I've heard if someone gives you a buckeye, it means that person wishes you good luck. So here's one to let you know that you'll be wished good luck every day while you're gone.

"Your friend,

"Charity Michaels."

His fingers closed around the smooth brown seed. He continued to hold it tightly as the train carried him to Pennsylvania. As their parents before them, neither he nor Charity knew the countless twists and turns their lives would take on the road to fulfillment of their own length of days.

About the Author

 How does one piece together the life events that make up a biography? How to choose this event or that one when one incident flows into another so subtly that, suddenly, decades have been spanned. The adult we are looks back at the child we were, and we shake our heads in wonder at the swiftness of the journey.

I was born in Willows, California. My family moved to Southern California when I was eight. Grade school, high school, junior college. A weaving of memorizing Shakespeare in English class, playing clarinet in the high school marching band, and getting an "A" in gym class one semester—my sole physical education triumph. Marrying. Moving to Ohio and back to California. Moving to Washington State. Working nights in a nursing home for six years so that I could be home during the day with my children. Completing a secretarial degree and finding employment in an attorneys' office. Divorcing and forging a new life for my daughters and me. The opportunity to complete my college education "at home", instead of having to travel over two hundred miles, came when Western Washington University opened a branch campus at our local junior college. I graduated with my bachelor's degree in 1992. In the years since, I have studied sign language and learned to square dance. I served as secretary of our local square dance club for six years and was my club's editor of *Footnotes*, our state square dance magazine. I served as the Publicity Representative for our county unit of the American Cancer Society for twelve years. Each time I decided to quit and let someone else do the job, another person I cared about and loved was stricken with cancer, and I *couldn't* quit.

I had always enjoyed writing, but never dreamed that I could do it for real. When my younger daughter was three months old, I decided I wanted to do something for me that was inexpensive and could be done at home in my "spare" time. I began writing my first novel. Through the years, my quiet time became a source of much comfort in periods of stress and chaos, even when my characters were ornery and, refusing to do what I told them, went their own ways into situations *I* would never have willingly led them. I told them so, but they wouldn't listen.

My first novel, *The Longing of the Day*, was published in 2000, just a month before my younger daughter's twenty-fifth birthday. My "spare" time turned out to be a lot sparer than I had imagined! Since then, I have had four more novels published, *Day Star Rising, Days of Eternity, Day*

Unto Day, and *Children of the Day*. Each novel tells its own story, but the individuals' lives are bound, each to each, in ways they could never have foreseen.

ALL THINGS THAT MATTER PRESS

FOR MORE INFORMATION ON TITLES AVAILABLE FROM
ALL THINGS THAT MATTER PRESS, GO TO
http://allthingsthatmatterpress.com
or contact us at
allthingsthatmatterpress@gmail.com

www.ingramcontent.com/pod-product-compliance
Lightning Source LLC
Chambersburg PA
CBHW051636260626
47170CB00004B/1199